About the publisher

Dragonfall Press is a small independent publisher located in the Hills of Perth, Western Australia. Commenced in late 2010, their goal is to get unknown Australian authors known and to publish books like this, that otherwise may never have made it into your hands.

Also published by Dragonfall Press

THE LEGACY TRILOGY:
The Young Magician
She Who Has No Name
The Ancient Ones

The Tree Singer
The Dreaming

Harmonica & Gig

RJ Astruc

This is a work of fiction. All the characters and events portrayed in this book are fictitious and any resemblance to real persons is purely coincidental.

HARMONICA & GIG

Copyright © 2004, 2011 by RJ Astruc

Except as permitted by the Copyright Act 1968, no part of this publication may in any form or by any electronic, mechanical, photocopying, recording, or any other means be reproduced, stored in a retrieval system or be broadcast or transmitted without the prior permission of the publisher. All rights reserved.

Published 2011 by Dragonfall Press
www.dragonfallpress.com

Cover by Chameleon Print Design

ISBN: 978-0-9806341-4-3

'Are you alive, or not? Is there nothing in your head?'

A Game of Chess, T. S. Eliot

0

(2042)

All night I am running on stiff fleshless legs toward a distantly luminous day. Aware in motion that motion also occurs, concentrically, around me. For each of my strides the land leaps a mile. This primitive world is expanding digitally, casting out ripples of primordial computer code that web and solidify; that seethe into bundles of spitting neon static; that assume clumsy, irregular shapes which splinter too easily on connect.

We call this place the qverse—it sounds hipper than virtual reality. Q stands for question and for quorum; also for quartet and queen. And also, perhaps, for quick, quick like electronic evolution. Within a month those flailing, foetal code-bundles will be recognisable as objects. Simple structures at first, such as cubes and spheres; then, domestically, chairs and tables. Later houses, streets, people, cities, worlds. But at this moment—the moment of this memory—there is only the code and me. Me, running. On legs as artificial as the ground they cover.

Q.1 What am I?

My Self is not a single identity but a collection of parts. I am a digital construction that I constructed. I am a computer program designed by my human hand. I am not dead but neither am I living. I have, however, been close to both. I have seen the light (dimly) at the end of the tunnel. But with my arms outstretched I reached beyond myself, forcing through the coarse corporeal pith and away from that dark internal cinema where the squeal/scream of brakes and the Crash repeated, over and over, like the rhythmic percussion (and re-percussion) of a tumultuous sea.

Call me an escapee, then, a physiological refugee. Just another displaced ghost in the virtual reality machine. Running toward a brightness that grows larger with each laboured breath.

Q.2 Where am I?

At this moment-of-memory? Historically, on the cusp of the qverse revolution. Geographically, in GreaterAsia. Specifically, in SouthAsia. The real SouthAsia, not to be mistaken for Thailand, or Cambodia, or even Singapore. As we are always explaining to curious foreigners, our world—our external, Asiatic world—is no longer a fractured thing. Migration and assimilation has made equals of us, has made *brothers* of us. I am in Brisbane, Queensland, SouthAsia, on a landmass recognised, in previous centuries, as a colony of the British Empire.

Simultaneously (this is where notions of a singular Self begin to degrade) I am also in the qverse, and consequently have the option of being everywhere at once.

Q.3 Why am I?

Why am I? Because I *think*. Therefore... Therefore I avoid existential debate and continue to the practical. Why am I here, why am I running? Simply: because I am lonely. Because I am an electronic ghost who craves company. Who would trade an eternity in this computer-code labyrinth for a mere hour in the outside world, exposed and naked to the onrush of humanity.

A ghost who runs not in space but in time, toward the promise of human contact, toward the day that someone—that first intrepid qverse explorer—comes for me.

Comes, and holds me.

And says, 'You are not alone.'

* * * *

Twenty years later...

THURSDAY – FRIDAY

1

harmonica

The hack wore a rabbit skin—a lop-eared caricature with curious bristling whiskers and a perpetually dopey expression. Harry tagged it nosing codemines inside WestAsia Bank's southern defences. Twenty-four security fences ringed the WAB, each codeshell specifically designed to fry auspicious hacks. The rabbit had expertly penetrated the first eight in under forty-five minutes without triggering an alarm.

A trace confirmed Harry's suspicions: Gig, or one of his associates. No surprise there—Harry recognised his style. Thorough, quick, brilliant. In the past few years she'd lost three secop contracts to the precocious little fuck, and didn't relish the thought of surrendering another.

That he'd chosen a rabbit skin disturbed her. In the qverse a rabbit—used as a symbol or a skin—commonly foreshadowed a virus outbreak. Would he dare infect her systems? No, not Gig, Harry reassured herself; the kid was reckless, but he wasn't stupid. His mind and methods tended to the fantastical, not the piratical. If the rabbit had meaning, it would undoubtedly be a covert jibe at her expense: an in-joke, a mythical reference, a fable...

Harry blanched. Of course, Aesop's 'The Hare and the Tortoise'. Slow and steady versus fast and narcoleptic.

So *that's* what you think of me, is it? Harry mused. A belligerent, predictable, old lizard?

More fool you, then, for sneaking under *my* shell.

Thumbing the loudspeaker option on her secop control menu, Harry cranked the volume to its limit and then deep-breathed into the microphone. Amplified, the noise resonated through the fences like a localised thundercrack. The rabbit jumped a foot.

When the echoes had died away, Harry calmly readjusted the volume. 'Hi there,' she sneered. 'This is Harmonica, your friendly qverse hall monitor. Your unauthorised breach of security has been noted, and the compromised sector will be put into virtual stasis. Business will resume in five minutes or so, depending on how long it takes me to read my mail. Thank you for your time.'

Without waiting for a reply, Harry snapped the area into stasis, effectively immobilising the rabbit between reams of intractable plaincode. A recent survey of qverse clientele had revealed that four users, out of the sixty million polled, could read plaincode, the complex cipher sequences that formed the building blocks of the qverse's virtual reality.

Regina 'Harmonica' Carter was one of them.

The whizkid hack Gig was not.

While Gig stewed in a morass of indecipherable cryptograms, Harry coolly browsed her evening's correspondence. An eclectic jumble clogged her mailbox: pay slips, in-house memos, complaints from disgruntled secop underlings, a mysterious job invitation from INTROMET couched in obtuse platitudes, and a sickeningly cute letter from twelve-year-old Lucas:

> Hi Mum! I hope you are well! I would really like to catch up some time. I miss you. If you want I can come and see you, so you don't have to argue with Dad. I have a shuttle pass. School is still boring. Dad bought me a puppy. Nicole and Lyn are doing fine. Looking forward to seeing you. Love you a lot, Lucas. XOXOXOX

Lucas Carter-Soo was a lingering memento of an ill-fated extra-marital affair with a twenty-something Swedish masseuse. Harry haemorrhaged cash to her ex-husband to ensure the boy's keep. Real 'guilt money'—in an uncharacteristic bout of self-disgust she'd offered an inordinately high alimony, twice what she bled for the two girls. Unlike Nicole and Lyn, who returned their mother's bitter antipathy in kind, Lucas aroused a worrisome sentimentality in Harry's stony heart.

Not love, but its close cousin, shame.

She dictated an abortive attempt at maternal affection into her mail program and sent it before she had time to regret it. The effort left her emotionally exhausted. She was tempted to log out of the qverse altogether and prepare herself a nice, hot bath, but the persistent flickering of lights in her secop control panel reminded her of her duties.

Oh, yes. Gig.

The work of a security operative was never done. Flipping back to WestAsia Bank, Harry found the rabbit patiently waiting in a sarcophagus of frozen code. Any other hack would have logged out the moment he was detected, but over the years Gig and Harry had developed a certain antagonistic repertoire. Was it Aesop you wanted, my lad? Harry thought, combing through her vast wardrobe of skin files. Then Aesop is what you will get.

It wasn't a tortoise skin that she eventually settled on, but the skin of a tortoise's very distant ancestor: the scaled body of a prehistoric colossus modified to greatest effect. Its blunt muzzle clashed with an array of sharp, rabbit-mincing teeth; eyes like coals glowed red beneath heavy, squamous brows; the swoop of its long neck mirrored the swing of its prehensile tail.

Harry struggled a moment to grasp the basic controls—piloting a dinosaur was far harder than anything human-shaped, and required many manual manipulations. *The things I do to make a point,* she thought, mildly amused by her own pigheadedness. *Can't stand to let anyone else have the last word.*

Once she felt comfortable with the dinosaur skin, Harry closed the stasis-bubble surrounding the rabbit into a tight cocoon and ported in next to it. The rabbit made no outward sign it registered her presence. Harry rolled her long neck down to fix it with a red eyed glare.

'Oh my tail and whiskers,' said the rabbit nervously.

Harry leaned closer, until the thick musk of her dinosaur breath began to fog the stasis cocoon. 'Gig, isn't it?'

'Yes sir,' came the pert, respectful reply. In her presence Gig often adopted the role of overzealous student to her overbearing teacher, a habit that Harry had to admit flattered her no end. 'Are you impressed?'

'Are you?'

Gig was silent.

'You should have run when you had the chance,' Harry told him.

'Running isn't my style, sir. If I log out of the qverse I lose everything I used to get here. I can't rig up a storage room in virtual stasis. I could escape and lose my tools or stay and lose my dignity; I chose the latter.'

'That's terribly optimistic of you. What makes you think you can't lose both?' Harry shook her head. 'Mind if I run a strip search?'

'I'm in no position to stop you, sir.'

The search revealed a miscellaneous bundle of goodies, including a unique corkscrew-shaped arrangement of doctored freecode that explained, in part, the strangely shaped breach lights her fences were belatedly displaying. Harry copied it all for her hack trophy room. The corkscrew in particular would look great stuffed and mounted on virtual wood.

'You still haven't run,' she observed.

'The corkscrew cost me six thousand; the modifications are brand new. I'm not letting them go. You'll release me anyway. It's basic secop policy. Like a pirate code of conduct. If a hack cracks you successfully, you let them go. I can tell you where the flaws in your system are...'

'There are *no* flaws in my system.'

The exchange had begun to bore her by this stage; Gig wasn't his customarily entertaining self this evening, falling too quickly into the pathetic bargaining routine common to the other hacks she caught. He hadn't bothered to complement her dinosaur skin, either. The whole thing was a farce. She should have fried him right at the beginning and taken her damn bath.

Harry discarded the dinosaur skin and slipped into a more comfortable, human default skin. Stifling a yawn, she reached into her files for her favourite gun—an impressive, streamlined laser which offered, as far as she had found, the very best electrical conduit for burning out someone's hardware. Her qverse handle, HARMONICA, was etched into the barrel in crisp silver lettering. In the rabbit's plain view, Harry clicked the laser on and began to charge it.

'That's a Benny Soo laser!' Gig said, with a breathless, boyish excitement, as if she'd permitted him a glimpse of a much-desired toy. Which, she reflected uncharitably, she probably had. 'Those things go for millions,' he nattered on. 'I didn't think even *you* could afford one of them. How did you manage it?'

The laser's little red light flashed: charged and ready for action.

'Are you sure we can't talk about this?' Gig tried, the rabbit eyes bulging. 'Look, you've already copied my gear, you don't need...'

Harry fried him—a hard, clean eyeball shot with enough surge behind it to shatter the delicate metal circuitry of his neurocap. The rabbit skin trembled and promptly vanished. Harry imagined Gig emerging rapidly from the qverse in a rush of halcyon colour, coughing and spluttering into a painful reality. She guessed he'd be picking pieces of plastic out of his hair for the next week.

Served him right, too.

That was Thursday afternoon. Business as usual in the qverse, the same old virtual reality code-grind.

* * * *

She left her heart on the twenty-first floor—that INTROMET elevator had an almighty powerful kick.

The job invitation from INTROMET's CEO had been heavy on flattery but scant on detail. That in itself implied Harry would be dealing with some top-secret corporate business. Evidently INTROMET was scared its two rivals, the qverse companies TEEK and SWIFTWATER, would hear news of the venture, and was playing its cards as close to the chest as possible. Naturally, Harry had no objection to working in secrecy. The pay for classified contracts was always spectacular.

She was to rendezvous in the ninety-seventh floor lobby for a briefing. Stepping jelly-legged from the elevator, Harry saw two men already waiting there, presumably job competition. One was a skinny, suited Anglo in his late thirties, whose pronounced front teeth and rounded jaw gave him the unfortunate aspect of a beaver. Nervous twitches visibly twanged the muscles of his upper arms.

The other had the sweet, regular features of a movie-star ingénue, and a soft lazy body perfectly suited to draping itself over furniture—as he was doing now. Ordinarily Harry would have pinned him in his teens, but given the situation she supposed he couldn't be younger than his mid-twenties. Under his suit he wore baseball boots, their rainbow coloured laces hopelessly frayed.

'That's three,' he said as the elevator glass swept back.

Harry nodded politely and sat opposite them. An ill-advised Renaissance theme predominated the lobby's décor, heavy on gold cherubs, thick picture frames and red velvet cushions. All utterly ridiculous, especially when you considered that INTROMET's pervasive advertising campaign promoted the company as the 'new face of the future'.

But this *is* INTROMET, Harry reminded herself; the qverse's economic titan. TEEK may have mothered the qverse, SWIFTWATER may have designed it, but INTROMET alone made it profitable. Replete with emblems of majesty and power, the lobby's archaic style denoted INTROMET's place in the qverse hierarchy—as its greatest benefactor and uncontested queen.

'Quaint little pad, ain't it, luv?' the pretty boy said in a faux-cockney accent, noting Harry's scrutiny of their surrounds. 'I plan to have my bathroom done up much the same.' He chuckled and leant forward, offering a slim hand. 'I'm Felix McGuiggen, and this is Lloyd Hong. I guess you're either here to brief us, or you got the letter too.'

They shook firmly. 'I got the letter,' Harry said. 'I'm Regina Carter.'

'I bet you work in qverse security. Either that or software and hardware design. Hong and I both dabble in that field—strictly small-time operations, mind. I work out of my mothers' basement, Hong freelances for INTROMET. Nothing in the league of Harmonica, say.'

'Can't stand that bastard,' Lloyd complained, his voice reedy and nasal. 'He fried me twice.'

'Harmonica?' Harry asked, straight-faced. 'What did you hack?'

'A shipping corp; I only made it under the first three fences before he wrapped me in stasis. The other time I was loitering around a chat room and he traced me, recognised me, fried me with one of his Benny Soo guns. Complete chance meeting. Melted my neurocap to my *head*. I had to shave my hair.'

Like all hacks and secops in the industry, Harry avoided revealing anything of her personal life to the qverse populace. Generally men presumed she was a man under her skins. Harry found Lloyd's ignorance charming. Although she recalled neither of the events he'd mentioned, she had to concede that it definitely sounded like her M.O.

Shoot first, ask questions later, with Benny Soo guns blaring all the way.

'What did you say your qverse handle was?' she inquired casually.

Lloyd Hong bridled. 'I can't tell you that, Carter.'

'Too intimate for you?'

'It's my handle. *No one* tells their handle.'

'If you say so, Rumpelstiltskin.'

Lloyd bristled but wisely did not reply.

Having satisfactorily demoralised half her potential competition, Harry turned her attention to the pretty boy. Throughout this exchange Felix had said nothing, but gave the impression he remained interested. As she watched him he puffed out his belly and drummed it absently with long, slender fingers; a narrow belt of luxurious brown skin flickered between his waistband and the loose shirt tails.

His appeal was casual, impulsive and unhurried—a 'maybe sex, maybe later' kind of boy. Harry had encountered his type before, lounging in neon-lit jazz bars, heavy-lidded eyes not stoned but romantically dreamy, a perpetual teenager caught in a poetic cycle of melancholy and exhilaration.

Intrinsically fuckable.

He was beautiful and Harry realised then she wanted him, sensing he felt the attraction too, an immediate phenomenal magnetism. Libidos meeting across a room. She crossed her legs and caught his smile. Watch it, Regina, she cautioned herself. Remember what happened with the masseuse. After all, you're almost old enough to be his mother.

'What's *your* handle?' Felix asked.

She bit back a flirtatious response (I never tell on the first date), and then nearly succumbed to another (I'll show you mine if you'll show me yours) which was infinitely worse. Stuck between answers, Harry was relieved when a door at the end of the lobby opened. A man wearing the familiar navy uniform of INTROMET's indentured employees appeared and bowed politely before them.

'Ms Singer will see you now.'

He bowed again and exited. Harry was the first out of her seat and after him, Lloyd Hong running a distant second. Forget the pretty boy for a moment—Harry had a business deal to close, and first impressions counted in the high-speed world of qverse corporations.

As she tailed the employee down a long corridor lined with mirrors, Harry made some last minute dress arrangements: subtly shifting the black seam of her stockings, reaffirming the crease of her cuffs, pulling the clip of her necklace to her nape. Behind her Lloyd exhaled loudly into a cupped hand to check his breath, and Harry nearly sniggered.

But the sound caught in her throat as the pretty boy stepped alongside her, one overlong sleeve brushing her knuckles. In the mirrors she saw they certainly made an interesting couple: hawk-nosed, bitter looking Harry with her dark hair wrenched into a severe, corporate bun, and the young, plush-lipped innocent with his trailing basketball laces and scruffy brown curls.

'I feel like I know you,' said Felix in an undertone. 'I feel like I know you, only I don't remember your face. Does that make sense?'

'Only in the qverse,' Harry replied.

Up close she could smell him. He smelt a little like sweat, but mostly like toothpaste.

She'd always been a sucker for a nice, white smile.

* * * *

Viger Singer, CEO of INTROMET and possibly the richest woman in SouthAsia, turned out to be an incredibly beautiful creature with pale, unblemished skin, waves of thick, black hair, and a magnificent figure. Some feat indeed, given that the woman *had* to be pushing fifty, if not sixty. Harry supposed that when you were that rich you could afford to be a scalpel addict.

Or bathe in the blood of virgins, for that matter.

'Before you is a briefcase containing elements of a real-life logic problem,' said Viger. She sat like an olde world schoolgirl at the conference table, knees together, fingers clasped, head curiously tilted. 'Each briefcase contains slightly different contents: our resources and information were divided between you as equally as possible. Opening the briefcase means that you acknowledge and agree to the security conditions listed on the lid. It will also ensure your primary payment of five hundred thousand dollars; you will receive the final five hundred thousand upon providing us with a feasible report of your findings. Is this arrangement understood by all parties?'

Clause time. Harry nodded and the two men did likewise, their responses recorded for posterity on the state of the art camera by Viger Singer's left ear. Although Harry's interest had been piqued by Viger's personal involvement—surely a CEO had better things to do with her time?—she was now bored. The money was great, but the job sounded suspiciously like some kind of corporate game, or a scavenger hunt, or even a bad plot stolen from a B-grade movie.

Will the contents of the briefcase lead us to our first clue? she mused bitterly, thumbing open the briefcase's catches. Jacked by springs, the lid shot up to reveal a variety of items wrapped in plastic and bubble wrap. On the top lay a list.

1. 1 x Neurocap
2. 1 x Suit
3. 1 x Watch (biocheck)
4. 2 x Address Sheet (Qverse, Real world)
5. 1 x Memo Photocopy (SWIFTWATER internal memo)
6. 1 x Disk (Crime scene footage)
7. 1 x Blueprint (Qverse room design)
8. 2 x Testimonies
9. 1 x Autopsy report
10. 1 x Complimentary INTROMET Hardware Pack

'Good grief,' said Harry.

She checked the others' responses. Lloyd Hong was shaking his head in disbelief. Felix McGuiggen looked on the verge of laughter.

'Two months ago a member of our staff 'committed suicide' in incredible circumstances,' said Viger, curling her fingers to denote the quotation. 'He died whilst connected to the qverse. Since his passing, two other employees working on the same project have come forward and given statements. Each firmly believes that they were put under some kind of mind control as a direct result of logging into the qverse. In fact, they go so far as to say that they were *hacked*.'

Surely this cannot be happening, Harry thought.

Surely any moment now a man in a silly hat will jump out from behind a potted fern, and yell, 'You're on SouthAsia's Candid Camera!'

Surely a woman who controls over sixty percent of the qverse isn't telling me that she believes someone can hack her *brain*.

'I can see you find the idea ludicrous,' Viger said, with a knowing smile that revealed faint traces of scalpel scars below her flawless cheekbones. 'Our official company line is in complete agreement with you. Hacking the human body is plain science fiction...but then brainmapping and the concept of 'q' itself was science fiction not so long ago. And I am sure you will find some of the evidence in the briefcase quite... compelling.

'We at INTROMET require the three of you to investigate the alleged *hackings*. We cannot conduct an internal inquiry for fear of arousing unnecessary alarm within the company. Nor do we wish to entrust this to the police. And we certainly don't want to risk TEEK or SWIFTWATER getting wind of our concerns. I dare say we'd be laughed out of the industry.' The CEO's molded face creased in another near-perfect smile. 'Do you have any questions?'

'You're paying us a million dollars to find out...' Harry began uncertainly, feeling like she still hadn't grasped the punchline.

'That's right, Ms Carter. A million dollars to find a rational and scientific explanation for the phenomenon we've encountered. Or, if you prefer, a million dollars to prove that a person's brain *cannot* be hacked through q code.'

'Is this some corporate issue? Do TEEK or SWIFTWATER have a similar problem?'

Viger looked away, bothered. 'Actually,' she said quietly, 'we rather imagined that one of them might be causing it.'

'You're nuts,' said Harry, slamming the briefcase closed and pushing it away. 'I work for a secop company, not a conspiracy theorist. Forget it.'

'We could give you an answer now, Singer, without looking into the briefcases,' Lloyd said, trying to keep the peace. He drew a handkerchief from a breast pocket and passed it across his brow, where a faint patina of sweat glimmered. 'Everyone knows q only works one way. Just because you can transform electrical brain signals into code, it doesn't mean you can transform code into brain signals. That would be like saying you can turn a pig into a sausage, so why can't a sausage turn into a pig? The worst anyone in the qverse can do is fry your neurocap...'

'Actually, q has the potential to work both ways,' Felix interrupted him. 'Didn't you see it on the news a few months back? Some crazy hardware fanatic in NorthAsia spent years modifying his neurocap so his wife could operate him doing the dishes. Called it the q-inverse. It's the same principle SWIFTWATER is using for its new robotics line, according to their press releases. Hong, Carter, you're asking the wrong questions. The first thing you should have found out was, why us?'

A good question, Harry had to concede. Even Viger nodded approvingly. 'A policeman investigates the physical: people, places, things,' the CEO explained, removing a streamlined electronic file from its socket below the conference table. 'A qverse detective investigates code. A hardware specialist investigates machinery. It is exceedingly rare to find an expert in all three areas. But that is what you all are, isn't it? Secops and hacks?'

Harry stiffened as a premonition of *badshit* chilled her spine. Keeping the file's luminous screen out of sight, Viger toyed with the display. 'I know how much you all treasure your secrecy,' she said. 'You, with your double lives and your intricate codebarriers. But while you may be able to hide from the users, from your employers, and even from each other, you cannot hide from us. We *own* the qverse, and we see everything. And we've been watching you.'

She spun the file around. Harry goggled. Reams of text scrolled beneath a montage of faces: candid shots of Felix, Lloyd and herself interspersed with grainy, qverse skin photographs. Harry recognised some of her favourite skins from the mix—including, she noticed, the dinosaur.

'We've seen you deal with all sorts of cases,' said Viger, 'and q related problems. We know how you operate, and we *like* it. That's why we specifically asked for you.'

'How did you know we'd come here in person?' Lloyd asked hoarsely. 'I usually send associates to deal with these sorts of cases...'

'Which one of you could resist meeting the CEO of INTROMET face to face?' Viger laughed. 'Ms Carter, Mr Hong, Mr McGuiggen. There is no need for pretence here; it is INTROMET's wish that you have the opportunity to work together with full knowledge of each other. So allow me to reintroduce you. Ms Carter may be better known to you as the inimitable Harmonica.'

Oh *hell*.

Harry had known it was coming, but it still burnt. Never before in her life had she felt so exposed. She sweated it out: their horror, their grudges, their admiration. Can I get a lawsuit out of this? she wondered, forcing herself to stare straight ahead. Revealing my qverse handle—that's practically as bad as ordering my assassination!

'You can't tell them that,' she mumbled, recognising her words as an echo of her earlier exchange with Lloyd. She got to her feet unsteadily. 'That's my bloody handle, Singer...'

Viger raised her voice, drowning out Harry's protests. 'In the qverse Mr Hong goes by the name of Talobos—a reference to a WestAsia cartoon character, if I'm not much mistaken...'

'Oh *God*,' Lloyd mumbled.

'...while the plainly unimaginative Mr McGuiggen,' Viger finished, 'refers to his qverse incarnation as Gig.'

'Talobos!? Gig!?' Harry looked askance at Felix.

Looking completely unruffled, Felix winked at her. Harry sat down, hard and fast. Gig! she thought wildly. You're Gig! You're the hare to my tortoise. You're the pupil to my teacher. You're the whizkid hack who stormed through three of my systems, and very nearly scored a fourth. And you're...

You're nothing like I expected.

She rested her forehead on her hands and groaned. How to get her head around this? At least Talobos made sense. They had bumped heads regularly in the qverse, besides the two meetings he'd mentioned, and Lloyd Hong presented in real life as he did in virtual reality: neurotic, boastful, and far too eager to rise to challenges. But in her mind Gig had always been an obsequious type, with thick spectacles and a dark sense of humour wasted on those around him... nominally, a geek. Harry's preconceptions were irreconcilable with the unapologetically pretty reality.

'Do you understand me now, Ms Carter?' Viger asked coolly, breaking the silence.

'I'd have to be a fool not to,' Harry muttered. 'Qverse Blackmail 101. If we don't investigate, you'll reveal our names to the rest of the qverse. You must want our skills pretty badly, if you're prepared to go to such lengths.'

'I just don't like people saying *no* to me. Call it a personal problem.' Viger laughed again. 'Really, you're being dramatic. I don't think you realise how easy this is for me. Here at INTROMET, we've always known. We just never had a reason to mention it until now.' Her voice was suddenly thick with condescension. 'You realise what you have to do now, don't you?' she said.

'Take our briefcases and go?' Harry asked.

Viger beamed. 'I shall await your reports with bated breath,' she said, as the conference room's automatic doors slid open. 'A pleasure doing business with you, Ms Carter, Mr Hong, Mr McGuiggen.'

* * * *

The long walk to the elevator was as morose as a funeral possession.

'She didn't have to do that,' Talobos gibbered. His handkerchief was drenched in sweat; he wrung it fitfully in both hands. 'We would have done the job anyway. For that kind of money, who wouldn't? But that stunt...she just wanted to show what power she had over us. Like a queen. A qverse queen...'

'Shut up, Hong,' Harry snapped, resisting the urge to rabbit-punch him in the back of the head. 'Singer will be watching us on the security cameras. Don't give her something to gloat about.'

Three elevators waited in the lobby. Before either Gig or Harry could react, Talobos had darted into the closest and rammed the doors shut. Gig shook his head with feigned disappointment as he stepped into a second elevator. 'I guess that means we won't be working together,' he said. 'Such a shame. I really was looking forward to comparing notes with Lloyd 'Talobos' Hong, the only professional hack to idolise a cartoon frog.'

He held the doors for her. I *could*, Harry thought in a rush. I could join him, and forget about all the times we've battled through the qverse, about the contracts he's stolen, about the stupid games he's played and the idiot he's played me for. I could forget all that, because there's something…something *chemical* between us. And the qverse is just a job, after all…

She realised she was whittling down her objections to the million-dollar question: is he worth my pride?

'I'll take the other,' she said, stepping back.

Gig sighed. 'You're cold, sir.'

He punched the buttons. Harry's stomach turned. 'You don't look like I expected,' she said feebly, as the elevator doors closed.

'*I* don't look like you expected?' Gig mouthed through the glass. 'I always thought *you* were a man.'

* * * *

SATURDAY

2

gig

The radio called it for what it was—typical Melbourne weather. Sunglare lanced the shuttle-port's Venetians; a hesitant rainbow lurked in the sky's lower right corner. Five minutes earlier golf-ball sized hailstones had punched the busy street outside, imprinting the smooth chrome of automobile bonnets with irregular depressions like acne scars. Fleeing vacationers currently clogged the international routes from Victoria to Japan, leaving clouds of black shuttles stranded in holding patterns across the breadth of GreaterAsia.

Predictably, the Aotearoa Direct was running late; the monitors overhead tossed about optimistic ETAs. Gig wolfed a fastfood lunch in the passenger zone's cafe, Viger Singer's briefcase open on the table. A little yellow dog that had somehow evaded the shuttle-port's quarantine officers waddled up beside him, tail limply wagging, a look in its eyes that said: Feed Me. Gig shouted it a handful of fries and half a dim sim.

His vidphone shrilled unexpectedly and the dog spat out a mouthful of grease to emit a feeble answering yip. Gig opened the phonecase to find Ruth Nameri blinking crossly at him on the miniature screen.

Ruth was a distant European cousin who'd migrated to SouthAsia during the 'q-boom' in the early forties. Theoretically she worked for Gig's secop company; practically she *ran* it. Three years earlier, when Gig hit the hack big-time (crashing the previously invincible Harmonica twice in a row did wonders for the 'street cred') Ruth had helped him use his newfound reputation to ignite his own secop business. He was glad of the assistance; he'd never had a head for accountancy or management.

Currently fifty-six corporations owed him allegiance, and he ran—*Ruth* ran—a full-time global staff of twenty-four. Only Ruth knew that the organisation's official headquarters were located in Gig's mother's basement.

Twiddling with the vidphone's reception, Gig stifled a groan. 'Lord, Ruth, what crisis is it *now*?'

'Don't get smart with me, pretty boy,' Ruth hissed, jabbing an accusing finger at the vidphone as if trying to poke out his eye. 'Where are you? I've got Adam Tran and the Italians from the car depot on vid conference, and they both want to speak to you. What the hell is so important that you think you can blow off some of our best clients?'

'Good grief. I've only been gone for an hour...'

'Worst possible time you could have done it, too. We've had a major outage in NorthAsia—someone went nutso in TEEK's virtual Paris. They're in lockdown. Nothing we can do about it until TEEK gets its act together and flushes the little bastard out. But that's not what I'm worried about.' She glanced away for a moment, uncharacteristically nervous. 'Gig, we're being watched. There are beeps from INTROMET all over our operations. Bloody spooks. They aren't even bothering to conceal themselves. Did you do something illegal? Are we under surveillance?'

The hounds of INTROMET, Gig thought bitterly. The spooks had been tailing him from the moment he stepped into the qverse that morning: a host of faceless INTROMET skins that reminded him obscurely of the masked chorus of a Greek tragedy. No matter what stunts he pulled, no matter how much double-backing and trace-bouncing he did, they continued to follow. Even when he hid inside the coils of his own codebarriers, they hovered outside like a pack of thirsty vultures.

The normal rules of the qverse obviously didn't apply when you were dicing with its queen. Viger Singer again, proving exactly how much of her weight she was willing to throw around.

Gig winced, shook his head for the vidphone's benefit. 'No, Ruth. They're just making sure I do my job.'

'They aren't all we're picking up. Got a loner, too. Hangs outside our codebarriers and moves like a hack. Caught him on the fringes of three of our security systems. He's been seen stalking the WestAsia bank too—Harmonica territory—and that takes some serious balls. Zhadesh says it could be the froggy bloke who crashed Umbeya Corp last year.'

'Talobos. And he didn't *crash* us. He *inconvenienced* us for half an hour.'

'He ripped up our codebarriers, stole six months' worth of design work, fried four employees *including* me, and infected Umbeya Corp's message system so badly that every internal memo they sent opened with the line, "Frog For President."'

'But it only took him half an hour, didn't it?'

'Christ, Gig, you're terrible. Can you at least tell me what you're up to? There's a rumour going round the qverse hackchats about some million dollar INTROMET contract. A hack showdown; the best of the best.' She looked suddenly shifty. 'I hear you met Harmonica.'

Harmonica. At the mere thought of the woman, Gig's cock hitched involuntarily against his jeans. He didn't know whether it was excited or trying to hide. 'How in the hell—'

'Like I said, it's a rumour floating around the hackchats. Guess you just confirmed it for me.' Ruth grinned, pleased to be right. 'So c'mon, Felix. Everyone wants to know. What's old Harry like?'

He considered denying everything, but knew she'd see through him. 'Big nose,' he ventured hesitantly. 'Angry eyes. Hoarse voice. Tall. Long legs—'

Ruth screamed and clapped her hands. 'She's a woman! I *knew* it!'

'How could you possibly know it?'

'It's *obvious*. All the male secops I've ever met are neurotic freaks—the first sign of a hack and they're in panic-mode. Only a female secop would wrap a hack in a stasis cocoon and leave him, only to return later to steal his code, flirt with him mercilessly, and finally fry his sorry hack backside into the real world using the sort of laser a kid like you would sell his mothers for.'

'Speaking of Harmonica,' Gig said quickly, 'can you resurrect any parts of my fried neurocap? It took me three months to perfect the handling on that thing, and the manual controls were coded down to my little finger—'

'The woman blasted it with a Soo-laser. I may be a hardware expert, but I'm not a miracle worker. You're lucky you still have your hair. I've heard of people dying from shock after getting burnt out of the qverse. Do it too often and you could wind up permanently damaged. Not that that would be such a bad thing.' Ruth showed her teeth. 'Don't think I didn't notice you changing the subject there, Felix McGuiggen, because—'

Gig scrunched up his paper dim sim packet, simulating digital static. 'You're breaking up, Ruth, I'd better—'

'That trick doesn't work on vidphone, Gig.'

'Honestly, I've got to go! The shuttle's just arrived!'

It was true: a sinuous stretch of opaque metal had detached itself from the others circling overhead and now glided smoothly alongside the platform like a glossy black bat, little gusts of dust and steam spitting from the chinks in its frame. A tone sounded and several doors in the shuttle's body shot open, disgorging steel gangplanks first, then a bustle of palely disgruntled passengers. Giving the dog a fond farewell pat, Gig grabbed his briefcase and dodged in.

On the vidphone Ruth rallied an unbroken stream of curses. Gig switched her off.

The first shuttle-compartment he entered held three people: two geeky teenagers hooked into the qverse, a third flipping boredly through a shiny SWIFTWATER brochure. More casualties of SWIFTWATER's latest advertising campaign, Gig thought cynically, eyeing their cheap plastic neurocaps. It was no secret in the qverse business that SWIFTWATER's colourful qverse designs were aimed at the susceptible 'Y' market: yuppies and youth. Their latest range of neurocaps boasted cute neon goggles with pitiable resolution, trendy rubber earphones with tinny sound, and exceptionally poor manual control.

Gig slid onto the opposite bench as the shuttle took off. The geek with the booklet caught Gig's eye and grinned. 'In the market for a new cap?' he asked.

'Yeah, but I'm not a SWIFTWATER fan.'

'I've got other booklets,' the geek offered, brandishing a pile of glossy pages. He had the look of a fanatic about him: the lenses of his glasses were already fogging in excitement. 'We just came from a q-hardware expo in Launceston. You ought to check out the latest from INTROMET. A new range of modifiable skins, some intense cap designs, and built in vidphones. I hear they're trying to lure Benny Soo into the company; he did work on their new codebarriers...' he paused, frowning. 'You *do* know what I'm talking about, right—'

'I've got one of them,' Gig interrupted, pointing at a booklet's centrefold.

The geek studied the page at length. 'You can't have,' he said shortly. 'That's a biocheck watch. They aren't due to be released until next month.'

Gig sprung his briefcase's lock and dug around for the complimentary INTROMET pack. He shook out its contents onto the low metal table between them, unearthing in sequence a neurocap, a biocheck watch, and six labelled disks. In short: basic showbag junk, factory-line rejects impressive only to the qverse underclasses, and pitiful to anyone with a good solid hack-head on their shoulders.

Potentially fun to play with, though.

As the geek jealously ogled the pile, Gig snapped on the watch. A series of electronic calculations (blood pressure: great, heart rate: fine, daily calorie intake: beyond belief) lit up the tiny screen. According to the watch, Gig was either massively overweight or as hyperactive as a speed junky. Whoever was the brains behind INTROMET's biocheck watch clearly hadn't made allowances for people with Gig's unlikely metabolism.

'Are you somebody important?' the geek asked warily.

Gig laughed. 'I just have a few friends in high places. You want this?'

'You're kidding, right?'

'The way I eat, I'd probably overload the thing. Go on, take it. You can keep the cap and the disks, too. What's on this one?' Gig flipped it over to check the label. 'Sixty new skins,' he read. 'Well that should keep you going for a while. Oh, look, this one has a cap storage expansion. Couple of basic barriers on this one, and some softcore lasers...' He broke off; the geek was looking even more uncomfortable. 'Kid,' he said, 'if you don't want to take it, then I'll *trade* you for one of your shoddy SWIFTWATER caps. That make you feel any better?'

It did. The geek surrendered his cap and immediately began scooping the INTROMET hardware into a dufflebag. 'You're a hack, aren't you?' he said. 'I've got a cousin who's a hack, he talks just like you. Let me think—' And he raised his hands, index fingers and thumbs outstretched, and held them tip to tip in a triangle formation. 'For Q,' he said proudly, intimately.

Gig recognised the gesture immediately as the motif of the liberationists. This geek kid had evidently been hanging with the old school hacks, revolutionaries who wanted to make their own, corporation free q-worlds. Free Q, For Q! A nice idea, but hopelessly idealistic. Topple one Viger Singer, or even a Phoun Swiftwater or a Rebecca 'TEEK' Descartes, and another would step in to take their place. He rubbed his wrists distractedly. 'Yeah. For Q.'

'You know!' The geek beamed. 'I've actually met Malachy Memphis personally. Did you know that the q-corporations make millions of dollars every *day*? What hackchats do you use? Hey, I heard some crazy stuff in them today. There's a hack challenge on the cards: Talobos, Gig and Harmonica battling it out for some major-league INTROMET contract. Best of the—hey, are you okay, mate? You don't look so well.'

Gig swallowed bile. Beneath him, the shuttle lurched sympathetically. 'Must have been something I ate,' he said.

* * * *

The cops at the Wellington precinct mistook his secop workcard for a high-level clearance. They sent him into the field with a two-man escort. Conversation in the policecar was coarse and acerbic—beat cops rarely concealed their antipathy for hacks. The escorts juggled geek jokes and made much of Gig's dainty fingers, his slender shoulders, his rainbow laces and scuffed out sneakers. Despairing of civility, Gig hung out the window and watched Aotearoa's afternoon sky flash with advertisements for SWIFTWATER gimmicks.

HOLIDAY IN HAWAII EVERY AFTERNOON!
EVER WANTED TO BE A SUPERMODEL?
WITH OUR SKINS, YOU CAN!
GET YOUR 'SWIFTWATER' CAP IN SIX AWESOME COLOURS!
HACK PROBLEMS? FIND A SECOP IN OUR DATABASE TO SUIT YOUR NEEDS!

The cops are right, he thought morosely. People like us don't deserve respect. No matter which way you look at it, we're virtual reality parasites. It's a bitter business. You begin work as a hack, a virtual reality mercenary with a rudimentary knowledge of q-code and an aptitude for creating trouble. You attack a corporate security system. You fail, and a secop fries you. You break in, and the corporation ditches the secop and offers you their job.

You become a secop, and set up shop on the *other* side of the fence. You organise your clever security systems and wait until a hack attacks. You catch the hack, you fry them. You miss them, and they take your job. The more corporate contracts you get, the bigger your operation grows. Your operation gets big enough, and you begin taking on employees, becoming a corporation in your own right. Sooner or later you're forced to hire a secop to protect *your* corporate security, and the cycle repeats.

In this dog eat dog world, our kind *thrive*.

Five minutes later, the police car was cruising through middle-class suburbia. Ahead flashing blue lights ringed a classy white mini-mansion with a hydroponically green lawn. The escort ditched Gig in the street outside and beelined for the closest deli. Gig wished he had the guts to forget about Viger Singer and join them.

'You want DI Karlsen,' said the policeman standing sentinel by the cottage's front door. 'One of INTROMET's SouthAsian consultants, right?'

Gig flashed his credentials. 'You got it.'

'The DI's been waiting for you. Didn't expect you'd drop by during work hours, mind. I hope you have a strong stomach.'

'God, no!'

'We'll see if we can find you a paper bag, then.' The policeman smirked. 'Walk this way.'

Blood spattered the cottage's loungeroom walls, but fortunately the bodies themselves were long gone, sparing Gig the need to copiously vomit. Behind the red-tape cops crooned crime scene blues—lost my notes, the tape's run out, someone melted a hat on the radiator. Forensic photographers struggled to frame it: picture-perfect police incompetence.

Detective Inspector Karlsen turned out to be a bulletproof Maori with biceps that made Gig's knees weak. *Bitch could break me with one hand behind her back*, he thought, and felt considerably more cheerful. His mothers had always maintained he had a 'thing' for powerfully built women. Powerfully built women and women with power—it sure explained the 'Harmonica' attraction.

'Do you mind the interruption?' he asked the DI. 'I could come back later.'

'No point. The business here is closed as far as I can tell,' the DI replied, peeling off a pair of rubber gloves with a strange blend of precision and flippancy that made Gig's heart skip. 'Domestic murder-suicide. Paperwork and cleanup duties from hereon. I can certainly spare a few minutes. But I warn you that you'll probably be disappointed. I can only tell you what I remember, and in this job I forget as much as I can as fast as I can. Will you be taking notes?'

Gig shook his head. 'I'm not expecting a breakthrough.'

'Me either,' the DI admitted, shrugging. She spread her hands wide. 'Here's the skinny: Arnold Lee is found in a pool of his own blood with seventeen silver-steel knives sticking out of his body. Door unlocked, no signs of a struggle, naked except for a neurocap and bodysuit. Best case scenario the forensics can come up with is that *Lee did it to himself.* He's sat there in his swank Wellington apartment and calmly inserted seventeen implements into his torso, one after the other, twisting them savagely now and then so the blood comes faster. Steak knives, bread knives, butter knives—he's raided his kitchen for the tools. You'd think a man intent on committing suicide would find a more pleasant way to go.

'Landlord talks Lee: a quiet bloke, regular with his rent, no loud parties, a perfect tenant. Wife reports their marriage was romance and roses all the way. INTROMET wires a tribute: hard worker, loved by staff, certainly not the 'suicidal type'. We've got nothing to go on until a teenage constable suggests he might have actually been in the qverse when he died.

'We hear stories, see—mind control, body hacking, viruses and lasers that can burn holes in your brain. Science fiction and urban legends, but in our present circumstance they seem as valid an answer as any others we can come up with. Unfortunately due to budget cuts we lack the resources to fund a proper consultant, so the case gets sidelined and finally forgotten, until you show up here with INTROMET's blessing.'

So this was Viger Singer's real-life logic problem: an implausible death paired with an impossible theory. Frankly, Gig felt disappointed. He'd heard better premises for conspiracy theories in two dollar tabloids. In his head he rearranged the scenario in equation form: Man Stabbed + Baffled Cops = Brain Hacking, and felt his stomach churn again. 'Are they paying you to tell me this?' he asked dubiously.

The DI raised her eyebrows. 'Should they be?'

'It just sounded...rehearsed. I'm sorry. Forget I asked.'

The DI laughed. 'Rehearsed? You're lucky I remember that much of the case. I probably wouldn't have if the whole thing hadn't struck me as incredible. Who stabs themselves seventeen times with kitchen knives? Not just his torso, but his arms and legs, too. Guy looked like one of those spiky critters you SouthAsians have—'

'Echidna?'

'That's the one. Never seen anything like it in my life. Although I have to say...' She broke off, rubbing her chin.

'What is it?'

'Look, call me a crazy old lady if you want, but when you work this job long enough you gain a kind of intuition. Sometimes you can pick the guilty man by the expression on his face; even by the way he fixes his collar. Sometimes the answer to a case hits you out of the blue—forget evidence, forget motive, you just *know*. I had a moment of intuition when I saw Arnold Lee. I felt...I felt like it was a set up.'

Like squeezing water from a stone, he thought; you really *do* have to ask the right questions. 'Set up by who?' he tried.

The DI was offhanded. 'If I knew that you wouldn't be here, kid. Like I said, it was just a feeling. Hell, they told me you got the autopsy reports and the crime scene footage. You've got enough to work on without my input.'

He hadn't yet touched the autopsy reports or the crime scene footage; lurid images of high school biology class haunted him every time he thought of it. 'Sure,' he muttered.

'Look, I could have told you all this over the vidphone. I've already conferenced with one of your friends—you know Mr Hong, right?' She took his horrified expression as confirmation. 'I don't know why you bothered to travel to Aotearoa.'

Gig thought about INTROMET's qverse hounds, and the persistent note of worry in Ruth Nameri's voice. 'I guess I just like to talk to people face-to-face,' he lied.

'I know the feeling,' said the DI, nodding. 'Never did much like vidphones or the qverse; barely been in it, really. Tried to get a neurocap calibrated once—a complete failure. Couldn't grasp how to orientate myself. Kept moving forward in the real world when I was supposed to be *thinking* myself forward. Waved my arm instead of *thinking* a wave. They say it's like lucid dreaming—for me it was a lucid nightmare. All I managed was stuttering, disjointed movements; I felt like I was watching a movie with missing frames.'

'You have a neurological disease,' said Gig automatically.

'Parkinson's,' said the DI. 'Diagnosed two weeks later. Of course, with treatment the symptoms barely show, but it still fouls up the calibration. Guess my brain just basically isn't mappable. When the folks at the qverse shop heard that, they suggested I stick to manual controls. Or work in a body suit. I didn't like the sound of either; only people I know who wear body suits are perverts. And can you imagine manual on a Parkie?'

She raised a hand, exaggerating the tremor, and Gig laughed. 'You're beautiful,' he said. 'Can I call you?'

The DI fumbled for a business card. 'If it helps with the case, sure.'

He interpreted that as blow off—she probably had a six-foot Kiwi husband waiting at home who treated her much better than a skinny SouthAsian geek ever could. 'Thanks for everything,' he said, stuffing it into his wallet.

'Good luck,' said DI Karlsen. 'You'll need it.'

* * * *

He killed time in the qverse on the shuttle-ride home. Plugging into the geek's SWIFTWATER neurocap probably felt a lot like the DI's abortive first steps in q: stuttering images, discontinuous sound, and occasional bleats of static that made Gig's ears ache. What was Ruth always telling him? *Never* wear a cap that wasn't calibrated specifically for you. The brain may be mapped but the template sure isn't one-size-fits-all.

It wasn't that the reactions weren't there, but that they were horribly distorted; he felt like he was operating his body whilst drunk. Switching to manual brought a pleasant surprise; the geek's hand co-ordination almost perfectly synced with Gig's own. Better manual than nothing, Gig thought. He chose a suitably innocuous skin from the meagre range the cap supported—the body of a popular WestAsian movie star—and slunk into the qverse.

He'd half expected to be swarmed by faceless INTROMET goons the moment he entered, but the geek's neurocap, for all its lousy handling, seemed to be doing a good job of hiding his identity. Perhaps the fact he'd entered an area of the qverse that belonged to SWIFTWATER helped, too. Viger Singer's omniscience only extended within the limits of *her* land. Out in SWIFTWATER and TEEK territory she was as fallible as anyone else.

Why didn't I think of doing this earlier? he chastised himself. At least thirty-five percent of the qverse is safe for me!

He jabbed a room destination at random from the cap's pop-up menu, and the Spartan interior of the qverse entrance portal instantly dissolved. A second later Gig stood in the midst of an idyllic SWIFTWATER paradise: a stretch of sandy beach densely populated by bikini beauties, adonite lifeguards and polkadotted parasols. Yellow-headed surfers paddled languidly in the shallows; motorboats tore choppy white lines across the horizon. A group of nudists played at the water's edge under a swarm of flashing censor banners.

Steps led from the beach to a wooden promenade lined with gaily-painted shops. Gig stopped beside an icecream stall and squinted out to sea. A triangle symbol printed on an offshore buoy caught his attention; he understood the message immediately.

'Hackchat nearby,' he muttered.

Finding and entering mainstream hackchats was easy, provided you knew what you were looking for. Gig prowled along the promenade checking shop names for synonyms. An icecream parlour, a bar, a surfboard shop, four Italian cafes, a fish and chip shop, and a pool hall called the 'Four Cues'. Four Cues, For Q… Close enough, by Gig's reckoning.

He pushed inside. The interior was tarted up in gauche twenties retro—luminescent neon coils wormed over the furniture. A girl dressed as an old-time pop singer sidled up with a billcard and asked him if he wanted to play for money or kicks. Gig ignored her and ploughed through the crowds, which clustered shoulder-to-shoulder about the pool tables. It had to be here *somewhere…*

Ten minutes of searching later, he found the For Q symbol again, this time in the glowing triangle designating the ladies loo. Who the hell takes a crap in virtual reality? Gig wondered, annoyed he hadn't spotted the absurdity earlier. If this were an Intelligence Test, I'd have failed ages ago.

Behind the toilet door was a gloomy corridor, its dimensions slightly but noticeably distorted—not an intentional artistic flourish, Gig thought, just bloody bad coding. At its far end, a formidable metal door with a grill inset barred the way. Gig knocked and waited. Two bright eyes with vertically slit pupils appeared at the grill and peered out at him.

'What's the password?'

'Fuck you,' said Gig.

The cat skin bridled. 'I beg your pardon?'

'For Q,' Gig repeated, more clearly this time.

'Bloody smart alec,' the cat skin grumbled, unlocking the door. 'Do you know how often I hear that one?'

'Clearly not often enough.'

Bad move—hackchat bouncers were renowned for their inability to take a joke. Gig hugged the wall as the cat skin lashed out at him, all bristling fur and flashing silver claws, then dashed past it at a crippled half-run. A laser-flare scorched suddenly past his left ear; he felt its corporeal heat sing through the neurocap's wires and into the electrical pith of his brain. Instinctively he hit the ground, rolling along the corridor until his feet hit the hackchat's floor and he was safe.

Note to self, he thought: Don't be an asshole unless you're packing superior weaponry.

He picked himself up and looked around. The hackchat was a real junkpile; its walls and furniture cobbled together from random qverse trash. Aside from the few funded by TEEK, most hackchats were created by exploiting room design flaws. Disconnected panels of freecode lay scattered about the qverse like leftover bricks at a construction site; collect enough and you could piece them together into a sort of patchwork structure. Look too long and you could even see glimpses of plaincode adhesive strung tight between the panels, taut as elastic...

The bad resolution of the SWIFTWATER goggles made the discontinuous panels all the more jarring. Damn you, Phoun Swiftwater, and your bloody awful hardware, Gig thought, wading through the throng of hacks. With his manual controls, third-rate cap and default skin, he felt terribly conspicuous. Even the cheapest hacks rarely skimped on skins. He caught the other hacks' smug looks: devil skins, angel skins, fairy skins, ghost skins, a supernatural multitude quietly sniggering at his expense.

Ashamed and thoroughly outclassed, Gig dropped back into the room's shadows and eavesdropped. The snatches of conversation he heard alarmed him:

'Battle of the hacks? I'll put my money on old Harmonica *any* day. He was there from the very beginning, the sly bastard knows his q...'

'Sure, Singer wants the best of the best, but the only thing Gig ever did was crash Harmonica. He's not exactly top-of-the-range secop material, is he...?'

'Talobos might be crafty, but Harmonica has the firepower—weren't he and Benny Soo partners in the old days?'

'I heard that there were contracts out on their heads; if they fail, they get fried. *Forever.*'

'Get this: Malachy Memphis reckons it's not a contest at all but a punishment. Heard him talk about it in the TEEK quarter a few hours ago...'

Oh, God. Gig scrabbled for a vidphone socket by the wall and punched in Ruth's number. 'Okay, Ruthie,' he blurted into her answering machine. 'It's me, Gig. I'm sorry, I need your help. Please pick up. They're talking some crazy shit in here. I don't know what I've gotten myself into. You're right, I'm wrong, I'll say anything, I'll give you

Harmonica's bleeding home address if you answer the damn phone...'

'Gig? My, my. Small world.'

Gig looked over his shoulder. A statuesque movie-blonde stood aloof and smoking by a rickety shelf of 'For Q' propaganda. She lowered her chin to lock gazes with him, deliberately posing her long body in a provocative three-quarter turn. In the neon light the arch of her thigh seemed to blur into the ridge of her spine. Breasts as hard and immutable as fists strained her red evening gown. She was both beautiful as a siren and sexless as a mannequin, and as Gig watched she rounded her lips into a perfect blow-up doll O.

'Nice skin,' said Gig.

'Nice cap,' the blonde retorted, and laughed bitterly. 'Is that the best you could do? Why, Ms Singer really picked a winner with you. I'm almost offended to be running against you.'

Gig blanched. 'Talobos?'

'The very same. Sorry to dash your hopes.' The blonde casually examined her nails. 'Boy, oh boy. A two-dollar SWIFTWATER cap and a two dimensional default skin. You're out of your league, Felix. Viger Singer is going to nail your skinny arse to the wall.'

'Look, *Lloyd*, I really don't care what Viger Singer does.' Gig felt incredibly weary all of a sudden. He hung up the vidphone. 'What's the best threat she can offer? She's going to spread my real name—big deal.'

He made to leave, but the movie-blonde clamped an iron hand about his upper shoulder. 'Yes, it *is* a big deal,' Talobos sneered in the skin's terrible, husky falsetto. 'If you don't care about your anonymity, little Felix, then you're just not bright enough to understand it. Don't you see? Without a name, there is no culpability; without a name there is no responsibility. Hacks lose their names in order to become truly free. Call it transcendence. Call it a clean slate that never attracts fresh dirt. That's what Viger Singer is threatening to take away. How many companies have you razed in the past few years? In here it's all just a big game, but out there? Think lawsuits, kid, think jail-without-bond. This is some high-level corporate piracy we're into.'

'I know the law. We're within our rights to hack in the qverse.'

'Remind me again who *makes* the law? Begins with V, ends in Singer; because she's not our queen at all, Felix, she's our bloody God. This isn't about money; it's about power. We've abused her system, we've fed off her people like fucking parasites, and now she's letting us know exactly how vulnerable we really are. How pathetically small. How pathetically weak.'

Gig relaxed. 'You're drunk,' he said.

'Check your mail and tell me that I shouldn't be.'

'What are you talking about?'

The movie-blonde's face wore a pained rictus. 'We're being watched. And don't kid yourself into thinking her omniscience doesn't extend to the real world.' He broke into song, suddenly, his voice rasping on the high notes.

'She knows when you've been naughty; she knows when you've been good...'

'Talobos—'

'I said, check your fucking mail.'

It took Gig a minute to access his qverse mailbox via the unfamiliar SWIFTWATER cap. Three messages from the top was a letter from INTROMET's administration. Gig opened it.

MCGUIGGEN
KEEP UP THE GOOD WORK
SINGER

Viger was keeping tabs on him. He'd heard before that the big league companies sometimes had their contractors followed, but there was something obscene about the fact she was letting him know. A snide reminder that he'd renounced his right to privacy the moment he'd walked into her office—although maybe he'd given that up the first time he'd logged into the qverse. Gig stared blankly into the movie blonde's vapid, thick-lashed eyes.

'Stupid fuck,' Talobos swore drunkenly at him. 'Do you really think you're ready to match wits with *her*?'

* * * *

3

harmonica

'So Viger Singer has you chasing moonbeams,' laughed the vampire. 'Brain-hacking! Now I've heard it all. What did you say the dead bloke's name was?'

'Lee. Arnold Lee.'

'Sounds familiar for some reason. But then you SouthAsians are all Lees and Soos and Chans these days.' He toyed with the ornate silver handle of his cane. 'In my opinion Viger's using this conspiracy malarkey as an excuse to get chummy with you, Harry. You're hot property, one of the talented four who can read plaincode. You, Benny, Rebecca and Phoun. Viger tamed the other three, but you're still on the loose. Loose like a canon, if you don't mind me saying. Maybe she's looking to buy you out. Or buy you in. Appeal to your ego.'

'That's certainly the way to do it,' Harry agreed.

'Must be nice to feel so wanted. Me, I've tried to break the plaincode cipher countless times. Spent hours sitting in stasis waiting for the answer to reveal itself. It never did. I don't feel too bad about it, mind you—celebrated geniuses the world over can't figure it out either. Even the idiot savants are stumped.' The vampire bared glossy white fangs. 'No offence, love, but how in hell did *you* manage to crack it?'

'I'm a woman scorned,' said Harry. 'I'm extremely good at channelling my hatred in pro-active ways.'

'Translation?'

Harry patted his pale, gnarled hand kindly, pitching her voice at an old-crone warble. 'Back in the old days, little boy, we had a manual.'

He was an ex-lover. All the best people were. Outside the qverse the vampire was known as Joaquin Magdellin, a twenty-four-year-old TEEK code designer currently based in NorthAsia. The exquisitely rendered Dracula skin was a pet project of his: classic twenty-first century retro. Dead eyes glinted from a sallow, sunken face; white hair fanned from the high forehead like a shell. Ridiculously huge fangs overlapped the garish red lips. A brand circling the bony left wrist marked it as property of TEEK Inc.

Harry had stumbled upon this young TEEK protégé six years previously: they'd been allocated neighbouring seats at a "For Q" conference. Ill at ease in a suit and tie, Joaquin had jiggled throughout Malachy Memphis' onerous speeches, all wispy blond nerves and teenage insecurity, at one point knocking Harry's purse onto the floor. It was a random, forgettable incident, and Harry had thought little of it at the time.

But later Joaquin sought her out and apologised profusely, his soft Anglo face flushed with shame and sunburn. Against her better judgment, Harry had let him buy her a glass of champagne, invite her to his hotel room, show her a sketchbook filled with embryonic skin designs and adolescent dreams, hold her hard hand in his tender one and finally, at around three o'clock on a fresh new conference morning, fall sheepishly in love.

It proved a short-lived affair: enjoyable but wholly unsustainable. At the time they were both going through 'transitional' phases; Harry's divorce papers were in the mail, and Joaquin had just finished high school. He was a toy-boy, she the older-woman. The break up was amicable, understandable, and they'd remained friends—perhaps even *best* friends—to the present day, catching up every Saturday to exchange news of tribulation and triumph.

This Saturday they were doing coffee in Paris. The coffee was fake, but then again, so was Paris. Originally Harry had scheduled their morning rendezvous for the Valley of the Kings, but on arrival they'd found the place swamped with badly conceived celebrity skins. Blond bouffants and cowboy hats cheapened Egypt's historic majesty. Skateboarders in brand-name bandanas tricked off the pyramids. Abseilers monkeyed down the Sphinx's truncated profile.

Disappointed—but not altogether surprised—Harry had suggested Paris. Joaquin embraced her choice: Q-Paris was TEEK territory and his home turf. He'd selected the café, an open-air shuttle that hovered over the *Avenue de Suffren*, its hulking metal frame comically dotted with red and white parasols like feeder-fish clinging to a whale. A tinny background track played orchestral renditions of *Sur La Pont, D'Avingnon* and *Frere Jacques* on an eternal loop.

'You've got to do something about that music,' Harry muttered.

'I'll do something about the music when you lend me a manual.' Joaquin leant back in his faux-wood chair and smirked. 'Want to see my latest trick, old timer? You'll like this. Ripped straight out of INTROMET's secret files—their resident secop is a blundering idiot.'

A blundering idiot? That was some arrogance. Who did he remind her of?

Gig. That was it.

Gig. And Talobos.

And all those other naughty little boys who'd surfed in on the tide of her triumphs.

'As far as I know,' Harry said, 'INTROMET's resident secop is Viger Singer herself. A woman who hasn't fallen to a hack since the late forties. And that hack was *me*.'

Joaquin deflated somewhat. 'Fine. Let's just say I got this file off a friend. Fell off the back of a q-truck, on a q-super-information-highway.'

'Translation?'

'I conned it out of a deadbeat INTROMET employee who needed the cash. But you keep that under your hat. Could cost me my job.'

Shaking her head, Harry stirred her fake-coffee with a finger. 'I don't care about your corporate spies, Jo,' she reminded him. 'I'm not barracking for any team. TEEK, SWIFTWATER, INTROMET, hell. Far as I'm concerned, you're all as bad as each other. Go on, then. Tell me about your trick.'

'I'll have to show it to you. Can I plug you into my goggles?'

'Do you have to?'

'Christ, Harry, I'm not going to stare down my pants or anything.'

Harry made a face. 'Fine, fine, do it.'

Plugging into someone else's reality always struck Harry as perverse, a form of 'assisted' voyeurism. She was only too aware that the external-view function of qverse goggles had been installed primarily to attract sex industry investors. As Joaquin connected the feed of his goggles, her aerial view of Paris' cluttered streets vanished. A few seconds of static later, Harry found herself looking at a drab TEEK office building crammed with a honeycomb of tiny cubicles. Joaquin stood up and slowly turned around, treating Harry to the full three-sixty.

'Behold ze Vorkplace!' he said, affecting a barely passable Transylvanian accent. 'As seen through ze eyes of Jo Magdellin, who can currently be found loafing off in ze design department with ze rest of TEEK's creative drones. Velcome to my hell!'

At his last word the scene changed, and Harry was somewhere else entirely: a rubbery, cartoon hell carpeted with fire, filled with altars and severe, black rocks. A pair of stylised demons skulked in a corner, pointed tails swinging ominously. Something about the regularity of the rocks' placement immediately struck Harry as odd. If you ignored the jagged edges, they almost looked like…

Like a honeycomb, she realised.

'It's some sort of filter,' she said, unplugging into q-Paris. 'Hell-coloured glasses.'

'You're the first person to recognise it,' said Joaquin, with grudging admiration. 'The program recognises and defines shapes in the real world, and then translates them into a theme. You can create and save an entire new room without having to build up a foundation from plaincode—it practically invalidates the need for plaincode in the first place. In addition to 'hell', we also have options for 'heaven', 'pleasure-pad', 'farm', 'beach', and 'haunted mansion'. To name but a few. Easily the most sophisticated program I've ever had the pleasure of stealing.'

'It's incredible. You sure INTROMET came up with this?'

Joaquin shrugged. 'They had help. I heard Benny Soo was involved. The hackchat grapevine claims he sold his scruples to Viger Singer for eight million. All donated to the charity of his choice, of course. Mr bloody Philanthropy. It was a sad day in TEEK when the news came through, let me tell you. All that time we'd thought he was on *our* side. Rebecca Descartes was crushed.'

'I hope the bitch chokes.'

Her venom clearly surprised him. Joaquin recoiled like a slapped child, knocking over the table's sugar bowl with the flared sleeve of his shirt. 'Remind me never to piss you off, Harry,' he muttered.

'That's easily avoided. Just try not to fuck anyone I'm currently married to. Call me overly sensitive if you like, but for some reason that always gets my goat.'

'Right. Right. How are the kids, Harry? Nicole and Lynette and Luke?'

'Lucas. They're fine. What on earth do they have to do with anything?'

The vampire skin's pale features were frozen in a hideous, forced smile, but Joaquin's voice maintained its laid-back drawl. 'Just making conversation. Are you with anyone at the moment? Rumour has it you're having it off with that Gig kid—'

'I beg your par...'

She stopped. Joaquin was writing in the sugar with a clawed, vampire fingernail.

SPOOK

Harry tensed. 'Where?'

Joaquin transported their vocals to a private, direct line. 'You've got at least fifty of them tailing you,' he blurted out as soon as the connection was secure. 'INTROMET goons. I can read their traces—they're sending them off every five damn seconds. Some in the street. More on the roofs. A couple at the table opposite. Some in chameleon skins are hanging off the shuttle's wings. Bloody good skins, too, since I sure as hell can't see them outside of the control screen. It's a hack fest, Harry. What the hell have you done?'

'Give me room control, now.'

'I can't do that. I'd lose my job. Only TEEK employees with level seventy clearance and over—'

'I said, give me the damn room control.'

He handed it over and moved twitchily on his chair. 'What are you going to do?'

On Joaquin's control screen the INTROMET spooks registered as blinking red dots, connected to Harry—a depressingly blue dot—by thin, sparkling trace lines. All variations of hacks, too, she observed; everything from the invisible chameleons to the pair of celebrity skins calmly drinking fake-coffee under a nearby parasol.

Sneaky little bastards. Harry palmed a laser as she considered the situation. How *did* you nuke fifty people at once? she wondered. Stasis cocoons were no use; furthermore, they lacked the satisfaction of a laser-flare between the eyes...

'Harry?' Joaquin tried feebly. 'You're not going to do anything stupid, are you?'

Harry grinned. 'Be right back,' she said.

With the laser dangling at her hip, she loudly excused herself from Joaquin's presence and walked to the celebrity couple's table. On the surface they appeared female—big breasted fantasy women with identical leopard-print skirts and streamlined limbs that utterly failed to replicate natural motion. According to the control screen data, the duo had been tailing since her first stop in q-Egypt. Those tacky skins disguised some mighty powerful hack code.

They looked up silently as she approached, thick eyelashes springing open to reveal ridiculous pastel blue irises like those of antique china dolls. Smiling, Harry leant forward and wrapped her arms around their shoulders in a one-sided group hug, as if they were old friends reuniting. As she'd hoped, neither spook had been anticipating this. One stiffened in surprise; the other mumbled a warning.

It mumbled the warning again a split-second before Harry fired her laser. At this close range the charge blasted straight through the skull of one spook and buried itself in the other's. Bullseye. A nimbus of light foamed about the spooks' heads and hands, something crackled, distantly; then they vanished from the qverse, leaving behind a couple of loose threads of freecode and two lukewarm fake-coffees.

That was two down, forty-eight to go. Nicely done Regina, Harry congratulated herself. Didn't even have to break a sweat. Rising, she checked the café's patrons and was satisfied that no one had noticed anything suspicious. Localised dropouts weren't uncommon, and at any rate, TEEK territory was notorious for its hackfights. Who'd care about a couple of fried strangers?

Recharging her laser, Harry swung a leg over the wooden fence that closed off the café area and jogged briskly along the shuttle's sloped right wing. Thanks to the control screen she could pinpoint the precise location of the chameleon skins, even if she couldn't see them. Six lay prostrated against the matte black metal, hands interlinked, breathing in unison, eyes fixed on her. Obviously they had no idea she knew they were there; if they *did*, they'd have run by now.

Harry had always found chameleon skins offensive on some level. Anonymity in the qverse was fine, but actual invisibility took it a step too far. Bloody voyeurs. She snapped out her laser a second time, drawing it quickly across their line at neck-level before the shapeless critters had time to react. Instantly the chameleon bodies seizured, then lit up like Christmas lights, spurting an array of liquid colours before exploding into dazzling blobs of white light. Harry had to admit the special effects were classy. She could almost smell the plastic-burn, neurocaps fritzing and melting, dribbling down their receptor spindles, as their owners were painfully birthed into the real world...

She checked the control screen. The remaining spooks were located on ground level. Some, aware they'd been rumbled, were already beating a retreat into safer, INTROMET areas; others ganged together in preparation for battle. The spattering of red dots had begun to fuse into a single mass.

A host of enemies, seemingly insurmountable odds... it was just how Harry liked it. What was it Malachy Memphis had once told her? Hacking and frying came to her like breathing; it was too easy to be this damn good. And didn't the For Q underground still call her the mother of hacks? The queen of q, q's serpent, the black bitch, the black witch—affectionately in her absence, bitterly to her face. Even after she'd fallen to Gig, not once but three horrible, humiliating times, the hackchats had never doubted her skill. Gig was just some fool whiz kid who'd gotten lucky. Harmonica was, simply, the best.

The spooks think I'll run, Harry realised, running her fingers over the control screen. I guess old Viger forgot to tell them I'm not some run-of-the-mill hack who can be easily intimidated.

Especially not when *I'm* the one with room control.

She danced four balletic steps left then vaulted, spinning, off the shuttle's wing, free-falling seventy feet as the earth rose to catch her, the body of her skin held tense and trembling as a harp string. Her bird's eye view of Paris' intricate laneways dwindled rapidly to a rush of grey stone and upturned faces. Below the café a crowd of curious skins had gathered on the street, presumably drawn by the laser fire. Harry landed easily on the fringe of the group and shook herself.

No matter what people said about the qverse being like a dream, you never died when you hit the ground.

She was still regaining her bearings when a bulky bodybuilder skin shouldered through the crowd and prodded her urgently in the side. 'Are there fireworks?' he asked in a squeaky adolescent voice.

Harry shook her head. 'No, kid. Just some lunatic frying folks.'

'Oh.' The bodybuilder bit his lip. 'Should I leave?'

'And miss the fun? Gracious, no!' Harry pumped her laser one-handed, switching to manual to explore the limits of Joaquin's room control.

'I just got an error message from TEEK,' said the bodybuilder. 'Technical difficulties.'

Harry experimented.

'I got another error message,' said the bodybuilder, sounding less and less certain of himself. 'It's telling me to... to shut the hell up.'

'Not bad advice,' Harry commented dryly.

The bodybuilder made to go, then stopped in his tracks, pointing. 'God,' he said, and stifled a silly, childish laugh. 'Who do those folks think they are?'

Across the road, the remaining spooks were waiting for her. They were an ill-matched bunch: some playing it cool under cheap default skins, others resplendent in all INTROMET's glorious panoply. Cat skins brushed flanks with dogs, harlequin-clad jesters stood beside foreign kings. If it wasn't for Joaquin, Harry thought, I might have gone all day without suspecting a thing.

She was angry then for the first time. Really *angry*, not just mildly annoyed or a tad frustrated but stirred to actual violence. Because they'd *nearly* got the better of her. Because they'd made her feel vulnerable—even for a moment. Beneath her skin's calm façade Harry spat and seethed like a wildcat in a cage.

Anger. Which wasn't good, not if you were a professional secop and hack. Neurocaps responded badly to strong emotion; once you lost control your reflexes went to hell. Secops who got mad quick got fried even faster.

So the aftermath of the Rebecca Descartes incident had taught her.

Harry battled through unfamiliar control screens, cursing INTROMET, cursing herself. The spooks shifted forward stiltedly, happy to do some frying of their own, but hesitant to be in the front ranks. Their approach reminded Harry of a stylised sequence from an old zombie-flick—those dull-eyed dead lurching from the crypt in interminable waves. Odd and mis-paired as they appeared, their movements united them, the trained synchronicity of many months—perhaps years—of working side by side. She sensed they'd done this before, slipped automatically into the role of pack animal, goading each other to pick off stray hacks on the vast plains of q-space...

I'm doing the world a favour, Harry thought, and fried them.

It was, as she'd later explain to Joaquin, a merging of two simple room functions: the supply of power to the room's visual surroundings, and the room secop's 'eject' button, which allowed TEEK employees to swiftly boot troublesome users into other qverse territories. As she stumbled backward, an entire panel of q-Paris crumpled in on itself like a combusting star, vacuuming the howling spooks into its white code-core. They clutched at nothingness, arms and legs flailing; then the earth trembled; reams of ruptured plaincode spluttered dizzily from the gash; and they were swallowed up. A huge, symmetrical zigzag fractured from the strike-point up the road; code burst its seams and washed into the guttering in lashes and fronds. Around Harry civilian skins screamed and fled, the smarter ones porting directly out of q-Paris, the less techno-savvy escaping on foot, scampering for the safety of houses and shuttles, clutching their shoulders as they ran to limit skin-damage. Shudders wracked the city in bursts like seismic tremors, aftershocks, folding archaic buildings into two-dimensional panels, which in turn folded into nothingness...

It was perfect chaos and Harry stood on its edge and breathed as deeply as she dared.

'You just fried Paris,' said Joaquin Magdellin.

He was beside her, his Dracula cape flaring out rivulets of blood-red lining. He took the room control screen from her unresisting fingers and examined it. 'That's twenty-nine INTROMET employees and twenty percent of TEEK's most popular room,' he said bitterly. 'Really, Harry, I'm surprised at your prudence. Why in hell did you stop the carnage there?'

Harry wrinkled her nose. 'Someone's at my door,' she said.

* * * *

'Hi, Mum,' said Lucas Carter-Soo, dimpling on the doorstep.

Reflexively, Harry shut the door.

'Mum!' Lucas yelled.

Harry opened the door. 'Hi,' she said.

'I got a shuttle pass,' he explained, brandishing it.

'Great.'

'How are you?'

'Fine.'

'You look well.'

'Thanks.'

'Can I come in?'

Harry stepped aside. Lucas bounced around her and vanished down the hall.

When she found him again he was in the kitchen, Viger Singer's briefcase open, its shiny contents scattered across the table. She observed him warily from a distance. Always a handsome child, Lucas had inherited his Swedish father's fairer colouring and finer features. Two insuperable cowlicks puffed his black hair above his temples in little humps which looked, to Harry's jaundiced eye, like incipient devil horns. As he flipped through Viger's carefully collated files she noticed that the fingernails of his left hand were clumsily painted black with magic marker. Stencilled on his knuckles was the word HACK, each letter circled with a flourish.

Harry watched him a minute longer before her nerves got the better of her. She went to the fridge and cracked open a beer. She found a packet of cigarettes in a shelf cupboard and lit one off the stove. She kept track of his movements out of the corners of her eyes. For the life of her she did not know what to do with him in her house. She felt utterly *derailed.*

It was ironic, really. Fifty INTROMET spooks armed to the hack-teeth had failed to off-balance her; her prodigal son had managed to do so in less than five minutes, equipped with nothing save a charming, slightly buck-toothed smile.

'Heard about this on the hackchats,' said Lucas, looking up, a bag of INTROMET goodies clutched in a plump hand.

'Never knew some guy was actually murdered, though. Arnold Lee. Didn't he design some second-rate code barrier in the late fifties? This is an awful lot of evidence you've got here. Why didn't Singer go to the cops? Do you have a list of suspects? I bet TEEK had something to do with it. Don't care what Dad says, Descartes is one sneaky customer. What with the rivalry and that new system the old man designed for Singer, I reckon—'

'What the *hell* are you doing here?' Harry asked.

Lucas pouted, hugging papers. 'I got a shuttle pass, Mum. I wanted to see you.'

Harry smoked, stared, and said nothing. It was an old trick. All her children talked a lot—their father's influence. Even pinch-faced Lyn chattered up a storm to her perm-headed friends. Silence unnerved them, loosened their tongues.

A minute passed. Lucas squirmed, spluttered psychiatric jargon: 'Dad and I are having problems with our relationship.'

Harry snickered. 'You and me both. Did he hit you?'

'Hit me, hell! He's going to flipping kill me. I'm going to get flipping expelled.'

'What'd you do?'

He picked sheepishly at his black fingernails. 'Fried my teacher.'

Fried your *what*? Harry put down her cigarette in surprise. Pride struggled against obligatory exasperation: mentor versus parent. And there I had him pegged as boring, as much of a chore as the other two, she thought with a sudden glee. But he's growing up just like me. *Wicked.* A surge of post-Paris-frying excitement returned to her. Aloud she said, 'Hasn't your dad told you not to play with his lasers?'

'Wasn't *his*. I made my own. Dad's stupid.' His eyes were huge, their colour cutting a pretty contrast to his milky-coffee complexion. Some occidental throwback of her diverse genetic history had ringed his pupils in deep-sea green. 'Dad shouldn't've taught me code if he didn't want me frying things. His fault, see... Mum! Stop that! It's not funny. I'm in awful trouble.'

'I'm not laughing,' said Harry, who was, her mouth straight but her body shaking. The whole situation appealed to her dark sense of humour. Frying a teacher. Lucas the penitent running to *her* for help. And to think her bastard ex-husband had the audacity to accuse her of being a neglectful parent. After he'd taught Lucas plaincode? 'Tell me what happened,' she suggested, schooling her face in concern. 'What'd the teacher do?'

'Wasn't our regular teacher. A substitute bloke. He bugged me. Got in my face, see. Stuff about Dad. He was some For Q fanatic. I told him to leave me alone and he told me to go to the principal. So I fried him. I was mad. I was just so mad. Then some stupid girl went to find the principal and he came in, caught me. I told him this guy was just *crazy*, he'd even left For Q leaflets on the desk. The principal got in my face, then. Said I'd be expelled. I said I didn't want to go to his stupid school anyway, so I crashed the whole stupid place and ported out. Now Dad is going to kill me and it isn't even my flipping problem; it's *his* flipping problem. They shouldn't employ revolutionaries in a stupid school.'

The juvenile truant had spent the entirety of this monologue glaring into the briefcase, elbows propped on the table, fists kneading his cheeks, still smarting at the memory. Now he appealed to Harry directly. 'Mum, I got to stay here for a few days. Please. Until Dad calms dow—'

'So you fried your *entire* school?' Harry said.

'Yeah. I guess. Wasn't hard. Their secop is some nutty EastAsian Public Relations graduate who buys all his codebarriers in hack markets. Only speaks bloody Japanese. I'd had access to their room control for wee—'

'Cool,' said Harry. 'Want a beer?'

'Mum! I'm fourteen years old.'

'Fourteen? I thought you were twelve.' Reaching out, she steadied his round chin in her hand, examining him at arm's length. Fourteen, and no sign that puberty would be raising its acne-riddled head any time soon. Despite the fact that both his biological parents hovered around the six-foot marker, Lucas was barely more than four feet tall. Suddenly it wasn't too hard to imagine why her ex-husband had insisted the kid learn plaincode. Even in a virtual reality q-school, children could *smell* weakness, picking out the ugly, the short, and the fat by some ineffable teenage sixth sense.

Woe betide any school yard bully who'd pick a fight with *my* boy, Harry thought smugly, and wanted—for the first time in her life—to hug him.

Instead she casually scuffed his hair and was quietly charmed by the pleasure written on his face. 'How about we trade, kiddo?' she suggested. 'I could do with some new codeware. You got anything by way of barriers and lasers? Your old man's junk is getting dated.'

'I done some okay stuff recently,' said Lucas, one hand see-sawing in a so-so wave. 'Touched core on nearly all of Gig and Talobos' companies. If you want assistance on *that* front.' He looked toward the briefcase; she saw he was itching to root through the jumble again, to unearth more gossip titbits for his hackchat friends. The kid sure made the most of having a famous mum and dad.

'I've already touched core on *all* of Gig and Talobos' companies,' said Harry firmly. 'Especially Gig's.'

Lucas looked confused. 'But he crashed you. Three times. Why didn't you get him back?'

'Gig is a hack, not a secop. If I want to prove I'm better than him, I have to withstand him. Not go smash up his cheap codebarriers—codebarriers that I'm sure he doesn't design himself. That would be vindictive. It's all about principle and knowing how to really get under other people's skin. Take your dad for instance. If I cut him off completely from my life, he'd get over it and move on. But if I keep up the charade of friendship, I get—'

'Er, are you sure you should be telling me this, Mum?'

God, thought Harry. The first time I talk openly to someone in years, and it's my son. Which was no bad thing, really. The very fact of his presence here established that his loyalties lay with her, not his father. Even if it was something of a crisis situation. Whatever did I do to deserve that? she wondered, touching his chin again and staring into his odd, ingenuous eyes.

Perhaps it was better not to ask.

'You can stay here,' she decided.

'Thanks!'

'Sleep in the guest room. No getting in my way, no messing with my gear, no resetting my vidscreen controls, no going through my wardrobe—'

'Can I help you on the case?' Lucas wanted to know.

'The case?'

'Arnold Lee. The murder. The hack showdown! The news is all around the qverse! Don't tell me you haven't even looked through this stuff!'

Harry glanced at the briefcase again. Yesterday she'd flicked through the crime scene footage, and had swiftly tagged Arnold Lee's death a schizoid special. The term was Malachy Memphis'—he'd used it to describe his wife's suicide. A schizoid special: some poor fool so strung out on their own unique depression that they'd kill themselves with anything that came to hand. Schizoids pulled off the best deaths, the most insanely disturbing ones. Lee's was an average mania, with an above-average application.

'The guy just killed himself,' she said. 'No big deal. If Viger Singer wants to make a fuss, she can. But I'm not going to be part of it.'

'What about your name? Won't she spread it?'

The hackchats had all the details, it seemed. Obviously someone—probably Lloyd 'Talobos' Hong—had spilt his guts to the wrong people. Harry sighed. 'Viger's not the only one with leverage. I've got it figured out. She threatens to spread my name, and I'll threaten to type up an entire plaincode manual and publish it across the world. Let's see her maintain control of the qverse when people start creating their own code.'

'For Q,' said Lucas, mockingly, and made the triangle salute.

'Damn straight. I'll even give Malachy the first copy.'

Her grin was reflected in miniature on his face. It was a sobering moment. Harry stubbed out her cigarette in the kitchen sink. 'You want to go someplace, Lucas?' she asked, rolling a stiff shoulder. 'A gaming arcade? A park? Hawaii? I don't feel like going back into the qverse today.'

Her son beamed. 'I've never been to a real gaming arcade before. Dad says it rots the brain.'

Harry smirked. With a hand on his shoulder, she guided Lucas out into the warm, SouthAsian sun.

* * * *

SUNDAY

4

gig

Harmonica was an animal in the bedroom—not any one animal in particular, Gig amended, but some sort of sexed-up, sauced-up hybrid. Long, gazelle legs snared his waist with impossible strength; clawed tiger-fingers tore his chest; hard reptilian eyes fixed him with an inscrutable stare. Above him the smooth black ribbon of her body gleamed, breasts small yet somehow gravid, her hair unwinding in a slow, single curl to her waist. He caught a handful. It was as soft as silk.

God, Harmonica! The queen of q, the black witch. So aloof in person, so damned *untouchable* in q, but here, finally, in the debauchery of his dreams, the mother of hacks had consented to his whims. She wrapped her hands about his jaw and fed her tongue to his lips; and he trembled and reached for her, as a small child might; and she pulled away and looked at him in an odd fashion, as if seeing him clearly for the first time.

'You still haven't run,' she said.

'You know me, Harmonica. I never do—'

But then fate—never a friend to Felix 'Gig' McGuiggen—kicked in again, thrusting him rudely back into the real world. Sudden light rawed his eyes. Sweat pooled slickly on his chest. A large and furry object launched out of nowhere to land on his lap. Purring loudly, it needled its claws into his thigh. Gig yelped and sat up, only to see Ruth Nameri standing in his bedroom doorway, a clipboard tucked under her arm. She was fucking with the light switch.

On. Off.

On. Off.

On—

'Get lost, Ruth!'

He always found himself slipping into a kind of sibling rivalry with his cousin, a rivalry which inevitably devolved into an extended game of Who-Can-Annoy-The-Other-The-Best. More than once they'd left smart-suited corporate drones gaping while they volleyed curses across boardroom tables. Childish behaviour, of course, and probably detrimental to business on the whole. At this point Gig didn't care. He threw a pillow at her, shortly followed by the cat.

'I should report you for cruelty to animals,' said Ruth.

Gig growled. 'Give me a few minutes, and you'll be able to upgrade the charge to homicide.'

'Aww, poor Fuffypoo,' Ruth crooned, turning her attentions to the cat. 'Did the nasty Felix man hurt you because he's a bad-tempered so-and-so? Poor wittle Fuffy.'

But Fuffy plainly wasn't interested in her consolations. After treating Gig to a withering feline glare, the cat trotted out the door with his nose in the air. Off to lick his wounds in private, Gig guessed, and far from keen to become yet another casualty of a Gig vs. Ruth battle. Fuffy was one smart cat. Gig's mothers had maintained for years that Fuffy could smell a bitchfight from a mile off.

'What are you doing here?' Gig asked.

'I'm here to motivate, inspire and assist,' said Ruth.

'You said that with a straight face. I'm impressed.'

'I'm serious. I've done some research on your behalf,' Ruth said, settling cross-legged on the end of his bed. 'Turns out Viger Singer's theory isn't *that* farfetched. Aside from that 'q-inverse' stunt in NorthAsia, I've found over thirty medical reports in which neurocap malfunction is cited as the most likely cause of permanent neurological damage. Also nabbed a bunch of articles on a phenomenon known as 'AR in VR'—altered reality in virtual reality. Sources say it feels like you've taken a hit of LSD: the world distorts, you get visions, paranoia, strange physical sensations, numbness, the sort of crazy hippie shit your mothers are into. There's suggestions it may be caused by certain radio frequencies or areas with high magnetic fields...'

She paused to reorder her notes, giving Gig a chance to speak. 'You looked in the briefcase?' he groaned, groping one-handed under the bed for his boxer shorts. 'Don't you know there's a confidentiality clause? I could be sued.'

'Let me be frank with you, dear cousin.' Ruth spread her hands. 'In the race for INTROMET cash you are the underdog. Much as I'm loathe to take tips from hackchat bookies, I do feel that in the company of such big shots as Harmonica and Talobos you might be a tad outclassed. Now we *need* this million, and I will not jeopardise our chances by leaving it in your less-than-capable hands.'

Sneaking the boxers under his blankets, Gig affected a discreet bum-wiggle into them. 'Playing along to get Singer off my back, that I understand. But why do we need money? I thought we were doing all right.' He stared at her, suddenly appalled. 'We *are* doing all right, aren't we?' he pressed.

'For the moment. But Gig...'

'But Gig what?'

'But I'm not bloody Harmonica, that's what!' Ruth snapped, smacking the back of her clipboard impotently against the mattress. Predicting an outburst, Gig had moved his legs just in time. 'Don't you get it, Gig?' she cried. 'Every time we secure a new contract, I can't just *create* codebarriers out of nothing. I have to buy parts from one of the qverse corporate trinity. Hunting down pockets of loose freecode is a mug's game; I don't have time for that kind of scavenger hunt. If we want to expand and evolve with the changing needs of our client-base, we'll need the money to fund it.'

Gig found he couldn't meet her eyes; they brimmed with expectations. Instead he crawled from the covers and sought out a pair of jeans from the chaos of his wardrobe.

Recently his mothers had placed a housekeeping embargo on his room, reasoning that at twenty-eight their son was fully capable of performing such tasks as vacuuming, tidying, and laundry. Matching socks and ironed suits were now a thing of Gig's past. He rifled clumsily through the mess for a clean top until Ruth, taking pity, tossed him a tee-shirt.

'I've taken the liberty of reorganising your schedule for today,' she said. 'You'll be double-checking the testimonies of Arnold Lee's co-workers in the afternoon. After that it's a shuttle to Perth and a visit with Lee's widow the next morning.'

'Why?'

'What do you mean, why? I've told you why. Because we're going to find out how they brain-hacked Lee, and we're going to *get* that million dollars.' She snapped the clipboard closed. 'I'll leave my notes with you; you can read over them while you change.'

'Sure,' Gig lied, accepting the clipboard. He didn't put much stock in Ruth's research. AR in VR, neurological damage, magnetic fields—he was sure he'd read similar 'facts' on arcade gaming billboards. At any rate he'd already eliminated brain-hacking from his list of possible causes. If you hacked an INTROMET employee in an INTROMET neurocap in the middle of INTROMET territory, chances were that Viger Singer would know about it. There would be recordings and traces and codelogs, none of which Viger had supplied in her briefcase of bollocks.

No, this wasn't about brain-hacking. And Gig was not an objective investigator but an element of the puzzle. Because Ruth was right—he wasn't in the league of Harmonica and Talobos.

Why me? He'd been asking the right damned question from the start. Why the hell did you choose *me*, Viger Singer?

'One little job for the CEO of INTROMET and my life is no longer my own,' he lamented, fumbling for his sneakers. 'At least I'll be able to have my breakfast in peace. Right?'

Ruth shook her head. 'You have guests.'

'Oh, God!'

'No one quite so prominent, I'm afraid,' Ruth replied, smirking. 'Just a few of our local clients.'

'Oh, geeks!'

Ruth rolled her eyes. 'You can be such an unlikable prick sometimes, Felix,' she said, spinning on a heel. 'You're lucky I'm too busy to tell them you said that.'

And what would they do if you did? Gig wondered as he laced his sneakers. Their only local clients *were* geeks; he doubted any of them would dispute the fact. In the late forties the small group of qverse addicts had pooled resources and founded a thriving little piracy business on the outskirts of TEEK territory. The sole purpose of their business was to sneak freecode samples out of INTROMET and SWIFTWATER.

And back in again.

Dirty work, as Ruth liked to say, but *someone* had to do it.

Corporate spies had never impressed Gig, but his company had been the geeks' first port-of-call when they began head-hunting for a secop. Possibly because he was one of the few mid-range secops who could turn a blind eye to code-piracy occurring right under his nose. Possibly because they were impressed by tales of the Harmonica wars: he *had* crashed the queen of q and secured the most coveted belt-notch in the hack-circuit. Or possibly (and probably) because his bitchy cousin was having it off with one of them—although what she saw in those fleshy mulattos was beyond him.

After all, Gig noted bitterly, people saw nothing in *his* fleshy mulatto backside.

* * * *

Three geeks sat around the McGuiggen family dining table, posed at different stages of pancake consumption. At the kitchen cooker Gig's mothers performed their forty-year-old double act: Honoria cast as the brazen neo-feminist, Sandra playing the belaboured, world-weary domestic. Ruth had once commented that Gig took after both his mothers. Which meant, Gig supposed, that he was a double act unto himself.

So conflicted.

'The qverse is the world's first and only example of anarcho-capitalism,' Honoria was reading aloud from a pamphlet, 'a system regulated and controlled by three corporate CEOs. Unlike its poorer relative, the internet, the qverse cannot be physically expanded without hands-on assistance from these CEOs. The qverse's construction base, "plaincode", is a closely kept secret. It is the mission of For Q to discover how plaincode operates, thereby liberating the qverse from its capitalist oppressors—'

'No Malachy Memphis at my breakfast table,' Gig grunted, falling onto a chair.

Honoria shook her head. '*My* breakfast table?' she said. 'Hark at the lad, Sandra, and his antiquated patriarchal compulsions. Claiming and conquering. I suspect he'll be colonising the living room next.'

'Comes from your side of the family,' Sandra said, sliding Gig a fresh pancake and a pitcher of bitter lemon-syrup. 'My family were *never* the colonising type.'

'My stars, listen to this now.' Honoria was at the pamphlet again. 'Our For Q revolutionary has moved onto familiar ground: 'Men built the qverse but their good intentions were subverted by the three women who now rule it.' Why, I'd say that harks back to the myths of Adam and Eve, wouldn't you?'

'Only if Adam was a Mormon,' said Sandra, staring balefully into the frying pan. 'Or a Muslim. Aren't they allowed a lot of wives too?'

'I'm certain I don't approve of it,' Honoria sniffed. 'It's all absolute poppycock if you ask me. Blatant exploitation of women. When our boy gets married he'll only have the one wife, you can be sure of that. Then again, considering he can't even convince a woman to *date* him...'

'Oh dear,' said Sandra, covering her face. 'Not in front of the guests.'

The geeks tittered nervously until Gig glared across the table at them, his whittled-down ego desperate to pick a fight he stood a chance of winning. And the geeks were easy pickings. Society's dregs, the lot of them: weak-wristed asthmatics in faded jeans and baggy t-shirts that failed miserably to conceal their post-pubescent pudge. In hack circles the local crew were notorious for their fondness for qverse buzzwords and For Q propaganda.

No prizes for guessing where Honoria's pamphlet had come from. Stupid bastards.

His own anger surprised him; it felt horribly out of character. All Ruth's fault, Gig decided. The bitch had deprived him of sex. With *Harmonica*... Gig froze. Hang a tic, he thought. I'm angry because I missed out on dream-sex with dream-Harmonica?

Good God, I must be the saddest man on earth.

While his mothers bickered on about Gig's shortcomings, the geeks conferred amongst themselves. Presently one raised his napkin, waving it in a hesitant semaphore that Gig translated as an apologetic 'Pardon me, sir...'

'What?' he said, glowering over his third pancake.

'Er, Gig?' the geek mumbled.

'Not Gig. Felix. In *there*, I'm Gig. Out *here*, I'm Felix. Got it?'

'Sorry. Felix.' The geek hung his head into a hammock of chins. 'Look, what I came to say—what *we* came to say...

See, we're not here about business. I mean business is fine. We've had no problems from hacks. Ruth's been very helpful. Thank you. Er. What we're here about, you see...' He lowered his voice to a conspiratorial whisper. 'It's the INTROMET affair. The battle of the hacks. It's very important that you join For Q.'

Gig didn't laugh in the geek's face; a credit to his self-control. 'What's your name?' he asked.

'Phatman.'

'So your parents predicted your future glandular problems? How uncannily astute of them.'

'Felix!' Honoria warned, tuning in at precisely the wrong time. 'Manners!'

Gig showed his teeth. 'I'm so sorry, Phatman. I hope I didn't hurt your feelings, Phatman.'

'Bradley,' the geek admitted, his blush eclipsing his acne. 'Bradley Ah Chow.'

'Right, Brad.' Gig stifled a burp. 'Well I don't know what my cousin told you, but I'm not interested in For Q. Frankly I think you're a bunch of cranks. And code-pirates to boot. There isn't a high-level hack or secop anywhere in the qverse who'd design to speak to your type. Hell, I wouldn't join For Q if Malachy Memphis asked me himself.'

'He has,' said Bradley.

'What?!'

At first he imagined it a joke: get back at pretty boy Gig for being such a moody asshole. But Bradley's expression was fatly sincere. Why me? Gig thought—and realised belatedly that he knew the answer to that one. Sure, it wasn't every day that one of the qverse's major players extended a personal invitation to him. But then again, it wasn't every day that Viger Singer plucked him from a host of wannabe hacks and turned him into a bonafide qverse celebrity.

It was like being touched by a god, Gig thought, his stomach turning.

May the saints preserve me from the attentions of earthbound deities.

'Last night we went to see Memphis speak in a hackchat conference,' a second geek explained. 'He was talking about the battle of the hacks. Obviously, he mentioned you in his speech. So during the question time Bradley stood up and told Memphis that we knew you. In real life.'

'Thanks, Phatman,' said Gig.

'Memphis wants to talk to you,' Bradley said miserably. 'He was concerned about your well-being. We're just passing on the message.'

'I said *thanks*, Phatman.'

'Anyone else would be pleased by the news,' the second geek muttered. Eric, Gig remembered suddenly. The second geek was Eric, and the quiet one was Zhadesh—the kid Ruth was dating. 'This is Malachy Memphis we're talking about. The man who created the neurocap. The man who all but mapped the subconscious. Benny Soo would still be a mid-level systems administrator if it wasn't for Memphis. Hell, when you think about it, Memphis is the *real* father of the qverse.'

'If Malachy Memphis is so great, why doesn't he know plaincode?'

'Because Benny Soo betrayed him...'

'Uhuh. And then Rebecca Descartes betrayed him. And then Phoun Swiftwater betrayed him. And then Viger Singer bought the lot of them out.' Gig snagged a fourth, fifth and sixth pancake from the pile Sandra had conscientiously rolled. 'My heart bleeds for the guy. Either he has extraordinarily poor choice in friends, or he's a bloody unlikable bastard.'

Eric reared up indignantly. 'Just the sort of response I'd expect from your type,' he snapped. 'You take advantage of hackchats and freecode trading, and everything else that For Q has petitioned TEEK for. But when it comes to giving a little back in return, you bite the hand that feeds you. Well I'll tell you something for nothing, Felix, Gig, whatever you want to call yourself—'

'I want to know what happened.'

It was Zhadesh who'd spoken. He smiled calmly at Eric, which off balanced the geek so much that he sat down with a bump. Zhadesh turned his smile on Gig, then. It was a quietly *knowing* smile, the expression somehow reminiscent of those spaced-out guru children that washed up on India's shores every couple of years. Skinny shaven-headed Buddhas. Gig translated the smile as a smug, 'You talk a big game for a twenty-eight-year-old who still lives with his mothers,' and was suitably abashed.

'Please, Felix, forget what you may think of Memphis,' said Zhadesh. The guy even *talked* like a guru: all big lazy vowels like a guided meditation tape. Or like a NorthAsian martial arts master from a twentieth century kung-fu movie. 'Isn't your curiosity motivation enough? We've all heard the stories of the beginning. The Q-genesis. But a lot of it doesn't make sense. I'm sure you've noticed that too.'

'Actually, I—'

'For instance, how did Soo and Memphis meet? Why was Rebecca Descartes chosen as the first person to enter the qverse? We know Descartes believes in For Q's message, so why doesn't *she* teach Memphis plaincode? Who is Phoun Swiftwater and why do no records of her exist anywhere in GreaterAsia? And where does Harmonica fit into all of this? The mother of all hacks is the mother of all conspiracy theory headaches. He-or-she writes plaincode and carries Soo lasers. But he certainly didn't figure out plaincode on his own. And despite his undisguised hatred of Descartes and occasional destruction of TEEK property, Harmonica has no connection to any of the main players. Right?'

The geeks stared at him patiently until Gig realised that something was expected of him. 'Are you asking me?' he managed.

'Of course. You're the one who met him,' said Zhadesh, raising an eyebrow. 'Don't tell me you didn't even *ask*.'

Gig knew when he was beat. 'What's Memphis going to do?' he said sullenly, swiping all three remaining pancakes out of spite. 'Invite me around to his house for a few drinks? I've got a busy social calendar. Checking brain-hacking testimonies. Interviewing grieving widows. Being Viger Singer's gofer is a full time occupation.'

Zhadesh chuckled, and even over-anxious Bradley cracked a smile. Digging in his pocket, Zhadesh withdrew a square copper q-cache and skimmed it across the table. 'The password for cache access is For Q,' he said. 'Check it after seven tonight. I expect that Malachy Memphis himself will tell you what to do from there.'

* * * *

'It happened in q-Topia,' Tweedle Dee began. 'SWIFTWATER territory. I was walking through one of those star-portal tubes and everything suddenly went dark. I'd been feeling dizzy for a while beforehand, but didn't think anything about it—I was probably coming down with something. I figured that the blackout was just a power surge; SWIFTWATER isn't the most stable territory. A second later the lights came on again. And I saw that I was somewhere else entirely: a long dark hallway…'

'Like one of those ancient old mansions from the twentieth century,' Tweedle Dum elaborated. 'Of course Seran didn't port out immediately because he was curious. The area was completely unfamiliar to him—and Seran here has seen a *lot* of the qverse! So he kept walking down the hallway in the hope of finding out where he was.'

'A few minutes later the hallway vanished again, and this time it didn't reappear,' said Dee. 'I took off my neurocap and discovered to my horror... that I was in my lounge room.'

Gig stared.

'He was in his bedroom to begin with,' Dum explained, once the silence had moved from simply uncomfortable to downright embarrassing. 'While he was travelling through this strange house, someone *possessed* his body and brought it into the lounge room. If he'd been in the trance any longer, they could have made him jump off his balcony. Dead! I had virtually the same experience. Except in my case I was in an alien spaceship and they were putting words into my head subliminally.'

'I felt it!' said Dee. 'I felt myself being taken over. I was hacked. We both were. Our bodies were being controlled by some external power. God's honest truth. You can ask anyone here; they'll tell you Pat and I aren't the type to make things up.'

Now *that* I don't doubt, Gig thought, clutching Viger Singer's briefcase to his chest. If I ask anyone here, they'll corroborate your story.

Probably word-for-word.

Tweedle Dee and Tweedle Dum. Their real names were Seran Yee and Patrick Young. Despite the fact that one was blond, their facial features were so similar they might have been twins. Corporate INTROMET clones in identical pinstripe suits, all they lacked were the Tweedle-trademark propeller beanies. Their shared mannerisms and inflections reminded Gig of sitcom odd couples, people who'd lived or worked together for so long they could finish each other's sentences.

From the beginning of the 'interview' it had been made absolutely clear that Gig would only be allowed to speak to them *together*. All attempts to separate them were met with smiles and polite laughter. As a fan of old cop shows, Gig was positive that this sort of open collaboration wouldn't cut it in a real police station. Even worse, not only were the two sticking to their 'brain-hacking' stories, but they were sticking to them to the point where they were actually quoting bulky sections from their written testimonies.

Viger Singer is playing with me, Gig thought. She's giving me authority and then putting limits on it, as if I'm some spoilt kid who needs taking down a peg or two. And these two fools *know* it. They're sitting there, laughing at me behind their corporate smiles.

Damn the Tweedle-twins. Damn the geeks. Damn Ruth Nameri. Gig calculated today's running score in the Game of Life:

WORLD : 3
FELIX 'GIG' MCGUIGGEN : 0

'I think hacking our brains was a practice run,' said Dum. 'They were testing to see how far they could go. If their methods worked. Maybe they hadn't got control yet of all the body parts...'

'...we were guinea pigs. Pawns. I expect they did it with some sort of virus. Like the ones you have in lasers, but more powerful. One that could corrupt the neurocap itself. Which narrows down the field of suspects. There are only four people in the world who could write a virus like that. The four people who can read plaincode. Benny Soo, Harmonica, Rebecca Descartes and Phoun Swiftwater.'

'And Viger Singer,' said Gig.

Dee looked shifty. 'Well, no one really knows if she...'

'Viger *bought* the qverse off them. Would you buy a plastic aeroplane kit without a construction guide? Viger is a smart woman. I'd be bloody surprised if the purchase didn't include a manual.'

The Tweedle-twins exchanged concerned looks. Disgusted, Gig rose from the table and walked to the window. In the tinted glass he saw his face—round, distraught—superimposed on the scape of Sydney, the once majestic waves of the opera house dwarfed now by INTROMET's gleaming blue towers. Five of them ringed the harbour, their lean bodies slightly bowed as if accommodating the weight of the sky. A fitting testament to Viger's megalomania.

How often do you look down on your towers, Viger Singer? Gig wondered. How often do you curl your fingers to shadow their span?

And more importantly: Does it turn you on?

'What do you know about Arnold Lee?' he asked, turning back.

'We worked with him for a short time,' Dum offered. 'After his last design project was completed Lee moved into Biocheck development. Biocheck watches—I'm sure you've seen the advertisements for them. Lee seemed a very nice man. A little on the loud side, though. He didn't fit in particularly well with our sector. We're often called the conservative chapter by the new blood.'

'That wasn't why he didn't fit in,' Dee said. 'It was because of the rumours. There was a ruckus in the design department before Lee was moved into hardware. We heard he was a double agent.'

'Funny,' said Gig. 'I thought they were all made redundant after the Cold War.'

'A *corporate* double-agent,' Dee corrected himself. 'Ms Singer discovered that quite a few of his designs were similar to recent SWIFTWATER work. And vice versa. Of course SWIFTWATER denied all accusations of code plagiarism, just as we did...but after that no one really trusted Arnold Lee. I have a feeling he was brought to us so we could keep an eye on him. To see that he didn't get into trouble.'

'I guess you failed.'

'He was already in trouble. It was just a matter of time.'

Gig gnawed on the remnants of his fingernails. 'Are you insinuating that SWIFTWATER killed Arnold Lee over code-piracy?'

The Tweedle-twins shrugged in perfect unison. 'Code-piracy is worth millions each year,' Dum said. 'One dead spy... or two... is an excellent deterrent. Let's just say that if SWIFTWATER did kill him, well, it wouldn't be the first time. Allegedly Phoun is connected to EastAsian gangs. Y-A-K-U-Z-A. Those people have ways of...making things happen.'

Back to square one of Conspiracy Theorem 101. Gang warfare meets the qverse? Phoun Swiftwater calls in Japanese heavies to settle virtual reality scores? From the way these two were talking, it was a minor miracle that Zhadesh and the local geek crew were still breathing. The entire notion was absolute poppycock, as Honoria would say. Gig stifled a groan. 'Fine, okay,' he said. 'But where does brain-hacking come into—'

He stopped. His hand dropped from his mouth.

Hang on a moment.

Where am I? What am I doing in here?

For the first time he took in his surroundings. The Tweedle-twins had chosen an odd little room to stage their 'interview'. Too large for an office, too small for a boardroom. Uncarpeted and featureless, its Spartan furnishings consisted of a distilled water dispenser, four chairs, an ashtray and a plastic table. A pretty ordinary layout for the lower floor of a corporate building, right? But they were on the fiftieth floor, the stomping ground of INTROMET's middle-management. Most of the rooms they'd passed on the way had been lavishly decorated, every spare inch of wall occupied by a showcase of INTROMET's business triumphs.

So what would a multi-billion dollar company like INTROMET need a room like this for?

Not to welcome clients, and certainly not to work in.

In the fickle world of qverse politics, there was only one feasible purpose for this room.

Interrogations.

That *was* it, wasn't it?

Gig took a deep breath. The Tweedle-twins schooled their faces in patient understanding. No, not twins, Gig realised. A set of identical twins where one was Asian, the other plainly Anglo? Genetically impossible, even in SouthAsia. The slippery little creatures must have been *cut* that way, right down to Dee's fake epicanthic fold.

A pair of scalpel addicts. Just like their employer.

'What did I do to INTROMET?' Gig blurted.

Dee blinked. 'I beg your pardon?'

'What did I do to INTROMET!' Hysteria tweaked the pitch of his voice to an unflattering shrill. 'It's a simple question. There's got to be a reason *why* Viger is doing this to me. What made her choose me? Why am I on this wild goose chase? Why is everyone who's *anyone* suddenly fascinated by my every move? Hell, why did Malachy bloody Memphis send me a cache?'

'Malachy Memphis sent you a cache? I don't see—'

Dum's reassurances were interrupted by a screech from Gig's vidphone. Paranoia made Gig clumsy: he almost dropped the thing twice. Once he'd read the text message flashing on the screen, Gig almost dropped it a third time.

URGENT MESSAGE FOR 'GIG'

WE NEED TO TALK OK!
YOU HAVE TIME FOR ME?
I SEE YOU MONDAY. WILL SEND SHUTTLE
OK BYEBYE! XOXOXOX

SENDER : PHOUN SWIFTWATER

Gig took another deep breath. Then he turned off his vidphone and walked out of the interview room, ignoring the Tweedle-twins' spluttering protests. He caught an elevator to ground level. He caught a taxi to the shuttleport. He caught the 4.09 shuttle bound for Perth, and somewhere over Alice Springs he dropped Malachy Memphis' q-cache into the shuttle's disposal unit and pressed the PURGE button. With his nose pressed to the glass, he imagined he could see the tiny square shooting across the backdrop of redlands like a miniature comet.

Gig spent the remainder of the journey being sick in the toilet. Those pancakes and lemon-syrup came up much the same way they went down: yellow, bitter and soft.

* * * *

5

harmonica

Game, paused. On screen an anime pin-up whistled theme songs through dot.com lips, balloon breasts bobbing to the beat. Tacky eroticism. Harry didn't have to look at the game's packaging to know the manufacturer. "Shuttle 3XV" had Phoun Swiftwater's name all over it: fast cars, sexy chicks, copious drug references and designer guns. Amazing, how a Catholic Japanese princess could so perfectly intuit the triggers of the average male libido.

'Are you sure I can eat Malaysian for breakfast?' Lucas popped his head round the kitchen door, looking dishevelled and tragically effeminate; he'd spent much of the morning blundering about in Harry's pink silk nightgown. 'Dad said that take-out gives you germs.'

'Yes dear, but Dad is full of bullshit. Malaysian food only kills you if you leave it out on the bench for a week.' A multitude of cardboard take-out boxes littered the lounge room floor—last night's gourmet dinner for two. Harry flipped the lid off one and sniffed its contents. 'I eat this damn stuff every day. Do I look germy to you?'

'I guess not.' Reassured, Lucas vanished into the kitchen again. 'Can we do some investigating today?' he called. 'Please? I've got a heap of theories. We should go to INTROMET and hunt down Arnold Lee's friends. Better yet, visit his widow.'

'Kid, I told you yesterday that I'm not going to be Viger's lackey.'

'Muuu-um. It'll be fun! Heaps more fun than having you beat me at console games all day.' Lucas' voice creaked: the words came out half little-kid whine, half throaty teenage complaint. 'The Arnold Lee murder is like a real life detective story.'

Harry snorted. She was about to get up when the anime pin-up on the wall screen dissolved into static. Vidphone message incoming. Which was odd, because to Harry's knowledge she hadn't approved the call. Nor was she likely to, at this early hour.

'Luke? Have you been fiddling with the vidphone? I told...' She stopped. 'Oh.'

There was a man on the wall screen. A man or a bastard, depending on your choice of social sub-category. Even with folded arms and clenched jaw, he looked like an oriental adaptation of those saccharine cherubs on old-fashioned Hallmark cards—soft-faced, round-eyed, with a crest of silky curls. The shtick would have been cute if he was, say, eleven, but at fifty-something there was a sprinkling of wrinkles at his hairline and yesterday's puppy fat had slowly but surely matured into today's middle-aged spread.

Li Ben Nee Soo. Benny Soo to the qverse riffraff, That Cheating Swine to the ex-Mrs Soo.

'Hi, lover,' said Harry. 'How's the conscience?'

'What the hell do you think you're playing at, Regina?' Benny raged from the lounge room wall. 'INTROMET has you under heavy-duty surveillance and Rebecca called to tell me you've been crashing TEEK again. Normally I wouldn't give a shit who you chose to harass, except at some mid-point in your destructive warpath you also managed to kidnap my son.'

Locating a clean chopstick amongst the floor's detritus, Harry stabbed it at the vidphone's remote control. Benny's image didn't so much as flicker. Evidently her annoyingly prescient ex-husband had managed to override the vidphone's manual controls. Short of killing the power to the entire apartment complex, there was nothing Harry could do to shut him up.

'Did Viger put you up to this, honey?' she asked, re-examining the remains of yesterday's take-out mee goreng with a critical eye.

'Don't be a fool.' Benny's voice trembled with that early-morning frustration she remembered so well. 'You know I've kept my connection to you out of Singer's radar. With luck it will stay that way, unless you choose to blab your life history to hackchat goons. Wouldn't put that past you—you've never been the model of discretion. Where is my son?'

'In the kitchen, getting me a beer. Look, love, do you mind getting off the screen? We were in the middle of a game of Shuttle 3XV and I'm winning by sixty thousand points.'

Benny's eyes rounded. 'You sent my son to *get you beer*?'

'Yes. Please note: that's *beer*, not crack cocaine. And it's in the damn kitchen, not down at the local pub.' Harry plucked at a morsel of wilting tofu. 'Really, it's not as if you can talk about responsible adult behaviour. You're the one who taught him—' but hesitated there, uncertain, because at that moment a guilty-faced Lucas had appeared in the kitchen doorway, beer in hand. Safe outside Benny's vidscreen periphery, her son shook his head with a vehemence. Harry winced.

Oh, Lucas.

You disappoint me.

'You're the one who taught him... how to swear,' she covered lamely.

'Swear? He's never cursed in front of me.'

'The boy has some mouth on him,' Harry said. 'But I think I've beaten that impulse out of him. There's no habit a bit of the old birch can't break.'

Benny looked faint. 'I'm going to send a cab over to pick him up.'

'The hell you will. You've always said I should try to bond with the children. Well I'm doing it now, aren't I? Honestly, Benny—Lucas is fine here. We're getting along okay. I'm not beating him or getting him hooked on drugs. Just let him stay for a few days. Please?'

An interminable silence passed before Benny would concede a 'Huh' in reply. Huh, Harry decided, was as close to approval as she was likely to get on this matter. Benny wouldn't say *yes* outright to her. Saying *yes* wasn't part of Benny Soo's style. Best to change the topic now, before he could turn that Huh into a No Bloody Way.

'The grapevine says you're working for Singer now,' she said. 'What's it like to sell your soul to the devil?'

Benny smirked corporate argot: 'We have a beneficial business relationship—'

'How does Rebecca feel about that?'

The smirk died. 'I am not going to talk to you about Rebecca.'

'But the bitch is free to talk about me, right? Don't deny it—you said yourself that she called. Poor woman. I almost feel sorry for her. Siding with the INTROMET enemy must put a strain on your relationship.' Harry raised a hand and Lucas, recognising the cue, tossed her the beer. Instinctively Benny's dark eyes darted sideways, straining to peer beyond the limits of the screen's 80x60. 'Guess old Bec's luck is running out. She's managed to evade me thus far, but one of these days we'll run into each other, and when we do—' Harry mimed a merciless assault-by-chopstick.

'I am not going to talk to you about Rebecca.'

'Well, if you're not up to discussing your much-denied affair with Rebecca Descartes, let me nominate a conversational tangent.' Party trick moment: Harry's forearm, the beer-cap, a sharp twist and the satisfying hiss of expelled gas. 'Business. If you're really in Singer's pocket,

I bet you have the inside track on INTROMET's side-projects. Don't suppose Singer mentioned a bloke named Arnold Lee and a very ill-advised blackmail threat?'

'No, but she did mention that you'd been buggering about on her time. Let me tell you something about Viger Singer. She holds grudges. You, Talobos, Gig—the three of you are mercenary little fucks. You in particular have ripped INTROMET off time and time again. My advice is that you do what she asks. Then stay the hell out of her territory.' The vidphone's reception zigzagged. Benny battled static to get in the last word. 'By the way, Regina, I'd warn your mate Gig to avoid the hackchats. Jealousy breeds revolt amongst the unwashed q-masses. Tall poppy syndrome—it's a SouthAsian epidemic.'

Then he was gone. The vidphone crackled a death-wheeze and subsided into blackness. Harry looked at Lucas—a good long squirm-inducing stare.

'I did fry my school,' Lucas blurted, 'but I didn't get caught. I did learn plaincode, but Dad never taught me. I'm not in trouble, but when I heard about the battle of the hacks I needed to help you win. I didn't want to lie but I didn't want you to send me back, either—'

'Hm,' said Harry.

'Honestly, I learned it myself! Dad keeps all his old programming notes in the attic. And once you know how to view plaincode, it's easy. I've been playing with q gear for years. Hardware *and* software. I'll be an asset to the case, not a hindrance. And maybe if I solve this, you could get me part-time work as a secop...'

Harry returned her attention to the mee goreng.

'Mum! I'm not like Nicole and Lyn. I didn't lie to you to get some sort of petty revenge. They only lie to you because they think you hate them. Even our stupid therapist thinks you hate us. But I know you don't. I understand you.'

'Oh?'

He knelt beside her and folded his hands over her knee. 'You don't hate us,' he said. 'You just didn't really want a family, that's all.'

And suddenly she was off balanced again, feeling small and pathetic. Way to go Lucas. That was the second time he'd done it in as many days. God, this time it really *hurt*; not a guilt-hurt but something finer and deeper and difficult to define. Weakly, Harry reached out and touched the side of his mouth. 'Go have a shower while I call Jo,' she said. 'Then we'll go be detectives, okay? We can visit your Lee-widow and interrogate her.'

Her son beamed, kissed her cheek, and skipped off to the bathroom in a whirl of pink silk. A minute later Harry heard the water running and Lucas yodelling some neon-pop refrain. Too cute for his own damn good, she thought sourly, reaching for the vidphone remote. She tried Joaquin Magdellin's number twice but got no response. Typical of the little git—he was probably screening calls. Or had a girl over.

Or had been ordered not to associate with Regina Carter by the embittered Ms TEEK-Descartes, who was still smarting over the destruction of her precious q-Paris.

Joaquin's answering machine recommended that she leave a message after the prompt, and he would get back to her at the soonest opportunity.

Never an optimist, Harry just hung up.

* * * *

An air-traffic blunder caused a three hour delay just over the western border. In-flight entertainment consisted of a badly dubbed Kong-fu joke. Worse still, some infrequent flyer had holed up in the nearest loo and was vomiting loudly enough to drown out the shuttle's engine. Apparently this kind of airborne catastrophe was business as usual for economy shuttle passengers. A crying shame, Harry thought, that first-class travel required a two day pre-booking.

'Q?' Lucas suggested, fishing an adulterated INTROMET neurocap from the 'detective bag' he'd packed. 'Catch you in SWIFTWATER q-Topia in a minute.'

Harry had misgivings. The idea of cavorting about the qverse with Lucas in tow felt somehow *inappropriate*. Wasn't q about escapism and the shedding of responsibilities like motherhood? To enter with her son would be contrary to the system's basic tenets; it blurred the boundaries she'd so carefully constructed between her real and virtual lives. But the kid was already *in*, goggles on, deaf to anything external to the cap's earphones. It seemed the decision had already been made for her.

Grumbling, Harry snapped on her own neurocap. A control prompt began to buzz the second she connected, loudly informing her she had new mailbox messages. The majority of these turned out to be impersonal business queries; it took a matter of moments to reroute them to the right employees. Two letters of For Q propaganda gave her pause. For Q spam was commonplace—practically epidemic—but the sender in this instance claimed to be one Malachy Memphis.

'Still haven't given up on me?' Harry murmured, reading:

> M'lady Carter.
>
> It's been a long time; longer than I'd like. Of course (forgive me my impertinence!) I still think of you as an old friend, although your opinions of me may not be as favourable.
>
> How go the hack-battles? You've always made your position on For Q perfectly clear, but I wonder if present circumstances haven't made you reconsider your apolitical bent. You can't be a lone revolutionary all your life. Sooner or later you'll have to pick a side, and with Rebecca gunning for blood and Viger breathing down your back, now's as good a time as any.
>
> I have enclosed some reading material you may find enlightening. Please contact me.
>
> Yours, MM.

Cute. But not, Harry reflected, cute *enough*.

Especially not from the man who'd coined that unshakeable 'black bitch' epithet.

She deleted both letters, closed her control screen, and ported into q-Topia.

God, SWIFTWATER country! Benny had once remarked that Phoun Swiftwater had a Fauvian attitude toward city planning and interior decoration. Everything she created was larger and louder and brighter than life. Her rooms were a mishmash of cultures, their elements spliced haphazardly together.

According to SWIFTWATER's marketing department, q-Topia was a faux-futuristic gaming arcade and youth hangout, spread out across a network of skyscrapers. A grand city of curves and spade-headed towers, the place owed as much to the Taj Mahal as the B-grade sci-fi movies it sought to emulate. Lime green turrets spoked the sky, ripped from some acid-inspired fairy-tale. Translucent, tubular walkways flowed between them, forming an incredible, interwoven cat's-cradle of passages; a testament to both Phoun's planning genius and her complete lack of taste.

Beyond the towers, on the world's outer rim, a great sun gleamed over distant waters, its colour a gross egg-yolk yellow. Within its swollen eye, bright letters flickered, morphing into and out of religious placard maxims. PRAISE JESUS. LOVE THY NEIGHBOUR. GOD SO LOVED THE WORLD... and others, warring for subliminal control of the live-fast culture thriving beneath.

Harry landed, randomly, in a middle-floor arcade. Default skins clustered about archaic gaming apparatus, cheering every time the machines whoop-whoop-whooped a high score. Above, glossy screens looped pop-concert footage: some gross SouthAsian simulacra of Americana. Uncharacteristically modest cupids flitted near the ceiling, their baby-fat bodies garbed in what Harry supposed was Phoun's artistic riff on a ballerina's tutu.

Gingerly she threaded her way through the masses to a walkway. Tiny luminescent tumbleweeds with smiley faces rolled down it toward her. Impulsively Harry kicked one—it exploded in a shower of confetti. As she wiped her legs clean, it occurred to her that locating Lucas amongst the hubbub would be next to impossible. His trace was unfamiliar to her; he hadn't even described the skin he planned to use.

Damn that boy. Annoyed, Harry cast out a handful of traces like a fisherman's nets, hoping to catch someone—*anyone*—she recognised in the vicinity.

Felix 'Gig' McGuiggen showed up on her screen almost instantly, a blue light blinking at her from a nearby café. Harry investigated. The café's interior was nothing short of nightmarish. Fluffy anime monstrosities covered the walls; the chairs and tables were shaped like dumpy, googly-eyed animals. Harry found her hack nemesis tucked away in a wallside booth, cloaked in a simple default skin.

'Gig?' she prodded.

The skin giggled nervously. 'Er, no. It's me, Mum.'

'Lucas?'

'Yes. Sorry.'

Harry slid onto the bench opposite him. 'But you... My trace...' She took a breath. 'How the hell did you do that?'

'It's called masking. All traces identify me as someone else; it's like wearing a stolen face. The hackchats say the very concept is science fiction, but as a matter of fact Dad perfected it about eight years ago.' Lucas giggled again. 'So I stole it, replicated it. Pretty complicated hardware manipulation, even if you do know what you're doing. Necessary, though. Couldn't have Dad catching me tramping about the qverse on my own.'

'Why Gig?'

'I usually mask as mid-level secops and I've had Gig's details for ages. I figured you'd probably run a quick search for him because of the hack-battle.' He grinned. 'If you hadn't, we might never have found each other. I don't have a tracer on this cap. I hope you don't mind...'

'Of course not,' Harry lied. In truth she'd have been more comfortable catching him trying on her bras than trying on Gig's identity. 'You haven't gotten Gig into any trouble by wearing that...mask, have you?'

'I think he's got *me* into trouble. Dad was right about the tall poppy syndrome—hack folk have been tracing me since I ported in. Seems like they're itching to pick a fight.'

'Then shouldn't you—'

'Mum! You're *Harmonica*. Why should I be scared with you around?'

The kid had a point. Harry sighed and looked away. As her gaze roved the café's technicolour jumble she spotted a still, dark skin in the crowd. Instantly it shrunk away, cognisant of her interest; it shuddered in disgust; then it unfolded thin arms and lurched forward. An old woman— no, a *widow*-woman costumed in elaborate mourner's attire, pale face obscured by a dark veil. Something of her bent-backed progress recalled the Fates of Greek myth.

She stopped at their booth, gnarled hands cradling the knob of a walking cane.

'We're busy—' Harry began, but the widow-skin cut her off with a hoarse, wicked-witch cackle.

'Felix and Regina, well, well, well. Fancy running into you two here. Getting along famously, I see.' Shiny red lips gleamed beneath the veil. 'May I sit? Of course I may. We're old friends now—co-workers, really. Vying for employee of the month. Employee of the year. Employee of the damned dynasty. God, what a morning! I've been running all over on this fool's errand, from testimony checks to hardware queries to a tête-à-tête with one of those insufferable Lauren Fang women... Why if these legs were real I dare say I'd be unable to take another step.'

Talobos. He pulled up a chair—a pink, elephant-eared monstrosity—and settled on it, prissily rearranging the skin's voluminous black skirts. His audacity blew Harry away. Daring to sit with her without invitation! That was a frying offence, at the very least. But even as she reached for a laser, a maternal axiom looped through her mind: you're the adult; set a good example for the kid. What sort of behaviour patterns would Lucas learn from a mother who nuked people at the slightest provocation?

Reluctantly Harry settled back in the booth. 'What are you and your skin mourning, Lloyd?' she hissed. 'Your qverse survival instincts?'

'Gracious no! Have a heart! There's been a death in the family. *Our* family, I should say—our great big extended hack family, God love it.' Talobos fanned himself with a lace-edged handkerchief. 'Remember Yeunify? Real name Nelly Georges. Company drifter, but a damn decent hack. Ex-TEEK, Ex-SWIFTWATER, last seen working an INTROMET secop round to pay off a beach house mortgage. Suicide, poor dear. Completely unexpected. Just climbed out of her bedroom window and jumped. Thirty-second floor apartment. A tragic end. I knew her well—better than these miserably inadequate virtual tears would have you think.'

Harry glared. 'Pardon me. Can I help you with something?'

'No doubt a humanitarian would offer their condolences. But obviously such a gesture would prove too taxing for the great Harmonica.' The widow-skin drooped backward in a dramatic half-swoon, black skirts pooling about its waist—a dark stain on SWIFTWATER's rainbow canvas. 'Ah, why am I not surprised? If the qverse has taught me anything, it's that the mother of all hacks has a heart like a swinging brick. Still, it's a shame you two weren't close, Regina. You might have liked Yeunify. She shared your regard for authority. That is to say: she had none.'

In the qverse Harmonica, mother of hacks, smiled a grim smile. Outside in the real world, Regina Carter kicked the carriage bench opposite her.

'I've been drunk since Friday,' Talobos gurgled on. 'No, I tell a lie. There was a regrettable sober interlude on Saturday morning. Don't think me a lush, my dear hack den-mother, I *need* to be drunk. Helps me to see round corners. A different perspective, if you prefer to think of it that way. When drunk I feel like I am...as if I am outside my body, you see...as if I am watching one of these delightful prototypes of womanflesh—' Snickering, the skin slapped its thigh, the noise resonant and quite authentic. '—act out the part of Singer's pawn. Quite autonomous of me! So while the womanflesh plays, I sit beyond the proscenium and analyse each move, each thought. I am terribly empathic, you know; and sometimes I am in the skin's head, and sometimes I am in the killer's, and at others I imagine I see the world through Viger Singer's scalpel-cut eyes...'

'You think Arnold Lee was murdered?' Lucas asked, before Harry could stop him.

'Of course he was, darling boy!' Talobos squeaked, clapping his hands. 'If he wasn't murdered we wouldn't be on this mission, this daring jaunt through q-space! Dashing detective that I am, I've already narrowed the cause-of-death field to two possible scenarios.' He beckoned Lucas closer with a bejewelled finger, pitching his voice at a passable, if somewhat slurred, falsetto. 'Either something went wrong,' he crooned into the boy's ear, 'and we have to find it. Alternately, something went right, and we have to *not* find it. Have to not find it, haven't to find it, have to avoid it, is what I mean. The answer.'

'Is that some kind of hack poetry?' Harry gritted out. 'Your attempt at existentialism?'

'God no. Haven't you been listening to me? This is all very straightforward, or as straightforward as q can ever be.' He paused. 'Wait. Tell me that you *have* been investigating. That you've at least looked into the briefcase.'

Harry shrugged. 'Detective stuff isn't really my thing. The kid's more interested than I am.'

'Oh, I know little Felix has toed the line. Toed the line and then some. Easy to track down, this second-rate hack friend of yours.' The widow-skin blew casually on its fingernails, then fixed Harry with a tearful stare. 'You know he's part of it too, don't you? McGuiggen, I mean. He's not one of *us*, so he has to be one of *them* or one of something bigger. A bigger picture...'

'I *am* right here, Lloyd,' said Lucas. The kid was getting into the role, God love him.

Talobos slapped his forehead. 'Ha ha! I quite forgot. Are you spying on us, Mr McGuiggen? Saving and logging our pathetic conversation so that Singer may peruse it later at her leisure? Oh, don't look that way—I'm no paranoid.' He sighed a deep, histrionic sigh. 'There is this wonderful old foreign movie you two should watch. I thoroughly recommend it! Regrettably I forget its name, but names are so swiftly becoming irrelevant these days... In this movie, a beautiful young woman invites three past lovers to her house. All have betrayed her in some fashion and of course she desires revenge. But it isn't enough to murder those cheating bastards. First she wants to *use* them, as they used her...'

This was becoming ridiculous—no, check that. This was ridiculous. 'You're drunk,' said Harry, giving Talobos' chair a firm push away from the table. 'You're making a fool of yourself. Leave, for your own sake. Get out of the qverse, have a glass of water, and go to bed. Hell, go light a candle for your hack friend if it helps.'

'And leave you two vultures to reap the glory?' The widow-skin rose haughtily, sniffed, then staggered a few uneasy steps to the right. 'Fat chance. I doubt you'd work it out anyway. You don't have the minds for it. Because it's not about q, see. It's about people. I think... I think I can *feel* the edges of it, even through all this Singer-orchestrated bullshit, but there are still pieces that don't fit...'

'Your metaphors are as scrambled as your brains. Go home, Lloyd.'

'Go home, Lloyd,' Talobos echoed in a sing-song voice. 'Lloyd go home. Home, Lloyd go. Go home Lloyd—oh, you precocious bitch! You may know plaincode, but that doesn't give you the right to order me about; no, that right is reserved for that unholy Singer creatur—'

The widow-skin seizured and vanished.

'Oh come on, Mum,' said Lucas cheerfully, tucking away a laser. 'He *was* asking for it.'

* * * *

They flagged a yellow cab outside the shuttleport. Lucas claimed shot-gun and tucked himself in beside the driver automaton, knees wedged against the glove compartment, face pushed to the window. Reaching between the seats, Harry tugged him back down.

'Don't put your lips there. You don't know who else has been smooching the glass.'

'But I've never been to Perth...'

'Have you ever been to Beijing? If you've been to Beijing, you've been to Perth. Why do you think the Anglos call it Perking?' She gestured to the west where the city rose to meet the sky in compacted rectangular lumps. Municipal planners termed these ugly edifices 'Chinese apartments'. A typically NorthAsian answer to overcrowding—they just kept building *up* until the foundations began to protest, then started over. Like metal jenga blocks, Harry thought; pull one block out from underneath and it would all collapse.

On some level the notion of a collapsible city excited her. Such an act of vicious, easy terrorism appealed to the hack in her heart.

'Only to the qverse version,' said Lucas, 'and it's not really the same.'

'After you've finished your investigation I'll take you to China,' Harry promised. 'You speak Mandarin? Cantonese?'

'No.'

'That's okay. Neither do they... Hey. What's happening up there?'

At this time of night Harry had expected to find Perth's streets virtually deserted, frequented only by corner-stop whores and insurgent youth. But as they entered the city centre the place came suddenly alive with people. The road ahead thrummed with the systolic pulse of feet, a crazy tilt-a-whirl of partygoers, drunkards, overcoats, evening gowns, milling before the cab like cattle on a railroad track... A festival, Harry supposed; some foreign Anglo caucus stranded far, far from European shores.

The cab crept forward against the onrush and the scene outside shifted along slowly, like a slide on one of those ancient microfiche projectors. In an alleyway's mouth a troupe of musicians played a gypsy concerto, shadows collected around their shoulders like shawls. An anorexic blonde woman stabbed her way through a throng of laughing suits, her progress serenaded by an abrasive vidphone ringtone. By the stoop of a newspaper stand a small boy crouched, feeding pieces of orange peel to a one-eyed beagle. A man dressed in jeans and a cowboy hat flanked the cab for a time, swaggering along with a long cigarette in his mouth, size eighteen feet squeezed into ridiculous high heels.

Eurotrash, Harry thought, tapping lacquered nails against the window in irritation. The streets were awash with their detritus: stale popcorn, plastic wrappers, crumpled flyers. Perth locals watched from the sidelines, orientals and mulattos struck dumb by culture-shock, their heads bobbing like surprised pigeons. Outside an Asian take-out a goofy looking Chinese dragon roiled in a foam of cigarette smoke and car exhaust, its huge eyes silently amused by this Western chaos.

'It's *brilliant*,' Lucas breathed. 'Can we get out and walk?'

'God, no! We don't know these people.' Harry rapped her knuckles against the driver automaton's metal skull. 'The closest hotel. I don't care where it is.'

'Shangri-Lair,' said the automaton, pointing. 'We are right outside it, ma'am.'

Harry paid with a fistful of plastic-cash and dragged Lucas out, past red-cheeked hotdog vendors, past shrieking blondes, past teary flag-clutching geriatrics, and up a muddy red carpet into Shangri-Lair's cramped foyer. An acne-speckled hotel clerk smiled over the front desk at her, apology ready:

'No vacancy, sorry.'

'I don't care what the cost is,' Harry snapped. 'I need a room for two.'

'No vacancy, sorry,' the clerk repeated, still smiling, still apologetic. 'Big party night tonight, whole place booked out. Maybe another time, okey?'

'I'm not going to be here 'another time'. I want a room *now*.'

Lucas tugged at her. 'C'mon Mum, let's find somewhere else.'

'I give you number of different hotel, okey?' the clerk tried, rustling papers. 'You go there—'

'I will not go back out there into *that*. The entire city is filthy.' Harry jabbed a finger at the door, at the crowds, at the horrible confusion of it all. 'I don't even care what sort of a room it is—I've braved economy shuttle so I'm sure I can make it through a night in a twinshare. What do you people want from me? Look, I have credit cards...lots and lots of credit cards...'

Obviously the clerk had been trained to deal with situations like this: melodramatic businesswoman with kid in tow, lost and angry in the big jenga-block city. His smile did not falter an inch, but his hand strayed dangerously close to the desk's vidphone alarm. Not a threat. Just a sad inevitability. 'No vacancy, sorry,' he said. 'You go now, okey?'

Harry slammed her fist off the counter. 'Jesus H. Christ—'

'You can stay with me, sir.'

Harry turned around.

'I've got bunks,' said Gig. 'Do you mind bunks?'

He had a rough, unshaven look about him tonight; still pretty, but in a washed-out kind of way, like a child model past their celebrity use-by date. His choice of clothing fascinated her: novelty-tee shirt (I ♥ MELBIN!), worn jeans scissor-cut at the shin, one sock pulled up, one sock pushed down, and both unmatched. The rainbow lace of his right shoe had come undone.

'I think there's a couch-thing that folds out, too,' he said. 'You can sleep on that, sir, and your...'

'My son,' said Harry. 'Lucas.'

'Your son can sleep on a bunk. It isn't the nicest room in the hotel, but we're on the sixty-second floor. Great view.

Or would be a great view, if we weren't in bloody Perking.' He jammed his elbow into the elevator button behind him, adding thoughtfully, 'If you're worried about my motives, please rest assured that I won't steal your notes on the Singer case or undermine your investigation. I've just had an absolutely awful day and I hate being depressed on my own.'

Harry nodded dumbly. I'm in shock, she realised. No, not in shock. I'm in *surprise*—practically the same thing, but somehow more pleasant.

Beside her Lucas squirmed, craning up to whisper. 'Mum, who the hell is this guy?'

'Hi, Lucas,' said Gig, before Harry could answer. 'I'm Felix. Coming?'

He bent over and held out a slim brown hand. Lucas eyed it with distrust. 'I'm fourteen, not four,' he said. 'I don't need to hold your stupid hand.'

'I don't need you in my stupid hotel room, but I'm a big believer in not being a rude little shit to people.'

Lucas grinned. 'I like you, Felix,' he said, detaching himself from Harry and linking fingers with Gig. 'You're a lot more fun than Dad. Of course Dad isn't my real dad, my real dad lives in Sweden...'

'You have two dads? That's two more than I ever did.'

'What about your real dad?'

'This is the sixties, kid. I don't *have* a 'real' dad. I have two mothers, a pleuroplasmic Y chromosome and a laboratory guarantee. The chromosome alone cost twenty-five thousand, but my mothers figured it was worth it. They already had six girls.'

The elevator dinged its arrival. Gig entered, Lucas following, and jammed the door with a lace-trailing sneaker. Lucas still looked doubtful. 'Dad says every boy needs a strong male role model.'

Gig fixed Harry with a level stare. 'I *thought* I had one,' he said. 'Funny how things work out, ain't it, Carter.'

Harry smirked. 'You talk too much, McGuiggen,' she said, stepping into the elevator.

'Thank God you got in, sir,' said Gig, and pressed the button. 'If you didn't, I think I might have cried.'

* * *

SUNDAY – MONDAY

6

gig

It started making sense when the kid flashed a shiny new shuttle pass. At first glance the thing was innocuous enough: standard issue student concession, black emboss, unflattering passport snap wrapped up in greasy laminate. But the name? LUCAS CARTER-SOO. Carter-Soo! The mother of all hacks and the father of the 'verse itself, the two titans of q captured together for the first time! Could this child be the panacea for Zhadesh's mother of all conspiracy headaches?

Caught in the middle of unfolding the sofa bed, Gig gaped openly at the shuttle pass until a spasm of contracted bedsprings sent him ass-over-head to the floor. He sprawled across the grotty hotel two-ply, playing dead until the kid condescended to lend a hand. It was a small, soft hand with black-painted nails. Gig sat up and squeezed it tight.

'Hey...!' Lucas muttered.

'Carter-Soo, kid. Is that Soo as in...?'

Lucas rolled his eyes and pulled free. 'Yeah, yeah, Benny Soo. But I told you, he's not my *real* Dad. But he was still married to Mum when she had me, so he's my *legal* Dad. See—' and he tugged a small gold locket from the front of his shirt and popped it open for appraisal.

It held only one photograph—Benny's. Gig had seen pictures of the man before. Geek magazines regularly bore Benny's face—he was the closest the qverse had to a posterchild. On their glossy covers the creator of the qverse appeared as an austere geek archetype, suited, smart, with a round and somewhat anonymous face. But the locket photo presented him in a more human light: this was Li Ben Nee Soo as the frazzled father-figure, dredging up a token smile between the twin heartaches of divorce and infidelity.

Gig thought, I must be going mad. This has to be a dream, some sort of stress-induced vision. Getting up close and personal with the qverse's tyrannical overlord, that I could accept. Sharing a cheap hotel room with my virtual reality mentor was a stretch, but I'm coping fine. Running into the son of q's creator, the man who *made* a universe from the numbers-up, who revolutionised how we view the brain, how we view the world, and how we view ourselves...well, okay. I'll admit it. *That* comes as a bit of a surprise.

'He still loves Mum,' Lucas continued matter-of-factly, tucking the locket away again. 'He wanted to stay married, but Mum said no because he had an affair with Rebecca. You know, Descartes, the one who runs TEEK. At least Mum says he had an affair with Rebecca, but Dad says he didn't.

Rebecca got a restraining order put on Mum for the longest time, even though Mum never met her. Hey, was that a present from Viger?'

Gig followed the kid's gaze to the black INTROMET briefcase, which he'd left absent-mindedly by the sofa bed. 'I guess you could call it that,' he said, shrugging. He felt weirdly disorientated, as if the very balance of his brain had been offset by the all those qverse connection revelations. Christ! he thought. There was me thinking it was some sort of complicated corporate hush-up. Instead it's a bloody soap opera. Complete with angry ex-wives, bizarre love triangles, secret affairs, sexy Swedes, and precocious bastard offspring.

'How'd you get it?' Lucas prodded.

'Get what?'

'The briefcase, Felix. Weren't you listening to me?' By this stage the kid was kneeling on top of it, flicking the catches with bitten-down fingernails. 'Cripes, it's just like the one Mum got. You're a qverse geek, right? Wait, what am I saying—all Mum's friends are qverse geeks. So you know about the battle of the hacks, yeah? Well, my Mum said that I could investigate it. I've got all these brilliant theories about what happened, and—'

The kid paused at this juncture, his monologue interrupted by a short, terse expletive from the adjoining room. Shortly after their arrival, Harmonica had commandeered the wallscreen in the cramped space that passed for a kitchen in this budget hotel. Last time Gig looked in, the woman had been alternating between seven separate vidphone windows, waving the wallscreen remote as if she were the conductor of some digital orchestra. Before Lucas dragged him away, Gig had watched her unnoticed for a time, reflecting on the long curve of her body, one leg raised and braced on the wall, trousers riding up to expose a slim ankle posed balletically in its high black heel. She'd discovered a bar fridge, too; a beer nested in the crook of her elbow, an ashtray on her lap.

Talk about making yourself at home. But her rudeness did not offend him. He hadn't expected her to be social; she was too rich and too busy to concern herself with 'making nice'. That she had conceded to suffer his company at all was a triumph. No matter what his bitchy cousin claimed, Gig could be charming when he wanted to be.

Or, at the very least, inoffensive.

'—and my Mum says she'll let me be a secop for her company if I solve it,' Lucas said, picking up where he left off. Gig got the sense that the kid was used to being interrupted by the histrionics of adults. 'I reckon I will too. It's not as if I have much competition. A drunk qverse transvestite and some new guy who doesn't even set up his own codeshells…'

'Oh piss off,' said Gig. 'You sound like Ruth.'

'Who's Ruth?'

'Never you mind.' Sighing, he scuffed the kid's puffy dark hair. 'You want something to eat? I think there're complimentary sandwiches in the fridge.'

Lucas tailed him into the kitchen, dragging the briefcase like a much-loved teddy bear. From the looks of things

Harmonica's seven-way vidphone conference was over; she'd loaded a local shop directory onto the wallscreen. At some point she'd also changed out of her day-clothes. Gig had expected her nightwear to consist of exotic, pseudo-gothic lingerie or an Amazonian leopard print number, and was surprised to find himself even more excited by the pair of drab men's pyjamas she had on. Freed of its conservative bun, her hair was shorter than his fantasies had led him to believe.

Gig opened his mouth, but nothing intelligent came to mind, so he closed it again. This woman has just jumped out of my dreams and into my hotel room, he thought unhappily, and I have absolutely no idea what to say to her. Thankful for the distraction of the voluble Lucas, Gig looked over his shoulder, only to discover that in his brief lapse of attention the kid had managed to pry open the case.

'I didn't say you could look inside that,' he began hopelessly.

But it was too late. Round-eyed, Lucas held up the case's contents list. 'You're Gig?'

'I'm Gig. But I *prefer* Felix out here...'

Still shocked, the kid looked to Harmonica for guidance, but found none—his mother was too busy scanning the vidscreen's listing of nearby Chinese take-outs. 'Er, hi Gig,' Lucas said, in a faintly worried voice. Gig guessed he was used to negotiating with bullies, too. 'Sorry about what I said about you earlier. I mean, I kinda like your style...'

Gig raised an eyebrow. 'I have a style?'

'Of course you have a style, McGuiggen,' Harmonica interrupted loudly, without turning from the directory scroll. 'You're not like other hacks. You've got talent—but everyone has talent. The difference with you is that you hack a *person*, not a barrier. Call it a feel for human error, like a poker player watching for his opponent's betraying twitch. Talobos has a similar method; sadly, like Freud, the idiot always ends up fixating on himself. But you? Well, I almost enjoyed being hacked by you because you made it personal. You weren't trying to get into a heap of code, you were trying to get inside *me;* it was visceral and intense... Am I embarrassing you?'

Merciless woman! Gig's face and ears grew hot. Harmonica callously ignored his plight and jabbed at the remote. 'Now that you're here and the subject's come up,' she said, 'I've a question for you. As far as I remember, you managed to crash me three times in your glorious hack career. The first time you were just damn lucky—a hardware short-circuit on some godforsaken WestAsian island disrupted my shields. A four-year-old could have made it through that mess of broken code and touched core. The second time it was entirely my fault; I'd been up all night recoding company barriers and fell asleep before I could activate them. But the third time? I never worked it out.'

Gig rubbed his temples. 'And you expect me to tell you, sir?'

'Of course.' She sneered in profile. 'Or is now not a good time for you, dear?'

'I don't give away my hack secrets for nothing, sir. Even to the great Harmonica.'

The sneer faded. 'Suit yourself. How do you feel about Chinese?'

'I can take it or leave it, sir.' Gig considered the wallscreen options. '*Specifically*, I can probably take numbers 24, 25, 37, 39, 40, and 41 with a side order of 12, and leave the rest. If that's okay with you.'

Dutifully Harmonica punched in the numbers and added a few of her own. Tossing the remote onto the kitchen counter, she retired to the equally cramped lounge. Within moments of her touch the previously intractable sofa bed had subsided into something vaguely bed-shaped. Lucas shot Gig a rather wicked grin and pranced off to share the bed with her. Gig wished jealously that he'd thought of doing that first. Or had the guts to try for third place.

'Bloody Ruth's right,' he muttered to himself. 'Got no damn balls.'

The Chinese take-out had arrived by the time he mustered up the courage to enter the lounge—that was some *fast* fast food. Lucas passed him a teetering skyscraper of plastic boxes. His mother twirled chopsticks with practised ease. With her legs crossed and her face tense with concentration, she might have been the descendant of some ancient WestAsian fakir.

Snake charmer. Ha bloody ha, McGuiggen.

They ate. Lucas talked about Viger Singer and Arnold Lee, theorising the maybe-murder in prepubescent terminology, a hip remix of the crappy twenty-first century detective pulp Gig had read as a kid.

And through it all he felt Harmonica there, sensing her presence as a palpable *heat*, like a small domesticated sun.

* * * *

Later she said, 'You want to come outside with me?'

Gig ran a finger around the inside of a plastic box and sucked on it. 'Give me a moment, sir.'

She waited for him on the balcony. When he stepped out she passed him a cigarette—some creamy-brown filterless brand. Not a regular smoker by any means, Gig only managed to light it on the third try. She smirked at him and said nothing. She stood with her back to the city, one elbow crooked on the railing, picture-perfect against a backdrop of grey concrete and steel. Behind her the sturdy peaks of Chinese apartments broke clear from the industrial smog like mountain peaks above mist, like mythical islands ringed by sea. Bilingual neon signs sparked below, the downward sweep of Chinese characters regularly broken by horizontal English words. Typical Perking pidgin. Like a crossword of cultures, Gig thought, and one more damn puzzle to add to the mix.

Still puffing self-consciously on the cigarette, he glanced back into the apartment. Taking advantage of their absence, Lucas was comparing the contents of the two INTROMET briefcases.

'He's a cute kid,' said Harmonica. 'Pity he doesn't know when to shut up. Don't worry about your briefcase. I told Lucas I'd spank him if he tried to sabotage it. He knows me—I don't lie.'

'Really, sir?'

She shrugged. 'Try me.'

'Benny Soo. You were married to him. That's how you learned plaincode. He taught you.'

Clearly she hadn't expected him to take up the challenge. 'God no,' she replied, frowning. 'I taught myself. Benny didn't think I had the 'smarts' to understand plaincode. Wasn't college educated like the rest of them, you see; didn't have a swag of certificates to flash around. They were a company of geniuses: Dr Memphis the neurologist; Descartes the law graduate; Dr Soo the marine biologist; Hayashi the child-protégé. Then there was me: high school drop-out, perpetually unemployed, living off Benny's largesse. Worse still, the daughter of American expatriates. You can be sure I wasn't invited to participate in their discussions.'

'Wait, who's Hayashi?'

'Hayashi Misoka. Of course the kid calls herself Phoun Swiftwater now. Wanted to sound less like a Jap and more like a European fairy-tale princess. Princess Phoun Swiftwater. Becomes more pathetic when you pronounce the Phoun as she intended: Phoun like 'fun'. Memphis managed to talk her out of becoming Princess Phoun Lovelyflower, although I'm still not sure which one is worse. The imperial title is fitting, mind. Only ever met her a few times, and the kid was a *royal* brat. In the old days Benny used to threaten to feed her to his sharks, and I'm sure he was only half joking.'

'Dr Soo, marine biologist,' Gig reflected. 'I thought Benny worked in computers...'

'He *did* work in computers. Computers and marine biology. Believe it or not, the two can be complementary. Benny... Benny liked dolphins.' She laughed then, but it was a quiet, self-depreciatory laughter. 'Sorry. I'm used to talking in riddles when it comes to plaincode and q.'

What relevance dolphins had to plaincode was beyond Gig. 'I know you've probably been asked this before, many times,' he said. 'By many other, far worthier hacks. But I *have* to try myself. Will you teach me to read plaincode, sir? Give me a hint, at least?'

She shook her head. 'You hacks never understand. It's not about learning to read it. It's about knowing *how* to view it. What you see now when you look at plaincode is a series of weird hieroglyphs. What you have to be aware of is that, on some level, it all makes perfect sense.'

'Well, *obviously*...'

'No, not *obviously*. If what I just said to you was obvious, everyone in the world would be writing their own damn plaincode. Like mirror-writing, like invisible ink, like chalk on wax, the most difficult—and simultaneously, the most easy— translations are those that require you to think outside a formula. A genius may be able to break complex military ciphers, but give them a page written in a child's magic-pen and they'll be stumped.'

'You're telling me there's a trick to it.'

'I'm telling you that I'm not telling you.' She yawned. 'But it was brave of you to ask me. You're very cool. Laid-back, I mean. Calm and collected.'

Gig hid a shameful grin in a chin-rub. Lady, you think Talobos is bad? he thought. I have more neurosis and complexes than Freud himself. Hell, even as we speak I'm sexing you in my head while simultaneously worrying about what my mothers would say and whether or not I would spare myself a lot of future embarrassment if I just threw myself off the balcony right now; and at the same time I'm wondering if this balcony and the view of Perking could be considered romantic, and if it could, do *you* think so too, and suspect I've brought you up here under false pretences—or rather licentious ones—which brings me back to the sexing...

'Oh, snap out of it,' she said. 'Do you want to ask me anything else? Or have you got your twenty questions' worth already?'

He held up a finger. 'One more. Before we met in Singer's office, what did you think I looked like?'

'A geek.'

Gig felt himself flush. 'Well, I am—'

'Pretty? Is that the word you were looking for?'

He floundered under her gaze. 'No, sir. Not at all.'

She was silent for a long time. She closed her eyes and mouth and vanished for a moment into the darkness of the night. The black bitch, the black witch. Gig wanted to fall into the vacuum of her, to be sucked into the fathomless depths of her body... Then she opened her eyes and smiled, the whites of her eyes and teeth sudden and almost luminous, and was returned to him. She reached out a long arm and touched her thumb to his cheek, rubbing there like a mother wiping clear a tear. Tremors in him crept from his skin and rippled down her arm, a sexual current shared.

Harmonica said, 'You like me, huh.'

'Greatly, sir.'

She slapped his cheek lightly and straightened. 'You're a bold kid, McGuiggen. You'll come with us tomorrow to visit Lee's widow. I rather think my Lucas has taken a shine to you.'

With that she took her long legs and nice tits to bed, leaving Gig to agonise over his short-comings in relative privacy. Feeling lanky and somehow *elongated*, he hung over the balcony railing and watched the world below, the city's crowds blurred by distance and smog. Exploding firecrackers splintered the street's festive lull. Gig remembered textbook trivia: the NorthAsians had discovered gunpowder long before the Europeans. But they'd used it to make celebratory crackers, not guns.

Crackers and guns. Now there's an idea, McGuiggen. If an entrepreneur like Viger Singer hadn't bullied her way into Soo's circle, would brainmapping be used for something else entirely? You could be sure that the qverse think tank hadn't set out initially to make a quick buck out of virtual reality games. Perhaps Gig could bounce that notion off Zhadesh the next time he saw the modern-day guru in person, or get his not-distant-enough cousin to pass on the message...

His vidphone chose that moment to shrill. Speak of the devil—Ruth Nameri on line one.

'What the hell do you want from me now?'

'Nice to see you too, cousin,' Ruth said placidly. 'Thought I'd give you a buzz before I went to bed. Have some bad news and I'd rather you heard it from me and not the mindless idiots you associate with in the hackchats.'

'Christ, you called me about *hack* shit?'

'Remember Yeunify? Real name Nelly Georges. Met her once at Zhadesh and Eric's place—some dumb house party.'

Gig vaguely recalled an incorrigibly drunk European who'd made a particularly discomforting attempt to seduce him. The fact that he—the great unlovable—had turned her down said a lot about the woman on the whole. Her capacity for projectile vomiting rivalled even Eric's. 'Name rings a bell,' he said. 'That crazy hack-thief, right? Nicked a heap of hardware a month ago for the gee—I mean, for Zhadesh, Eric and Bradley. That was one of the stupidest things—'

'She's dead, pretty boy. Suicide. Bradley is over here bawling, and Eric is all riled up, and Zhads is being very *zen* about it but I can tell he's inches from cracking...' His ever-sympathetic cousin made a face that efficiently summed up her disgust for sensitive males. 'Anyway. I thought you might want to check her out. Yeunify was a depressed alcoholic, sure, but I've heard rumours she jumped whilst wearing a neurocap. According to Zhads, Yeunify also did a stint in the Biocheck technical department before moving up the INTROMET ladder to liaise with Benny Soo. Of course, it was about *then* they found out about her hardware theft and fired her. Still, it's some co-incidence...'

'Ruth. Not everyone who dies is part of a massive qverse cover-up.'

'Oh come on! Use that brain your mothers gave you! The two deaths are obviously related.' She looked downward at her lap; evidently she was reading notes from one of her beloved clipboards. 'One last thing before I go. My research turned up another juicy titbit you should consider in the case. Quite a few hospitals in the NorthAsian area currently use neurocaps to dull pain in terminal patients. Completely illegal procedure, but no one's complained about it so far, which suggests the method has some merit. From what I can tell, an electronically unstable neurocap can temporarily confuse the pain receptors in the brain—an amplification of the AR in VR rot I mentioned yesterday. There's a lot of medical jargon involved, the kind of rubbish Malachy Memphis probably jerks off to. But basically what it means—respective of the Arnold Lee situation—is that the bloke could have stabbed himself fifteen times without feeling a thing.'

'Seventeen times. He stabbed himself seventeen times.'

'Seventeen times then. And you don't even have to change the wiring of the neurocap. It's manipulation of external magnetic and radio fields. Adds an interesting twist, doesn't it? I'll just bet that Yeunify and Lee had enemies in common, given that they both worked on the same project. You might want to bring up the hack back-history with Yeunify's family when you visit them—'

'When I *what?*' Gig spluttered. 'You want me to poke through the girl's dirty laundry in front of her grieving relatives? Do you think interrogating Lee's widow won't rack me up enough bad karma? Seriously, Ruth—leave me alone. Go look after your boyfriend. Call me back tomorrow.' He hung up, then furtively switched his vidphone off to avoid an inevitable Ruth vs. Gig reprise. Poor Yeunify, he thought, stuffing the vidphone back into his pocket. A shame I never got to know you better. But in fairness, you *did* puke all over my trousers...

Good God, he checked himself. I'm as emotionally barren as my evil cousin.

He went back inside. Harmonica and her son were sprawled on the sofa bed; Lucas whiffled softly into the pillows with each breath. Quiet and cat-footed as a burglar, Gig tiptoed over. Sleep failed to soften Harmonica's face. She looked much the same as she did awake: hard, untouchable and strong.

* * * *

Tara Lee lived in Sticksville—an over-grazed property twenty kilometres from her closest neighbour. Out in the *real* SouthAsia, the bucolic 'outback' that coast-dwellers tried to deny existed, its desertscape as uninhabitable and barren as the terrain of mars. Erosion and drought had ripped almost all nutrients from the soil, but the orange-red sands still sprouted the occasional tuft of harsh wild grass. The weathered colonial residence at the end of the winding driveway was more hovel than home. Its veranda was shaded by a sheet of green corrugated plastic, a meagre canopy crippled by sun-warped posts.

The taxi's digital counter registered a heart-stopping three-figure sum. Super-rich Harmonica flashed a swag of credit cards at the driver automaton while Gig and Lucas exited the vehicle. The heat came at him like a punch. He imagined he could smell his own flesh sizzling in the sun, ripe and succulent as fresh bacon. God, and to think of the times he'd bitched about the weather at home! This perpetual summer was infinitely worse than the ever-changing Melbourne climate. Clutching Lucas' sweaty hand, Gig beat a quick path to the veranda's pithy shelter.

There was a woman waiting to receive him—a tiny, prematurely wizened blonde creature dressed entirely in mourner's white. Obtusely she reminded him of the eucalypts they'd passed on the journey out, bleached tree-skeletons, paperbark peeling like bad sunburn. She possessed that same combination of fragility and strength. If the hardships of outback life and the loss of her husband had momentarily defeated Tara Lee, they were yet to break her.

'You're Felix McGuiggen,' she said, voice a large ocker drawl. She cocked her head toward the gate. 'And that's Regina Carter. You're here about my husband.'

'That's us.'

He felt her size him up: the young face, the unkempt clothes, the shameless bed-hair. Pretty city boy, a long way from home. She said, 'I won't tell you anything you don't already know,' the emphasis suggesting a threat rather than a promise.

Somewhere a wild bird trilled, its call echoing with a sound like chiming bells. Harmonica strolled over, dangling a cigarette, composed as ever. But that was to be expected; the Carters were Sydneysiders and humidity was nothing new to them.

'I suppose you want to come in,' said Tara Lee. Adding, after some thought, 'The kid can come too.'

'Gee, thanks,' Lucas muttered.

She led them through a house filled with trinkets and assorted collectables: kitsch china kittens, wilting magazines, mismatched handmade furnishings, pseudo-aboriginal dot paintings, vases stuffed with plastic European flowers, the obligatory didgeridoo used as a prop for a broken shelf. In the living room two yellowing sofas lay in uneasy parallel like stifled lovers, wheezing tufts of stuffing from their battered seams. More magazines covered a low wooden coffee table between them.

Hardly a home suited to a techno junky like Arnold Lee, Gig noted. Too rustic. He couldn't see a power point, let alone any obvious signs of qverse hardware. But this wasn't Arnold Lee's home, he realised a second later—intuition finally kicking in. Wasn't Arnold's house and never had been. Tara Lee must have moved here after her husband's death. A retreat from the hi-tech world that had killed him.

'He wasn't depressed,' said Tara Lee as they all sat down. 'Arnold liked his job and had no enemies outside his qverse circles. I don't know the names of anyone he associated with, but I do know that he regularly stole and traded qverse software. Nicked from INTROMET, SWIFTWATER, and even the little TEEK group when he had the chance. I think the term you people use is a corporate spy. I never objected to his dealings. You can't be put in jail for code piracy.'

Looking bored, Harmonica lit another cigarette. Lucas said, 'Do you think he was murdered?'

'My husband was a pussy when it came to pain. No matter how badly he wanted to die, he wouldn't have topped himself with seventeen kitchen knives. A gunshot to the head or a jar of pills; that would have been Arnold's preferred method.' Tara Lee's face hardened. 'How fucken old are you anyway, kid?'

Lucas was spared the ignominy of answering when Gig's vidphone began to squeal. Tara Lee gestured to a sliding door in the far wall. 'Take it in the kitchen,' she said. 'I hate listening to people talk on mobiles.'

Gig slunk off to take the call. It was Ruth—her routine morning check-up. Sometimes Gig wondered if the sole purpose of his vidphone was to help his cousin keep track of him. In recent days it had surely seemed that way.

'Hi, pretty boy. I thought you'd have called me before you left the hotel...oh good grief.' Ruth's mouth twisted in a grimace.

'Did you have to call now? I'm in the—'

'Shut up, Felix. I can barely hear you. The reception I'm getting is shocking. You're ninety percent static and ten percent motion blur right now.' A clenched fist swung in and out of focus on the vidphone's screen. Ruth Nameri, hardware troubleshooter. 'Are you hugging the shuttleport control tower or something? You know their electrics muck up vidphones.'

Gig rolled his eyes. 'I'm at Tara Lee's house—Arnold Lee's widow. Does it look like a shuttleport to you?'

'The hell if I know! All I can see is your big stupid head.'

'How about you call back when you're not malfunctioning,' Gig suggested thinly. 'Oops, I mean dysfunctioning. Oops, I mean when your *vidphone* isn't malfunctioning.'

'Your mothers have said it a hundred times and so have I. You're just basically not funny. Give up the comedian gig; try your hand at mime. I promise to support your career all the way. Oh, damn!' Her image vanished from the vidphone, replaced by a skewed close-up of diagnostic hardware. 'Well, Felix, I'll have you know that there's nothing wrong with my vidphone. The problem is all on your end. You must be in a factory neighbourhood. Near an old power plant. Beside a radio station. Close to underground cables. Maybe Tara has stockpiled some serious electrics in the garage. Her husband probably had a mountain of hack junk—'

'I'm on a fucking farm! We're in the middle of nowhere! She has a wood burning oven!'

'Then explain to me why every troubleshooter program I'm running is telling me you're inside a high density electrical field? Either you're slap bang in the middle of an incredibly complicated computing system or you're being stalked by a radioactive cartoon villain. Don't talk back to me about hardware, pretty boy.'

Normally Gig would have backed down at this stage of the argument; hardware had never been his forte. But for once pride won out, his confidence bolstered by Harmonica's proximity and the stark absurdity of Ruth's claim. 'Fine. I'll believe you when you show me this damn system.'

'Don't get your panties in a knot. I'll call it for you. Hot or cold.'

'Fine! Do that!'

Holding the vidphone at arm's length, Gig marched the kitchen's perimeter, a victim of his own tenacity. Ruth called *cold* at the room's centre, but *hot* beneath the solitary fluorescent lamp; it was *warm* by the chopping bench and *warmer* still at the sink; the cabinets were *hot*, as was the wooden dining table; a survey of the saucepan rack chalked up two *warm*s and a *cold*; a stack of recently washed china plates bordered by a floral motif were a definite and disheartening *cold*; the small showcase of glassware registered as *warm*; and *warmer* when Gig stuck his hand inside; *hot* when he stroked the hinges; and Ruth declared she was positively *burning up* when something small, rectangular and metallic tumbled out of the cylindrical axis and into his cupped and waiting palm.

Gig lifted the thing into the sights of the vidphone.

'It's a bug,' said Ruth quietly.

'Are you sure?'

'Yeah. Yeah, I'm sure.'

'And the rest of the house...?'

'All signs point to yes.'

'Oh.'

'I'd tell you to put it back, but it's a bit late for that now.'

'Oh God.'

'I don't think I've said anything incriminatory. Have you?'

'I don't know.'

'Great. Just great. You're freaking out. I knew you'd freak out. I knew I should have waited until you were out of there before telling you. Jesus, Gig, sometimes you act like a bloody six-year-old. Pull yourself together.'

'Ruth!'

'I'm on the other side of SouthAsia and I can't come in and rescue you. You'll have to get out of this on your own. Are you listening to me?'

'Yes. I think—'

'What you have in your hand is an extremely sophisticated auditory bug. Their use is usually limited to the upper echelons of the North and WestAsian military, but it's not unreasonable to assume that they can also turn up on the GreaterAsian black-market. You can disable the bug by holding the tube at both ends and twisting until you hear a click. Careful, they're very sensitive instruments. When you've done that, put the bug in your pocket. Turn off the vidphone. Go back to Tara and tell her you have to go. Be polite. You don't know why she's been bugged. Hell, she might have done it herself. I want you to make some excuse—doctor's appointment, forgotten funeral, sudden bout of syphilis—and then I want you to get the hell out of there. Can you do that, Felix?'

'Yes.'

'Good boy. See you tonight.'

She cut the call—a blue-text prompt redirected him to the vidphone menu. Gig disabled the bug with shaking fingers. He put it in his pocket, as per instruction. He turned off his vidphone, as per instruction. He walked back into the lounge room. The others stopped talking. Tara Lee looked up. He saw it in her eyes just as she must have seen it in his—that impotent anger at forces beyond their control, at controls that undermined their force.

He said, 'Ms Lee, I have to go.'

She stood up. 'Before you do, Mr McGuiggen, I want you to have something of his.'

'Um. Okay.'

Feeling foolish, he held out his hand. The widow lifted a magazine from the coffee table's strategic display—a photocopied For Q quarterly, replete with Memphis dogma—and gave it to him. And froze, in the act of giving. With eyes wide in sudden horror. With mouth tensed. With skin pale and growing paler still. What an odd tableau we must make, Gig thought; both clutching at the same paper like a celluloid still from an old slapstick.

'You're genuine, aren't you?' said Tara Lee.

'I'm looking for the truth.'

Tara Lee released the paper. Somewhere, far, far away, Gig heard the mother-and-son pair harmonise a relieved sigh.

'It was nice of you all to visit me,' said Tara Lee. 'Now please get out of my house.'

* * * *

MONDAY

7

harmonica

On the way back Gig stretched a skinny arm across the taxi, fingers unfolding to reveal a tiny metal capsule nestled in the crevasse of his heartline, cold and malignant as a bullet. 'We were being watched, sir,' he murmured. 'The whole house was bugged.'

Harry sighed. 'We're *always* being watched,' she said. 'A bug here, a bug there. You work for the big names, you get used to it. People like Viger Singer like to know where their money is going; and more importantly, who with. Bugs, spooks, phonetaps, private investigators—you name it, they'll do it. Many a dishonest hack has been caught maxing a company expense account on the sex, drugs and rock and roll trifecta.'

'I'm not altogether sure the bugs were there to keep track of *us*.' Her hack protégé gnawed the heel of his palm. 'Tara Lee knew about them. That's why she gave me the magazine—I saw it in her face when she held it out to me. She wanted to tell us something, but couldn't say it aloud for fear of Them listening in. So she found a way to say it through the magazine. Except...'

Except. For conspiracy theorists, there was always an *except*. 'Except she didn't put anything inside the magazine, did she?'

'Christ! It has to be in here somewhere. I know I'm right, damn it; I'm just not intelligent enough to work out what 'it' is.' His quick brown fingers flickered across pages overflowing with Memphis maxims: FREE Q, FOR Q; FOR Q, FREE Q. 'Perhaps it's an article we're supposed to read. Or one of the trade advertisements in the back. Or maybe she gave me it simply because Memphis is—was once—a neurologist, which suggests Ruth's theories aren't so far from the truth...'

'Pardon?'

'My cousin, sir. Has some crazy ideas. Not brain-hacking but brain-*altering*. Numbness of the senses. Dizziness and disorientation. I understand the overall sensation that results is a little like being terribly drunk or stoned. You could probably kill someone in that state without them noticing. Until they were killed, that is. My God, sir,' he exclaimed, lifting his chin to look her in the eye. 'You have no idea how nice it is to talk. Just talk. And not be interrupted or corrected every damn second.'

Something about his gratitude, his frank and earnest smile, charmed her the way no well-spoken Romeo could. Oh Gig, Harry thought fondly. What an odd character he was! At their first face-to-face meeting she'd pigeonholed him as a 'geek-Casanova' in the mold of Joaquin Magdellin.

Mid-twenties playboy, young, cute, clever and *nouveau riche*, with a conversational repertoire limited to q and girls. An easy mistake to make, based on first impressions.

But Gig lacked a Casanova's bravado, a Casanova's easy style, a Casanova's resilience in the face of adversity. He was vulnerable, intensely so—you could see it in his soft brown eyes and his long gentle hands, in his oversized, mismatched clothes and his slightly lopsided smile. He was a mix of eras as much as a mix of races; he was part anachronism and part supra-modern; he possessed both a newborn's frailty and a sage's cynicism; he was a romantic and a dreamer and probably a certifiable neurotic.

This was a boy she could hurt, *really* hurt, and Harry no longer wanted to fuck him. Instead she wanted to open her arms and take him to her breast, the way she'd never been able to with Nicole or Lynn or Lucas. She wanted to use her body as a shield—as a codeshell—to protect him from the tragedies of the real world. She wanted to hold him like a child, to kiss his forehead and cheeks in a parent's benediction.

How nauseatingly *Oedipal*. But hell, weren't those the roles they'd been cast in from the beginning?

He was a hack. Qverse idiom maintained that she, Harmonica, had mothered him.

She reclined her leather seat and watched him puzzle over the magazine with a biro, the nib hopping every time they hit a stretch of the uneven road. Above his bowed shoulders the redlands of Tara Lee's provincial sanctuary receded into the distance, and up ahead the Ondanaroo-

Perth highway branched out tributaries into suburban delta. Billboards bigger than houses strobed advertising jingles from the wayside. The largest of them announced the impending release of INTROMET's Biocheck watch. Underneath the animated countdown (12 DAYS TO GO!) some hick lackwit had scrawled a graffiti addendum: 'TO THE END OF THE WORLD'.

Conspicuous, she thought; the absence of traffic. Conspicuous, like Lucas' silence in the passenger seat. Conspicuous also, the metallic flash in the lap of Gig's jeans, the zipper of his fly bouncing at a provocative half-mast. He yawned and drew one knee to his chest and she glimpsed a gasp of shameful grey underwear. Pity, that. She could better picture him in a thong.

She said casually, 'Bet you two hundred dollars I can tell you what Tara Lee put in the magazine.'

He wrinkled his forehead. 'I don't have that kind of money, sir.'

'A hundred, then. Fifty. Twenty. Come on, McGuiggen, be a sport.'

'Fine, twenty.'

They shook on it, solemnly, formally. Then solemnly, formally, Harry took the magazine, rolled it into cylinder and craned forward between the front seats. Lucas had been dozing fitfully since their departure, his forehead pillowed by the yellowcab's plush leather dashboard. It took four smacks with the magazine to rouse him. He sputtered awake gracelessly, rubbing his eyes. The first word out of his mouth was an abject, 'Muuummm...'

'Felix needs your help, sweetheart,' Harry said, shaking out the magazine to its centrefold: 10 REASONS WHY Q MUST BE FREED on one side, the other a collage of unflattering candid shots of Viger and Phoun (PUBLIC ENEMIES NUMBER ONE AND TWO!). 'See anything unusual about this?'

Lucas deadpanned, 'Memphis has really toned down his style?'

'Don't be a smart alec.'

'It's a message in code,' her son concluded after a brief once-over. 'Tara Lee put a tiny black dot underneath the letters she wanted to use. Tried rather unsuccessfully to make it look like an ink fault of the printer or typesetter. Yes, Mr McGuiggen, that's some pretty complex encryption you have there. Think tank, military genius standard. Almost impossible for the mortal man to solve. If the mortal man were blind. Or stupid. Or a baby. Babies would find it very hard... Look, give that biro here; I'll transcribe the entire thing.'

Gig threw up his hands as Harry sat back down. 'God, you're a bitch! Both of you.'

'What can I say? The kid's a genius.' Harry grinned. 'Lighten up, pretty boy. You never struck me as a poor loser before.'

'Pretty boy? You sound like my cousin, sir. She calls me that all the time.'

There was a hint of sadness in his laconic drawl and Harry sensed she'd accidentally struck a nerve. Was pretty boy really such an offensive epithet? Perhaps, she supposed, but only if he didn't believe it... And he *didn't*, she recalled suddenly. They'd touched on this on the hotel balcony last night. 'Pretty? Is that the word you're looking for?' she'd joked, and immediately a blank, lost look had crossed his face. He'd replied seriously, 'No, sir. Not at all.'

As if the very idea of it disturbed him.

It was a small wonder that Gig remained ignorant of just how good-looking he was. Then again, you often got that with test-tube kids—a psychological peculiarity Malachy Memphis termed 'appearance apathy'. They'd look in the mirror and see not a person but a *construction*, a laboratory technician's fusion of catalogue DNA. Poor Gig. Even his masculinity had come from a bottle. Was the act of sex an unpleasantness for him then, a process reduced to the minutiae of intersecting cells?

These impossible designer children, resting uneasily in their designer genes...

She patted his leg in a consoling fashion and he gulped and blushed and tried to sulk and smile at the same time. It was cute. He was cute. She forced a grin and swallowed a laugh and the urge to bounce him on her knee and took out her vidphone and dialled Joaquin Magdellin's number on impulse, because she needed a jolt of reality *fast* and preferably *hard*, and if there was anyone who knew how to nip a fantasy in the bud it was smarmy, pragmatic Jo.

'Just remembered a business appointment, sir?' Gig asked.

'What?' It took her a moment to realise he was referring to the vidphone in her hand, the ringtone peep-peeping plaintively half a continent away. 'Oh, no. Just a friend who deserves an update. You might know him. Ever heard of Joaquin Magdellin, TEEK's baby-faced goldenboy? Built q-Paris and the majority of TEEK's default skins. Does room and skin design—'

'And buys a lot of black-market code?'

Black-market? That inquiry jogged her right out of her comfort zone. Think fast, Carter! she thought. Heads up! Remember that this guy has a knack for reading people and you have no guarantee he doesn't have an ulterior motive for befriending you. Better to play it safe. You didn't get to where you are today by telling secrets.

'I really wouldn't know,' said Harry stiffly.

Gig laughed. 'I really would,' he replied, and she felt instantly guilty for doubting him. 'Put it this way, sir, Magdellin doesn't mind slumming it down my end of the qverse. Rubs shoulders with the bottom-feeders who hire my cheap-and-nasty secop services. I'm surprised Descartes hasn't fired him for code theft, but then TEEK does take a more liberal attitude toward piracy than SWIFTWATER and INTROMET. And, for all his transgressions, Magdellin is a brilliant designer.' He looked at her coyly then—coyly, if she could believe he'd ever intentionally be coy. 'My cousin met him once. Said he was very charming.'

'Did she indeed.'

'Very charming, sir. And greatly appreciative of the company of women. But not charming and appreciative enough, it seems, to answer his phone.'

'He hasn't for the past two days,' Harry grumbled, cancelling the call. Much as she disliked to admit it,

Joaquin's continued absence was starting to niggle at her. 'Bet it's Descartes' doing—she never approved of our friendship. Bitch probably showed Jo a bit of leg, flashed a scalpel-shaped tit or two. Let him see the face and flesh of her, the body she hides away from the rest of the world. No wonder Jo hasn't returned my calls. How could I compete with Descartes in the real world or in q? I'm an uneducated hack; Rebecca is the q-Eve to Benny's q-Adam...'

She was cut short by a growl from her disgruntled son. She had read somewhere (possibly in one of those pastel-bound guides to 'Motherhood' Benny reproachfully sent her each year) that children needed more sleep than adults to function. Lucas' bloodshot eyes and manic expression suggested that the six-hour snooze on the Shangri-Lair sofabed hadn't been sufficient.

'Here's your stupid message,' he snapped, pitching the magazine onto the floor by Gig's feet. 'Want me to summarise? Blah blah blah, Arnold Lee is a paranoid For Q advocate, blah blah blah, his wife isn't much better. Now you both might as well give me your phones. Get your money's worth out of me while I'm still eligible for the junior wage. After all, I may not be a super-cool secop feared by the qverse masses, but I *do* know how to rewire and signal-jam a vidphone. If only because my father is a control freak and my mother never returns his calls.'

Harry blinked. 'Signal-what, dear?'

'Override someone else's call-reject option. Dad did it to you yesterday, remember? You can even pull a Big-Brother-

Is-Watching-You stunt if you like... Gee, don't look at me like that. I'm offering to do you both a favour.'

More to distract him than anything else, Harry offered up her vidphone. Gig followed suit a few seconds later. Optimistic that this new task would occupy the boy for a good ten minutes at least, Harry flicked through the magazine for Lucas' transcription.

> X THS IS THE TRUTH. MY HSBAND WAS MURDRED, HE KNEW TOO MUCH. HE STOLE CODE, HE TOLD SEKRETS. THEY KILL HIM, SWIFTWATER, INTRMET. THEY WILL DSTROY TEEK. THEY AFTER SPIS, PIRATES. HACKS FOR Q CHECK. WATCH FOR PARK. INSONIAM SUFERING. THEY BUGED MY HOUSE, THEY WANT POWER, THEY WANT CONTRL, THEY WANT RVNGE. YOU ARE PART OF THER GAME. X

The message's confusion, limited spelling and extreme, Memphis-influenced content was more disappointing than amusing. 'Odd. She didn't strike me as a For Q fanatic,' Harry commented, and handed the magazine over to Gig. 'Just goes to show you never can tell.'

'You're telling *me*?'

Five minutes down the road Lucas spotted a suburban shuttleport: a great white tower ringed by a loop-de-loop of transit lounges and thoroughfares and landing zones that in turn flowed into overpasses and underpasses and reminded Harry obscurely of those quaint 'marble run' contraptions of the previous century. Or a toned-down version of Phoun's graceless, labyrinthine q-Topia. Harry barked an order at the driver automaton—syllable by syllable—and directed the yellowcab to the Sydney departures terminal.

They stopped at the passenger drop-off. Harry got out. Lucas got out, hugging his detective bag. The small drop-off platform was air-con cool and hospital-bland and overspilled with travellers and their personal effects. Colourful polyglot people hugged and wept under colourful polyglot signs. When she turned around for Gig she saw he was still in the taxi. He wound down the window.

'I guess this is goodbye, sir,' he said.

'Right.'

'If my Cantonese is correct, the Melbourne terminal should be on the other side of the complex.'

'Right.'

'I need to see you again, sir,' he said.

'Of course you do. You owe me twenty dollars.'

He signalled the driver automaton to start the taxi again. He looked back and might have been on the verge of saying something more when Lucas cried, 'Wait! Your phone!' and tossed it through the window. Gig caught it two-handed, clumsily—then the taxi sailed on to the Melbourne terminal and he was gone.

'Nice guy,' said Lucas, and giggled. 'I bet he'll go far.'

Harry sighed. 'You did something else to his phone.'

Her son didn't even have the common decency to look ashamed. 'This is a hack-battle,' he pointed out. 'The rules of hack war apply—and that means anything goes. I don't have to play fair. Even if Gig plans to tackle things honestly, you can be sure that Talobos won't. So I checked Gig's mail.

Viger Singer buzzed both of you a few minutes ago. Wants you to visit her 'at home in q'—which I assume means her qverse castle in that dumb swords-and-sorcery haven. Obviously, I deleted the message from Gig's vidphone after I read it.'

'Why bother? You said I got one too.'

Lucas preened. 'That's right. *You* got an invitation. *I* didn't. Didn't until now, that is.'

'You're an evil conniving little sonofabitch,' said Harry, with grudging admiration. 'I think you have the makings of a brilliant secop.'

* * * *

My dear Ms Carter,

Recent events have caused me to re-evaluate my position and the task I have set for you and your fellow secop/hacks. Upon receiving this message, I request that you join me *immediately* in sector C-4 of the Badlands (INTROMET central territory) so that we can reassess your situation. I shall await you in my haven—the 'Black Castle', as the sword-and-sorcery clientele like to call it.

Thank you in advance for your prompt response,

Viger Singer

The Badlands. Because every haven has its hell. Six square q-miles worth of sword-and-sorcery hell, to be precise—a barren desertscape bordered by black boulders and overcast by a blacker sky. Viger Singer's medieval castle sprouted from its middle like some perverse centrepiece. The qverse heart of INTROMET was a distorted mirror of its real-world contemporary. Five fingers of stone rose from the battlements to perfectly frame a distant red sun.

'All right for a holiday,' said Harry, 'but I wouldn't want to live here.'

'Better here than SWIFTWATER,' Lucas-as-Gig returned philosophically.

'Barely. Much as I'm loath to admit it, Descartes is the only qverse matriarch with any aesthetic taste.'

Mother and son sat opposite each other in a Perth-Sydney shuttle compartment; they stood side-by-side before the great gate of INTROMET's castle. In the far distance fabulous q-beasts clashed with intrepid q-heroes; swords and armour flashed amongst the scrub. Scalding zephyrs chased tumbleweeds and the less courageous across an ocean of tessellated rock. Stalks of burnt-out vegetation strained from fissures, little more than withered husks of bark. Despite their appearance, Harry knew from experience that these could cut just as surely as any bravo's blade.

In all her years in the qverse Harry had never understood the attraction of swords-and-sorcery games. If you wanted a battle of wits, wouldn't it be smarter (and cooler) to hit the poker tables of the q-Lounge, TEEK's idealised reconstruction of an American speakeasy in the 1930s? If it was action you craved, SWIFTWATER's q-Metropolis offered a dystopic cityscape populated by the gangs of the future. And there were a thousand other, smaller gaming territories tailored to suit the qverse's various niche markets, from superheroes to furries to erotic adventures...

So why choose swords-and-sorcery? Was it the horribly simplified battle between good and evil that appealed? Or did people genuinely enjoy beating up creatures that looked, for the most part, like the waste product of failed genetic experiments?

Like all sword-and-sorcery territories in the qverse, the Badlands were populated by a veritable menagerie of virtual beasts. Unidentifiable reptilian things scuttled between the rocks; incredible scintillating insects buzzed over the bones of slain monsters. There were creatures with tentacles, creatures with eyes on stalks, and even creatures entirely composed of mud. A huge dragon-vulture crossbreed swung lazy circles overhead like a malevolent, red-eyed shuttle. Plumed in shadow, talons like knives. Something limp and many-limbed dangled from its beak, twitching. Lucas-as-Gig tracked its progress across the sky, raising a hand to his face out of habit.

'I wonder if that thing poops as ominously as it flies,' he commented. 'Amazing that they don't have more trouble cleaning all that Pure Evil off the roof.'

'You're so jaded,' said Harry, and knocked.

She had no sooner taken her hand away from the door when it sprouted a less-that-medieval scanning apparatus, a neon purple bar joined to the castle by an umbilical of wires. It extended like an antennae and hovered up to her face. There it flashed twice, obnoxiously, and then drifted on to size up Lucas. Harry was filled with a sudden paralysing fear that the scanner would see through Lucas' "Gig" disguise. Fooling her own scanners and tracers was one thing; fooling Viger Singer's quite another.

But it seemed that her son was as good an engineer as he liked to think. The scanner elongated to form a screen, on which the scan results appeared in block letters:

HARMONICA - REGINA CARTER
GIG - FELIX MCGUIGGEN

Above the dragon-vulture let out a shrill, banshee scream and flapped on into the Badlands' perpetual dusk.

Lucas sighed. 'Well that sounded promising,' he said.

Instantly the huge wooden doors folded inward to reveal a neat, twenty-second century boardroom. The juxtaposition of Badlands and office-space was jolting. Standing at the threshold felt weird, as if balanced precariously on a fence between the past and the present, the mythical and the hyper-real. Inside two skins sat restlessly at opposite ends of a long table like a feuding married couple. The closest was a classic Renaissance beauty dressed lavishly in courtly attire—a woman who, with her heavy-lidded eyes and other-worldly expression, might have stepped out of a Da Vinci painting. Her curly brown hair was threaded with tiny pearl beads.

The other skin was Viger Singer. Not just Viger Singer in a skin, but Viger Singer *as* a skin. Harry blanched. Wearing your own face in virtual reality was surely the height of egotism.

'So they arrive, finally!' cried the Renaissance woman, in Lloyd 'Talobos' Hong's drunken twang. 'And together, at that—do I sense a touch of romance in the air? A joint investigation and a jointly shared hotel room...so rumour has it. Well don't stay hovering in the doorway, do come in. Ms Singer and I have been waiting for you.'

Harry elected not to fry Talobos on the spot for judicious reasons—it would only further delay the meeting. She settled on a seat at the table's midpoint, Lucas at her side. A low hum sounded from behind her. Turning, she saw the huge castle doors erupt into a sequence of fractals like a combusting hypercube. Streamers of plaincode burst from the hinges and entangled themselves across the once-wooden beams. The image held for a long moment—a birthday present wrapped in code?—before crumbling in on itself and vanishing altogether.

'Cute trick,' Harry said.

'Ah yes, my magic doors.' Viger laughed. 'You like them? The design was Benny Soo's. You know him, don't you, Regina? On a personal level. I've noticed he often censors your qverse conversations—won't tell me why, of course. I can't tell if he's trying to protect himself or you.'

'Perhaps he's trying protect *you*,' Harry suggested.

'Perhaps. Either way, I don't suppose it matters.' She leant back in her chair—the faint leathery squeak it emitted was at once believable and too good to be real. 'Now you are all here I can explain why I've arranged this meeting. At present I am trying to decide whether or not to suspend your little investigation. Perhaps permanently. Somehow it has managed to receive rather too much public attention. The hackchats are ripe with speculation—yes, I do visit them from time to time. Furthermore I have received word that certain security conditions have been—how can I put it? Let me say simply that INTROMET has been compromised and that this may affect the case to its detriment. Have any of you seen anything odd in the qverse recently?'

'Odd? My God,' giggled the Renaissance woman, '*everything* in the qverse is odd. Why just a few minutes ago I saw a great feathered dragon—the wicked creature nearly took my head off in a jet of flame!'

Talobos erupted into gales of hysterical laughter and Viger's practised smile grew visibly strained. 'I mean something different, Mr Hong,' she said coldly. 'Something odd. A strange program. A strange piece of code. A strange skin. Something completely new that you'd never seen before.'

'Are you talking about something in particular?' Lucas asked.

'Yes.'

'Then why don't you tell us what it is?'

'Telling you may alter your interpretation of the case.'

'The lovely Miss Singer likes to have about her an air of mystery,' Talobos simpered, stretching out a long pallid forearm heavy with virtual jewels and then pressing it, theatrically, to his forehead in a sweeping motion befitting a diva. 'For if the lovely Miss Singer did not, we might find out too much, and what we find out might hurt us...'

'So it'll alter our interpretation of the case,' Lucas pressed on, ignoring him. 'What's wrong with that?'

Viger said tersely, 'This case is strictly confidential.'

'I'm aware of that. But what's wrong with altering our interpretation of the case? And exactly what does 'altering our interpretation' mean?'

Harry had heard enough. Talk of altering interpretations and compromised security conditions? That was business jargon she recognised. Viger, Phoun and Rebecca rarely used such phrases outside the context of qverse violence; it augured either an impending attack by mercenary hacks or imminent inter-company warfare. For example:

> THEIR ACTIONS AGAINST US HAVE *COMPROMISED OUR SECURITY CONDITIONS.*

Alternatively,

> OUR FRANKLY UNDERHANDED ACTIONS AGAINST THEM MAY *ALTER YOUR INTERPRETATION* OF OUR COMPANY POLICY.

'It means Viger's playing with us,' Harry snarled, rising from her chair. 'Maybe Tara wasn't so far wrong after all.

Something is going on with INTROMET and TEEK. Another power struggle between the titans. Viger can't spare us questing hacks any attention; she's too busy trying to run Descartes out of business.'

'Goodness, Carter!' Viger spread her arms. 'What an imagination you have! I'm not trying to destroy TEEK. Honestly, there's no point—TEEK's days are already numbered. Both Phoun and I have received confirmation that Rebecca Descartes will soon be leaving the qverse in pursuit of greener pastures. Of course I can't say that the news particularly upsets me. It will be sad to see TEEK go, but the benefits that Phoun and I stand to gain through Descartes' retirement certainly overcome any feeling of sentimentality. I'm sure Descartes' decision will be made public within the next few months, but I'd prefer you three kept this information under your hat until then. At present not even her own staff know.'

Harry was inclined to believe her. The notion that Phoun would willingly forfeit her portion of the qverse was too outlandish a lie. Was that why Benny split? she wondered. Or is Rebecca quitting *because* Benny split? 'So you aren't planning on a TEEK takeover,' she said aloud. 'Is SWIFTWATER more to your liking, then?'

'How on earth did we get on to corporate takeovers?' Viger appealed to the others—still calm, still collected, still smiling with devilish composure. 'I merely asked if you had seen anything out of the ordinary in the qver—.'

'We haven't,' said Harry.

'And you're all completely certain of this? In that case I believe that you can continue your investigations without further interruption. Which is why—' Viger paused. 'Good God. What do you think you're doing, Carter?'

Harry looked down at her hand.

It held a laser.

'Do put the laser down, Ms Carter,' said Viger Singer. 'Even if that thing *is* up to Benny Soo standard, there is no way that it could do me any damage in the heart of INTROMET country. If you wanted to fry me you'd first have to fry fourteen nationally and internationally located INTROMET operating centres. I think you'll find that even Benny Soo would have a hard time managing that without his access codes. Don't even *think* about testing me on this one. You aren't the first disgruntled employee to spring a laser on me—or a knife or gun, for that matter—and I dare say you won't be the last.'

Oh, but I *could* be, Harry thought. Your spooks underestimated me. So have you. Don't you know who I am, Viger Singer? I am Harmonica. I was there at the beginning. I am the mother of all hacks. I am the father of revolutionaries. I am the black bitch, I am the black witch. I am q's serpent; I am the wicked thing that slithered into Eden on its scaly belly and bit off Rebecca Descartes' smugly smirking head.

And I warn you not to fuck with me, Viger Singer. You may be a god but I am a demon, and I will gut you if you try.

'This is a game,' she said, letting the laser hang slack and loose between her fingertips. Tara Lee's words felt strange yet somehow familiar on her tongue. 'This is your game.'

Viger's patient smile returned. 'It is my *request* of you. But I never claimed otherwise. And the rewards you stand to gain are significant.'

I did this wrongly, Harry realised. I respect my son's ambition and his Machiavellian instincts, but I should never have let him come in Gig's place. Gig may be a rotten secop and a substandard hack, but he has a gift I don't—a talent for spotting the weaknesses of others. And I know that he alone could tell me what I need to know right now.

What is going on inside Viger's head?

'I've crashed you once before,' Harry warned her. 'I'd do it again in an instant if I had even an inkling that you planned to—'

'Planned to what, exactly?' The woman's condescension was so thick Harry could almost *taste* it—a salty flavour similar to blood. Airily Viger snapped her fingers. 'No, Carter, I don't think you'll crash me. I think that you will do as I tell you to. Not for the money. But because you value your dignity, and because you couldn't stand to lose out to a drunk has-been like Hong. This meeting is over,' she added, as the magic doors reached long tentacles of code out of the blank office walls like an emergent Cthulhu. 'I think you'd all better go.'

* * * *

'**W**hat was that, Mum?' Lucas wanted to know as he pulled off his goggles. Crushed beneath the neurocap's spindles, his hair puffed out over his eyes in a ridiculous quiff. 'You pulled a laser on Viger Singer! Viger Singer! That's almost on par with challenging Dad to a qverse duel. You shouldn't have done it. Dad is always saying you're impatient. I bet Viger would have told us all about the 'mysterious code' if you hadn't challenged her—'

'Isn't today Monday?' Harry asked.

'I think so.'

Wearily Harry reached for a cigarette. 'In that case, kid, I'd advise you to shut up before I remember that today is a school day.'

* * * *

8

gig

The shuttleport vending machine ate his small change without coughing up so much as a biscuit. Six dollars and forty cents down the corporate drain. The machine's ridiculous neon decals and nonsensical jingle ('DRINK POP! BE POP!') seemed unnecessarily smug to Gig. 'Waiting for a second course, are you?' he asked it, pushing his knuckles firmly, but not aggressively, into its smirking chrome facade. You never knew what shuttleport security would consider an act of wilful property damage.

'You are standing too close, sir or madam,' the machine piped. 'Please step away.'

Its voice was a stern Scottish brogue, unnervingly similar to the schoolmarm tone Honoria McGuiggen took with her son when he failed to load the dishwasher, clean his room, or find a nice girlfriend. Gig sulked off, mouth puckered like a surly teen. God, it was times like these that he truly hated life. Here he was, thwarted by a bolshie vending machine who sounded just like his mother, while somewhere, out *there*, Harmonica was boarding a shuttle that might well take her out of his life forever.

Ms Regina Carter. Of course his mothers wouldn't approve of her. She was the sort of woman they despised, a far cry from the earthy, homely daughters-of-friends they continually foisted on him. They wanted him to settle down with a soft-hearted, big-hipped vegetarian, the kind who believed in physical labour, socialism and growing your own organic food.

While Harmonica was a woman of big-business, quick qverse cash and fast food. Harmonica, with her big nose and her white teeth and her insufferable, smart-mouthed son. A woman twenty years older, twenty years smarter, twenty years cooler. A woman who had married Benny Soo, stood up to Viger Singer, bitched out Malachy Memphis, and numbered husky blond gigolos like Joaquin Magdellin amongst her closest friends…

Who was he kidding? What chance did he have with the likes of her?

Feeling thoroughly demoralised, Gig checked his timetable. The next Perth-Melbourne shuttle was due to arrive in thirty minutes. Ample time, then, to stretch his legs and take a piss. An advertisement for Biocheck watches spanned the length of the connecting thoroughfare. On it a twenty foot tall interracial couple cheerfully compared their daily cholesterol intake, surrounded by all the modcons of suburban myth. A closer inspection revealed that their eyes had been photoshop-enlarged to resemble those of an anime character.

So *kawaii*.

The bottom portion of the poster was freckled with bright red FOR Q stickers like an outbreak of measles. In a moment of whimsy Gig peeled one off and stuck it on the front of his beat-up denim jacket. He thought of Malachy Memphis' discarded q-cache then, that little copper square he'd last seen spinning end over end down to the red earth of Alice Springs, a miniature metal meteor... Or had he only imagined that?

It was becoming harder and harder, he noted, to differentiate between the qverse, reality, and his flights of fancy. The first sign of madness, anyone?

He found the men's toilets in a between-platforms shopping area, the entrance bookended by a pizzeria and a newsagents. Inside a group of sunburnt youths were telling tall qverse tales around a bathroom dryer like boy scouts around a campfire. They wore tacky oversized Akubra hats complete with swinging corks and neat plaid shirts. Geeks on holiday. Probably the idiots responsible for the FOR Q stickers. Gig skirted clear of the urinal and bagged a stall. When he came out they were still there.

'Betting odds have Harmonica making it at 2:1,' said one. 'Talobos is going at 5:1 but people say the stress has really gotten to him. Guy starts drinking from the moment he wakes up. But I still say that your money is safe on anyone but Gig.'

That was a line like a cowboy's lasso—it fell on him from above, gripped him round the gut and reeled him in, buckle-legged as a wayward calf. Gig stopped in the doorway and slowly turned around. His heart beat sudden and loud in his temples.

'Guy is a total fraud,' agreed a second geek. 'No talent and no style. Reckon he paid his way into the competition. Maybe even blackmailed Singer. It's possible—he's got connections to the some of the major codepirates.'

'Blackmailed Singer or sold someone out. You know that chick Yeunify died, right? Just after the battle began and in mysterious circumstances to boot. Suspicious or what?'

'Coward has been keeping a low profile in q, have you noticed?' another laughed. 'Probably knows that everyone is gunning for him.'

'Why is everyone gunning for him?' Gig asked.

The geek nudged him in the side, evidently mistaking Gig for a member of the crew. 'Because we all know he doesn't deserve it,' he said. 'So he crashed Harmonica a few times? So what? He's a lousy hack and an even lousier secop. Everyone I know who's spoken to the guy says he has the personality of a slug. Unfriendly snob reckons he's better than the rest of—'

Gig hit him. He had never been in a fight before but somehow it seemed the right thing to do. He hit the geek with his briefcase and the geek fell down and Gig fell with him; they rolled and the geek was Viger, Ruth, Tara Lee; he planted his knees on either side of the guy's gut and smacked him across the face, right, left, right; the geek reached for his neck and Gig bit his hand and tasted not blood but *meat,* a matter of texture rather than flavour; they rolled again and Gig was aware of the rushing whiteness of the bathroom tiles; and the walls distorting and bloating before his eyes until it was no longer a bathroom but a coliseum, and around them a jeering, cheering audience; and someone yelled, 'Release the lions!'; and someone yelled, 'Jesus, guys, break it up!'; and Gig looked down at the frightened face beneath his knuckles and realised that the geek wasn't all that much older than Lucas Carter-Soo.

Just a kid.

He stood up shakily and the other geeks backed up fast and the geek on the floor started to cry in a quiet, self-conscious way. Gig felt like Viger, Ruth, Tara Lee. He touched his mouth and it came away bloody. He took a step forward but they shrank away from his open hands.

'I'm sorry,' he told them, 'but you don't understand.'

He picked up his briefcase and limped out of the toilet. The shuttleport's intense fluorescent lighting numbed his anger, his pain. By the time he'd reached the Perth-Melbourne platform he had begun to doubt the fight had actually happened.

A woman stood alone by the vending machine that had stolen his money. Their gazes locked as he passed her. Was that a flash of recognition he saw in her face? Gig was certain he didn't know her. She had sharp, clever features like a rodent, offset by large, almost *bovine* brown eyes. Hair in a cute cyberbob—midnight black dye shot through with blue streaks. A Celtic tattoo unravelled in loops from her jaw to her neck; and presumably it continued on below her collar, dancing across ribs, ringing a nipple, sliding dark sinuous tendrils between the cleft of her buttocks—an intricate body-weave of Irish symbols. She wore an ill-advised silver lamé jumpsuit and ridiculously huge astronaut boots.

Neo-clothing. For people too rich to care about being cool.

He stopped. She walked up to him, smiled, and bowed.

'Felix McGuiggen,' she said. 'My name is Jane Cragg. I am here to take you to SWIFTWATER.'

* * * *

He had never been in a private shuttle before. In fact, up until a few minutes before, Gig hadn't even known they existed.

The oval-shaped compartment interior was larger than the bottom floor of his mothers' house and decorated like an open-plan bachelor's pad. A natty, 1960's themed bar dominated the fore, crammed with psychedelic artworks and kitsch bubble-furniture. The rest was given over to a lounge set upholstered in bright red tartan and a state-of-the-art entertainment system which featured, amongst other things, a wallscreen twice as tall as Gig himself. As usual Phoun had appropriated the most colourful aspects of Western culture and assiduously incorporated them into a visual grotesque.

God, what was it with these qverse women? Phoun Swiftwater was a psychotic interior designer and a fairy-tale princess. Viger Singer was a megalomaniac with delusions of omnipotence. Rebecca Descartes was a recluse, a virtual reality hermit who'd not been seen in the real world for over twenty years. Had power corrupted their minds, or merely *contorted* them?

Gig settled uncomfortably on a high-backed 1960's stool with legs like wriggly straws. Jane Cragg sat opposite him and lit a cigarette. Behind her, framed by the compartment's largest window, clouds the colour of candyfloss boiled to a froth like the wake of a powerboat.

'You like SWIFTWATER products?' she asked.

'Well, I'm not the biggest fan—'

'No. You never use SWIFTWATER caps. Maybe you think that just because something is pretty it cannot be functional. Some of the top secops in the game use modified SWIFTWATER caps. Here.' She tossed something shiny onto the bar between them—a slick black neurocap, aerodynamically curved like a cyclist's helmet. 'Phoun left it for you. No need for calibration. She checked your trace files and personally calculated your brain-map.'

Gig lifted the cap in one hand. It felt light and strong and inexplicably *his*. He turned it over. Within its matte plastic shell a fine carpet of metal spindles quivered. The average SWIFTWATER neurocap contained around forty spindles. This one held hundreds of thousands, perhaps thousands of thousands, each delicate electrical conduit primed to interpret the mechanics of his brain, to intercept and redirect the firing of individual neurons.

Curiously he ran a finger across them. They rustled to meet his touch, a sensation alternately like a host of tiny sucking mouths or sifting through a layer of fine sand. With a cap this advanced, who needed plaincode? But Gig felt apprehensive rather than pleased. Did Arnold Lee once accept a gift like this? he wondered. Did Nelly Georges?

'Bought off the shelf, that cap would cost you more than a car,' Jane remarked. 'Perhaps more than a house, depending on your choice of suburb.' She pursed her lips and exhaled a long ribbon of cigarette smoke toward the ceiling. 'As a shuttle is to a kite, so it is to the caps you're used to. You'll find no better handiwork in all of GreaterAsia.'

'I really can't—' Gig began, before remembering the lesson he'd learnt from Viger Singer.

In Rome, do as the Romans do.

In the territory of a qverse matriarch, do whatever she commands.

'Thank you,' he finished weakly.

'I feel close to you, Mr McGuiggen,' said Jane. 'You and I are very much alike. I, too, worked for INTROMET—a long time ago now. I was an accountant in those days, although not a very good one. Managed to get myself into trouble with the law—Viger Singer's law. Very dicey business. In the end I was forced to make a choice: either work for Singer or risk several years in jail for fraud. So... better the devil you know, as they say. Did you want champagne?'

Mutely Gig shook his head. Shrugging, Jane poured a generous amount into a tulip-shaped glass for herself. When she swallowed the Celtic tattoo on her neck undulated like the body of a snake.

'Singer asked me to 'investigate' a system she had constructed: a set of accounts that were an exact duplicate of a set in the WestAsia Bank systems. Every day I was to review these accounts and report any unusual changes or errors. The first fortnight passed without event. On day fifteen I noticed a subtle change in the books: a dummy account with a name almost identical to one of the wealthiest customers. Naturally I immediately contacted Singer.

'When I looked back the next morning the dummy account had vanished. This occurred four more times during my investigation. Each time I told Singer and each time the accounts had returned to normal when I checked again. She was testing the waters, you see—finding out what she could get away with before she was likely to be caught. What manipulations would the accountants at WAB notice? What would they overlook?

'I tell you this, Mr McGuiggen, because you need to understand the kind of woman you are working for. There are two types of genius in this world. There are women like Phoun who are truly brilliant, who can decipher any problem or puzzle within moments. Then there are women like Singer, who *make* puzzles. Women like Singer are simultaneously aware of both the bigger picture and its individual elements. In her puzzles we are mere cogs, mere jigsaw pieces; we mean nothing outside the context of the whole.'

'You know about the case,' said Gig.

'We know about the case and we know about Arnold Lee. We are as interested in the cause of his death as you are. Lee worked for us, stole from us. Surely you saw the SWIFTWATER memo? I'm sure Singer supplied it along with the other red herrings. Check your briefcase. NO STAFF MEMBER IS TO HAVE CONTACT WITH ARNOLD LEE UNTIL HE CAN BE LEGALLY TERMINATED. Does that ring any bells?'

It did. He had glanced over a duplicate of that memo briefly, 'evidence' of Phoun's complicity sealed and tagged in its own special laminate pocket.

5. 1 x Memo Photocopy (SWIFTWATER internal memo).

'How did you know?' he asked.

'Because we keep track of what in-house memos find their way into Singer's hands. She only sees what we wish her to see. We're a close knit group at SWIFTWATER. It's only the wildcards like Lee who pose us any security threat. And men like him don't last long.'

'Not if you murder them, no.'

Jane curled her lip. 'If that was a joke it was in very poor taste.'

'I know. I'm sorry. Pretend I never said it.' He forced a goofily apologetic grin. 'Can you tell me about Yeunify? Real name Nelly Georges. Did she work for SWIFTWATER too?'

'With a name like Georges? I very much doubt it. We *are* based in EastAsia, Mr McGuiggen. The number of Anglos we hire can be counted on one hand. Phoun requires all her employees to be fluent in at least four languages or dialects.' She stubbed out the remains of her cigarette with a sharp, deft movement that made Gig think of a striking cobra. 'A lot of people claim to work for SWIFTWATER. It is fashionable to be associated with Phoun. But in truth the company employs little more than sixty people full time. A first class secop—like your friend Harmonica, for example—would hire far more. Most of SWIFTWATER's business is outsourced to national and international temps or handled by Phoun directly.'

'That must be a phenomenal workload.'

'My employer is a genius, Mr McGuiggen. In addition to her invaluable assistance in the construction of the qverse, her other works and theories have revolutionised the industrial and economic world. Even the engine of the shuttle we are flying in is Phoun's creation, a design conceived when she was a mere eight years old. No single individual since Da Vinci has advanced the human race in such leaps and bounds.'

'Shame she's colourblind,' said Gig.

Jane Cragg's sharp face grew sharper still and the candyfloss clouds churned into angry, Rorschach shapes against the window. 'You are a bitter young man,' she told him. 'I wonder if I will enjoy working with you after all.'

* * * *

Stepping into the executive foyer of SWIFTWATER headquarters was like entering an underwater grotto.

Literally. One moment Gig was racing an EastAsian monsoon across the shuttle landing pad, jacket rucked up over his ears. The next he was blinking stupidly around a room—no, a *cave*—that echoed with the muted splash of waves and smelt strongly of the sea. Beside him Jane Cragg calmly folded up a black umbrella and wiped her astronaut boots on the mat.

The sea! And people said reality-to-qverse transitions were bad! Bug-eyed, Gig ventured in ahead of his guide. Coral stalactites jutted out of the high ceiling, sculpted from foam rubber. Lush ferns in rhythmically vibrating pots simulated seaweed fronds caught in an ocean tide. Revolving lamps beamed ripples across the floor and walls. Long aisles of aquariums housed pretty tropical fish, their scales iridescent as oil slicks. Charmed and awed, Gig touched his nose to the glass. A speckled yellow fish trailing glorious golden streamers swam to him and wriggled its fins in greeting.

Gig wriggled back at it. The fish drifted closer, curiously, then suddenly darted away as Jane's face appeared to rise from the depths, bloated and distorted on the other side of the glass.

'You are not here to have fun,' she mouthed.

He trailed her to the elevator, casting more than one yearning look over his shoulder as he went. Jane ushered him inside, pushed a button, and stepped out again moments before the doors closed. Obviously her part in the 'Journey to SWIFTWATER' odyssey had ended in the aquarium. Gig had no time to react to her vanishing act. He was still gaping like an idiot when the elevator hummed into action.

As his stomach sagged into his knees, it occurred to Gig that he might be being kidnapped. Perhaps that had been Phoun's plan from the beginning. Lure Singer's lackey into SWIFTWATER and keep him prisoner until all demands were met, all ransoms paid in full. But he couldn't take the threat seriously. Tough qverse chicks and handcuffs—the idea was bizarrely arousing. Bring on the Stockholm syndrome!

Depriving him of any further elaborations on *that* daydream, the elevator doors snapped open. He was back in the aquarium again—no, not the same aquarium, Gig quickly realised, although the basic décor was identical. This new aquarium was a pigsty, littered with wads of crumpled paper, chocolate wrappers, clumps of computer hardware, caved-in neurocaps like black split oysters, and completely incongruous furniture: an overstuffed settee here, two bubble-chairs (one swiftly deflating) there.

An underwater garbage tip. Less pretty, but much more realistic, if those Greenpeace magazines his mothers kept quoting were anything to go by.

There was no sign of anyone around, no sound save that of the ersatz sea-side. Emboldened, Gig decided to explore. For the first time he noticed that his sneakers left wet patches on the floor—still moist from the downpour outside. That, and his still-damp hair, somehow added to the authenticity of the grotto. He crept over the mess and on, arms extended so his fingertips brushed the aquariums on either side. Blue light fell on his face, shivered over his chest.

'Annyeong? Hou's aw wi ye?'

A girl's voice. Gig turned. A skinny, pig-tailed school girl stood in front of the elevator, grinning up at him from beneath a fashionable hack-and-slash fringe. One hand tweaked the hem of her pleated tartan skirt. The other flirted with a large silver crucifix exposed by the low v-shaped neck of her blouse. Right sock pulled up, left sock hanging about her ankle, casually over-casual. Cute kid. Maybe too cute—there was something contrived about the sparkly pink mascara, the silly patent-leather shoes. Where she had come from was anyone's guess.

'Annyeong? Hou's aw wi ye?' she repeated, tilting her head on one side. 'You no speak your own language? Too bad! Your heritage Korea-Scotland right? That some crazy mix. What the odds nice Korean girl meeting nice Scottish lady? Not fond of dykes but okey live and let live. I hear all you chromosome kids is infertile like asses. Barely man at all! I speak fifty-eight language, close to hundred-fifty dialect. Not to show off. I just make you at home, okey?'

Fifty-eight languages to choose from and she'd picked an Anglicised variant of Perking pidgin. Gig winced. 'I'm here to see Phoun Swiftwater?' he tried. 'My name is Gi—Felix McGuiggen.'

'Yes yes, I know! Hi, Felix. Not so bad looking! I seen worse. But ee-fem-enit. You like the fishies?' Giggling, the girl spread her fingers on the glass. 'My favourite is dolphins. Know what cool about dolphin?'

'Well, no...'

'Sonar! It a clever thing dolphin do. Send out soundwave, they reflect on object. Come back. Dolphin think, okey coral reef coming up. Or, okey shoal of yummy fish hiding in sand! Super! Dolphin can see without seeing. Sense place, sense figure, sense motion. Bats do also. You know Benny Soo do that in q? Plaincode, it all same principle. Brain sense objects. Falsely. An entire operating—why that face?'

Gig was struggling. 'You think that's the secret of plaincode? Sonar—'

She slapped both hands on her flat belly and faked a big Santa laugh. 'Ha ha, you okey funny boy. Sonar *is* plaincode. That how hack like Ray-gee-neh can see through wall and jump over tall building. Sonar not tricky. Tricky part is seeing in plaincode. Qverse is construction of rules. Rules say gravity here. Rules say colour there. Rules say this place full, no more admission. Only without rules you really see in plaincode. In plaincode you make own rules. Hey, what up funny boy? You make that silly face again! Maybe a little penny dropped in little Felix brain?'

Had it ever! Jesus Christ. *This* was Phoun Swiftwater? Suddenly everything made sense and didn't make sense at the same time. Genius, visionary, protégé—it all seemed horribly incongruous with this simpering, giggling creature. Yet not, Gig remembered, with Harmonica's cynical observations of the girl's character.

Kid sure was a *royal* brat.

Watching him, Phoun turned her toes inward and twirled a pig-tail. So *kawaii*! He could tell she was relishing his confusion. Funny boy is super bewildered, ha ha! Gig grimaced. So this was how millionaire whiz kids got their rocks off—by playing mindgames with the cerebral underclasses. Already he resented her. Maybe hated her, and they hadn't even gotten to the subject of her horrendous qverse designs yet.

'Everyone think Princess Swiftwater just some crabbid old lady like Rebecca and Viger and Ray-gee-neh,' Phoun chirped. 'Big sillies! I am super much younger than you!'

By six months at the *most*, Gig thought. You might not be middle-aged, Misoka, but you sure aren't a school girl. No matter what your plastic surgeon would like me to believe. 'Look,' he said crossly, 'you brought me here to talk to me about the Arnold Lee case. Can we get to it?'

The self-appointed princess shrugged her skinny shoulders. 'Okey you listen. You hear rumour of triad gang, huh? Ninja warrior? Secret assassin? I pay martial artist to do dirty work? They some crazy story! Viger is evil bitch. She want to blame Lee on me. I fire him, okey, that make me suspect. What he take from me? Nothing. What he take from Viger? Plenty. Code and program. Costing her more money than me. Know the old saying? Here is to my enemies' enemies? If Lee is hurting Viger I think him A-okey! I not get much trouble from codepirates. Everyone love me!'

'Except Viger and Ray-gee-neh,' Gig muttered.

She heard him. 'I not speak to Ray-gee-neh,' she pouted. 'We have row okey. Stupid woman fry me when I working. Say I help Benny cheat with Rebecca. Benny with Rebecca? Last time Rebecca get intercourse, folk music still popular, ha ha. Ray-gee-neh is just some dumb American. And Talobos just some dumb SouthAsian. He once a pirate, you know that? He one slippery character. Rip plenty code from INTROMET. Little from me also. Idiot. But not half so bad as you! You protect plenty pirates. INTROMET code, SWIFTWATER code, TEEK code, your little FOR Q friends steal all. What they called? Zhadesh Patel. Eric Nui. Bradley Ah Chow. Those bad boys better watch out!'

Hand on hip, a mock-stern Phoun waggled a finger at him. 'Ha ha, you look super mad! You hate me? Oh no, Felix hate me. I cry! Ha ha, not really. So you super hate me! What you plan to do?'

'I *can* leave,' Gig hissed.

'How you do that, funny boy?'

Good question. Even if he managed to start the elevator, Gig had no idea what floor the landing pad exit was on. Maybe his kidnapping idea had been right. 'Please, Phoun,' he tried, ashamed of how ready he was to beg. 'I don't know if this is some test, or if it's to prove something to me, but I've had enough of these games from Viger. Any more and my head will explode.'

The princess pushed out her bottom lip. 'You no think I cute?'

'Honestly? No.'

Deflated, Phoun sat down with a thump on the floor. Papers gusted up on either side. 'All men like Princess Phoun,' she said uncertainly. 'She's the Phoun-nest girl around!'

Oh.

God.

'Not this one,' Gig said, matching his voice to the soothing cadence of the pseudo-sea, amazed at his own patience. 'This one wants to talk to Misoka. The business woman who runs SWIFTWATER. Do you think I could speak to Miso—'

'I'm not a fucking multiple personality headcase, you retard.'

The retort was bitter, shocking, offensive. Certainly not the sort of outburst you expected from someone who professed publicly to be a devout Christian. Then again it followed that if school girl Phoun was an act, staunch moralist Phoun was probably one too...

Gig started to like her a whole lot more.

'I wanted to do this my way,' the princess spat, lurching to her feet. 'You were supposed to play with me. But you just fucking couldn't, could you? No sense of entertainment.'

No sense of entertainment? Was the cutesy Japanese school girl shtick still in vogue in EastAsia? Or did her SouthAsian investors *expect* this kind of saccharine teasing, this gimmicky I-no-speak-English-good routine? Or was it a personal fetish... Gig realised he'd rather not know. 'Do you want to talk about Arnold Lee now?' he asked. 'What's going on between SWIFTWATER and INTROMET?'

'Not SWIFTWATER and INTROMET. SWIFTWATER and INTROMET and TEEK.' Under the shifting ocean lights her expression was no longer angry, merely cold. 'It's about territory. Aren't all wars? The three of us—Viger, Rebecca, and Benny on my behalf—signed an agreement eighteen years ago, long before we had any idea of the commercial potential of the qverse. We could build our empires, but Rebecca allocated the space we had to realise our dreams. The qverse was divvied up like heathen lands between Roman centurions. Our ratio? 3:2:1. 3 for Viger, who had money. 2 for me, at Benny's request—kind-hearted bastard probably thought it might act as kind of trust fund for poor little Misoka. And 1 for Rebecca, who had the final say in everything.'

Great. Another cryptic rehash of 'old school' qverse, certain to leave him with more questions than answers. We made an agreement—why? Why invite Singer on board at all? What did you use the qverse for *before* it was commercial? The veterans never told the whole story, just those snippets immediately relevant to the situation. Leaving Gig with a narrative tapestry as riddled with holes as a Swiss cheese.

'We might well have signed that contract in blood,' Phoun continued obliviously. 'Not even Viger's legions of lawyers can find a loophole. As it stands, INTROMET and SWIFTWATER can grow only as TEEK grows—no faster. Until, of course, TEEK falls. And TEEK will fall. It could be months.

It could be days. But when Rebecca leaves it will crumble, leaving us to expand to our hearts' content...'

'That's a good thing, right?'

'If you're me, yes. If you're Viger, probably not. She may be starting out ahead, but these past eighteen years I have been plotting, saving, constructing. The moment Rebecca's departure is confirmed, SWIFTWATER territory will expand to sixteen times its size. Stock market values will soar, we'll gain thousands of new investors, and Viger will be all but washed up. And Viger knows it.'

'How?'

Phoun laughed. 'We *told* her. Dumb bitch is running scared.'

He believed her, utterly. She was a woman of many faces but when it came to business and control there was nothing duplicitous about her. Jane Cragg had been right—Phoun Swiftwater was a genius. Albeit an evil genius in a school girl's uniform. And at that moment Gig could actually *visualise* her plan unfolding like an origami rose—cornering the market, becoming even more fabulously wealthy, playing some malicious mindgames on her nemesis.

Power and money and cruelty, these were but a few of Phoun's favourite things...

'Which brings us back to the matter of Arnold Lee,' said the princess. 'Poor Mr Lee. Nuked in the qverse. Brainhacked, if you believe Viger's PR. You can see now why she would want to frame us for something like this. Why she would love me to be implicated in Lee's death. Someone *died* in SWIFTWATER? People would be fleeing my territories like, like—what is your clever SouthAsian saying...'

'Rats fleeing a sinking ship? Hacks fleeing an activated codeshell?'

'Either one. Of course I don't blame Viger for trying. If I was desperate I might make a similar attempt to discredit her.' Slim fingers worried at the silver crucifix again; her smile was abruptly rueful, self-pitying. Around her the fake-sea heaved in the throes of a sudden fake-storm. 'Aren't women funny, Felix?' she murmured. 'You want to hurt a man, you do it physically. You want to hurt a woman, you ruin her reputation.'

'I've heard that before.'

'Unsurprising. In the qverse, everyone has heard everything before. Life imitating art imitating life. After a while you start noticing the reflections. Get lost in the fantasy—which is the reality—which is the subconscious, the id, ego or superego—and then, in due course, you turn into Rebecca Descartes. Who isn't really *real* in the first place and hasn't been for quite some time. The qverse is filled with riddles, isn't it? Riddles and rumours.'

She was toying with him again. She sashayed to him, half-airhead and half-genius. She was getting her rocks off. The sounds of the ocean rose to a crescendo.

'You could join us, okey?' she cooed. 'Viger see po-ten-shul in you. Maybe you are super hack? Not hack deadshit after all! When Rebecca go, qverse will middle-split. And then, Felix, you will be forced to choose a side. Go for Princess Phoun! She always win! Naturally your FOR Q crowd won't last in *my* qverse, but to be honest you owe them no loyalty. Crazy bad boys, they all go to hell!'

'Please, don't start this—'

The princess cut him off with a giggle. 'It pretty late, Felix! You stay here tonight, okey? Princess Phoun make you very comfortable indeed!'

* * * *

TUESDAY

9

harmonica

In the summer of 2057 a nineteen-year-old Joaquin Magdellin had chased a whim and a peroxide blonde down a stretch of WestAsian coastline. After five days without a word his over-anxious parents contacted the police. For weeks their plight headlined internet dailies and six AsiaNational television channels. But if Joaquin had been remiss in advising his family of his plans, he had not forgotten to tell Harry, phoning her collect from a cut-rate backpacker hostel in Bombay.

'Missing your legs, baby,' he'd slurred into the vidphone, sunburnt and cheerful. 'These Indians are a fucken riot. Want me to bring you back a cheap carpet?'

He called her again in 2060 before embarking on a four month lone odyssey through barely-charted bushlands—a journey to *find himself*, he explained. Self-awareness, SouthAsian style. He sent her a series of postcards via vidphone, posing barechested and openhearted against backdrops of ghost-tree gullies and featureless plains of red sand; she watched him clamber up razor-back ridges and down dunes from the comfort of her living room.

Twice he wrote to say he still loved her—hopeless, rambling letters, his brain addled by heat and solitude. He referred to her as 'the Virgil to my Dante,' 'the muse of my artistic soul,' 'my one true love,' and once, lasciviously, as 'my favourite wet dream'. His feeble attempts at poetry failed to enchant but Harry was secretly delighted that he had chosen her, of all his many friends, as his sole confidant.

But in 2062 he hadn't called or written. He had simply vanished. His cramped NorthAsian apartment held no clues. It was as chaotic as usual, crammed with technical junk and sci-fi pulp fiction, its walls buried behind kewpie-doll pin-up girls and comic strip enlargements. Joaquin had left no hint of his whereabouts, but he *had* left a note. Written in sloppy black capitals across the streamlined black surface of his wallscreen, his final message was blunt and rushed:

EM ROF KOOL T'NOD

'I see you forced your very first vidphone connection,' Lucas observed, peering over the back of the sofa. 'Thanks in no small part to my hardware genius. Remember that next pocket money day, won't you.'

Harry forced Joaquin's wallscreen recorder to pan right and the black letters listed to follow. The vidphone view scrolled past more hardware rubbish, a stack of empty pizza boxes, some unwashed clothes, and above them a half-open window. Its single curtain billowed and twisted. 'Don't look for me?' she said. 'Jo would *never* write that unless he was in serious trouble. Not if he thought I might be the one to find the message. Something's happened to him.'

'Like what?'

'Like whatever happened to Arnold Lee?'

Sighing, her son tumbled onto the sofa beside her. The previous night he'd been forced—for lack of choice—to don one of the frivolously pink nighties Benny had insisted on buying her during their engagement, a purchase most likely inspired by one of Memphis' bright ideas. ('If you want to make Regina a lady, Ben, treat her like one...') Privately Harry thought the garment suited Lucas a lot better than it had ever suited her.

'Nothing happened to Arnold Lee,' Lucas said, trying to pat the flounces on his sleeves into submission. 'Really, there's no way to control someone's brain via q. If there was Dad would have found it long ago. I guess you could twist their *perceptions*, if you did it externally. Used some nearby device, a radio maybe. But that wouldn't be enough to make someone write their name on a wallscreen—'

'I'm not talking about brain-hacking. I'm talking about some NorthAsian thug chasing Jo out of his own home. One of Phoun's heavies.'

'Mum, I've *met* Phoun. Last time I saw her, she taught me to make sushi and sing American show tunes. Then we played hopscotch and ate green ice-cream.'

'Then you went home to dinner and she went home to order an assassination and four corporate take-overs. The woman is twice as smart and a hundred times as wicked as Viger. The whole cute-little-schoolgirl thing is an act to keep you off your guard. And if it wasn't Phoun it was someone else. Maybe Viger. Maybe Rebecca. Bitch couldn't stand the fact Jo liked *me* better than—'

But she stopped there. I sound like a neurotic FOR Q nerd, she realised. All this talk of brain-hacking and conspiracies has rattled me. Think rationally, Regina! Much as you may love him, there's no denying that Joaquin is a skittish bastard. Chances are he's knocked up some wretched Chinese girl and is hiding from her parents. Or gone on a drunken round-the-world cruise with his TEEK workmates. Either way, it's nothing you should worry about. The lad is old enough to take care of himself.

'Mum?' Lucas asked, nudging her. 'Are you...?'

'I'm fine, kid,' Harry replied. 'You're right, I'm wrong. We'll solve one mystery at a time. Lee first, Magdellin second.'

In an effort to regain some good-parenting credits, she fixed them both a hearty breakfast of leftovers. Poppadoms with peanut butter, naan with vegemite, grilled samosas with tomato sauce. Appeased, Lucas cranked open Singer's briefcase and prepared to present his latest theories on Lee's death. His eagerness reminded Harry of Benny, or rather of *a* Benny, a Benny before the advent of q. An idealistic, excitable Benny, one who hadn't yet realised that no matter how clever he was, he still couldn't save the world or help the poor or cure the sick, and that his only lingering legacies would be a garish virtual reality game, a broken marriage and three spoilt kids...

God, it was too early in the morning for nostalgia.

So Harry tuned out Lucas' babble and thought of Gig instead. Gig and his long lazy body and gentle pianist's hands. If only she'd made some excuse to take him swimming—Perth's beaches had recently been cleaned, the sea-water filtered of tourist refuse. He would have been handsome there on the sand, his dishevelled hair windswept, his dark eyes creasing against the light. And handsome too in the water; slender, if not athletic; a sunbrown body gleefully battling the surf; and rising wet and silky in a spray of droplets...

'Mum, you're putting vegemite on the peanut butter,' said Lucas.

Harry snapped out of it. 'There's nothing wrong with—'

'On a samosa?'

Harry examined the mess in her hands, on the counter, stuck in gobbets to the sides of the grill. 'Ah, shit.'

Yes, it definitely looked like it was going to be one of *those* days.

To cover her embarrassment she bundled Lucas into an old tracksuit and sent him to the nearest convenience store with a shopping list of high-flyer essentials: four bottles of Merlot, a Cascade slab, a dozen European cigars, twenty packs of cigarettes and a week's worth of microwavable vindaloo curries. Alone, and guiltily thankful for it, Harry flipped through Singer's party-bag of paranoia. Nothing like a violent unsolved murder to keep the mind clean and pure.

A handful of crime scene photographs piqued her interest from a 'home renovation' perspective. Arnold Lee had died in a spiffy ultra-modern kitchen, one of those state-of-the-art chrome outfits with bubbly corners that looked improbably like the interior of a space-age butchershop. Matte black tiles. Nifty open grill. Lift-out barbeque. Oven-timer-cum-clock with digital readout. A long (retractable?) rack extended over the oven hotplates, its empty knife-shaped slots appallingly conspicuous.

Harry estimated the whole set-up had cost at least twenty grand, co-incidentally the same amount she was likely to get back on her tax return. She was still comparing her furnishings to the photos when Lucas returned, laden with a surfeit of bulging plastic bags.

'Can I talk about Lee *now*, Mum?' he whined.

'Did you get the cigars?'

'They're right there, Mum.'

'Then of course you can, my sweet.'

Who said nature beat nurture? Her son might not have had the benefit of super-brainy Chinese genes, but he'd sure mastered Benny's trademark hung-dog look. Shuffling forlornly to the briefcase, lower-lip drooping, Lucas was every bit his father's son.

'Short story is that I looked through Gig's briefcase,' he said. 'He also got a 'suspicious' neurocap to investigate. Figured that was a bit weird, since I thought *you* had the neurocap that Arnold Lee died in. So I checked the notes

Viger supplied him. Looks like Gig and Talobos got the neurocaps worn by the two INTROMET employees who also reported brain-hacking. Yee and Young. Which means that they're practically useless. Sure, Gig and Talobos have blueprints of the SWIFTWATER room as it was when Lee died, but they can't actually *get* there.'

'I thought Lee died in INTROMET territory.'

'No, not exactly. He died in an INTROMET territory *inside* SWIFTWATER. It was one of those SWIFTWATER rent-a-space rooms that people hire for special occasions. You can bring your own furniture and decorations from other territories. They call them party rooms but people usually use them for sex. Due to privacy laws, the contents of these rooms are deleted *immediately* after the patrons leave. Even Phoun wouldn't have a record of what happened in there. But the cap itself will. So I think you and I should go into the qverse, find the right rent-a-space, plug in the cap, and recreate a perfect 3D model of the room.'

Harry bit off the end of a cigar and spat it in the vague direction of the kitchen sink. 'You're starting to talk like your Daddy,' she observed. 'Like a little corporate parrot. You'll be getting chummy with Rebecca next.'

He resented that. Two spots of red rose in his cheeks and his green eyes glistened with an angry dampness. 'I'll get my cap,' he said, and left.

* * * *

They ran into Lloyd 'Talobos' Hong outside the rent-a-space reception hall. Lucas pointed him out—Harry would have missed him otherwise. The disgraced secop was squatting in the gutter of a remarkably low-key example of SWIFTWATER real estate, head tilted toward the rippling candyfloss-coloured sky. The skin he'd donned for the occasion resembled a feisty heroine from the cover of a newsstand bodice-ripper. Peaches and cream complexion. Eyes like limpid pools. Rosebud lips. Hourglass figure. The face was classically beautiful, fine features framed by waves of flaming red hair.

And that's not all that's flaming around here, Harry thought to herself, amused. She stopped in front of him. Talobos put his hands to his face, framing an invisible trumpet, and serenaded her with a sequence of ascending raspberries.

'Ladies and gentlemen, give a big hand for Ms Regina Carter and her trained monkey, Mr Felix McGuiggen!'

'Are you stalking us?' Harry asked.

'Certainly not. I am stalking answers. If you happen to have an answer in your possession, then that is merely a happy co-incidence.'

'Do we fry him now or later?' Lucas wanted to know.

Harry sized Talobos up. Even when fighting fit she had never considered him much of a threat. Drunk, he was harmless. 'That really depends,' she said, 'on whether or not Lloyd can keep his incredibly large mouth shut.'

After a moment to consider the alternatives, the colonial beauty pantomimed locking its lips and throwing away the key.

'I like you better when you're sober, Lloyd,' Harry told him. 'You have less personality then.'

With Talobos in tow they entered the rent-a-room reception hall. The place was cramped, the standing-space largely occupied by wet-dream window dressing. Looped holograms of big bosomed babes tottered past, fluttering their eyelashes, sashaying and flirting, whispering sweet-nothings and sub-clauses in sultry voices. Women to suit every occasion: jungle-Janes in leopard-skin bikinis, leather clad dominatrix wielding riding crops, skunk-eyed party girls in sequined dresses. Some shitty shag-score played in the background, its bassline pumping a porno soundtrack.

Boomcha-Boomcha-Babyyou'resobig.

Initially Harry had worried about bringing Lucas in—despite his worldly airs he was still only fourteen—but the 3D sex-advertisements that crowded them were more pathetic than suggestive. At any rate, she reassured herself, Lucas was the kind of boy who would steal a sex automaton just to take it apart and find out how it worked.

Dodging the overtures of several underdressed male fantasies, Harry pushed the service button on the front desk and waited. A few seconds later a clerk appeared: an Amazonian femme-fatale costumed in red vinyl. Beneath the SWIFTWATER logo embroidered on her collar was the name LAUREN FANG. Harry gathered that this was not the woman's qverse stagename but a moniker bestowed upon every employee unlucky enough to land front desk responsibilities.

'Room for three?' the Lauren yawned. 'Fifteen dollars per fifteen minutes. Best rate this side of the SWIFTWATER-TEEK border. Bonus discount if you refer a friend. All sex acts okay, so long as there're no kids, no necro and no animals. Company policy—'

'I want an hour in the room where Arnold Lee died.'

'Oh,' said the Lauren, disappointed. 'You're from INTROMET.'

'Contracted, actually.'

'Same bloody difference. Room fourteen, down the hall. It'll open for you when you get there. Have a nice day.'

And she vanished.

Room fourteen was an almost-featureless white 8x8m *space*, the blankness of its walls sporadically broken by small ridges and hooks, additions presumably used to secure whatever sexual apparatus the room's patrons might bring along. Some party room, Harry thought, as she walked its perimeter. It looked more like a boy's shower room than anything else—then again, that kind of location would probably float *someone*'s boat.

'I've been here before,' Talobos offered, one hand raised like a meek pupil. 'There's nothing. They delete all the records—it's something to do with the NorthAsian privacy act. Far be it for me to give you advice, but you're wasting your time.'

Harry glared. 'Did I say you could talk?'

'No, but—'

'Then shut up!'

Having cowed Talobos into silence, Harry went to check up on her son. Lucas was standing at the room's centre, deep in concentration. My boy at work, Harry thought fondly. Had he learned his skills as she had? Of course Lucas hadn't been motivated by anger but by a genuine desire for knowledge—but were their methods the same? Had he, too, peeped through the staircase railings as Benny worked below? Combed through old boxes of files and cast-away journals? Stolen pieces of hardware to reap the fruits of domestic espionage?

She moved closer to examine his work. He had connected Lee's neurocap to his own, somehow—Harry had long since given up on asking Lucas how he did *anything*. As he moved his fingers, its faintly transparent image resolved in the air between them. A ghost-cap to harness a qverse-ghost. Light gleamed suddenly at its front, brilliant and blinding, then cast out lengths of shimmering plaincode like guy ropes. Chains of it moored themselves to the walls, meshing around hooks and diving into holes.

And slowly Arnold Lee's room remade itself. First in simple silhouettes: the edge of this table, the corner of this cupboard, the vague ripples of buttons spread across flat vertical screens. Steadily the lines grew denser and the silhouettes gained depth and texture, ballooning to convey the natural curvature of a stylised knob, deepening to indent floortiles, growing loose and streamer-like to create racks and stands. Layer heaped upon layer heaped upon layer—it was like watching a spider spinning its web in time-lapse.

A laboratory? Harry guessed, as the code jumped to sketch a space-age console on the right wall. Between the flashing buttons a clock blinked out a Morse-code of numbers. A large metal structure—some 'scientific' innovation unfamiliar to anything she had seen before—all but eclipsed the left side of the room. Two vessels filled with effervescent liquid bubbled over hot-plate rings that jutted from its middle.

Above them sat a rectangular shelf; glowing metal rods (or handles?) emerged from slots in its surface. Harry could not tell their colour—plaincode stripped back all qverse constructions to basic blacks and whites—but her instinct told her that they should be a shiny, modern red, like the 'death-ray activating' levers in bad sci-fi movies.

Beside her Talobos panted, 'Is that…plaincode?'

'Yes. A plaincode reconstruction of the room as it was when Arnold Lee died.'

'So how can I see it?' he pushed.

'Because we're letting you.'

'Isn't that—but doesn't that—you mean you're telling me the secret?'

'No. We're just showing you the *answer*.'

Curiously she placed her hand against the closest fixture, a long laboratory bench with rounded edges. Instead of being hard to the touch, it hollowed beneath her fingers as if it were made out of dough. Lucas let out a warning yelp.

'Don't play with it! It's a reconstruction of plaincode, not *real* plaincode—the whole thing is about as solid as a memory. Lee's cap wasn't exactly high quality, so I can't hold it up for long. When it crashes it'll probably take the lot of us with it.' He groaned. 'Run a trace, would you, while we still have time? I need to know if Lee was alone when he died. Or three minutes *before* he died, which is the best I can manage from what's left of the neurocap's logs.'

Obligingly Harry flipped out her control panel and booted up the necessary programs. 'I'm picking up a pair of INTROMET skins,' she noted, when the tracers returned a set of propitious results. 'Corporate folk. Looks like the duo were from Biocheck division too. Good old Singer, she knows how to categorise her employees. S. Yee and P. Young? Those names sound awfully familiar—'

'The other brain hack victims!' Lucas squeaked. 'This could have been where it began! The site of infection. Like a computer virus, perhaps—'

'Pardon me, my dear friends, but when did Felix learn plaincode?' Talobos interrupted. 'One can't help but notice that he seems remarkably proficient in the area. Surely such knowledge is limited to the upper echelons of qverse society! Or is the aging Lady Harmonica now in the practice of selling her secrets in exchange for sex with pretty oriental youths—'

Harry did not have a fully-charged laser handy, but that didn't prevent her from slamming the handle of one into the colonial beauty's smugly self-satisfied face. The force of the blow sent Talobos spinning straight through a plaincode stool. Still only partially complete, the stool erupted on contact, its seat bursting into snaking tendrils of code like the head of a Gorgon. Lucas screamed; Talobos screamed. The entire room undulated—a real stomach-turning motion. A sharp twinge of pain at the forefront of her neurocap told Harry that another fast move like that was liable to end up crashing the room altogether.

'Are you *crazy*?' Lucas wailed. 'I just told you not to play with it!'

'Did that look like "play" to you?' Harry growled.

'Geeze, Mum! Fry Talobos if you want, but don't touch the code!'

'Charging my laser as we speak, sweetness. I swear I'll make that bastard sorry for ever setting foot into the 'verse…'

But Talobos was laughing. It was a horrible, hollow laughter and it spilled out of him between sobs.

'What the hell is wrong with you?' Harry demanded.

Talobos said, 'It's the same room.'

'What?'

'It's the same room. God, look at it!' The code shuddered again and the colonial beauty shuddered with it. 'The room in which Arnold Lee died!'

'Of course it is,' Lucas began. 'That's the whole idea—'

'No, no, no! The *real* room. Not the qverse room—God, no! It's real. Nelly said—Nelly said—Nelly *said* it—Nelly saw it…'

'What?'

'Naughty Nelly-Yeunify found a program, a very special program; she picked it up and put it in her pocket,' Talobos sang, and the colonial beauty clapped her peaches-and-cream hands in delight. 'Big hush-hush Soo project. Made the verse like the world and the world like the verse. Like *surreal*-coloured glasses. Your lounge room as a beach. Your bedroom as a bathhouse. Your garden as a forest. Like Arnold Lee's kitchen as a laboratory.'

The words on the tip of her tongue were, *You must be joking*. But as she leaned down to snarl them into his big stupid face Harry saw the edge of the laboratory bench curving—with dramatic somnolence—into a state-of-the-art bubble-corner. The kind you'd only find in a spiffy ultra-modern kitchen. Oven-timer, she thought, desperately—and found in on the wall in the guise of a digital clock. Hot plates? They were there, practically unchanged, albeit partially hidden beneath the bubbling beakers. The plain square floor tiles were identical.

And the knives he'd used to kill himself? Three minutes before Arnold Lee's death, the knives had been sitting idly in the rack, only their handles visible. Like red levers, Harry realised. Red levers to activate the death-ray.

It was the same room.

On the floor the colonial beauty writhed in the throes of some exquisite psychological torment. 'Christ, can't you hear them?' it whispered. 'Can't you hear them murdering him? Lisping in their wicked INTROMET voices, Mr Lee, Mr Lee, we want you to help us test our Biocheck watches. Could you take these little…little handles, rods, whatever...could you insert them into your body? Just here, if you please, and just there, and in your elbow—they may prick a little, but not to worry...'

Harry felt faint. 'That can't be right. First of all, Lee would feel it. Second of all, in the qverse you move with your mind, not your body.'

'But what if you *didn't*?' Talobos howled. 'What if he *didn't*? What if he was in here and out there, too? What if they showed him this virtual world in order to steer him around the real world? Not brain hacking but brain *fucking*, Regina, they fucked his head, they stood there calmly and directed his suicide, his ingenious and horrible suicide, like the conductors of some ghoulish orchestra. And he didn't feel it until it was too late. Until he'd run out of knives or virtual rods. God, just look around this place and tell me I'm crazy, woman! You're the idiot, not me. You are standing in the middle of Arnold Lee's kitchen on the day he died, and you say this isn't part of the conspiracy?'

'Why would Singer call us to investigate if INTROMET was responsible? Why would Benny Soo—God!' The very idea of his involvement floored her. 'Why would Benny Soo create a program with the potential to kill?'

'Why do either of them have to know about it? It's about *perspective,* it's about creative thinking. Think historically, my dear Ms Carter. Remember that the Chinese were using gunpowder for fireworks long before the Europeans got—'

'I know that, but—'

Lucas said, softly, 'He's right, Mum.'

'Of course I'm right, you insufferable piece of qverse trash,' Talobos wept, one white arm twitching and extended like a semaphore of surrender. 'Perhaps they sedated him first. Twisted his cap a little *too* tight, made some minor alterations. And then they took Lee firmly by the hand and led him step-by-step through the methodology of his own murder. Oh so helpfully! Oh so carefully! And he never suspected a thing; never felt it until it was too damn late. Saying, as he died, I feel a tad dizzy, kind sirs! Saying, Might I have a moment to catch my breath? Saying, I do believe I am leaking, sirs—'

'Stop it,' said Harry.

'I do believe I am leaking, and from a thousand holes! Your magic rods have perforated me! Struck me down in my prime!'

'Stop it.'

'The program. That's why they killed lovely Nelly Georges. Because she had it. Because she saw it. Because she knew the answer to Singer's riddle. Surreal-coloured glasses.'

No, Harry thought. Not surreal-coloured glasses.

Hell-coloured glasses.

Someone started to bang on the door, probably a concerned Lauren Fang simulacra.

Harry thought: It was Saturday morning. You were in q-Paris and he said he had something to show you. Fell off the back of a q-truck, on a q-super-information-highway. Conned it out of a deadbeat INTROMET employee who needed the cash. Wanted to plug you into his goggles so you could see it through his eyes.

'I can't hold this room for much longer, Mum,' Lucas panted. 'Don't have the resources. We stay here much longer and I swear the place will implode.'

Oh, Joaquin.

'What did Yeunify do with the program?' Harry asked.

Talobos giggled. 'I don't know. Passed it on to her Melbourne contacts, I suppose. They do a brisk trade in stolen code down there.'

'Did she say that?'

'No—but. Wait. She *did* mention it to me. Her guys in Melbourne managed to arrange a deal with some NorthAsian half-wit. A four figure sum exchanged hands. More hush-hush business. Pity she didn't have the chance to spend it on anything.'

'Mum,' Lucas screamed, distantly, 'I told you I can't hold this up!'

'Who was it, Lloyd? Who did they sell it to?'

'How am I supposed to remember, bitch? After all I'm just a joke, a laughable drunk...' But he sobered as her grip tightened and the blinking red barrel of her freshly charged laser levelled with his right eye. 'I really don't,' he whimpered. 'A corporate guy. Maybe. A borderline qverse personality. Almost-famous?'

'From TEEK?'

Talobos nodded. 'TEEK guy.'

'Room designer.'

'Yes, yes.'

'Called Joaquin Magdellin. Paris-boy.'

'I—yes. Yes, it was him, I remember now...'

Then it came down, the room, the qverse, *everything*, the last threads of plaincode unstitching themselves and vacuuming back into the ghostcap-core. And Harmonica was sucked down with them, hollow-eyed, gasping, feeling gravid and fleshy and hideously corporeal —*I'm a ship that's all hull*, she thought obscurely, and crashed, spastically, spectacularly; she fell like a star, she fell like a meteor, she fell like a planetoid, and even as she fell dark and unspeakable terrors orbited her shattered skull like unwieldy satellites.

* * * *

She called Benny. Nicole picked up.

'Hello stranger. What, is there some court-order forcing you to speak to me?'

'Just put Benny on.'

'Fuck you, Mum. Just fuck you.'

Ring-tone, static.

* * * *

She called Benny on his downstairs line. Lynn picked up.

'Geeze, Nicky said you called and I didn't believe it. What's happened? Are you in jail?'

'I need to talk to your father.'

'Let me give you a tip, Mum. We aren't your little messenger-girls. If you're going to neglect someone for seventeen years, don't expect them to turn around in an instant and do you a favour. Frankly, I don't want to know you. Nicole doesn't want to know you. Dad doesn't want to know you. Got it? Then do what's best for all of us and stay out of our damn lives.'

Ring-tone, static.

* * * *

She talked to Lucas. He helped pick pieces of melted neurocap out of her hair.

'It doesn't make complete sense, love. I know that. But I also know that it makes *enough* sense. Two identical rooms. A program that twists reality into code. Two hack deaths and one mysterious disappearance. At this point I don't care who or why or how. I've just got to find Jo.'

'What do I do?'

'You stay here, baby. You lock all the doors and you stay put until Dad or I come for you. And if you find Gig's vidphone number? Tell him to stay out of the qverse.' And then his face in her hands, her lips on his forehead. 'I'll be back soon, Lucas, I promise. Be safe.'

* * * *

10

gig

On Tuesday morning Felix 'Gig' McGuiggen woke yawning to a molten NeoTokyo dawn. Sunlight fell in warm streamers across his bed. Above the ceiling was as white and expansive as the sky. Pink-lipped orchids in a bedside vase swelled and dwindled before his eyes. He pushed their bobbing blossoms aside and rose to gather his bearings.

That Phoun Swiftwater sure knew how to make a man comfortable—five star EastAsian hospitality all the way! The previous night he had been ushered, with courteous schoolgirl aplomb, into a penthouse on an upper floor of the SWIFTWATER building. Apparently it was not unusual for business-types to stay overnight in Japan following a consultation. If the protracted shuttleflight into EastAsian airspace didn't exhaust them, conversing with SWIFTWATER's CEO and her jumpsuited minion certainly would.

Initially the mere idea of staying in a room designed by Phoun had him gagging, but to Gig's surprise the penthouse was pretty. And, dare he say it, fashionable. The French-styled balcony shutters matched the plain paper-screens that partitioned the room into kitchen, dining and bedroom areas. Swinging lantern-lights flattered the chessboard floortiles. The four-poster bed, although frivolously elaborate, was covered in a simple sheet marked by the Chinese characters for HOME, WEALTH and HAPPINESS.

Finally Phoun had achieved a perfect balance of East and West, a kind of cultural Feng Shui in which all parts were cohesive and harmonious.

He spent the first minutes of wakefulness in bleary pursuit of caffeine. A ransacking of the cupboards and fridge unearthed a congregation of mini-liquor bottles but no coffee. This minor oversight of his host annoyed him— maddened him, even. He stood shaking and shameless in his underwear and cursed Phoun, by all her names, in all her guises.

Early-morning irrationality: it was his cross to bear.

Discouraged by life in general he returned to bed. But sleep eluded him. Hundreds of metres below he could hear the insistent freon thrum of automobiles spilling from offroads and sidestreets into the helter-skelter of layered motorways that wove in and out of the city's skyscrapers. Curious in a touristy fashion he wrapped the silken bedsheets modestly about his waist and sloped out onto the balcony, feeling about as graceful and chic as a recently exhumed Egyptian mummy.

Uptown NeoTokyo was fast and horrible, an intestinal scramble of transparent tubing and eye-gouging billboards, a scrabble of modern primitives beneath a curdled froth of smog, a stinking spaghetti-sprawl of upperclass ghettos—in short, a smaller, louder, denser version of Perking.

Or perhaps a real-life version of the gamers' online paradise, q-Topia.

And which one *had* come first? Gig wondered suddenly; NeoTokyo or q-Topia? Fifteen years ago NeoTokyo still looked more-or-less like a city, not some mutant metropolitan waterslide; fifteen years ago bonafide schoolgirl Misoka Hayashi had launched q-Topia 1.0, a comparatively tame version of the contemporary. Had art really inspired life or was their relationship of a more symbiotic nature, the two feeding off each other, growing bolder and brasher with each new update, each urban overhaul?

The idea disturbed him and he was overcome by a sudden and absurd desire to be clean—although to be *cleansed* was probably closer to the mark. The women in his life had contaminated him somehow; Singer with her autocracy, Phoun with her trickery, Ruth with her cruelty, Harmonica with her world-weary cynicism. Angry, miserable, and feeling more of a pawn than ever, Gig staggered off to perform his morning ablutions in the stylish modern bathroom. A topographical relief of GreaterAsia ridged the base of the steel hot tub. Gig scooped up a handful of bathsalts and snowed a trail of musk-scented flakes across the mountains of Tibet.

He ran the water. It smelt fresh and new.

In Gig's opinion a good long soak required a good long book. Coffee omission aside, Phoun had also been remiss in providing reading material for her guests. Gig made do with Tara Lee's well-travelled FOR Q magazine. Flipping past the translation on the front page he headed for the FOR Q classifieds. Cap (INTROMET, L, V7.95) for sale, 2x2m{blue, flat} wallcode section needs a new home, 24/M/WESTASIA seeking hack-friendly girl, GSOH...

A scattering of blue spots on one entry caught his eye. Holding it up to the light he saw that they were clearly not printer malfunctions but precise markings made by a ballpoint pen. A pen the exact same shade as the one Lucas had used to decipher Tara's code.

Kid left me a message, Gig thought excitedly. Something he didn't want Harmonica to see.

Nabbing a complementary SWIFTWATER-branded biro from the bedside table, Gig returned to the tub and settled down to do his hack homework. Working backward from right-to-left he came up with:

```
CO{!3xY}    BASERED
SVOL    SOUNDTAG
ENTER42-SP206(SW.4.9)126.INTECT(857333.X432)    WALL1RECPT
857333.X432    WALL1
QWHATISQAMMBSMHRD
```

Gibberish or a code within a code? Having flirted with computers in secondary school the first two lines were immediately familiar. 'BASERED' and 'SOUNDTAG' referred to coding nuances of a popular animation-creation program.

Gig gnawed a soapy finger. At a guess—he'd have to check with hardware-savvy Ruth for verification—'WALL1RECPT' and 'WALL1' labelled sections of machine-language pinched from a neurocap calibration.

Cheered by these code-cracking victories Gig turned his attention to the final line and was instantly stumped. Even an application of rudimentary punctuation failed to clarify matters: Q, WHAT IS Q, AM MBSMHRD. With a ratio of three vowels to fourteen consonants there was no point in attempting an anagram. Which meant that either this was an acronym or Lucas Carter-Soo had successfully made a fool out of him.

I will *not* let a fourteen-year-old brat get the better of me, Gig told himself firmly. I am twice his age and I'm positive I'm not as stupid as my mothers and Ruth like to think. Just because the little bastard's daddy is the great and terrible Benny Soo, he thinks he can pull a load of BS—

And Gig got it.

Q. WHAT IS Q?
A. MM, BS, MH, RD.

Alternately:

QUESTION. What is q?
ANSWER. Malachy Memphis, Benny Soo, Misoka Hayashi, Rebecca Descartes.

Eu-fucking-reka.

He leapt from the bathtub in a tsunami of foam and sought out his fresh new SWIFTWATER neurocap; and crammed it on regardless of his damp hair; and materialised in SWIFTWATER's obnoxiously rainbow-coloured entrance portal; and brought up his control screen with trembling hands; and readjusted his view of the external world into the familiar jumble of plaincode static; and stared a while into the misshapen silver programming symbols that rarely, if ever, repeated; and took a breath; and released the breath; and typed in the first eight symbols of Lucas' message.

And then switched to manual; and lifted the symbols whole onto the canvas of rippling plaincode hieroglyphs; and guided them steadily across its gullies and tors, fighting the tides of its unpredictable seas; and sensed a strange, *planetary* gravity as the symbols fell into place with a satisfying click; and glowed; and became a handle; and he wrapped his fingers about it and pulled it and it came away, an entire layer of plaincode came away in his hands, leaving a sequence of hieroglyphs perceptibly less obscure than before...

Plaincode.

On some level, Harmonica had said enigmatically, it all makes sense.

And, *on some level*, it did.

Plaincode was not the key to the ultimate programming innovation but a 'cheat' password for a virtual reality game. It was a kind of back-stage pass into a rule-free version of the qverse: gravity, space and time all optional. There was no 'ultimate programming innovation'. Because the qverse had not been constructed from a single original code but an amalgamation of four plagiarised ones.

Like mirror-writing, like invisible ink, like chalk on wax, Harry had said, the most difficult—and simultaneously, the most easy—translations are those that require you to think outside a formula. Some bloody formula! Four geniuses had written four codes on four levels and compressed them to look like a sequence of mutating cryptograms, overlapping and entwining and intermingling like the GreaterAsian diasporas. Picking the individual strands apart was simple provided you knew enough of the building-block codes to muddle it out.

Forget chalk on wax, the whole thing was a damn hoax. Gig felt cheated. Betrayed, even—his morning wrath had matured into melancholy. They'd made it so damn easy, he thought. They made it so damn easy and then sat back to laugh at us, the fools paying top dollar for code we could have made ourselves. Maybe that's why Lucas showed me. He felt sorry for me—

'Funny boy been busy like bee, ha ha.'

Princess Phoun, checking up on him. Gig attempted to switch out of plaincode and into normal-mode in order to better facilitate the conversation, but found the controls of his neurocap had mysteriously jammed.

His SWIFTWATER neurocap.

'I've seen a plaincode adept with your trace in the qverse before,' Phoun cooed. 'Silly me, I always imagined it was one of the Carter-Soos playing games. But now you come into my world and into my house and have the audacity to parade about your ill-gotten skills. Who told you? Lucas, I'd bet. That magazine code was more his style than Regina's. Poor little rich kid just wants to be everyone's best friend.'

'You think I'm going to tell you—'

'*I'll* tell you something for nothing, funny boy,' Phoun nattered on. 'Your magazine code break, okey? This shit in biro: My husband was murdered, he knew too much. It a hasty translation. Also, grammar and spelling not so hot. Maybe you try again. Tara Lee woman is psycho, okey. But she speak more right than wrong. Also, if you explain plaincode to another living soul? I kill you and all your family. Pardon the cliché but I have business to run. And ridding the world of two dykes and seven genetic mutants is pretty okey by me.'

'What are you going to do?' Gig smirked. 'Hack my brain?'

'Why should I, if I can blow a hole through it far more easily?'

He tore off his neurocap. He was naked on the floor and she was standing over him. She wore no neurocap or bulky goggle set but instead a transparent partial helmet that enclosed the left side of her skull. A glass monocle covered her left eye, cyborg style. Through it a distorted mirror of the qverse appeared projected onto the surface of her retina.

She had a gun.

She said, 'Funny boy not so funny now. This real gun. It kill you super-quick. I am perfect shot. I think I shoot you in the head but maybe balls is better. I think you want to start talking straight. No more lies. So you answer everything quick and fast. Why you carrying around an INTROMET bug?'

'I found it in Tara Lee's house.' His voice came out high and pitchy. A knot of terror had taken his throat and he feared it might unravel at any moment, sending him stuttering and squeaking into abject hysteria. 'Someone was recording our conversations. Harmonica said it was common corporate policy. I switched it off.'

'Yes you did. If you hadn't you would already be dead. Nothing personal. Just common corporate policy.' Idly the princess scratched her cheek with the gun barrel. 'Ha ha, you do pull some funny faces. Okey next question. How close to finding Arnold Lee's killer? I need estimate in days. Okey, you are not super smart but I already give you big hints.'

Incredulity overcame his fear. 'What? *What*? You mean you worked it out?'

'Princess Phoun Swiftwater is super clever. Anyway I explain all before. This not battle of hacks but battle of corporations. INTROMET versus SWIFTWATER. You start off in her game but you end up in mine. Think of European stories. Beowulf. St George. Snow White. Always bad guy make some dumb move—attack town, eat damsel, make poison apple—and get killed. He precipitate drama. Good guy end it.'

'Am I the good guy?'

'You are the fall guy,' said Phoun, but not unkindly. 'Last question. You love Regina much?'

'Holy mother of—'

'I take that as fanboy-speak for yes. You do not deserve her. You dumb and weak and whimpering idiot. But Ray-gee-neh always have super bad taste in men. Dopey Benny Soo best example. I love you Ray-gee-neh,' she mimicked. 'Now stay home look after my kids, okey! Benny Soo got big things to do! So better you than Benny I guess. You have okey body. But I prefer natural men. Also I do not trust you. Big flappy mouth. You not so good at keeping secrets. I might have to kill you later. Lucas too.'

'Lucas probably didn't mean for me to find—'

Phoun giggled. 'I knew you tell me sometime. Lucas explain plaincode? He must have some super good reason. If not I smack his fat bum next time I see him.'

'Next time you *see* him?'

'Sure, funny boy. What lies he told you about me? Who you think taught him plaincode in first place?' The princess yawned deliberately and glanced over her shoulder, the gun now dangling casually at her side. 'Okey. We done talking now. You go home. You and Ray-gee-neh find out how Arnold Lee died.'

'But I—'

'Bugger off, that how you say it in SouthAsia? Put on clothes and Jane get you a shuttle home.'

Her manner was dismissive but held an undercurrent of menace. As Gig scampered to grab his things it came to him that he was in the presence of something large, a kind of historical anchorpoint. Like a spectator at the signing of the Magna Carta, the GreaterAsian treaty, the matriarchs' qverse agreement. Like a one-time diner at the table of a young Alexander, a young Napoleon, a young Attila the Hun. Like a hack at the feet of Princess Phoun Swiftwater, Gig sensed an inimitable and indefinite *significance*. The face of the qverse was changing and soon, soon, the rest of its denizens would be dredged up, squealing and terrified, by its formidable undertow...

He left silent and chastised. His whole body ached with knowledge he could never use.

* * * *

Ruth Nameri picked him up from the shuttleport in his mothers' powder blue Mitsubishi. She wore plastic pink sunglasses with tacky heart-shaped joints and a cool half-sneer that puckered at one side to accommodate a biro. As he staggered into the passenger seat she commented in her dry way on his shell-shocked expression, his jelly-legged walk, as if he were a sailor returning from a six month voyage across a volatile sea.

This image appealed to him—an apt simile. I have seen an ocean while I was away, he thought. I have been submerged in a great basin of unholy bullshit. And I survived it, almost, maybe; my pride the only enduring casualty.

They pulled away from the shuttleport and he sighed gloomily into the irregular thrum of traffic. Turning to toss his briefcase into the backseat, he discovered a surfeit of cardboard boxes crammed in on top of one another. All were printed with the INTROMET logo.

'The folks at INTROMET are practically throwing away stock,' Ruth explained when he asked, briefly taking one hand from the wheel to jab a thumb at the boxes. 'Went there to make a few subtle inquiries about Yee and Young. The reception staff were so anxious to get me out they coughed up a wealth of Biocheck freebies. Don't see the appeal of it myself. Who the hell wants to know their blood pressure in the 'verse?'

Gig shrugged. 'Everyone loves a good fad.'

His cousin pulled a face, then wound down the window to scream an obscenity at an overtaking automaton-driven vehicle. He noticed two glaring lovebites on her neck which suggested that Zhadesh Patel had done more than mourn Nelly's passing at the McGuiggen homestead. Gig wondered if the duo had sex tantric-style, with lit phallic candles and gut-trembling moans.

Very zen.

Ten minutes from the shuttleport Ruth swung abruptly into a side lane and parked outside a dense line of shops. Puzzled, Gig took stock of his surrounds: a bland inner-urban suburb, familiar but unnameable; most likely the stomping ground of the Melbourne geek crew. His confusion brought out Ruth's inner bitch in record time.

'Don't tell me you forgot you're seeing Memphis today,' she hissed, spitting the biro onto her lap. 'Didn't Zhadesh give you a cache?'

'Yes. I dropped it in a shuttle garbage disposal and flushed it out over Alice.'

Her forehead wrinkled. 'What, by accident?'

'No. Not by accident. I did it on purpose. Because I was angry and I was scared. Someone put a gun to my head today. Wait, let me clarify that: Phoun Swiftwater put a gun to my head. Joked she'd wipe out my family and suggested I'm still a chromosome short of being a man. Two hacks are dead and rumour has it there are more to come. Ruth, I don't want to do this anymore. I'm so tired, I'm exhausted right in my bones. The qverse, the geeks, the secops and the hacks, all of it. I'm *done*. I want to go live in the country and grow vegetables.'

'God, you never stop whinging,' said Ruth and raised a sandalled foot over the handbreak, shoving him with one deft kick out the door. 'This is an honour. So at least *act* like you deserve it.'

'Ruth!'

'Call me when you're done. *Then* I'll give you a lift home. Unless you want to try walking back to your mothers' place—no, didn't think so.'

She peeled his fingers off the door handle and drove away, redoubtable as a bitch goddess. Wearily Gig evaluated his situation. Stranded. Bullied. Pathetic.

God, he thought. You'd think I'd be used to it by now.

It wasn't hard to pick the right building: the massive tinfoil triangle in the front window gave the game away. He pushed open the door and entered a room divided. Half-hardware, half-propaganda, a real hack hangout. On the left towers of circuitry teetered like Chinese apartments at high winds. A Warhol-styled masterpiece enveloped the right wall, a thousand technicolour hands frozen eternally in the FOR Q triangle. Viva la revolution.

The Melbourne geeks were all there, Zhadesh, Bradley and Eric, hunched around a table constructed from old desktop computer parts. And another man, who had looked up as Gig entered and now studied him openly, almost searchingly, as if attempting (as Harmonica had before him) to reconcile Gig's real life identity with his qverse masquerade.

Memphis.

He was old—older than Gig's mothers, his face aged in a pattern of wrinkles that was almost symmetrical. No scalpel work there. The skin was leathery from exposure and folded in creases as definite as the flap of an envelope. Eyes hooded and aproned twinkled above an almost-smile almost-lost in the wilderness of a pepper-spiked beard. In concession to the formal nature of the occasion Memphis had donned a loose suit jacket. Beneath it his clothing was casual: a violently flowered t-shirt and jeans faded by negligence. The FOR Q motto covered both knees, lettered in black magic marker.

An unusually skittish Zhadesh made the introductions: 'Felix McGuiggen, Malachy Memphis. Mr Memphis, this is Felix.'

'Hi, geeks,' said Gig, hating them.

'Felix,' said Memphis, untroubled by the slight, and leant forward to shake hands, breath pungent with tobacco and rum. 'Me and the boys here were just looking over a few papers while we waited. Explaining to them a few of the obstacles facing the FOR Q movement.'

Gig bared his teeth. 'Don't let me stop you.'

'Ain't nothing you can't catch up.' Memphis tapped the page before him, a convoluted asterisk of qverse connections and intersections imposed over a map of GreaterAsia. 'The ladies've got themselves a sweet set-up here, chum. They all use the same power stations to generate their qverse territories; their local generators and wireless networks are shared. It's a matter of trust, innit? Three vote party system. No weak links. The girls could probably cut each other off if they dared—two against one—but some ethical code prevents it. Or perhaps they're just scared. Never know what the repercussions of bringing down a qverse matriarch could be, eh?'

The accent was a singsong BBC cockney that had surely died out before the turn of the century. UK, not US. Which surprised Gig because Memphis' brand of revolution, with its pervasive advertising campaigns and brazen personal attacks, smacked of American enterprise.

'A lot less qverse, I should think,' said Gig.

Memphis laughed. 'Bold answer from a bold kid. I hear you aren't too hip to the FOR Q philosophy. Surprises me, coming from a hack. Especially a hack like you. According to Zhadesh you don't mind them smuggling in the odd bit of stolen code. What part of FOR Q do you object to? The methods or the message?'

'The man. You and your little mates talk of communist insurrection like it's a God-given right. The qverse is a business, Memphis. It costs money to run. It costs money to buy. Someone is always going to be making money out of it and putting money into it. I don't care if you steal code or hack corporations. Just don't pretend you have a right to. So the matriarchs made a deal and cut you out of the pie— man, stick out your stiff British upper lip and get *over* it.'

'Kid, the qverse was made for the people. It should *belong* to the people.'

'No. It should be *used* by the people. It should be *enjoyed* by the people. It should *belong* to the people who are willing to service it and maintain it.'

Watching, the geek trio had assumed wise-monkey poses. Hear no debate. See no debate. Speak no word against their incompetent cult leader. If I'd been in this situation a week ago, perhaps even a day ago, Gig reflected, I'd have sat tight and nodded and smiled and waited until later to vent my frustration. But the gun episode had instilled in him a kind of reckless courage.

Pity he was still no hero. More like a chained dog snapping vainly at the end of its tether at random passersby, a fatigued boxer punching air in the wake of a faster, flightier opponent.

Reckless but ultimately ineffectual.

'So what happened to you, lad?' Memphis asked, playing it kindly-uncle style. 'Had a nice heart-to-heart with a couple of your matriarch mates? Far as I hear, Singer and Swiftwater've both shown an interest. That kind of attention would be flattering to a young hack, yeah? But don't let the million dollar surgery and the schoolgirl cute act win out over your better instincts. They're hardnosed business women, relics of the old Mafia and Yakuza law. They would kill you for money. Question their motives, peel back their saintly gloss, and you'll find yourself in—'

'If that's true, why are you alive?'

'I'm too loud, too well known.'

'I bet if you asked anyone today the names they most often heard in the qverse, they would give you three. And they wouldn't be Viger Singer, Phoun Swiftwater or Rebecca Descartes. Or even Malachy Memphis or Li Ben Nee Soo. The battle of the hacks is the biggest news on the block. I am big and I am loud, Mr Memphis, and I may be scared but not so scared I'll take the advice of a lunatic.'

The silence that followed was palpable and carried weight. In sporting terms these could be the heavily pregnant seconds between the clinch and the separation, the tackle and 'foul' call. And Gig remembered for the first time that wise-alec hack kid in the shuttleport bathroom and the satiating power of his own fists, and the way his anger felt, exquisite and unleashed.

Memphis said, 'Do you realise how long it's been since they let someone else on the inside? To get up close and personal with the main players? Not just Singer and Swiftwater but Carter, too. Who was always the key to everything: a woman in the know and on the loose. You could help us greatly by pressing Regina Carter to deliver the translation of plaincode...'

'What makes you think I don't know it already.'

'Beg pardon?'

'I can read plaincode.'

'Who taught you?'

Gig shrugged. 'Nobody you'd know.'

'Prove it.'

'No.'

'The FOR Q organisation would be happy to provide you with anything you might want—'

'Then I want to know why you did this,' Gig said. 'I want to know why you made it. I want to know how four over-educated brainiacs got together and came to the conclusion that this, *this*—' and his arms swept a broad sphere that strained to encompass everything, the defunct hardware, the FOR Q propaganda, the dumbstruck geeks and the unshaven ex-neurologist, '—that this was a good idea. Tell me that and I'll give you your plaincode. Hell, reveal all within the next five minutes and I'll toss my everlasting soul into the bargain.'

Memphis began, uneasily, 'We made it to help people. It was…an altruistic endeavour. Benny and I planned it using his sonar research and my perfected brain-map. Once we had the basics together Benny headhunted Phoun from the ranks of some ridiculous EastAsian gameshow—I think the literal translation of its title was something along the lines of CLEVER KIDS MAKE ADULTS LOOK DUMB—and taught her the rudiments of computer engineering.

'Initially I thought he was crazy to bring her in. Photographic memory or not, Phoun was only seven years old. Ended up eating my words a week later. Girl mastered every computing language we could throw at her. Things were moving along swimmingly when Viger Singer smelt the qverse's commercial potential and came sniffing at our door. She flooded us with cash, bought up our brains. We couldn't refuse; Descartes needed the—'

'Fuck your Descartes,' Gig interrupted. 'I don't believe she even exists. After all, she doesn't *need* to. The neurologist, the biologist and the whizkid designer fit, but a *law student*? What place would she have in the q-genesis? Let's face it, in the colourful orgy of qverse personalities Descartes is a burnt out rubber sex doll: faceless, shapeless, a character who exists only to please your egos and unstring your enemies. I bet she's some half-assed AI automaton that you and Benny knocked up to scare Harmonica into fidelity, or an urban myth, a ghost in the machine—'

'We made it for her,' said Memphis.

'Huh?'

'We made the qverse for Descartes. We made it to help people but primarily to help *her*. Of course her name wasn't Rebecca Descartes then, but who bothers with real names these days, eh, Mr Gig?'

'Who is she?'

'No one special.'

'A real person or some seminal psychological construct?'

'A real person.'

'Did Benny Soo have an affair with her?'

'Look, I ain't really—'

'I ask you one damn question and you can't give me a straight answer,' Gig snarled. 'I want to know why and you give me vague half-arsed stories. Maybe you don't want plaincode that badly. And maybe I don't really care to give it. Maybe I just don't want to be involved any more. Okay?'

And then he punched Eric Nui, who was nearest, and ran, out of the room and onto the street, where a yellowcab idled. He wrenched open the back door and spat out his address, the words coming out at a rapid-fire stutter, syllables ricocheting off his tongue. The yellowcab pulled away and he bounced onto his knees and stared out the rear window, hands cupped over his eyes to shield against the glare.

Seconds later the shop door burst open and the three geeks spilled onto pavement, nearly hysterical—their perfect Memphis-meet arrangement had backfired spectacularly. Yelling, they piled clumsily into their own tiny car like a trio of circus clowns. Good God, Gig thought, are they actually going to *chase* me down? In the driver's seat Zhadesh looked to be fumbling with the keys. Then he clapped his hands in triumph and rested a hand on the wheel and the tiny car's engine turned over.

And became flame.

The geeks' car was standard reinforced metal and contained the explosion efficiently; there was no jet of fire nor a melodramatic Hiroshima mushroom-cloud; instead the effect was more like staring into a modern glass-fronted fireplace. Even the sound of it was muffled—a distant thunder, a distant sea. Nose now pressed to the window,

Gig saw only violent reds and oranges and the car reeling up on its back wheels like a startled horse.

It was like something not real; it was too real to be real. It was a qverse kind of real and it made a funny sound come out of his throat that was part whimper and part scream. Behind him there came the scratch of a match, a second, smaller crackle of fire. Someone had lit a cigarette.

Gig turned around. In the passenger seat, beside the driver automaton, sat Jane Cragg.

She said, casually, 'Need a lift?'

* * * *

TUESDAY-WEDNESDAY

11

harmonica

Harry felt ashamed that she spoke only one language when the children lined formally outside the Guishen bus stop appeared reasonably fluent in at least six. They were of primary school age, dressed in identical smart navy uniforms and dapper peaked caps like a queue of marching cadets. Some carried lunch bags; others struggled with black instrument cases almost as large as they were. She smiled at them—it was hard *not* to smile—and they giggled and called out in near-unison, 'Hallo America! Hallo America;' innocently using plump fingers to dip their almond-shaped eyes into double-folds.

America, America. Hallo America. She could have been British, African, GreaterAsian, but they saw America in her. It showed on a subconscious, *unconscious* level, the American affinity, the continental connection. At the tiny Guishen shuttleport—less a shuttleport than a shuttle-sized plot of brown land—she had spotted another Negro face amongst the Anglos and Asians waiting for international flights. The Negro, a man, had been wearing a neat pinstripe outfit and carried a folded paper beneath one arm, a duck's head umbrella swinging from his bony wrist. Subtle side-parted cornrows tamed hair which, if loosed, was probably longer than her own.

He was English, she did not have to ask. Just as these Guishen children did not have to ask to know she was American. It was in the clothes, certainly, but also in the eyes and in her *carriage*—an embarrassingly old-fashioned word, but applicable here. Carriage: the way she held herself, the firm set of her chin, and her stature, statuesque.

Hallo, America.

It was a good thing to be American in Guishen. Joaquin had told her so the last time she—*they*—travelled to China's west. 'Better to be an American in Guishen than an American in SouthAsia,' he'd said, no doubt paraphrasing some long dead humorist, 'or even an American in America. Out here they're what you'd call bush folk, hicks in the sticks. You, the six-foot black bitch—you are fascinating to them, like the singers and movie stars they see on Global television. So when you step into their world—into *our* world—it's a bit like them stepping into your world, too.'

And he'd grinned and thrown back his blond fringe with one hand, boyishly—although he'd only been eighteen at the time, so perhaps boyishly wasn't the right word to use.

Thrown it back Joaquin-ly, then, and grinned a Joaquin grin.

'Hallo America. Hallo America!'

By now the children's' obedient crocodile had splintered into subgroups of curiosity. They gathered at her waist and gaped unashamedly upward, shocked and amazed that a woman could attain such an imperious height. One reached for her arm and caught it, marvelling in some Chinese dialect at the span of her hand, touching her skin lightly, inquisitively, as if to see what *black* felt like. The musically minded banded and sang the chorus of a popular Latin pop-tune, their intonation and timing as comical as their round, serious faces.

'You like sweet, American?' a boy asked, standing on tiptoes to offer a sugary square of something that smelt vaguely like honey. 'Bad for teeth. Yum, yum.'

'I have flower,' giggled another, pointing to the plastic tulip-shaped clip in her hair. 'Have many flower in America.'

'You sing music? You play piano?'

'How old are you? Which state? Florida California Nevada Texas...'

Fifty eager voices crowed insistently for her attention. Harry must have looked completely bewildered. A fish out of water, an American out of SouthAsia. Taking pity, a copper-haired girl toward the back of the crowd raised a hand and shyly called a suggestion.

'America? My sister is translator. Maybe you ask for help?'

'God, yes,' said Harry. 'Please.'

The girl offered a hand and Harry reached out and took it. A short but vicious power struggle ensued: two boys tussled to grasp her other hand and were only dissuaded by a sharp (apparent) expletive from the girl. Quick-witted in victory, the copper-haired girl swiftly led Harry away from the bus stop and the children toward a distant intersection, explaining as they walked, 'I am Ash Lee, this the shortest way, you enjoy our city,' like a cheerful tourist guide.

Ash Lee. Or maybe just plain Ashley, you could never tell with these Chinese-English names.

Ben Nee, Benny.

In this world, Harry remembered, the dashing blond womaniser Joaquin Magdellin was plain old Jong Lin.

'I'm Carter,' Harry replied, and shuddered as an icy wind ripped up a sidestreet and dusted her coat with a confetti-sprinkling of snow.

The intersection was a mess of flashing lights, blaring horns and conflicting signals. NorthAsians liked cars more than their shuttle-reliant SouthAsian neighbours, preferred the thrills of manual driving to the reliability and safety of automatic automaton control. Live fast, die fast. On the far corner of the road, by a pile up of tiny sardine-tin cars, an enraged automobile enthusiast was beating up a driver automaton with a wheel clamp.

Above his head an obsolescent Roman-scroll poster revolved, showing giant-sized women chirping happily over the latest domestic modcons. Cute motorised scooters—vauvoos, NorthAsia's thinner, faster version of the Vespa—whizzed through the stultified lines of traffic. Rich children on the way home from school rode smaller customised models, their streamlined vauvoo protective gear making them look like little helmeted dervishes.

Perfect chaos. Shame she hadn't the time to capture this classic tourist moment on her vidphone camera. Ashley/Ash Lee urged her onward and then down a sequence of seemingly identical sidestreets. Here and there she saw evidence of a kind of half-hearted gentrification: little yuppie flats with curly-tipped roofs, the odd 'mod' bar with twenties retro decor. Clean, healthy, wholesome, a life cookie-cut for Guishen's young professionals. Further on haphazard wooden homes nested between steel corporate buildings. Warmly dressed children played racquet-and-ball against their shiny facades, some city-living variant on squash. Beyond their game the flat thin road was blocked at its midpoint by a sprawling local market comprised of plastic tents and stalls. Light snow iced the tents' eaves.

Giggling, Ashley led her on. Two steps into the market, and the mouthwatering tang of exotic foods permeated the air. Even with her prodigious knowledge of Chinese take-out, Harry could name barely half the dishes. Vendors advertised plastic trays of shrivelled mushrooms, rice soups, and translucent bags of ochre powders the same dusky hue as the sands of SouthAsia's deserts. One trellis boasted a rack of boiled snakes, naked as worms, with peeled and staring yellow eyes. Nearby an unattended pot of rice boiled up over an open fire. A scraggy looking cockerel with a broken wing pecked timidly at the scattered grains around it.

A stall of jars caught Harry's eye and she reined in her little tour guide, curiosity prevailing over urgency. Within the glass, tentacled things sloshed in an oleaginous glue. Squid? Octopus? Mutant NorthAsian wildlife? The Chinese characters on the label were indecipherable. Even when she followed the lines of text from top to bottom, right to left, (remembering Benny's lessons) she could make no sense of it. Stocked beside these were traditional medicines, illegal bear bile and the sparkling skins of lizards.

'For hurt,' Ashley explained, tugging. 'For hurt and for pain.'

As they moved on Harry spotted a vendor selling hardwired neurocaps and personal calibrations on the cheap, as well as a remarkable range of presumably pirated music, music and video games. INTROMET merchandise with a few choice pieces of SWIFTWATER hardware thrown in. All in remarkably good nick, as far as she could see—not that she could see much amidst all these people. Who did not jostle the way SouthAsians did, she noticed, but instead moved instinctively with the flow of the crowds, like leaves caught in a breeze, a stick following a river's current. Maybe it was some Buddhist thing—or were they Muslim up here?

Harry caught one last memorable NorthAsian sight just before they broke out of the market and back into the street. An old Anglo woman dressed in a blood-spattered white labcoat stood by a stack of plastic crates, a cigarette hanging limply from her wrinkled, puckered mouth. Gnarled hands rocked a tattered baby carriage filled with fish. Flies packed about her in a dense cloud, crawling her clothes and face. As Harry passed the woman produced a long dirty knife from the voluminous depths of her smock and jabbered something in a Chinese/English pidgin. Harry heard the word 'money' and 'whore' repeated before the woman erupted into hacking laughter.

Then fresh air came barrelling into her face and Ashley was pushing her through a door into a clean tiled room like a doctor's surgery.

'Wait!' the girl instructed and bolted off down a corridor.

So Harry waited. She wasn't alone—a kid in a wheelchair sat in the corner, both legs held straight out in white plaster casts. He was plugged into the qverse via a second-rate TEEK cap. Probably hanging out with friends in q-Topia's roller coaster district, given the occasional surprised squeaks and chuckles that erupted from him. With the wind in his hair, the sensation of *fast* singing through his system, brain hotwired, tuned to the dips and turns, the fearful rattle as the coaster-carriage mounted its topmost peak... Harry leant forward, feeling a sudden vicarious excitement—

'He broke his legs in a vauvoo accident. A secretary's son. Ran out across the road after a ball. It's a bad break and will take another month to heal. For the moment he's stuck here. But he's making new friends in the qverse while he recuperates.' A tall sombre woman stood at the corridor's mouth. The sister, the translator—she shared Ashley's copper curls if not her lively disposition. 'My sister was supposed to be travelling to Korea for an overnight field trip,' she added. 'Evidently she thought the idea of helping out an American was far more interesting. She has a lot of American music—neon pop is the latest fad. Your name is Carter?'

'Regina Carter.'

'A very American name. I'm Kim Hills. SouthAsian originally; the family moved here fifteen years ago. I'm fluent in all local dialects and, of course, modern English. Oxford educated, if you've a discerning eye for tertiary qualifications. Did you simply require a tour guide or was your interest in my services of a professional or personal nature?'

'Personal. I'm here to find a missing friend. Joa—Jong Lin.'

'A missing friend. Perhaps your friend wants to stay missing.'

'Not from me.'

'Do you know where to start looking?'

'Mr Lin, Jong's fath—'

'How do you intend to pay? I charge by the hour for my services.'

'I have credit cards.'

'What was it you did for a living, Ms Carter?'

Being nice took effort, made her teeth hurt like too much candy did. 'Virtual reality, contract work. I met Jong Lin six years ago at a FOR Q conference. We've been close ever since. Rest assured I'm not a jaded ex-lover looking for revenge or a payout. I just need to find him. If you could talk to his father for me—'

'I could.'

Harry dipped a hand into her pocket and took out the square of paper she'd printed from a streetside internet directory: Mr Lin's home address in four different languages. Getting the information had been no big deal—NorthAsia had long ended the contrivance of 'silent' numbers. Ninety-six male Lins lived in Guishen, but the directory allowed browsers to cross-reference name with job-type, qualifications, marital state, country of birth and number of children (legally, one or none). Jong's father was the only widowed Lin in shuttle engineering.

'Is he expecting us?' Kim asked.

'No.'

The translator examined her watch, tongue pulsing impatiently in her right cheek. 'We'll take a taxi.'

Outside again, on the main street, Harry saw four bearded men playing a complicated card game around a table made from an upturned guitar case. If it wasn't for the chill and the intensity of traffic she might have been back in Sydney. Funny, how all GreaterAsian cultures seemed to merge into each other after a while, became interchangeable and indistinguishable. Joaquin had once commented dryly that there was no such thing as foreigners anymore.

Except, of course, Americans.

Kim Hills hailed a taxi, a tiny bug-like contraption with huge wheels that Harry guessed was the latest thing in transportation. They zipped through the city, flanked by white vauvoos, their riders looking small and slightly deformed, hunched up like some new breed of speedy turtle. Or tortoise. (Which brought her full circle, back to Gig the rabbit and Harmonica the prehistoric monster...) And as the sun sunk Harry was conscious of the passing city not in terms of its infrastructure or citizens but as a kind of complex code, each fluorescent sign linked symbolically to each instance of sprayed graffiti, each shout of polyglot babble layered illegibly over the next, and everything overexposed in whites and blacks like a photo negative, Guishen, China, NorthAsia, GreaterAsia pared down to the raw plaincode pith.

'I too am interested in virtual reality, Ms Carter,' said Kim Hills placidly, lighting a cigarette. 'I was deeply interested in linguistics at university. I even wrote a mock-thesis on plaincode. It fascinates me: a computing language that appears derived from a thousand other languages, an ultimate language, an impenetrable Babel. You know people have seen Chinese, Korean, Arabic and even Russian letters materialise in its midst. Others see human faces, often those of the recently departed. I think that the qverse is a poetic statement about finding oneself—'

'Bullshit.'

Kim raised an eyebrow. 'Pardon?'

I hired a translator, Harry wanted to say, not a damn philosopher. Instead she said, 'Lack of communication. You want to know what the qverse is? Lack of fucking communication. Like one of those damn refugee outposts populated by nineteen different communities with nineteen different languages and nineteen different religions and nineteen different ways to make pot noodle. Nineteen cultures compressed first into a tiny space and then compressed again into their individual spaces, not assimilated or integrated but stratified like the sediment in archaeological excavations. That's what plaincode is. Society in *mono*glot breakdown.'

'That's a very dark view to take. I always felt that a blend of different peoples enriched the world.'

'Who knows if it's enriching? Who cares? What I'm talking about here is the stratum, the codification of NeoAsia. When the depth of a bow has meaning. When a belch can be either a compliment or the ultimate faux pas. When taking a piss is an affair so shrouded in mystery that most tourists would risk piddling down their own leg rather than venturing into a public toilet. What I'm talking about is the inevitability of infinite misunderstandings. The meaning of things lose edges, lose specifity, lose context and eventually become nothing. Plaincode is the blueprint of an utterly meaningless world.'

'You seem a very angry woman,' the translator observed. 'Do you not like NorthAsia?'

'Put it this way, I've dated too many selfish Chinese bastards to enjoy the view.'

Kim smiled—humouring her—and turned away.

Ten minutes later they were out of the taxi's warmth and standing ankle deep in a sudden snow outside a block of yuppie flats. God, this infernal weather! Harry tugged up her jacket zipper—it made a raw, grating sound, like the closure of some mechanical vice. But there was no point in cursing. Blame global warming all you wanted, she thought, blame the depleted ozone layer, blame the 1980s and CFC-solidified big hair, but after you finished whining you were still bloody freezing.

Practical-minded Kim went for the intercom button, chattered for a minute through chattering teeth. Shortly the door of the bottom flat creaked ajar. Mr Lin. A French expatriate: wiry, sharp, nattily dressed, mop of blond hair shifting gracefully to a mature grey, a full two years younger than Harry. If the man had migrated to SouthAsia's coast instead of inner-west China he would have been a surfer, no doubt about it; one of those aging still-handsome champions who loafed into the waves after work the way lesser men slumped before the vidscreen. Lin looked like his son—strange, because Harry didn't remember the two being similar. But the very presence of boyfriends had a tendency to modify memories, rework them to fit an ideal.

'Mr Lin,' Harry said, stepping forward, forgetting etiquette, spreading her hands flat and wide. 'It's been years. Do you remember me? Regina Carter.'

Recognition. But finding the right words was harder. The almost insurmountable language divide… 'SouthAsia?' Lin tried uncertainly. 'Friend of Jong. How you say, close friend.'

'Girlfriend,' Kim advised.

The father nodded. 'Girlfriend.'

'I need to know where Jong is, please,' said Harry.

'My English not good, Regina—'

'Jong. Where is Jong, your son, where is your son—'

Lin struggled. 'He no live here.'

'I know that. But he isn't at home, isn't in his apartment in Beijing! Where is he now?'

'Regina, my English—'

Polyglot Kim took over the explanations, began a conversation inside the conversation, a glossary, a subtext. Harry stamped her feet on the porch until the numbness subsided. Lin said, 'No, no. Jong does not tell us where he go.'

'He hasn't called you?' Harry persisted. 'He hasn't visited? When was the last time you saw him?'

The NorthAsians conferred. Lin spoke at length. Kim translated: 'Monday night. He went into his old bedroom. Then he left again. Maybe he took something.'

'I need to search the room. Can I?'

'He says you can. He says you were always a very polite lady. Very cultured. He was sad when you and Jong broke up.'

'Tell him thank you.'

The translator bowed. 'I already did.'

So Harry entered the house, the cramped corridor, sliding past Lin in a breasts-to-the-wall crouch. And found Joaquin Magdellin's old bedroom, untouched since he'd moved out six years ago, still jam-packed with the debris of adolescence: an abandoned five-stringed guitar, a pile of EastAsian comics, a wardrobe filled with the clinging lycra-inspired fashions of the late 2050's, an outdated computer, a bookshelf of shamefully lewd science fiction and fantasy novels, a conspicuous roll of unused condoms, a blanket printed with the reclining image of a botox-lipped Korean film star.

And on the furtherest wall Harry saw Joaquin's life in photographs, a hundred snapshots running the gamut of boyhood, personal, intimate: naked Joaquin-the-toddler blowing bubbles in a ceramic bath; Joaquin-the-graduate in the sombre vestments of private school; Joaquin-the-teenager wearing a red vest and posing for a rugby team lineup; Joaquin-the-baby peeking cutely from a cocoon of swaddling cloth; Joaquin-the-prepubescent in a French beret, hand over heart, no doubt reciting some ode of the revolution; and finally, Joaquin-the-man, smirking out across a snow-filled plain, one arm around the only woman he'd ever truly loved…

Think, Carter. Which one of these is not like the others?

Harry ripped the last photo out of the collage. It had been taken during their last holiday in China. In it they held hands outside an old cabin that belonged to one of Joaquin's distant friends. Hardly a cute couple: she too tall, he too young. Some trick of the light had left her face surly and unfocused. Beside her the ever-photogenic Joaquin was a white elfin creature with thin and dainty hands. As protection against the chilly air he wore fingerless gloves, and wrapped about his throat was a bright red scarf, the tail of which, she remembered, had been snared in a constant battle with the wind. In response to each gust it had spooled its cotton body a little tighter about his neck, so that every few minutes he was forced to insert a finger between the rippling fabric and the pale pillar of his neck and tug on it sharply in order to prevent himself from suffocating.

She turned over the photograph.

There!

A date.

Last Monday.

2062.

And a message in the same black marker as that she'd seen scrawled in reverse across his apartment's vidscreen:

THERE I LOVED YOU LAST

* * * *

Kim Hills organised Harry's vauvoo hire before tallying up the bill. In all the translator's services came to measly ninety SouthAsian dollars. Harry paid with plastic cards, hopped on the vauvoo, and coasted out of Guishen into the sudden cloudless dark of a NorthAsian dusk. Veering from the main road (unpredictable by day, downright suicidal by night) she opted for the less travelled bike route. Her way was lit by a long train of white lanterns, each nestled in its own stone pyre.

Fast fast fast, she thought, and felt young again. Young, because of the wind in her hair and the stars in the sky and the bitter chill on her cheeks and this weird vauvoo weightlessness, almost as if she were accelerating on her own momentum, propelled by force of will alone, like a comet streaming through the great voids of space.

Fast fast fast and maybe free.

The cabin was on a hill some ten kilometres from Guishen's suburban fringe. Halfway up Harry discovered her vauvoo was a substandard vehicle—she had to coax it up a little bit at a time, encouraging it with timely revs. On the hill's final crest she dumped the bike, kicked off her heels, and walked up the path in her stockings. The snow, the ice. The cabin looked empty, smelt abandoned. THERE I LOVED YOU LAST. Harry thought: I am a long long way from home.

'Joaquin?' she called.

No answer.

'Jo? It's me. Are you there?'

She took a step forward and a brown furrow appeared on the ground between her legs, spat up a thin dirt boatwake. Moonlight glanced off something metallic at a window. She got the vague impression of something cylindrical, then it moved again and she saw it clearly. The barrel of a shotgun nosing out from underneath the curtains, ominous as a snake poked to strike.

'Jesus, Joaquin!' she yelled. 'You shot at me!'

'Harry?' His voice unsure.

'Of course it's me. I came looking for you. You left me clues.'

'Are you alone?'

'I'm alone.'

'They're after me, you know. That fucken program. Those fucken Melbourne geeks.'

She felt like weeping. 'I know.'

The shotgun disappeared.

'Well come on in, woman,' Joaquin said gruffly. 'What the hell are you waiting for, a written invitation? If I have to be on the run, I'd prefer not to run alone.'

So Harry ran to him. Through the door and into his arms; and they hugged like friends; and they kissed like friends; and he held her face; and his eyes were blue and tender; and she sneezed; and he blew on her cold curled fingers and laughed; and she started to shiver so he bundled her into a thick woolly blanket; and he put her to bed; and she lay there, one leg arched to touch the floor, and watched while he brewed soup on a tiny emergency gas-ring, a trick he must have learnt as a boy scout, if they even had boy scouts in NorthAsia.

'To warm you up,' he told her. 'You're bloody mad, vau*vooming* up here in this weather.'

'Oh piss off.'

'Monday morning,' he said. 'You left q-Paris to play hostess and someone knocked on *my* door. Clever me, I check the keyhole first. Two thugs outside, an Anglo and an Asian—maybe Japanese, I can't tell. Both in some kind of uniform. Exterminators? Cleaners? They call my name. Jong. Jong. Jong. I know I should answer but I don't. I have this eerie premonition: *badshit coming.* I wait. They mutter to each other. Then the Anglo says, in this reassuring hostage-negotiator voice, Jong, we just want the program. Don't be scared. We won't hurt you. We just want the program.

'So I know they know I'm there, I'm listening. Caught like a rat in a trap. No point in pretending any more. I say, What program? They say, *The* program, like I should know already. But I don't. I buy a lot of pirated code. In the last week I've picked up a whole collection of gems. A room skeleton. Six unmade chameleon skins. A high-class laser and some pretty nifty barrier-breakers. So it doesn't click yet. I say, What program? again. And they say—like they're not sure themselves, like they're repeating someone else's words—the program that makes life real.

'Okay, I say, playing dumb. The program that makes life real. But I'm not that stupid, I get the picture now. I also get that the two guys outside have absolutely *zip* idea of how qverse electronics work or what this mysterious program really is. Okay, I say. I've almost finished putting that real-life-making program together. If you give me five or ten minutes' peace it'll be done and you can take it away with you. But you can't make any noise while it's processing, otherwise I'll have to do it all again. Can you be quiet out there?

'Sure, whatever, say the thugs. We can wait.

'Great guys, I say. Thanks a bundle. Then I snatch up my neurocap, my wallet, and I climb out the window. I live on the sixty-ninth floor. But it's one of those new-fangled trendy-architecture buildings, all modern and fashionable with projections and external walkways and glass ceilings and ladders that go nowhere which I guess are supposed to be some kind of artistic criticism of corporate life. Anyway one of those walkways is outside my window. I get onto it somehow—God, I can't remember the details—and from there I kind of hook myself into this strange niche in an upturned projection, looks kind of like a coffee mug from the outside.

'It's at this point I realise that I am sixty-nine floors above the ground in a piece of modern art and I have a panic attack. Not very manly of me. But I swear I see my life passing before my eyes. The good bits, mainly. Our holiday to Jamaica featured prominently. As I'm whimpering in the cup, the thugs open the window. They look out. Mercifully they don't see me. They start yelling at each other, Where the hell do you think he went, that sort of thing.

'Eventually they come to the conclusion that I've managed to nick out while they were having their thug domestic. They leave. I wait half a bloody hour in the cold, in the cup, sixty-nine floors high. Finally I get my act together, hitch up my balls, and clamber back into my apartment. They've trashed all my qverse hardware. My spare caps, my caches, even my bloody computer. Ruins. I gather up some clothes. Then I write my message on the vidscreen and I run. Catch a taxi all the way back to Guishen, leave you a note there, then walk to the cabin on foot. Been here since Monday night. Which I guess leaves us with the million dollar question. Are you dating Gig?'

Are you *what*? Harry rubbed blurry eyes. Since when did a mad escape through China segue into a conversation about her relationship status?

'I've been in and out of the qverse during my enforced hermitage,' Joaquin explained. 'TEEK territory only, of course. Safety reasons. There's no chance of getting location-traced on my own home turf. That drunk asshole Talobos keeps harping on about you two. Harmonica and Gig. Gig and Harmonica. You shared a hotel room in Perking or something. According to Talobos you've been seen together. Is it true?'

Harry grunted, 'We shared a room in Perking. I think—'

'I met him once through the Melbourne geeks. Their unofficial head-geek, Zhadesh, is dating Gig's younger cousin Ruth. Real name Felix McGuiggen, right? Good name for the guy, Felix; he reminded me of a cat. Liked to drape himself over the furniture and hiss ineffectually when someone brushed his super-sensitive fur the wrong way. Spoilt city kid, Ruth said. His mothers' favourite. Genetically modified apple of their eye. Pretty, I'll give him that. Pretty like a girl. Pretty like a teenager. Pretty but vapid. Has no friends. Has no life.'

'You sound jealous.'

'I am.'

'He's just a boy.'

'*I'm* just a boy.'

She did not understand. She did not understand how Felix 'Gig' McGuiggen was relevant. She did not understand how he could sit there after a narrow brush with death, in this brief reprieve between frying pan and fire, and complain about her interest in a random mulatto pretty boy. She told him so. And he replied that if Gig was a random mulatto pretty boy then he was a random Anglo pretty boy. And then apologised, angrily, as if the word sorry soured his tongue.

And hugged her, as a friend.

And kissed her, as a lover.

It happened fast fast fast on the woolly blanket; she drew him in and pressed him on her, his skin warmer and softer than her own. Old sex. Familiar sex. Cloying sex. He whispered indistinct feathery things in her ear and she knew that this was as good as they'd ever get.

Later he said, 'I can't keep you.'

'It's nights like these,' Harry said wistfully, 'that I wish someone could.'

* * * *

12

gig

I am in shock, thought Felix 'Gig' McGuiggen. Shock is—believe it or not—a lot like being fried. Shock is an elevated pulse and a sudden dread as dire as an electrical powersurge. Shock is the fearsweat prickling your forearms and the inexplicable chill that rattles your ribs and teeth. The moistening of the thighs, the virtual synthasia. Shock is those tiny cerebral fireworks that you can feel erupting behind your temples, grey-matter going supernova, your neurocap's metal spindles ejaculating sharp static shocks into the mangled meat of memory.

The car explosion had become a solid thing in his mind: a moment framed and repeated, the colours and sounds retrospectively tweaked to perfect clarity. Reds were redder, blacks blacker; the detonation itself resonated between his ears like the deep, thunder-pulse of a drum. The scene even possessed a smell, not of gunpowder or synthetic compounds but the musky earthy odour of his mothers' basement, in which Gig had once been trapped as a small child. It was a smell he had long associated with feelings of helplessness and fear.

Horrible, horrible.

He rested his long brown fingers against the taxi window and stared blankly out at a sunset the same intense scarlet as the implosion's core. They had entered beachside territory and seemed to be closely following the voluptuous curves of the coastline. Infrequently he caught glimpses of blue craquelure between heritage-listed holiday homes. White seagulls hung dim and ghostlike in the upper-right corner of the sky, buoyed by an aircurrent whipped off the Tasman. Gig realised he could not remember Eric's last name.

'I'm a bad person, Jane,' he whispered, stretching out across the faux-leather back seat. With his eyes closed he could imagine he had been transported to the office of a 1980's shrink, safe and historically-neutral. 'People are always making excuses for me. They say it's biological, some inherent designer kid melancholia. Guess they're happier calling me a mutant than an asshole. But in the end I'm still a brat, no matter how you choose to couch the term. I'm malicious, jealous, spiteful, self-centred, cruel, I don't *deserve* to be—'

'It was not meant for you,' said Jane Cragg.

'What?'

'The car bomb. It was not intended to kill you.'

'How in hell do you know?'

'Death is a serious business. Those who deal in it rarely make mistakes.' She reached up to adjust the passenger mirror and he saw a flash of her pursed lips, burgundy and botox-plush. She said, 'I do not believe you are the only person in the world who is capable of attracting trouble, Mr McGuiggen. Your geek friends have been living on the proverbial edge since pirating their first code.'

Her tone was perversely matter-of-fact—a composed confession or merely a streetwise observation? Not that it made a difference either way. The geeks were dead. He was trapped. The qverse matriarchs and their high-profile acquaintances were swatting him back and forth like a tennis ball. The reason behind it all—if you could call it reason—no longer mattered. Let me go and I'll play your detective game, Gig thought weakly; shuttle me four hundred miles outside GreaterAsian airspace and I'll theorise and rationalise the situation all you like. Let my life off the line and I'll do my best to pretend I give a shit about your politics and your pompous female pride.

'SWIFTWATER policy, I suppose,' he said aloud, too distraught to be tactful, 'is murder Phoun's super-clever way of cutting down the competition?'

'Mr McGuiggen—'

'What about kidnapping! Where does that fit in to Misoka Hayashi's big plan for a better world?'

Jane laughed nasally. 'You were the one who entered *my* taxi. You are welcome to leave at any time. But for the moment I imagine you might feel a little safer in my company, under the watchful eye of SWIFTWATER. We take good care of our own, McGuiggen. We always have. And who knows where the next bomb will be found?'

He had disliked her at first sight, the sharp-faced corporate drone with her striking tattoos and officious manner. Now he hated her—irrationally, because she was right, because she was smug, because she was there. God save me from the agents of hospitality, he thought, slumping lower on the seat; God save me from PAs and PR. Send them off to mind their own Ps and Qs.

The taxi swung a hard right into a gravel driveway and stopped outside a supra-modern four storey house, the frontage panelled in technicolour plastics like an outsized Rubik's cube. Japanese characters arched over the front door like the Greek letters outside American fraternity houses. Hedges shaped into Greek numerals lined paths stoned with metallic crystals. A real rich-folk mansion: abhorrent to look at and inordinately expensive to build and upkeep. Could this house belong to anyone *but* Phoun Swiftwater? Gig mused as he climbed out of the car. It had to be one of the matriarch's many homes away from home, a SouthAsian mansion with views of the Great Ocean Road.

Distantly he heard the sea, its rush and fall, its gush and retreat, as steady as a human heart. And remembered—like déjà vu—those recorded ocean sounds in the SWIFTWATER building. Reflections. Within the qverse and without it. Oddly, he found the memory neither scary nor discomfiting, no more or less surprising than recognising his own face in a photograph. In the past few days he had come to expect this sort of duplication in the world.

Jane Cragg said, 'Come with me.'

He followed.

In the courtyard behind the house a pair of white-blond EastAsians lounged by an Olympic-sized pool on deckchairs printed with Barber-shop red and white stripes. Sleek, streamlined men ripped with lean muscle; the athletic type Honoria McGuiggen referred to dismissively as hard-bodied hunks. Gig presumed that made her only son a soft-bodied schmuck. The closest hunk wore an open suit-jacket and silver framed aviator sunglasses, the other running shorts and roman sandals that strapped to mid-calf. A pronounced similarity in their bone structure suggested they were related; first cousins at the least.

Bet they didn't get their Y-chromosomes out of a catalogue, Gig thought wistfully, his mind already running through a familiar litany of teenage self-criticisms. Too fleshy, too delicate, too damn pretty… beside their flawless physiques he felt like a fat circus donkey stabled alongside prize-winning stallions. As he shuffled after Jane the sandal-wearing EastAsian guffawed, a hoarse, faked laugh. His suited companion whisked a soggy towel from the back of his deckchair and cracked it whiplike in the air.

'Jane-Jane,' called the suit. 'What happened with this little one? You found it in the street and brought it home?'

'Who he is and why he is here is none of your business,' Jane replied.

'We know already,' said the other hunk, running a hand through cropped white hair. 'McGuiggen, Felix. SouthAsian geek. Phoun showed us photographs. What we want to know is *why* he is here. You think it is clever for us to be seen fraternising with Singer's gofers?'

They were speaking in Japanese—no doubt under the mistaken belief that this would cut him out of the conversation. How moronic and backward do they think we SouthAsians are? Gig wondered. I grew up in bloody Melbourne; I needed to master a minimum of six languages to manage the grocery shopping. Irritated on behalf of his countrymen, he glared down into the pool.

'It is not my fault,' Jane said; 'he got into my taxi.'

'You should have gotten him out again.'

'I am going to contact Phoun. She will advise on the situation. McGuiggen may prove useful depending on what Phoun has arranged with Descartes. And it should keep him out of Memphis' range.'

'You intend to leave him here?'

'You are under no obligation to fraternise. In any case I thought you were meant to be in Sydney by now.'

'We leave in the morning.' The suited hunk stretched—a better word for it would be *extended*—his body in a lazy yawn and Gig distinguished an odd shape bulging the man's side. New fear brought his concentration to a pinhole focus, an intense close-up like the qverse 'zoom' function. The suit rocked back on his heels and Gig caught the hard black sheen of metal and pearl nested close to his hip, almost but not quite hidden by his loose shirt.

And then saw another shape at the man's ankle, angular and knifelike. And saw also, on a poolside deckchair, a second gun wrapped like a baby in a cocoon of incongruously pink towel. And saw also the easy muscles of hunk number two's bare chest and the fine detail of a tattoo unravelling down his right arm, a tattoo that was a smaller duplication of the one ringing Jane Cragg's neck.

Not a Celtic design, he realised. But a convoluted weave of Japanese characters in the vein of the plaincode cipher. A gang thing. These were thugs, heavies, professional mercenaries. God, what would Phoun want with these guys?

But that was a stupid question—he'd *met* Phoun.

Who giggled about Yakuza connections and told him she'd kill him if he ever went astray.

Jane Cragg said, 'You should find out if she will be in Sydney first.'

'We should, we should. But we can wait for her, Jane-Jane,' the suit sneered. 'We are not as impatient as you. We know she will return at some point and Sydney is not an easy place to hide. Nor would she attempt to. What about the Singer gofer? Is he an actual part of this? Or is McGuiggen—'

He stopped. His gaze shifted to Gig. And stayed there until Gig's nervous blink betrayed him. 'Shit,' the suit said in English and spat onto the ground. 'You fool, Jane-Jane. The kid is a polyglot. He speaks Japanese. Right, McGuiggen?'

Briefly Gig considered denying it—but why bother? It would only delay the inevitable. 'Yes,' he said. 'I speak Japanese.'

Jane asked, frowning, 'Well?'

'Fluently.'

'So you—'

'—heard, yes. You're going to Sydney to kill Harmonica.'

'You misunderstood what we said. Phoun would never harm Carter. The woman is Phoun's rolemodel; she grew up idolising her.'

'You planted the bomb.'

'No.'

He was moving backward. His fingers, his hands, his whole face felt numb. 'Don't come near me.'

'We had no intention of doing so.'

'I'll call the police.'

'I very much doubt that,' said Jane Cragg.

Gig turned and ran, knowing intuitively they wouldn't follow. Not back the way he had come but onward, over the low iron railing that bounded the patio, over the chickenwire erosion fencing, over the thin green meshes that contained the sandbanks, over those final metres of powderwhite sand to the sea. Thinking, out, out, *out*, in rhythm with each footfall, each laboured breath, and that, too—that mad flight with his heart bobbing painfully in his throat—that felt like being fried in its own crazy way, some frenzied freefall back into the gravid density of his own body.

Crash, burn. He hit the sand and lay quiet. He was in shut-down mode. He watched the sky and those few stars visible through the smokescreen of smog, constellations shrouded in neon nimbus like streetlamps. His thoughts were rational and detached. If they wanted to kill me, he told himself, I would already be dead. If I wasn't meant to be here I wouldn't be. If this is a game I'm still playing it right—God knows how, but I'm doing it. I can't trust in myself but I can trust in Phoun's genius; I can trust that she will never, ever make a mistake.

The sea sent foamy fingers to flirt with the frayed ends of his laces. Gig thought of home and Harmonica. And riddles he could not solve, and questions that had no answers. And the shiny SWIFTWATER neurocap, and Phoun Swiftwater's cutesy pigtails, and the labyrinthine mesh of q-Topia's countless thoroughfares. And the black INTROMET briefcase, and Viger Singer's too-thin smile, and the five skyscraper fingers of INTROMET's headquarters stretching metallically to embrace a supernova sun.

His vidphone jumped suddenly in his pocket and then was still. God, please not Ruth, he prayed—replaying yet again Zhadesh's comic struggle with the car keys, those five seconds of everyday pathos before the geek vanished in smoke. The vidphone's screen was lit when he fumbled it onto his lap; he must have accidentally knocked the 'accept' button.

The caller was female—that fact alone filled him with a wary dread. On the up-side, she wasn't Ruth. Or Phoun or Jane or Viger or Honoria or Sandra or any of the innumerable other females with a stake in his body and soul. This female was just a kid, really, a skinny red haired thing with a smattering of freckles across her nose and expressive green eyes. Unapologetically homely: a rarity in this scalpel-cut world. One finger pressed her lips in the universal gesture for silence.

'Hello Hansel,' she whispered around it. 'Have I got you at a bad time?'

It was definitely Hansel she'd said and not the more predictable Handsome. Hansel, a name that conjured up childhood memories of wicked witches and bread crumb trails and freshly stoked ovens, all things quite relevant—in a strictly metaphoric sense—to his current predicament. Doubtful, then, that this was a random wrong number. By now Gig was convinced that there was no such thing as coincidence, not in the qverse. Everything was connected holistically, a mutant *asterisk* of intersections—you just needed to know where to pencil in the links.

'Qverse,' he said darkly. 'Christ. Who are you?'

'What a question! No one you'd know—the name's Eleanor Petegin.'

He tried to switch the vidphone off but couldn't. She was forcing the call.

'Sorry to barge in unannounced, Gig, but I need to speak to you—'

'Whose side are you on?' he snapped. 'SWIFTWATER or INTROMET? Or FOR Q?'

The question amused the girl. 'I'd like to think I was on my *own* side. But I suspect a cynic like yourself would find that hard to buy. So I shall be honest with you: I've had dealings with both Misoka and Viger in the past—and your friend Regina Carter. Dig a little in the annals of q-history and you may discover that I'm Malachy Memphis' first cousin. Estranged first cousin, I should say; you know what family politics is like. By virtue of birth and association I guess I am, as they say, old school 'verse.'

'Estranged first...what? Who are you?'

'I told you. My name is Eleanor Petegin,' the girl repeated, calm in the face of his hysteria. 'Have you been speaking to Ph—'

'Eleanor, I am in the middle of a very important breakdown. I do not have time for this.'

'I represent a large group of concerned people—'

'You look sixteen.'

She flushed scarlet. 'I'm nineteen.'

'What? Old school 'verse and as old as the 'verse? What kind of an idiot do you think I am?' He pushed his face to the screen and sneered when she failed to flinch. 'You're calling from inside the qverse, aren't you?' he said, examining her with a critical eye. 'You're a skin. A souped up qverse skin or maybe even a very, very convincing AI automaton. God, what happened to the good old days when the matriarchs had the good manners to send *real* minions to harass me? Petegin, Model 342. Mission: Seek and Annoy. Are you a Singer or a Swiftwater clone—or the brainchild of some unaffiliated party?'

'I didn't call to argue with you,' Eleanor said wearily. 'All I want is to know what happened. Could you give me a quick run-down of your investigation into the Arnold Lee death?'

'You must be joking.'

'I assure you that—'

Gig grated out, 'No, Eleanor, I cannot give you a quick run-down of my investigation. I agreed to a verbal confidentiality clause with Viger. And Phoun too, if you count the bit where she put a gun to my head and said she'd kill my whole family. Now please, please, do me a favour and piss off. You're as tenacious as a bloody telemarketer.'

'Six people associated with this investigation are dead,' Eleanor said stubbornly. 'Half died while plugged into the qverse. What I need to know is if this is real. That's all.'

'Define real. Real like Phoun's school girl persona? Real like Malachy's altruism? Real like Benny's clever code? Real like the ever-elusive Rebecca Descartes? Face it: you qverse people don't know the meaning of real. People are dead, woman. Zhadesh, Eric, Bradley, Nelly, Arnold, five, six, whatever. People are dead. Not qverse dead. Real life dead. Forgive me for sounding like a complete asshole but how more fucken real can it get?'

'I'm sorry. I didn't mean to suggest—I didn't mean that. Who do you think is behind the conspiracy?'

'Let's get one thing straight, Ellie—it's not a conspiracy, it's a game. All these people are pawns in the hands of the matriarchs. SWIFTWATER and INTROMET want TEEK territories and they're trying to run each other out of business. Killing in the qverse, ruining reputations, hiring Yakuza hotshots to decimate the hack competition. I made a dumb mistake at the beginning: I figured that it was personal, that it really mattered who Arnold Lee was. Truth is Lee could have been any back-sliding company slave. I cared too much about the *how* and conveniently forgot about the why.'

'And the why is...?'

'The why is the q.'

'Pardon?'

'The q. The fucken q; all the questions that have no answers. How did Arnold Lee die? Who is Rebecca Descartes? How did the qverse begin? Who really controls it? How do you hack the human mind? What manipulations will people notice? What will they overlook? How do you destroy a matriarch? How far can you push the virtual from the reality? Most importantly the who—that is, who in *hell* is asking these questions! Who wants these answers more than I do?'

She looked suddenly satisfied, Cheshire cat smug. 'You tell me.'

The vidphone was light in his hand. He'd never been a cricketer but he bowled a clean, mean overarm; the phone's flat rectangle skipped three times before the ocean closed in and swallowed it whole.

* * * *

At one-thirty a yellowcab picked Gig up outside a beige-fronted Anglesea newsagents. Previous driver automatons had refused his fare, citing sub-clauses from some abstruse 'taxi dresscode' rulebook. The soggy sneakers slung over his shoulder and the tourist logo on his crumpled t-shirt (GENUAHN AWWSIE KULCHA) gave him the bedraggled, culture-worn aspect of an inebriated NorthAsian foreigner who'd drunk more beer than his Asiatic physiology could tolerate. *No trouble, sir*, the automatons would bleat, and drive on. He'd heard rumours (probably from his neo-beatnik mothers) that the majority of automatons were programmed not to pick up anyone who wasn't wearing a suit after midnight.

Another damn corporate conspiracy.

By the time the yellowcab turned into his mothers' driveway it was close to three. Gig gave the automaton a credit-card IOU—acceptable in lieu of hard currency since the '50's influx of backdated cheques had crashed the free market—and dashed for the garage. Ruth had left Singer's briefcase in the Mitsubishi's back seat. Thank God for small mercies: the driver's door was unlocked. He fished out the case, yanked it open and gave the contents a wary once-over. The SWIFTWATER cap gleamed up at him from amidst the INTROMET propaganda, its curved helmet iridescent as oil on water. Something of its shape called to mind the panoply of comicbook heroes.

He took the cap to his room and sat with it on the bed, rolling his knuckles across the sensitive silver spindles inside. 'The only way I can warn Harmonica about Cragg&Co is through the qverse,' he muttered—testing to see if his logic sounded as preposterous out loud as it did inside his head. 'The only way to enter the qverse is through Phoun's cap. Knowing her, the cap probably has an auto-destruct button built in, primed for the moment I disobey her orders. But if Phoun seriously wanted me dead, then surely one of her peroxide boys would have shot me back at the mansion...'

Surely. Or perhaps the inscrutable Ms Swiftwater was saving him for later, an after-apocalypse snack to be consumed (or should that be combusted?) once she'd deposed Viger Singer.

Character expert that he might have been, trying to fathom Phoun's motivations hurt Gig's brain. In fact risking life and limb in the minefield of qverse politics was infinitely easier when he didn't think about it at all. If Lady Luck had gotten him this far with his major organs intact, he reasoned, she was unlikely to depart at this, his eleventh hour. Swallowing his misgivings, Gig crammed on the cap and plugged into the qverse. Later I'll look back on this and laugh, he thought dryly, as the world remade itself in the bold colours of SWIFTWATER's entrance portal.

Look back and laugh. If I'm not dead, that is.

The first thing he noticed about the SWIFTWATER cap—after sheer ease and precision of movement—was its superior location menu. In his eagerness to experiment with plaincode he'd overlooked the additional features Phoun had supplied. Gig saw now that the control panel offered direct access to all qverse areas. *Really* all of them: the line-up included normally hidden kink rooms, qverse company offices, high-class sex simulators and even the hackchats. No more fiddling around with obtuse 'FOR Q' synonyms or wrestling with implacable bouncers—he held the equivalent of a free-entry, all-zones-go, backstage pass.

A key to the city, a key to the whole damn virtual universe. The kind of thing the better class of hacks—think Harmonica, think Benny Soo—took for granted. Gig scrolled through the locations list, momentarily distracted by the number of restricted rooms' names that began with the words AAA HARDCORE TEEN. Six screens further up he found AAA HACKC 243223V, a room title which, while unappealing from a visceral perspective, would likely prove a more promising place to begin his search for Harmonica.

He clicked in. The design of AAA HACKC 243223V emulated a Roman colosseum, its huge shelved gallery sloping into a low arena. Unlike most hackchats its foundations were not made from dissimilar pieces of stolen code but had a uniform pattern. Surfaces and walls had been constructed of a tessellated virtual concrete that rippled gently with the same muted effect as rain on a midnight river. Dimly-lit, with appropriately low-volume background music, it was a perfect chill-out lounge. Hack folk gathered in clusters at the room's centre, elf skins rubbing shoulders with furries, movie stars chinwagging with demons. Others played it cool in the colosseum stands, eavesdropping on floor-level conversations or flicking through digitalised literature.

At this stage in events Gig's gameplan was simple: quietly enter, quietly find Harmonica, quietly warn her, and then get the hell out before triggering any matriarch warning bells. Easy, right? But already it looked as if he'd slightly over-estimated his blending-in skills. One step forward and his control panel's sensor screen erupted in digital fireworks, the luminescent sparks and spikes of locked-on hack tracers. Possibly these came from another coterie of INTROMET spooks, but from their number it seemed more likely that he was being tailed by unconnected qverse regulars, fringe-hacks keeping tabs on the penultimate qverse battle.

Well, let them keep their tabs, he thought, rounding his shoulders. I've got bigger things to worry about than my virtual fan club.

He'd made it halfway across the coliseum floor when an anime-styled penguin skin materialised some metres away and ran toward him at a speedy waddle, its eyes rounded in horror. 'Felix? Felix?' it panted, the snapping of its beak out of sync with the words. 'It's Lucas here. What're you doing? Don't you know how dangerous this place is for you? I don't even have a tracer and I knew you were in here. There's so much action heading your way that you're lit-up like a target.'

Greatly over-estimated his blending-in skills, then. But plainly the unwelcome attention had its advantages: reeling Harmonica's son was almost as good as reeling Harmonica herself. 'Got to find your Mum,' Gig explained briskly. 'She's in danger. Phoun sent heavies after her.'

'Mum's in NorthAsia. Guishen, China. Gone looking for Joaquin Magdellin. Why would Phoun send heavies... No, wait. Forget Phoun.' The penguin shuffled its stubby feet. 'Look, you haven't been in any rooms like the one you're really in, have you?'

'Haven't been in any... What?'

'Any rooms like the one you're really in?' the boy pressed, talking even faster than usual, as if something of Gig's urgency had infected him, too. 'Virtually real virtual reality? If you do—unplug. Fast as you can. It's some kind of duplication, see? Arnold Lee's death. Mind tricks. Smoke and mirrors. We worked it out—sort of. Then Mum went to rescue Magdellin and Talobos, I guess, went to claim his prize. Once he'd sobered up—'

Gig struggled. 'I have no idea what you're talking about...'

'I shouldn't really be here. Neither should you. You've got to get out.'

'Not until you promise me you'll tell your mother.'

'Huh? Tell her what?'

Utterly exasperated, Gig bent down to the penguin, arms spread in a motion of inestimable frustration, and was deliberating over whether or not to smack some sense into the kid when something white and lightning-fast swooped over his head, some glittering bird of electricity, beautiful and lethal, the drooping feathers of its tail sending a slight current sparking along his spine like a shiver. Laser-flare. Instinctively he hit the ground, bringing the penguin down with him.

Which almost instantly snapped out of existence, big dumb anime eyes and all, and Gig hit the floor alone.

He rolled over, distantly aware that the lights on his sensor screen were going batshit crazy. Someone was yelling. The ceiling rippled ominously. You've lost your mind, he cursed himself, fighting post-laser vertigo in the struggle to his feet. That jump to save the boy? Real heroic, McGuiggen. Real smart. Real impressive reflexes—if you were in the real world. Did you forget that the qverse offered a get-out-of-trouble free option? At the first sign of conflict a *smart* hack (think Lucas Carter-Soo) would have unplugged to save his skin—no pun intended.

So why hadn't he done it?

Because I want to know, he realised. Because if I'm going to die here in the 'verse, I want to know who'll do it. Cops get like this all the time, if the movies are anything to go by. Obsession. Cops risk their own lives to uncover killers.

Call it curious cat syndrome. I'm this far in, I *have* to know.

Clumsily he righted himself and they were all around him. *They*; not one killer but hundreds. Gargoyle skins, ghoul skins, demon skins, monster skins; others, testing the boundaries of good taste, in the black garb and cowl of medieval executioners. White laser flares glittered between them. Above, more popped into existence in the gallery, elbowing each other for front-row seats. From the arena it looked as if the audience was expanding like the ripples cast by a stone in water, or perhaps a vertical Mexican wave. News spread fast in the qverse, and no news faster than impending spook attacks.

Except according to his tracers these weren't spooks. They wore a range of neurocaps, from bottom-feeder SWIFTWATER designs to geek-trendy TEEK to the classier mid-range of INTROMET. Some with additions. Some with extra features. Some on bonus-plans and extra-speed-connections and full-colour-perspectives. Some hanging back, fearful. Others buoyed to the front ranks by adrenalin and wounded pride. Some without weapons and others in full qverse battle regalia.

They were hacks.

They were his people and they had come for him.

'You must think that you're just so damn good,' said a demon.

Gig said, 'You don't understand.'

'Who the hell died,' an elf smirked, 'and made you Soo?'

Gig said, 'You're all crazy. I'm not the one you should be—'

'Too clever and talented to hang around with the likes of us, huh?'

Gig said, 'I understand the tall poppy shit but this is ridiculous—'

And ducked as the lasers came out, the flare of one roasting directly through the space his head had been moments before. Automatically he raised a hand to shield himself—a pathetic, human gesture, a gesture rooted in the meat of him, the unspeakably outmoded *corpus*—and a ball of liquid light spat out of his palm, numbing his fingers in passing, and then unfurled loose tendrils like some digitalised cat-o'-nine-tails. And cast them out, multiplying and growing, each tendril reaching its apex only to sprout new hydra-heads; and some already snapping out to entrap the closest hacks, binding them into shiny cocoons like spider's prey; and others driving them backward until Gig, horrified by his neurocap's newfound facilities, closed his hand into a fist and the light vanished.

Things began to get muddled. Someone started screaming. A bit. And a group of hacks chanted something stupid—GET GIG GET GIG GET GIG—a real lynch-mob mantra. Three laser-attacks fizzled off his shoulders and face. A clown skin yelled curses. Some asshole called him a mutant and another asshole took up the cry. A sailor skin shouted drivel about shagging Harmonica for matriarch secrets. A back-row bastard tore up a piece of the floor and threw it at his head.

And despite understanding their anger. Despite understanding that jealousy and that frustration. Despite knowing that need to climb to the top of the hack pile. Despite that, Gig was struck suddenly by the idea that it might be fun to *fuck these guys up*. Test the limitations of his neurocap's power, say to hell with ethical procrastination and just shoot the shit out of people. Because that appealed to him in a raw, puerile way; it recalled those satisfying punches he'd thrown at that dumb geek kid, at pasty-faced Eric.

This arbitrary violence was part of him now, entrenched in his biochemistry like that ersatz Y-chromosome. Made him feel more solid. More sexual. Thanks to the neurocap, Phoun had given Gig something fourteen years of intensive gene therapy never had: *some fucken balls.*

Gig realised:

The *real* question in the qverse isn't who you are but what you're capable of.

So how far can I go? he wondered, unfolding a hand crackling with livid energy. How far can I go with you people? Because it's *always* you damn people—hacks, friends, geeks, mothers, cousins, women, whatever. You damn people. You've sneered at me, laughed at me, mocked my skills and now you're trying to fry me out of existence. Half of you treat me like some kind of genetic mutant and the other half like a simpleton. Maybe you think that under all this fucken *pretty* is a real soft touch.

Maybe you should come a little closer and try me...

But he couldn't do it. Couldn't do it and wouldn't do it and chose to run instead, not out of cowardice but out of mercy. (Because it was a gesture of *mercy*, he told himself, to save *them* from *him*. The ungrateful mob.) He bounded for the room exit like a gazelle and the mob growled after him like hunting-hounds; he took a sharp corner, a short corridor, and nipped past a startled, bear-skinned bouncer, and out, out, *out*, and into the adjoining room.

Where it was snowing.

He was on a mountain. Possibly Everest. Equally possibly Kosciusko—geography had never been his strong suit. But definitely SWIFTWATER. He was on a SWIFTWATER mountain and running up it, eyes slitted against the wind. Moving faster by the second in Phoun's overpowered cap, less a person now than a speeding bullet. His peripheral vision became motion-blur. Rugged-up skins in polar explorer gear stopped to watch him pass, pointing. Then pointed a second time toward the crowd still in hot pursuit, the hacks laser-waving in his wake.

Gig kept running.

At some point in his mad dash, some median place between utter desperation and utter despair, Phoun Swiftwater appeared—with an uncharacteristic lack of ceremony or surprise—and floated alongside him.

'Hi, Felix!'

'Hi, Phoun,' Gig wept.

'Boy oh boy! That cap sure look good on you! You keep it on, yes? What is crazy funny boy up to now? Making big trouble in little hackchat, huh? What a silly mess. Why are you not investigating? I am expecting double-quick results! You go find Harmonica; maybe she help you out?'

'They're chasing me,' he protested weakly.

Phoun looked up. 'Ha ha, so they are,' she said. 'You want for me to make them go away?'

'Please.'

Full circle in four hours: he'd run from her and run back to her and now he was at her feet begging for forgiveness and protection. Phoun giggled, patted his head. Good dog McGuiggen. She said, 'Okey, I take care of everything. You unplug now, do your homework! You promise?'

'I promise.'

And he unplugged. But not before he'd heard Phoun giggle one more time, and the embryonic rumblings of a SWIFTWATER avalanche.

* * * *

WEDNESDAY

13

harmonica

'I didn't hear that, Regina. I didn't hear a word. Not a single fucking paranoid syllable of it. Don't bother checking your reception—it's not a vidphone transmission glitch. Don't bother repeating yourself, either. Simple fact is, I don't *intend* to hear it. The program I designed for INTROMET was intended for management use only. If Singer's peon mislaid it, then it isn't my business. Nor is it yours. You may rest assured that if your name or your Chinese toyboy's comes up in connection with the program, I will plead innocence on your behalf.'

'Jesus Christ, Benny! What the hell is wrong with you? I told you this thing *killed* a man. Can't you do a bit better than deny personal liability?'

'Oh, 'Gina. We were married for eighteen years, and in that time you came up with—not to put too fine a point on it—a lot of really crazy shit. Then it didn't strike me as particularly odd, considering the near-lethal cocktails of pills you were downing. But I thought you'd grown out of it. Joke's on me, I suppose. Run me through your fantasy again, then, for old time's sake. You said I made an evil program that got lose and started murdering hacks, right? Shouldn't you be calling an exorcist, not a computer programmer?'

'I'm serious!'

'That's what worries me. But really, tell me straight. Who put you up to this? Was it Phoun? I understand that my 'defection' to INTROMET caused some resentment in the TEEK and SWIFTWATER ranks, but I certainly didn't think it was worthy of an entire conspiracy theory. (Nor did I imagine the retelling of it was worthy of my wife, but you live and learn, live and learn.) INTROMET wasn't a *personal* decision, you know. The reason I chose Viger over Phoun and Rebecca was simply because I felt INTROMET was a more mature company with a grander future and—dare I say it—a less capricious CEO.'

'Listen to me! For once in your life, trust me! There's something going on in INTROMET. Something really stinks. Your choice, your program, it all links back to Arnold Lee's murder. Honey, do me a favour and give me the hack lowdown. Rifle through Viger's laundry. I swear her employees are hiding a dirty secret.'

'There is no lowdown. There is no hack-work necessary. Viger and I are partners now. I have insta-access to the entire atlas of INTROMET territories—and *legally*. There is no killer program, Regina. There is no conspiracy. Most of all: there *is* no Arnold Lee case.'

'Benny—'

'Regina. Regina, Regina. You want to know what stinks around here? What really stinks? That you have the audacity to talk to me about trust. On the vidphone that I bought for you. While within the frame of your camera, in the not-so-distant background, through the cabin window, over your (conspicuously bare) left shoulder—yes, look, go ahead—I can clearly see your shagged out blond boyfriend practically fellating a post-fuck cigar as he scratches away at his hairy Anglo balls.'

'Benny,' said Harry.

And actually *felt* the word physically, the finality of it, as acutely as if this were the first time, the first betrayal.

Silence followed. Then Benny said, 'I can't do this anymore, 'Gina. Don't misunderstand me: I would love to continue. I would love to keep this up. I love the abuse. I love the madness. I love the hurt. I'd never have married you in the first place if I didn't get some kind of masochistic kick out of it. But I'm fifty-six. Maybe fifty-six isn't all that old these days, but you've got to remember that my own father only made it to forty-nine. And he lived a full life. He lived a *whole* life. I feel like I've lived a dozen whole lives—and I'm *sick* of them. I have three kids: a green-eyed half-Anglo that plainly isn't mine and two blAsians I'm too scared to blood test. I have a job that's eating my soul, my blood pressure has reached astronomical levels *and* I have no friends. There isn't room for you in this picture any more. There isn't a need for you. Life shovels enough shit onto my plate as it is. You wanted a divorce—great, sure, okay. Now please, please. Do what I ask. Give me a break.'

'Benny,' she said. 'You aren't listening.'

'Welcome to my fucking world,' said Benny Soo, and hung up.

Harry pocketed the vidphone without cancelling the call. Something about the muted dial-tone beeps was reassuring. As if the connection hadn't yet been completely broken, as if there was still room for second chances. Or third chances, or thirtieth chances. God, Benny, she thought. Of all the times. Of all the damn times to grow a backbone, you had to pick *now*.

She found Joaquin in bed, gazing intently at his vidphone, his slim body pale and elegant against the crumpled, greying sheets. Midmorning shadows darkened the hollows of his cheekbones, drew fine silhouettes of muscle along the arch of his calves, tinted his unkempt blond hair with patches of dusky brown. The remains of his cigar—*her* cigar—smouldered in a china saucer on the bedside table. That worried her. Not because he hadn't asked for the cigar but because in some equivocal way *he was too young to smoke*.

Poor Jo. Twenty-four and already a wanted man. Harry remembered the photograph's cryptic message: THERE I LOVED YOU LAST. And wondered if what Joaquin had really meant to write was THERE I LAST LOVED. And wondered, then, why leaving was always so easy for her and so hard for them and why men always fell in love like this: completely. Lucas is right, she thought. It's not that I didn't love Benny;

it's just that I didn't want a husband. It's not that I meant to hurt Joaquin; I just didn't want a boyfriend.

So maybe catty, bratty Gig is in with a chance. Because all he wants is to be told what he wants and that, *that*, I can handle.

She said aloud, 'Benny isn't going to help, Jo.'

Joaquin started and looked up at her, pushing a quiff of fair hair from his eyes. 'You think he's in on it?' he asked.

'I don't think he's in on anything.'

'He wrote the program.'

'He writes a lot of programs. Who called you?'

'It's a message from Descartes,' said Joaquin, running a guilty hand over his vidphone's screen. 'Harry, I don't know how to say this to you… but she's sending over a car.'

Rebecca, Rebecca. In the doorway Harry stumbled, her anger like sudden vertigo. 'The bitch!' she erupted. 'Can't leave you alone with me for a minute, can she? I have you a night and already the woman's scared I'll pervert your malleable young mind with ideas of corporate treason. Well, go if you want to. No hard feelings. But let me remind you that it wasn't Rebecca damn Descartes who came running to your assistance when—'

'Harry, please,' said Joaquin weakly. 'It's not me she wants to see.'

* * * *

All her instincts told her: *go*.

Go fix it. Go kill her. Go make things right. Go ruin everything. Go home, go away, go get even. Go, for the sake of your sanity: you need to know why, how, when, where. Go, for the sake of revenge: you're itching to get back the bitch who ruined your marriage. Go, for the sake of curiosity: Rebecca's real identity is the one code you've yet to crack. Go, because you want to, because you need to. Go. Just go.

And when she checked herself there was nothing inside her that said *stay*, nothing that held her back, no reservations, no fears, just this swollen, twenty-year-old impetus as insuperable as gravity.

Because she—Harry, Regina, the ex-Mrs Soo—was the kind of woman who didn't say no to a challenge. Who far preferred settling matters face-to-face, mano e mano, to the anonymous hit-and-runs of most qverse hack-battles. She was a physical person who needed physical resolution. And that was how she explained it to Joaquin: *calmly*. Rationally. In the fashion of Malachy Memphis. Staunchly avoiding the temptation to slip into trigger-words and western-suburbs slang. Harry didn't say punching that slag's lights out, she said, I expect some conflict. She didn't say she wanted to fuck up that ugly moll, she said, I need closure.

Outside the cabin it had started to snow again but inside Joaquin was sweating, red-faced, envisioning some ungodly bitchfight smackdown, Rebecca vs. Regina, complete with hair-pulling and eye-gouging and hysterical yells of, You stole my husband! and, You fried me out of q! A fight to the death in high heels—Jesus, Harry thought, any man with red blood pumping through his veins would find it a turn on! But Joaquin just sat trembling with his hands folding and unfolding on his lap, looking far more distressed than he had relating the story of his escape from Beijing.

'I respect you both,' he explained. 'I work for her, and you and me... well, we have what we have. I don't want you to hurt each other. Is Benny Soo really worth all this?'

'It's the principle of the thing.'

'God, you women,' Joaquin grunted. 'You never forget a slight.'

'No,' said Harry darkly. 'I won't.'

Shortly after eight a TEEK company car pulled up, a prehistoric American Cadillac piloted by a rusty, broken-nosed automaton. Harry got in. Joaquin got in. And as they sped along the great white road, China's major North-South arterial, banks of sleet fanned up to flank the car like arched wings. Even with an automaton at the wheel it was a ten hour drive to Beijing's commercial epicentre, and Harry took the time to sleep. Beside her Joaquin shifted furtively, his eyes watching—but not seeing—the passing streets, the disappearing mountains, the abandoned fields of rural NorthAsia.

They hit Beijing post-rush-hour and loop-de-looped through several Ferris wheel-like overpasses until they arrived outside a large, but otherwise unremarkable corrugated-iron warehouse. A TEEK headquarters, presumably, although not the only one. Harry remembered reading in a magazine that unlike SouthAsia's INTROMET and EastAsia's SWIFTWATER, TEEK had no single centre of business; there were TEEK factories and TEEK offices everywhere, from Cambodia to Turkey, from India to Aotearoa.

She got out, Joaquin following. The street was empty save for a handful of red-suited valets. Curious, Harry went to the warehouse door, pushed it, and met no resistance, mechanical or human. She turned to Joaquin.

'I'll wait outside,' he said.

Inside the walls were simply decorated with a border of Chinese characters and the only furniture was a low bench running the room's length. At its midpoint sat a grey-haired Anglo male, shoulders bowed and shaking. Tears formed tributaries along his gnarled fingers and stained damp patches on his jeans. There were letters there, across the knees, in black magic-marker capitals. FOR Q, FOR Q. Harry peered closer—and recognised, in spite of the grey hairs and the wrinkles, a phantasm of yesteryear. Memphis, she thought. Dr Malachy Memphis.

He did not look up so she did not feel obliged to greet him. Oddly she felt nothing for him—no anger, no hate, just a kind of vague irritation, the kind you'd reserve for a childhood foe. His presence did not even surprise her. All qverse roads led to the same place, inevitably, and TEEK was a common detour for those seeking answers. It's almost as if we're all coming together again, Harry thought, as we did twenty years ago. First Benny then Rebecca and now Malachy. An old-school qverse reunion.

She moved further into the warehouse, past Malachy and through a sliding screen-door. Here the floors were white and panelled in places with bathroom tiles; fluorescent lights gleamed above in chicken-wire netting. Disinfectant odours burdened the air. It occurred to Harry that the place must once have been a hospital, a relic of the class revolutions of the '40s, abandoned by the Chinese government and later remodelled as a warehouse.

Shortly she came to a small reception area—in another era, she supposed, the hospital's waiting room. A freckled, red-haired girl sat behind a neat desk, ankles crossed and hands clasped. Before her stood a triangular sign that read: ELEANOR PETEGIN.

'I'm here to see Rebecca Descartes,' Harry told the girl.

Eleanor's freckled cheeks dimpled. 'Yes. I am Eleanor Petegin, and you are Regina Carter. Also known as Harmonica, or—informally—as Harry. The greatest hack who ever lived. I am happy to meet you, Regina. No, no. Those are the wrong words. Rather: it is interesting for me to see you in the flesh and for you to see *my* flesh. Pardon the expression but this is the way my mind works, Regina. It doubles back on itself like one of those mobius strips. Sadly, most of the time I am the only one capable of appreciating the entire loop, the fully-formed thought. I have an unfortunate propensity for self-reference. When I say flesh I don't mean flesh, but at the same time—'

'It's the qverse,' Harry growled. 'I know what you mean.'

'Do I sound odd? It's been a long time since I've done this. Since I've entertained. Officially. In English. My first language and my *other* language. It gives me trouble, the English. It takes me a while to locate the right word inside my head and then, how would you put it? And then project it. Outwardly. So that it makes sense to both you and me, but perhaps more to me, because I understand on both levels. The internal and external.'

'Right, sure. Look, I'm here to see Descartes—'

'Yes. I'm the one who sent for you.'

Harry said nothing.

Then she said,

'You're Rebecca Descartes?'

'That's my pretend name. I'm a pretend person, see. Rebecca Descartes. Rebecca, which means bound. Descartes, as in philosophy. As in, *literally*. I think, therefore I am. Also the name Rebecca Descartes is a bit like Regina Carter, and Benny always did like to create reflections in his life, to have his life imitate art imitate life. So he would have me in the qverse and you on the outside, and when things were going badly between you he'd bring you into the qverse with him, bring all the issues you never spoke about. And I'd be Regina Carter, I'd be Rebecca Descartes, I'd be everything you weren't and he'd say to me everything you never heard.'

'You're younger than I expected,' said Harry quietly. 'And not as pretty.'

'I always thought you looked gangly in your photographs, Regina. Like a teenage boy. Not yet grown into your body. But now I see you in the flesh and you aren't gangly at all. And I know why he wanted you and why he

286

loved you and why he was obsessed about you. You are sexy. Not attractive by any means, but sexy. You're sexy like a whore and that always appeals to repressed, geeky NorthAsian men.'

Calmly, coolly, Harry picked up a chair.

Why?

Many reasons. Mainly because she'd had a rough childhood. Much like all American girls in foreign countries. Growing up, there was a prevailing expectation amongst your peers that you would fit neatly into a Hollywood stereotype: you were loud or tough or easy or big or dumb, and Regina Carter was all-of-the-above, standing a gawky five-ten at fourteen, always first to throw a punch and last to figure the punchline, and forever hanging out with boys (who wet-dreamed about her tits in secret, impossibly perfect under those regulation school blouses).

In her late teens she'd learnt to fight in the backstreets of Jarranoa—one of the 'deep west' suburbs of Sydney, a neighbourhood infamous for burglary and mugging. How to fight *and* how to fight dirty, which Jarranoa's larger populace understood as one and the same. Losing a front tooth in a girl-on-girl pub punch-up earned Harry the moniker she'd later bring to the qverse—some hard-edged urban poet claimed her mouth looked like a busted harmonica.

So Harry had never had qualms about rolling up her sleeves and getting mean, getting tough. Many of her initial secop contracts had been negotiated through a mixture of intimidation and force. Business meetings irked her; she had a tendency to throw things. She was forty-eight now but she was still hard, maybe even *harder*, and when a woman stole her man her first port of call wasn't her shrink. Harry didn't *do* ports of call. She just did tough.

Which came without any conscious thought, really—as she'd once explained to a startled and bleeding-lipped Benny—which came without premeditation. She was a woman who hurled rocks at cheating ex's cars and had once pushed Joaquin into a pool for making some wise-alec comment. The splash had taken her by surprise. One minute Joaquin was at her side, cattily remarking on the mentality of middle-aged women who took younger lovers; the next in the water, spluttering, blue eyes bugged in startlement, still clutching comically to his cocktail glass, the last relic of his lost poise.

The shove? It just *happened*. When she was mad her sense of reason was the first casualty. Anger bypassed her better nature, her better instincts. Sometimes it bypassed her brain altogether. Violence was a retrospective for Harry: it occurred in the past tense. She *had* punched him. She *had* pushed him. She *had* charged the laser.

She *had* picked up a chair.

It was a fashionable metal chair with an aerodynamically curved seat and when it hit Eleanor Petegin in the face Harry saw sparks. Seeing also, at this same moment, Benny's face, fixed in denial. And hearing, in concert with the blow's hollow thud, Benny's *Nos* and his *Nevers*. All this deceit, for the sake of one batty SouthAsian teenager...

So Regina hit Rebecca, but Rebecca did not fall, just slumped lower in her seat, expression never changing, and Regina hit Rebecca again, until the side of Rebecca's head hollowed, bloodlessly, into a strange metal dimple; and Regina saw sparks again, but they were the wrong kind of sparks, the *real* kind of sparks, and when she put down the chair and wrapped her hands around Rebecca's thin, freckled neck, she found a tiny slit just behind the girl's right ear that stripped skin and hair to reveal the transparent fibreglass dome of Rebecca Descartes' skull.

Harry stepped back. 'You're an automaton?'

Eleanor Petegin voice replied sadly, disembodied, 'And I was all ready to be civilised, too.'

'A *robot*?'

'Of course I'm not a robot, silly. That would make too much sense. Mind, your Benny is hardly the sort to strike up a relationship with an AI—they're far too *uncomplicated* for his tastes.'

'Then what are you? Where are you? You bitch; you hide behind some robot facade—'

'It's rather lucky for me that I did,' Eleanor commented, as Harry flung the automaton's peeled scalp across the room. 'Truly, I would love to meet you in the flesh, but your recent display does little to inspire my confidence…'

Harry wrenched open the first door behind the reception desk and found herself at a busy hospital intersection, a crossroad of corridors jammed with trolleys and fast-moving NorthAsian nurses. It was not logical, this scene; it did not fit. It was another trick, another Rebecca red-herring. Confident, Harry pushed on, ignoring the incomprehensible protests of the medics, pausing from time to time to peer into the wards. In some rooms small children lay prone beneath starched sheets; in others families gathered in white clothes of mourning; in others people wearing TEEK neurocaps held hands and conversed in lowered voices.

The last ward held only one patient ringed by massive metal machines. Harry investigated. And found in the hospital bed a strange, malformed shape, hairless, faceless, barely recognisable as human, the limbs stunted or missing, the spine grossly contorted, the torso furred with needles. Wires and tubes netted the air above it, drooping to pucker the patient's fine, paper-like skin. Horrible, horrible—it looked like a monster pinched from a B-grade science fiction movie, a twenty-first century Frankenstein, something unthinkable, something *unbirthed*.

She dry-retched, stepped back, sat down. Eleanor Petegin's voice drifted in, casual, cynical, '...Certainly, Regina, you can drop by any time.'

'Rebecca?'

'I was nineteen years old,' said Eleanor. 'It was a car crash. The Crash. It was spectacular. It came out of nowhere and I never felt a thing. I just saw a light. You can read my files. Complete paralysis. Third degree burns. Substantial brain activity. Uncle Memphis' field of interest—purist neurology. When I was little he used to sit me on his knee and talk about brain maps. Poor Ellie didn't get fairy-tales, she got ADVANCED PLEUROPLASMIC SYNAPTIC

ANALYSIS ON LIVING TISSUE 101. Such a co-incidence, me being me, him being him. In the early days I often wondered if he'd been the one driving—if my paralysis was premeditated, a crucial step in his glorious career arc. Which was rubbish, of course. But you do become terribly paranoid, Regina, when you're the only one inside your head...

'See, in the beginning the qverse was simply space, the palpable existence of space. Colour and sound came later. Contact came later. In the beginning there was space and I was a body—an entity—moving within that space; I had limitations and they made me *real* again. I was the first guinea pig—no, more like a lab rat, running circles in a mental maze. While they—Benny, Phoun, Uncle Memphis—watched and monitored. Took notes on my behaviour patterns. Measured my neurological activity. Programmed and reprogrammed my world just to see how I reacted to change. These days Uncle Memphis likes to pretend he's an altruist, a bleeding-heart, some kind of runaway genius who got pipped by the big corporations. Truth is he planned to market the qverse once it was completed as an emotional aid for other broke-backed cripples and their grieving families. The quadra-verse, perhaps. Doesn't quite have the same ring to it.

'But then I got sick—some crazy infection. Uncle Memphis' funding ran out at around the same time. So did Phoun's SouthAsian visa. What chaos! Memphis went door-to-door seeking a new sponsor. And somehow, somewhere, Viger Singer—patron saint of lost causes—

sniffed him out. Offered him money. In exchange for control. Make it a game, she said. People will play it. Like the internet with pictures—but Uncle Memphis didn't like the idea. Told her no. Didn't count on Benny— preternaturally soft-hearted Benny—to go behind his back. Why? Because Phoun was days away from being parcelled back to Japan. Because the q-code patents were all under Benny's name. Because I was *dying*. Because you were pregnant. Because Uncle Memphis was losing it, moral-wise, putting his personal advancement before my *very* personal disintegration. So Benny and Viger and me, we sat up late one night talking business, and ended up dividing the qverse into its disproportional shares...'

Harry managed, 'So you and Benny—'

'Never fucked? Never fondled? Never kissed? Oh, Regina, I couldn't honestly be sure. Maybe Benny did come up here, stuck his teeny doodah into this piece of sagging flesh. You know the old adage: Dead girls can't say no. Dead girls wouldn't notice that kind of thing, anyway—unless he knocked out a tube, tore some stitches, buffeted a lung out of shape. No; what I had with Benny was in my head, Regina, not between my legs. Me and Benny, we used to talk for hours. And I used to pretend in my head that he was this sweet little Chinese boy I met at a shuttleport in Beijing. It was the summer of 2040, and I was fourteen, and my shuttle to England was delayed, so this lovely Chinese boy took me to a café and bought me a square of sweet cake-bread covered in bright green sprinkles. Kissed my cheek when I said goodbye, but I never caught his name. So I thought of that boy when I spoke to Benny, and Benny thought of you when he spoke to me. It was an unspoken arrangement and it made us both happy—the computer geek in the failing marriage, and the lonely girl in the failing body. Or maybe I mistake the question. Maybe you want to know if I loved him? Well, sure I loved him, honey. Sure I did. Because he was the only one, Regina. The only one in the whole damn qverse. Him and me, testing how well this virtual reality game worked. We were like Adam and Eve in the garden of Eden. Until…'

'I don't regret frying you,' said Harry.

'Oh, Regina. Oh, Harmonica. The snake-in-the-grass. The black bitch, the black witch. The slut. The nymphomaniac with her harem of pretty barely-legal boys. Babylon. With your stolen neurocap and your intolerable pride. You, who came creeping, creeping, creeping, because you thought darling hubby was cheating, cheating, cheating. Did you know that Benny originally made lasers to get rid of malfunctioning programs? An energy virus that acted like a digital eraser. Never in his wildest dreams did he imagine that someone—least of all his borderline-personality-disorder spouse—would use it on a person. But it's an old story, isn't it? The Chinese and their gunpowder firecrackers. Broke-backed Eleanor Petegin and her virtual reality walking frame. You understand what you did, Regina, don't you? You bust into our world and you fucked up a *cripple*, Regina. You fried a dead woman. You drove a dagger into the only part of my body that still worked.'

'I hit your automaton with a chair, too. I've never claimed to be the most rational woman in the world.'

'So calm. So cold. So brutal. Benny always said that was your biggest problem. You couldn't see other people's pain for your own.'

'My biggest problem was that my husband lied to me.'

'For me! For a poor sick girl! He was so scared that people might try to hurt me. When they found out what I could do. That I might become a pawn in some corporate game. Benny believed in me, the dead girl. He wanted people to believe I was real, too. If I was real then Viger and Misoka could never have power over me—'

'Oh, spare me.'

'You aren't shocked, are you?' said Eleanor forlornly. 'By me. By any of this. Jesus wept, but hard old Harmonica? Nothing fazes you. I tell you everything you ever wanted to know and you can't even thank me. Do you know that, in my innocence, I actually thought I'd make you cry? When we met. When you saw me. When you understood. I thought, *Surely*. I thought, *She's not made of stone*. But here I am, proven wrong. By some snippy American housewife, no less. You know I'm going to die, don't you? It's in the cards; it's in the stars; it's on my medical record. Modern medicine, for all its marvels, just can't work me the miracle I need. And let's face it, the doctors don't have much left to work with. Eighty-five percent of my bodily functions are regulated or performed by machines. I'm a cyborg—in a strictly post-modern sense. Perhaps when I'm gone for good they'll make an AI for me. Recreate the Rebecca

Descartes experience for qverse anthropologists. I don't mind dying, you see. The way I see it I've already had an extra twenty years. A bonus. Any more and I'd just look greedy.'

Harry pressed a hand to her forehead to ward off an encroaching migraine. 'I'm busy,' she said. 'I'm busy with my *life*. I don't have time for this.'

'Listen, Regina. I'm talking about your life. Before I die, I have unfinished business to deal with. Rather: I have to *finish* business. Our agreement—mine and Benny's and Viger's—ends the moment I leave the picture. And when that happens? Phoun and Viger waiting like vultures in the wings, desperate to claim sole control of the qverse. And they're going to use you to get it.'

'I won't let them.'

'You don't understand. There's no longer a middle road. We're long past the point at which revealing the plaincode sham would significantly alter the power struggle. You waited too long to blow your secret. The qverse is too big these days. No single organisation has the resources and the know-how to challenge the matriarchs. Even Uncle Memphis is resigned to the fact: Phoun and Viger are unstoppable. Whatever happens, one of them will win. But—'

Harry rolled her eyes. 'There's a but?'

'But I think. I think. I think maybe, Regina? I think maybe you get to choose the outcome. Because I'm not going to mediate this one. I'm out, out for good. I've said to them: Do what you will. I've said: Do what you want. I've said, No dead woman will ever change the course of history. But you? You're alive. And strong. And...'

'And there's no one else,' said Harry quietly—who understood. Who'd finally picked up on the subtext, read Rebecca's epitaph between the lines. 'You're guilty of waiting too long, too. Now Benny's already picked a side, and Malachy was never a player to begin with. Which leaves you a little lost. Lost, and clutching at straws. Because you don't think Benny was right, do you?'

'I know what Viger did. Phoun told me. Your friend Gig confirmed it.'

'What did she do?'

Eleanor said, 'She started the game.'

'I don't get it.'

'It's a very clever game. You aren't supposed to.'

'Are you talking about Arnold Lee?'

'Are you?'

'I know what happened. Benny's program and Viger's assistants. Probably a set up—'

'You disappoint me, Regina. You're a virtual reality veteran, a plaincode adept. You should know by now that you don't find answers in the qverse. Just more questions. You've been making it difficult for yourself. You haven't been true to character—I blame Lucas' interference. Remember who you are: Regina 'Harmonica' Carter. The hack who doesn't fear the matriarchs; the hack who's too damn arrogant to be blackmailed. Start to think outside that square and things start going wrong.'

'Is this some kind of riddle?'

'No, Regina,' said Eleanor. 'This is not a riddle. This is the real world. This is real life. Much more difficult to predict than the qverse. Especially when people resolutely refuse to play their parts. Silly Harry. You weren't meant to be interested in Arnold Lee. You weren't meant to accept the challenge. You weren't meant to decode Arnold Lee's neurocap. Benny's program wasn't meant to be stolen. Tara Lee wasn't meant to get that magazine to Gig. You weren't meant to be Benny's ex-wife or Joaquin's ex-lover. What you need to do, Regina Carter, is look at all this from the right perspective—'

Harry hissed, 'What *is* the right perspective?'

'Who! Who! Not what but who! Can't you see how you three should have played it out? And would have played it out, if you and Gig had bothered to play by the rules. If you'd kept your little black cases to yourselves. You were meant to be a vindictive bitch. Just as Talobos was meant to be a gossip. And Gig was meant to be a paranoid. A perfectly dysfunctional collection of characters. No, that's the wrong word. You're the *cast*, the main players in Rebecca Descartes' last hurrah. So the question you have to ask yourself is—'

On the tip of her tongue. In the back of her mind.

Harry said: 'What was the answer we were *meant* to find?'

* * * *

14

gig

It was Ruth who woke him, finally—he came crawling into the living world shortly after five. His body, waking, felt foreign to him and somehow unmade. Night terrors had frizzed his loose curls into an electrified afro and the coarse hair against his skin made his face feel bloated. Sitting up, Gig saw that an impression of his torso remained in the bed, an outline frilled with white sheets like a plush coffin, and longer and thinner than he remembered it.

Blinking rapidly he suffered a sudden moment of dislocation: he was outside his body, looking down, only to find that his body had ceased to exist, to occupy real space. Full form vertigo, an absence of flesh. Better: an absence of self. He, Gig, *Felix*, was missing. Backlit binary combinations flashed before his eyes when he shook his head to clear it.

'He's dead,' said Ruth.

Gig's ears rang with car-bomb playback. Zhadesh, Zhadesh. 'Oh Jesus, Ruth, I know.'

The hand he offered in comfort was summarily rejected. 'No you don't,' Ruth snapped. 'You don't know shit. You've been asleep for the past thirteen hours.' Bizarrely his cousin's mouth was fixed in a triumphant grin. Shoulders rounded, neck framed by a black pan-collar, Ruth looked like a fairy-tale harbinger of doom: part woman, part vulture. 'It's all over the net dailies, even made it to the AsiaNationals,' she continued. 'It happened in the qverse—in SWIFTWATER territory. No clue how they did it but folks have got a pretty good idea now who *they* is. You should check out the activity levels in SWIFTWATER sections. Q-Topia is like a ghost town. People have been fleeing to INTROMET and TEEK.'

Fleeing to INTROMET and TEEK? From what? This conversation lacked a logical connect—it felt awkwardly one-sided, like listening to someone else's secure phone conversation. Rising, he tried, almost pleading: 'I don't understand.'

'Hacks and virtual addicts are like sheep,' Ruth said. Her tone was wistful—cynical, but wistful all the same, as if recalling a peculiar and unique foible of a past lover. 'Like sheep. Or maybe like lemmings—those little American rodents that jump off cliffs in packs. You put an idea in one hack's head and an hour later they're *all* thinking it. Collective consciousness. Like those old science fiction movies. And now the collective figures that Phoun Swiftwater could strike them dead easy as blinking. Well, maybe she can and maybe she can't. But for once I don't blame them. With another death in the qverse, who wants to take chances?'

'It didn't happen in the qver—'

'Of course it happened in the qverse! They've already admitted as much on the news. God, no wonder Talobos got further than you. He had an entire file on the case, you know—at least, that's what I heard from the hackchats. Guy knew all SWIFTWATER's dirty business. Did you know Phoun was planning a corporate take-over? Wanted to run Singer out of business, rebuild INTROMET territories, crown herself the queen of q. Maybe eat Rebecca Descartes for dessert.'

Numbly Gig shook his head: playing dumb around Ruth was always the easiest option. And right now playing dumb didn't require much acting skill. 'So Talobos solved it?' he asked hoarsely. 'Singer gave him the million?'

'Haven't you been listening to a word I've said?' Ruth spluttered.

'Well—'

'You fool! Talobos is *dead*!'

That sank in slowly. A full minute later he was still standing there dumbfounded, clumsily fumbling for the right words while Ruth looked on impassively, no doubt wondering how someone related to her—however distantly, however genetically corrupted—could be so thick. Talobos. Lloyd Hong. Dead. Talobos, who had died in connection with the case he'd reportedly *almost* solved. Gig's stomach felt heavy in his sneakered feet. Now there's proof you're a certifiable paranoid, McGuiggen, he thought bitterly. You don't feel sorry that Talobos is dead—you're too busy worrying that they'll come for *you* next.

'Want me to give you a moment?' Ruth asked, uncharacteristically sympathetic.

'Yes please.'

Four minutes later, and fortified with coffee, Gig dashed to the basement to scan the headlines of Aotearoan news sites.

HACK SUICIDE: BRAIN WASHING OR TRANSEXUAL CULT?
LLOYD HONG, QVERSE PROGRAMMER, DEAD AT THIRTY-FOUR
HARMONICA, TALOBOS, GIG: QVERSE STARS IN DEADLY GAME
IS SWIFTWATER SAFE FOR YOUR CHILDREN?

'Officially it's a drug thing,' said Ruth, perching on the edge of his desk. He'd always hated that about her: the annoying tendency to commentate on tragedies, cheerfully alternating between colour and play-by-play. 'But that's just bureaucratic bullshit. The only reason the police haven't shut down SWIFTWATER territories altogether is because—*get this*—Descartes' lawyers got an injunction. Won't let anyone near the qverse's big red OFF switch. The whole thing is getting crazy: Rebecca Descartes standing up for Phoun! Bet the two of them were in on it: they were sick of playing second-and-third fiddle to Singer. Decided to wipe out some of INTROMET's employees. You're lucky Phoun didn't go after you. Then again you weren't exactly close to cracking the case and unmasking her scheme.'

'No.'

She swung her legs thoughtfully, pedalled them in space. 'There goes our too-cool million. Doubt Singer will be interested in hearing from us now that the police have moved in. That million was wishful thinking anyway. I was an idiot to believe you'd get anywhere with the case. Even with my help. Honestly, Gig, I'm surprised Singer chose any of you. Harmonica is too bloody rich and famous to care about the case; Talobos was a loose-lipped gossip; and you're a paranoid asshole. No offence, cousin, but you aren't exactly the most balanced person around. Mentally or genetically.'

'No,' Gig agreed—only half-listening, and too anxious anyway to take serious offence. 'I'm not.'

'Real hero you are. Real white knight material. First sign of danger and you're running for the hills. I'm surprised you went back into the qverse after I mentioned the AR in VR quandary. Bet that—'

He interrupted: 'Do you know what the first question I asked Viger Singer was?'

'I have absolutely no idea.'

'Why us? That's what I said to her: *Why us?*'

She took that as a joke: retrospective irony. 'Bloody good question.'

'Everyone said that. It was a good question. That's why I keep coming back to it.' He switched off the computer and reached around to disable the internet connection manually. The raging paranoid in him forbid him to speak openly in the vicinity of *live* hardware. Watching, Ruth's pinched face reflected an odd breed of pity and disgust. 'I think I'm looking at this from the wrong perspective,' Gig said. 'I think I've spent a week chasing a criminal who doesn't exist.'

Ruth protested: 'But Phoun—'

'Don't ask what the qverse can do for you, but what you can do for Viger Singer!'

He went back to his room and the briefcase, leaving a bewildered Ruth loudly weighing up the pros and cons of having her theoretical boss committed to an institution. Singer's briefcase was as he'd left it: half open and spilling techno-junk. Silently he considered each item in turn, weighing the neurocap and watch in his hands; examining, in detail, the carefully tagged and dated crime scene photographs. From inside *and* outside the qverse.

Inside and outside? Curiouser and curiouser. What had Harmonica's pudgy son told him that morning? Watch out for virtually real virtual reality? Was that like AR in VR? Some kind of duplication, and mirrors, and smoke, and rooms that looked like rooms—God, but that kid could be brutally vague at times. Frustrated Gig tossed the photographs aside and reached for the final item—not part of the original collection, but invaluable nonetheless. Tara Lee's magazine.

Gig read, again:

> X THS IS THE TRUTH. MY HSBAND WAS MURDRED, HE KNEW TOO MUCH. HE STOLE CODE, HE TOLD SEKRETS. THEY KILL HIM, SWIFTWATER, INTRMET. THEY WILL DSTROY TEEK. THEY AFTER SPIS, PIRATES. HACKS FOR Q

CHECK. WATCH FOR PARK. INSONIAM SUFERING. THEY BUGED MY HOUSE, THEY WANT POWER, THEY WANT CONTRL, THEY WANT RVNGE. YOU ARE PART OF THER GAME. X

Strange, that. Despite her isolation and her lazy country drawl Tara Lee hadn't struck him as uneducated. More like a troubled cityslicker seeking a pastoral-method redemption. And what kind of illiterate misspelled husband by forgetting the *u*? He remembered, then, that Phoun had briefly mentioned the magazine code in Japan: 'It a hasty translation. Also, grammar and spelling not so hot. Maybe you try again.' And if Phoun Swiftwater was always right, then it followed that Lucas Carter-Soo must be wrong.

Become one with the 'verse, Gig advised himself sardonically. If you want to crack qverse riddles, you'll have to rely on qverse logic.

Over the next half hour Gig re-examined Tara Lee's magazine, piecing together the code a second time. In his hurry Lucas had missed letters and approximated others; the punctuation, unspecified by the simple code, was entirely guesswork. The entire thing was riddled with inaccuracies: Gig lost count after correcting the first twenty mistakes. Of course that wasn't really Lucas' fault—the kid was young, working under pressure, and the accurate version of a sentence wasn't always the most obvious one. Further, Gig had the feeling Lucas' intimidating intelligence was limited to the field of virtual reality programming. Not exactly an A+ English student.

Finished, the revised code read (with uncertain or suspect sentences underlined):

> X THIS IS THE TRUTH. MY HUSBAND WAS MURDERED. HE KNEW TOO MUCH. HE STOLE CODE. HE TOLD SECRETS. <u>THEY KILLED HIM. SWIFTWATER, INTROMET: THEY WILL DESTROY TEEK.</u> THEY'RE AFTER SPIES, PIRATES, HACKS, FOR Q. <u>CHECK WATCH FOR PARK. INSONSIAM SUFFERING.</u> THEY BUGGED MY HOUSE. THEY WANT POWER. THEY WANT CONTROL, THEY WANT REVENGE. YOU ARE PART OF THEIR GAME. X

Check watch for park—or maybe just: check watch.

Check, like biocheck.

He read the message again, this time backwards. It didn't make any sense but for the first time Gig felt confident he was seeing things from the right perspective.

* * * *

He sent Ruth out on a bogus mission for chocolate and called DI Karlsen from the basement wallscreen. The policewoman answered on the third ring, looking remarkably fresh-faced and cheerful for six-thirty in the afternoon. By luck he'd caught her at work, in the downtown precinct's dismal excuse for an office. A landscape of scuffed metal tables like school-room desks panned out behind her in a kind of structured disorder that reminded him, weirdly, of 2D optical illusions.

Late afternoon at the cop-shop, and nothing was stirring—behind her bored police tilted back their chairs, twirled pens, took calls. A half-eaten burger was melting onto the table by the DI's elbow and he saw her eyes slipping sideways to it, guiltily, before they met his.

'McGuiggen? Didn't think I'd see you again. But I didn't think I'd end up scraping your little Chinaman mate off Aotearoa's sidewalks either. Poor bloke. Guess this past week has been one horrible surprise after another.'

It took him a moment. 'Hong?'

'Hong. Of course I'm not taking the case—he died on the south island, many leagues out of my jurisdiction. But we talk, we do—precinct to precinct. Thanks to the wonders of vidphone conferencing. When I heard the name Hong I thought of you and your INTROMET story. All you hacks dying. Call me a crazy old bitch if you like, but Hong, after Lee? Well it made me twitch—my sixth sense started working overtime. You know they're saying it was drug related?'

'No. I mean I heard a bit, but I didn't—'

'The guy was living a double life. Day-time Hong played a straight-laced programming professional. Night-time Hong liked dressing up in women's clothes and popping brain-numbing EastAsian drug cocktails. Bloke lived in a semi-derelict high-rise with a blonde go-go girlfriend who 'accepted' his deviant lifestyle. Encouraged, more like. The girlfriend is telling the cops it was all her fault; she botched some drug pick-up; blamed Hong for it. Hong killed himself rather than face the dealers—some mad, bad, Japanese gang.'

'But you don't agree.'

'I don't like coincidences. I don't like running into the same guy twice in a week. I don't like the fact he was wearing a neurocap when he died. Don't look at me like that—the information is no secret to anyone with a computer and internet access. The south islanders tried to keep it off the news, the hardcopy broadsheets, but the AsiaNational net dailies ran it: you can't stop those immoral fuckers from publishing gossip. And under GA law we can't sue them for printing the truth.

'Truth happens to be that our man Hong did his swan dive while hooked into the qverse. We've even got witnesses. Housewife on the second floor saw him fall— bugger plummeted straight past her kitchen window. Had this funny grin on his face, the housewife said. Like he knew something the rest of us didn't, she said. One of my southern mates sent me a copy of her interview transcript. The thing reads like a two-dollar romance novel: all 'wistful eyes' and 'masculine serenity'. We're talking about a transvestite suicide here! Look, I never met Hong in the flesh but I pegged him for the kind of guy who'd put up a fight to the bitter end: a battler, a biter, a hanger-on. I see the word serenity in a statement about a man like Hong and my first thought is: drugs.'

'But it wasn't drugs,' said Gig.

'Sure wasn't. Toxology came back negative for anything except mild traces of amphetamines. Probably from a couple of months ago. Which leaves me…no. Which leaves the boys in the south island with little to go on. Except virtual reality hearsay, and no one believes that conspiracy crap—'

'Was he wearing a watch?'

'Sorry?'

'Hong's watch. Could you check? Was Lloyd Hong wearing a Biocheck watch when he died?'

'I'm not sure…'

Of course she wasn't sure. He'd deviated from the script, added a new variable, a new angle, a new perspective. And derailed her. For by now Gig understood Karlsen was somehow complicit in the crime but not knowledgeably so, a minor cog in the murderer's deadly machinations— although the word *pawn* didn't suit the DI, sat awkwardly on those broad shoulders like an oversize jacket. Didn't suit her, just as it didn't suit Harmonica. Or, he supposed, Felix 'Gig' McGuiggen. He repeated, amazed at the calmness of his voice, 'Could you check?'

'Check for biocheck?' She seemed to find the phrase appealing, even comical, and repeated it a second time—it came out sing-song, like a child's schoolyard taunt.

Check, check, for biocheck.

He said, 'Please.'

'I'll see what I can do, kid,' said DI Karlsen. 'But I ain't promising you the world.'

She rose and moved away, her hips thickly sexual in regulation uniform. One look at that arse—*Christ almighty*—and he was suddenly crazyhorny. Talk about your unseemly urges! But it wasn't regular, random Gig-lust he was suffering; this was like in those stories you heard about complete strangers fucking away their fears in the face of impending death. Airline-disasters, sinking ships, Bonnie & Clyde style shoot-outs—this lust was desperate and tinged with regret, not for lost life or lost dignity but lost *sex*, for future conquests that would never now be made. Too easily that could have been *his* name in the daily's by-line: FELIX MCGUIGGEN, QVERSE PROGRAMMER, DEAD AT TWENTY-EIGHT BECAUSE HE GOT IN OVER HIS BIG STUPID HEAD.

So this was a last-gasp hard-on he was wrestling now— and it made him tear up a little. As a randy adolescent he'd compiled a list of women he wanted to 'do' before he died, predominantly movie stars and pop idols with the odd girl-next-door type thrown in. A decade later and he had yet to cross any of them off the list…and that was a real tragedy, wasn't it? To die and have done so little. To die and have done so few.

When she came back his eyes were damp and chills crawled the backs of his hands. She said, 'Crazy stuff, kid, but you're dead right. Your Hong man *was* wearing some kind of newfangled INTROMET watch. Bloke I spoke to said he'd never seen one like it before. State-of-the-art. Of course he wasn't a proper tech-head like you qverse folk.

More a hobby-hack—if that's the right term for it. You reckon these watches are important?'

Gig gazed at the re-translation of Tara Lee's message. '*Someone* reckoned they were,' he said.

'We get all electrics investigated by our tech department,' the DI mused doubtfully. 'Wasn't nothing amiss found with Lee's watch. And if it was it sure wasn't in the report. That's why we let that lady from INTROMET have it back. It was just some damn watch.'

'Maybe you'd only recognise it if you knew exactly what you were looking for.'

'What is 'it'? What are *you* looking for?'

'There's a rumour on the qverse grapevine that before he died Hong created a file on SWIFTWATER. He believed they were responsible for Arnold Lee's death. I don't suppose you could get your hands on that file—if it really does exist?'

'It does exist. And I could, yeah. But disseminating its contents willy-nilly through GreaterAsia would mean the end of my career here.' She framed her face with her hands, an odd gesture that brought his mind back to wise monkey statues: hear no evil. She said, 'I like you, McGuiggen. You're a good man. Good-looking too, and that'll get you further than you might think with a crusty old cop like me. I can't give you the file but I can tell you what the bloke from Brissie told me about it. Guy reckons it wasn't just SWIFTWATER Hong wrote about. Toward the front of the file—the most recent entries—he was naming INTROMET employees. Disloyal INTROMET cronies working for

SWIFTWATER. Way our man in Brissie figures it, Hong got too close to the truth: and either killed himself out of fear...or something more sinister occurred on that hotel balcony. Last call Hong made was to an unlisted, in-house INTROMET number, about fifteen minutes before he died. Which makes me think that—'

'—that Hong was going to tell Viger Singer what had happened to Lee, and was killed before he could reveal the answer by some shady SWIFTWATER goons. Right?'

'Right. But...'

'But there's the watch,' Gig pressed. 'But there's the watch. Which means something. And there's the file. Which means something too. And there's uproar in the qverse—my cousin says people are fleeing SWIFTWATER rooms in their thousands. Which means something too.'

The DI sighed. 'I don't get this virtual reality thing,' she said. 'All you kids running about in some funny computer game. What's the attraction to it? Wouldn't you all prefer to get outside for a bit, play in a park, go to the beach. Healthier for you too. Honestly, folk's fixation on the qverse makes no sense to me. And that isn't just sour grapes—even if I *could* use the qverse, I doubt I'd make a habit of it.'

'Which means something too,' Gig echoed, and re-read:

CHECK WATCH AND PARK. INSONSIAM SUFFERING.
CHECK WATCH AND PARKINSONS. I AM SUFFERING—

That was the right translation. DI Karlsen had mentioned her disease the first time they'd met, and he'd thought it curious then, implausible now. A DI with Parkinson's? Too much of a co-incidence. Which meant, certainly, that the DI was not only a purveyor of seamless crime-scene information but also a clue in and of herself. Because the trick to this—the trick to the Lee case, the trick to staying alive—was to think in the real world as you did in the 'verse, to make those far-fetched holistic connections, to accept multiple intersections, to examine, again, the confidences of total strangers, to treat the entire world like a goddamned children's puzzle book.

He said, 'Tell me about your Parkinson's.'

'That's a funny thing to bring up out of the blue. Me Parkies? There isn't much to tell, kid. Having Parkinson's these days isn't like it was, say, twenty years back when they had the shakes and the stutters something chronic. We got meds now, see, two yellow pills in the morning, a blue one at night, a white one with every meal. I don't experience nothing out of the ordinary—no shaking, no stutter, no—'

'Except in the qverse.'

She looked briefly crestfallen—odd, considering that mere moments before she'd been deriding all forms of virtual reality. 'Except in the qverse,' she admitted. 'I get dizzy, I get numb, I see things that aren't there. Didn't I tell you all this before?'

'If you hurt yourself in the real world, while you were experiencing virtual reality, would you be able to feel it?'

'Hah! Got a good story about that, actually—been dining out on it for months since. During the neurocap calibration tests I got up and walked into a wall before the techie-guys could stop me. Thought I was hop-skip-jumping through a meadow of flowers, light as a feather. Hop-skip-jump-*wham*. Broke my nose and didn't notice till they pulled me out. Bloody stung for weeks—'course, that didn't happen every time they stuck the cap on me. Just sometimes. Sometimes I felt it and sometimes I didn't. Ain't just Parkies like me who get that effect, mind. One of the techie-guys said that perfectly normal folks get dizzy and numb too if they hang out too close to power-sources. Electric stuff, radios, you know? Truth be told, it was remembering that story of his that made me think there might be something to the brain-hacking yarn INTROMET's been pushing.'

Gig felt weak. He said, 'Thank you, Detective Inspector.'

'Detective Inspector, still? My first name is Minna. Minna Karlsen.' The DI pulled a face—an expression midway between a frown and a pout. 'Hey kid. You know last week, yeah? We met, we talked Lee, and then at the end, just as you were leaving, you asked me for my number—remember that?'

'Yeah.'

'Were you meaning to ask me out?'

Instantly his cheeks burnt red—standard guilty-Gig reaction. 'N-no. No.'

'Pity that. I thought you were pretty cute,' the DI said and dredged up a too-loud laugh, forcing out the sound like a donkey's dissonant bray. 'Maybe a bit young but I'm done with blokes my own age—crusty old buggers that they are. And I can tell—I could tell you were single because you had real greedy eyes. Watched me close—my tits, my hands—

the whole time we spoke. I thought you were cute, cute like a cat, all purr and whipped cream, with that lazy long body of yours. When you left I sat down and had a long hard think, and I said to myself, Minna, you might've just let a good man slip right through your fingers—only I didn't, did I? Because you weren't meaning anything, and I'm just a batty old copper with too much imagination. Right?'

Gig started to cry. 'I have to go,' he said. 'Minna, I have to go.'

'Okay kid. Maybe we can catch up sometime?'

'Sure, Minna.'

He clicked off.

* * * *

Waiting for Ruth to return, Gig killed time with an Asahi six-pack liberated from his mothers' stockpile in the pantry. Honoria kept a good (and commendably multicultural) liquor cabinet, much to her partner's disapproval. Come the end of the world, Sandra had once sullenly remarked, we'll be doubly damned: starving and drunk. Consider *this* the end of the world and Sandra wasn't far off the mark. Starving and drunk. He couldn't remember the last time he'd eaten.

This minor problem was rectified when Ruth arrived with assorted dollar-shop groceries. Over a refreshingly civil supper of chocolate biscuits and mints, Gig repeated his conversation with the DI. Stressing the importance of the watch, the importance of Karlsen's Parkinson's. Stressing, above all things, the importance of being *Gig*.

'What's the point in following this up?' Ruth wanted to know when he'd finished. 'I doubt Singer intends to pay you now. I suspect Talobos already won the million—the money will go to his immediate family.'

'The man is dead,' Gig hissed incredulously. 'Do you think this is still about the money?'

'What else would it be about?'

'Me! About me! I went into the qverse last night and a horde of hacks tried to blow my brains out! Phoun Swiftwater threatened to kill me in person! I met honest-to-God ninja assassins! Talobos is dead, Harmonica is certainly on the blacklist, and I don't even want to talk about the Melbourne geeks and Nelly Georges...'

'Geeze, Gig. So you've made some enemies. What the hell do you want *me* to do?'

He threw a bottle-lid at her. 'Jesus!' he shrieked. 'Holy mother of Christ woman, just get a fucken watch and tell me what's inside.'

Unfazed, Ruth said: 'Enemies, whatever. Personally, Felix, I'd be more worried if you'd told me you'd made some friends.'

But despite her enmity she eventually conceded to do what he'd asked, dragging in her box of freebie Biocheck watches from the car and upending it onto the kitchen table. Together they hunted a suitable candidate for a mechanical autopsy, finally opting—at Gig's insistence—for the largest model. Screwdriver in hand, Ruth set about dismantling the watch while Gig downed a third beer. Tiny slivers of metal bounced and rolled across the table; one loosed spring performed a ungainly half-ellipsis to rest against Gig's elbow.

Ruth's final report was blunt, factual, acrimonious: 'It's a fucken watch.'

'Don't be a bitch. Look, I'm sorry. I shouldn't have snapped at you. These past few days have been rough, but that's no excuse—honestly, I'm sorry.' On so many levels. (Zhadesh, Zhadesh.) 'Please, Ruth, tell me: how does it work? You can access its information through the qverse, so is it connected to the qverse itself or does it feed off the connection of the neurocap? How does it find out about your body, your heart-rate, your blood pressure?'

Placated by his apology, Ruth slipped effortlessly into corporate-geek mode. 'The watch contains an advanced radio system,' she said. 'I figured as much—there'd be no other way to pick up accurate biological measurements and store them on equipment this small. From what I can tell, the watch picks up on the wireless-network generated by a neurocap, but transfers the information in sonic format, rather than digital. For such a little thing it's surprisingly powerful—give them a couple of months and I bet you'll be able to load anything onto the watch. Run games from it. Make phonecalls. Viger Singer has outdone hers—are you *crying?*'

'No,' said Gig, who was. Again.

'What the hell is wrong with you today? Did you and Talobos have some gay love thing happening?'

'You just don't *get* it, do you,' he blurted. 'There's some part of your brain that isn't letting this sink in. A block. Are you in denial? Why are you pretending that putting a lethal device in a wrist watch is perfectly normal?'

'It's just a radio, Felix.'

'It killed two people. Three people. Jesus, Ruth. You talk about AR in VR. The DI talked about Parkinson's; Lucas Carter-Soo mentioned duplication and mirror-rooms. Well this is your answer, Ruth. This is how it happened. If those things can send detailed information into a neurocap they can certainly alter the visual output. Brilliant, isn't it! Because no one notices watches, see? Because it's all fucken science fiction, see? And in a couple of years INTROMET will have flooded the market and everyone who's anyone will be wearing one. A little death trap that doubles as a cute accessory.'

Ruth looked so utterly nonplussed that for a second Gig had the terrible feeling *he* might be the crazy one, that all this conspiracy hunting had somehow unhinged his brain.

'You think Singer…'

'Say, Ruthie. Pretend that there's a qverse war. Look around you. Who do you think is winning?'

'Well…'

'I've been doing it the wrong way round. I've been following this *backwards.* I started with Viger, detoured at Harmonica, stopped in at Phoun's place for a plaincode playdate, wound up shooting the shit with Malachy fucken Memphis. Give me another few days and I'll be hanging out with Benny Soo—shortly before zipping off to the end-of-the-line, a coffee with the ever-elusive and probably imaginary Rebecca Descartes. What I should have done—what Harmonica should have realised, Christ!—was stay put. What I should have done was kept on asking that damn question. Why me? Because I'm *me.* Because I'm a paranoid with no friends, dubious but popular pirate-hack connections, and a history of reaching the wrong conclusions through the right means. Because I'm the perfect person to jump-start a conspiracy theory. Same way that Talobos was the perfect person to spread it. And Harmonica was the perfect person to give it credibility.'

Ruth said, 'I've never seen you cry before.'

'I've never been used like this before,' said Gig miserably. 'That's the worst part. That she knew I was a fool and played me for one at the same *damn time.*'

* * * *

THURSDAY

15

harmonica

Word had hit the streets: SWIFTWATER was down—but not out. Although its garish territories had vanished, the qverse spaces that once supported their architecture still sung with ungrounded power. Between the strongholds of INTROMET and TEEK a faceless, featureless new SWIFTWATER pulsed with internal pressure, its layers peeled back to reveal a heart of shimmering binary. In this it presented an equivocal contradiction: intensely vulnerable yet completely impenetrable. Phoun had redesigned her world not in plaincode but in *pure*code: this was prehistoric data, a parade of loosely paired zeros and ones, as incomprehensible in this post-java age as history itself.

That was Lucas' story, anyway, blurted out in stops and starts like a faulty radio. Clocks on the SouthAsian coast were rolling over on five a.m. and Harry, Joaquin and Lucas were talking revolution in the overcrowded food court of Sydney shuttleport, bunked down behind the faux-oak balustrade of a discount EastAsian diner. Safety amongst numbers, Lucas had explained when Harry questioned the choice of venue. Safety first—which was fine, sure, okay, but the noise levels inside were proving a real test of Harry's self-control, chafing nerves already ragged from travel.

Of course she could tolerate normal chaos—and indeed, often precipitated it—but this was commercial chaos, at once ugly and amateur. The food court was arranged in dwindling, descending rings (reminiscent, Harry thought grimly, of Dante's hell), each level rimmed by shop fronts. Shuttleport wait-staff costumed in the gaudy panoply of their corporate sponsors yelled orders over the beetle-click of chopsticks on Styrofoam, the polyglot buzz of international commuters, the loudspeakers overhead announcing impending departures. Squint just so and Harry could well have been seated on the fringe of a badly organised funfair, an unchoreographed big-top spectacular. That brought back childhood memories: the tears, the lights, the emetic mash of smells, the hundred-thousand bodies queued sheeplike and squabbling between metal rails…

Gloomily Harry sipped her coffee and concentrated on maintaining her cool. Concentrated on her cool and concentrated on Lucas, too. Because it was hard not to look at him; under the neon lights his cheeks glowed a fiery red and his green eyes sparkled with childish excitement. Funny, she thought—the way this adventure had energised him, illuminated him, turned this juvenile malcontent into a dynamo. Harry supposed this was the sort of once-in-a-lifetime opportunity pudgy geek-boys like Lucas fantasised about: the chance to fight evil and authority with streamlined laser-guns.

Her maternal adoration was dampened significantly by the knowledge that it was his fault she was in this mess—bloody Lucas and his damned enthusiasm. There was a lesson to be learned in all this, Harry decided; an old lesson, probably, but a pertinent one. At the present moment she couldn't decide which was more apt: 'Curiosity killed the cat' or 'Children should be seen but not heard.'

'Phoun is running but she's not running scared,' Lucas babbled on. 'It's a smart move, Mum: it means she won't be held liable for future qverse murders. How can they accuse her of killing someone if her territories aren't even functional? If Viger tries to bump off another hack, she'll have to do it the old-fashioned way: up close and personal. Unless she wants to run the risk of implicating herself in her own grand scam. Phoun knows—she's buying us time.'

'Buying us time for what?' Seated on Lucas' right, a fast-fraying Joaquin Magdellin was peeling the label from a bottle of BE POP softdrink. 'Buying us time to say our goodbyes to loved ones? Buying us time to make a last will and testament? Buying your mother time to finish her bloody cappuccino before a mafia assassin arrives to blow off her head?'

'Gracious no,' said Lucas, giggling. 'Silly, I meant buying us time to get rid of Viger Singer. Gee, Mr Magdellin, anyone would think you hadn't been listening to a word I'd said.'

Horrified, Joaquin appealed to Harry. 'Don't tell me you approve of this, Regina? Singer is a bloody corporate colossus—you'd need an army to topple her. What we three should do is go to ground as soon as possible. Find some secluded EastAsian island and work on our tans—well, *my* tan—until the heat blows over. We can't beat her but we can—'

But he stopped—he'd seen and understood the look in her eye. Calmly, coolly, Harry put down her coffee mug.

'Do you know what I did when I found out about Benny and Rebecca?' she asked. 'I didn't scream and I didn't break anything. Instead I sat down, and I had a coffee, and then I stole Benny's notes and studied them. I did it very calmly and I did it very quietly. And I was calm and quiet right up the point I smashed into the qverse and shot Rebecca between the eyes. You might think I look very calm right now, Jo. The reason I'm very calm is because I'm very angry. So I am going to have my coffee, Jo, and then I am going to destroy Viger Singer's charmed Euro-trash life.'

'Jesus, Regina—listen to yourself! How the hell are you going to get to Singer? The woman is untouchable.'

'I'm not sure at present,' said Harry. 'But when it comes to revenge, the details usually seem to work out by themselves.'

'You're mad.'

'Mad? I'm fucken *livid*.'

'Did you know that if a corporation was a person, they'd be a psychopath?' Lucas began, in a voice too cheerful, too *obviously* an attempt to undercut the black fog of tension developing between the adults. 'I read it on the internet. Most CEOs of major companies demonstrate pathological behaviours in order to maintain their position and hold of the market. Take-overs and take-downs. Buy-ins and buy-outs. Psychologists reckon that if these CEOs brought those tactics home with them—'

'Shut up,' Joaquin hissed. 'Just shut up. If I'm going to die, I'm going to die. Just—for godsake, Luke, Lucas, whatever—just don't *analyse* it. Unless you've got a bright idea to get us out of this mess, I don't want to hear from you.' For a short time he glared into the distance, apparently seeking answers in the mass of squawking international arrivals. 'Regina,' he said finally. 'You're bloody lucky you saw Rebecca in the flesh. She usually entertains under an AI alias—only Memphis and Benny ever got to see her face. If she made the effort to appear, she probably had some kind of plan brewing. She didn't tell you what to do, did she?'

Rebecca had said, *Break her.*

'She might have given me a tip or two.'

Joaquin snorted. 'Tips and hints—fat lot of good that'd do us. Tips and hints are what got you into this mess in the first place. I guess it wouldn't matter, really, what she said. You'd need an army to really get Singer—like I said before. Need enough power to fry her out of the qverse. Enough to seriously *damage* her twisted INTROMET brain. But for that you'd need a thousand hacks. Maybe even more. Maybe *all* the hacks. And even then she could flush you out of the territories at any moment, at the touch of a button. Not that it matters: you don't have an army to begin with. All you've got is me. Maybe Lucas here, at a stretch.'

'Who needs an army? I've won plenty of battles on my own. Battles against Viger Singer, no less.' Harry drained her coffee. 'There's Gig too,' she added. 'Provided he's still alive.'

'Gig? God, you still think that guy's some kind of whizkid! What did he do that was so clever? The little bastard is an opportunist—that's how he got under your defences. Sheer bloody luck. He was in the right place at the right time.'

'What about the last time?' Harry pointed out. 'The third time he—'

'The third time? When he touched core in that cheesy little soft-drink company? Gee, Harry, that's a tough one. Especially considering your spectacular resources and brilliant codeshells. And him a qverse outcast with novice-level programming skills.' Exasperated, he shoved his palms roughly against the Formica table-top. 'Sometimes I think you don't hear half of what comes out your mouth, Harry. Isn't it bloody obvious how he did it? *He had someone on the inside.*'

'A what?'

'Someone on the inside, damnit. A spy, a sleeper, a mole; a disgruntled employee with level access codes and union immunity. Think human error, think human corruption. Think about your pretty boy and his established modus operandi. Maybe Gig paid them off, maybe he sucked them off; I've heard some cute shit from Zhads about the big-boned butch tricks that skinny fuck has turned. In the end the bastards *must* have let him in. Or maybe they just handed over the passwords and sat back to watch your carefully crafted shells come down in flames—'

'Benny,' Lucas blurted: it seemed the word had popped out at the same instant it occurred to him.

Joaquin glared. 'Benny? What the hell does Benny have to do with this?'

But Lucas was looking at Harry. And was smiling, triumphantly, his face as optimistic and open as his father's had once been. And Harry saw Benny in Lucas then; saw in Lucas all of Benny's genius and all of Benny's hope. (And loved him for that. For once. Because although Benny was still a liar, a ruthless liar and an unforgivable bastard, Rebecca/Eleanor had exonerated him of that worst crime: the affair. And perhaps, Harry reflected, there was something thanklessly noble in what he'd done—*except you were worried about the wrong woman, Benny, you fool, you were worried about the wrong damn one...*) Her son scotched his plastic chair to hers and stretched up to whisper in her ear. 'Dad,' he said breathlessly. 'Dad. I have his *face*.'

'What?'

Quick-fingered Lucas had already pulled out his neurocap and snatched hers from her travel bag. Dumbly Harry watched as he pried open the covers of both with a complimentary plastic spoon and began to hotwire their interiors. His mouth moved as he worked, forming small, soundless half-words twice drowned by the cacophony of the food court: words like redi- and under- and reco-. She realised what he was doing after a minute, although she couldn't tell if it was a brilliant idea or a terrible one. But brilliant or terrible, this was definitely a *hack* idea: dirty, low, and an abuse of both knowledge and power. On that level, it appealed.

'I'd feel strange,' she said.

'That's better than feeling shot, yeah?'

'You can't come in with me,' she warned.

'I'm not going to. I'm going to get Dad.'

'Who'll help me? I can't just waltz in there alone.'

Lucas shrugged. 'You've got Gig and *him*.'

'I'm not bloody doing anything if Gig is involved,' Joaquin snapped from the sidelines. 'And I especially won't pull some crazy hack-job with him. Going after Singer is stupid, we all know that...'

'You done with the cap, kid?' Harry interrupted.

'I guess, Mum.'

'Give it, then. I need to think. Away from this noise.'

Yes—away from this noise, and away from both of you, too. Their bickering was intensifying her migraine. Harry took the briefcase and the neurocap and pushed her way out of the food court. From there luck guided her to a near-empty corridor, one of the many transparently tiled overpasses that looped between shuttle platforms. She laid her cheek against the cold metal screen of a BE POP vending machine (it protested mildly at this contact in a nasal, Scottish accent) and counted seconds until the purple ache in her head dimmed to a dull red.

Stay cool, Carter, she told herself. I get mad, I get fried. I lose it here, I make one wrong choice, and I'm as good as dead. And I'm being asked to make a choice right now, she realised; I'm being asked to make *the* choice. We could run now and wait until Benny arrives and fixes everything—like he always does, like he always has. I could rent a hotel room and spend a couple of nights in bed with Joaquin, watching movie re-runs. Or we could fight. Which I've always done but never (to be honest) done *well*, never done *gracefully*. But I could fight with Gig—Gig with his slippery mind and his slippery brown body—I could fight alongside Gig, and we might win...

Of course in the end this wasn't a choice of tactics but a choice of men. Compatibility in a time of crisis.

Which made the answer obvious. If not necessarily sensible.

On her way to the Melbourne departure lounge Harry stopped in a newsagency to pick up some cigarettes. There was a queue for service: two muscle-bound Japanese with a newspaper order, and a fat woman with a bottom as disproportionate as a medieval bustle struggling to control a trolley of baggage and three over-excited children. There but for the grace of God go I, Harry thought.

One of the Japanese glanced her way—a quick, coy appraisal over the silver rims of his aviator sunglasses—then did a double take. After a murmured word to his companion, the two returned the paper and left the queue.

Harry guessed she'd offended them in some way. The Japanese could be funny like that.

* * * *

She chased a red dawn across the stateline. From her window seat the black bat-swoop of the shuttle's wing cut a dark gash on the sun. The woman beside her—a *zaftig* blonde with luminous blue eyeshadow—exchanged fifteen of Harry's cigarettes for a handful of caffeine pills. 'I know what it's like running the interstate circuit,' the woman confided, mistaking Harry's suit for an official corporate sales uniform. 'Sixteen meetings in sixteen hours. Surprised you're still alive.'

Harry knocked back the caffeine with a vodka chaser, thankful Lucas wasn't around to see. The 5:30 Sydney-Melbourne EXP touched down just after six. Juiced up on pills and complimentary in-flight coffees, Harry bounced out onto the street and enthusiastically flagged a yellowcab. It was only when the driver automaton requested a prompt that she realised she didn't know Gig's address.

'Would sir or madam like to consult a directory?' the automaton chirped in its digital twang. 'All yellowcabs come fully equipped with regularly updated online maps and local listings. Should you wish to tour famous sites of Melbourne, I would personally recommend—'

'Just give me the damn directory,' said Harry.

Felix McGuiggen wasn't listed by the online directory but Toorak-dwellers Honoria and Sandra McGuiggen were—the only female couple on the screen with a common surname. Playing to a hunch, Harry cross-referenced their address with registered business listings and discovered that the McGuiggen family home shared tenancy with GIGQC, a qverse consultancy situated on the McGuiggen's ground floor. Which was telling on two accounts: firstly, it seemed Gig really didn't care who found out about his virtual reality identity; and secondly, the guy still hadn't moved out of his parents' basement.

Some men *never* grow up, Harry thought, amused, remembering in counterpoint Jong Lin's untouched adolescent bedroom, Joaquin Magdellin's adult bachelor pad. It was cute, though—wasn't it? A twenty-eight-year-old dicking about with computer gadgets in the basement in the same fashion middle-aged men ran model railways in the attic. And Harry got a measure of him then—who Gig was, and why she liked him, and what made him such an easy target for the likes of Viger Singer. A little boy in his own little world, both fearful and excited by the propositions of strangers...

Then the cab hit the overland freeway, the open road, the high road, and her idle musings were drowned out in a crescendo of wind.

Toorak was an affluent suburb a quick four minutes from the city centre, its constituency divided between apartment dwellers, terrace renters, and the owners of ornate country manors. From the look of their house (mock Tudor, classic) and its sprawling lawns, the McGuiggens fitted into the latter category. Unsurprising—Harry had pegged Gig as upper-middle class from the first moment she'd seen him. These days only bums and spoilt rich kids dressed in op-shop rags. And who else but the fabulously wealthy could afford the luxury of designer genes?

The yellowcab ditched her at the front door. No answer was forthcoming from the intercom. Harry wandered around the side of the house and discovered, mid-way down the east-facing wall, a wooden door set flat in the earth like the ingress of a bomb-shelter. A door to GIGQC headquarters? Harry dragged it open. Below she heard music (NorthAsian pop trash) and smelt that familiar sweaty-smell that meant: Geeks Nearby. Stone stairs led down into darkness.

She was one step shy of the bottom when someone swung a cricket bat at her. Reflexively she raised the briefcase to deflect the blow. The bat hummed away again as if it had struck rubber, and Felix 'Gig' McGuiggen came stumbling blind-eyed into the light.

'Hello, rabbit,' said Harry. 'You greet all your customers that way?'

'I assumed you'd come here to kill me, sir,' panted Gig. He looked *wrecked*—think rockstar at the arse-end of a year-long countrywide tour, five steps from another spell in rehab...but his voice was steady, refreshingly sane. 'A natural mistake on my part—murdering hacks seems to be all the rage these days.' Still shaking, he lowered the bat by degrees until it rested peaceably against his thigh. 'I had hoped you'd come, sir,' he admitted. 'I had a wonderful fantasy about you riding in on a great white beast— probably some sort of dinosaur—throwing me over your shoulder, and then carrying me off to a safe place. Mind: a safe place that wasn't my mothers' suburban basement.'

'You're cute,' said Harry finally, 'but you're fucked in the head.'

'So I was brought up to believe, sir. Please take a seat. Somewhere. My home is your home.'

His 'home' was a converted basement easily as big as her Sydney apartment. Harry figured the content ratio was hack standard: ninety percent hardware, ten percent furniture. At one time she supposed the room had been a feature of the house; years of geek living had changed that. Brown stains (soda? beer? pizza?) discoloured the beige carpet; light from the classic screen lamps above was overwhelmed by the blue-brilliance of some thirty LCD monitors. These were arranged haphazardly; some on desktops, others on the floor, some piled by the wall in the fashion of wallscreen security feeds. Around them computer cords and cables unrolled like bunting. Evidently Gig did a lot of work outside the qverse; most hacks found it easier to program without distractions.

Harry found a seat on a steel computer chassis. 'Are you okay?' she asked.

'I'd like to say yes but I'd be lying. Frankly I'm not very good at coping with stress. I'm small-time, remember? Until Singer called, my job consisted of fixing faulty cap calibrations and approving my cousin's codeshell designs. This whole death by corporation thing has taken me a little by surprise.' He slumped onto a chassis opposite her, discarding his bat in favour of a neurocap—an expensive unbranded SWIFTWATER contraption. 'And I suppose now you want to fry her,' he said. 'And you want me to help. I mean you're here, and I'm here, and I don't think—wildest dreams aside—that you'd come looking for me if it wasn't for a purpose, if I didn't have some use, and I think the only thing I'm good at is being a hack. Of course I'm assuming here that you've already worked out what Singer was up to, and did so long before I did; you know about the distortions and how the matriarch has been playing us like a—'

'Yes.'

He looked exhausted but he also looked eager, like a marathon runner summoning his last reserves for the home stretch. He was drunk—she could smell it on his breath—but he was hiding it well. She thought right now he was maybe-beautiful in a strung out kind of way, the kind of way frail, desperate things were always beautiful. 'I want Singer dead, sir,' he said, and the formal pupil-to-teacher effect gave his voice a sinister edge. 'I want her dead partly because she is evil and she killed people—some right in front of me. But most of all I want her dead because she made me feel stupid and I *hate* that. I must sound like a child but that's how it is, the honest truth. So—I want to *get* her but at the same time I don't want to end up like Talobos. What if she gets clued into our plot and tries to kill us, sir?'

'It's virtual reality, lad.'

'And my point still stands.' Slim fingers curled around the chromed lip of his neurocap. 'I suppose you have a plan?'

'I thought I'd go in and pull her plug while you distracted her,' said Harry.

'How do I do that?'

'Throw rocks at her windows? Call her dumb names? I'm sure you can think of something.'

Gig pressed his fingers against his mouth, his eyes. 'Is this how you plan all your attacks?' he asked, disappointed (she could almost read his thoughts: *Some dinosaur-riding heroine you turned out to be!*). 'You just run right in with no clear plan and do stuff loudly until something works? I don't mean any offence by that—the concept is just completely alien to me. I tend to plan everything out beforehand, see; I even schedule it, I write lists, I set watches, I compare notes, I research and revise...'

'It's just another hack. We're just frying some chick and killing her system. That's all.'

'That's funny. And by funny I mean funny-strange, sir. You don't seem—forgive me, sir, but you don't seem to be taking this very seriously. The way I see it Singer has us marked for life; we're doomed to a brutal death the moment we emerge into the sunlight. While you, on the other hand, are acting as if you've just had a little tiff with a schoolgirl chum and you want to teach her a lesson. And I don't quite understand—I mean Talobos is *dead* sir; is a *corpse* sir; is the definite indefinite article. And Viger Singer has virtually unlimited resources and a real knack for unconscionable crimes, and—'

'I thought you said you understood people,' said Harry. 'Wasn't that your party trick?'

'I understand people. But I could never get my head around Singer. Singer or Swiftwater. Their minds operated in a different kind of space from yours or mine. In *corporate* space. But I see some things.' He rubbed his temples, unconsciously massaging in the same, circular motion with which he'd stroked his neurocap moments before. 'I understand that Singer is weak. Because of all the qverse power-players she's the only one who hasn't changed. If you know what I mean.'

Harry did—and it was odd that this hadn't struck her before. Viger had stayed Viger. Misoka had become Phoun, and Eleanor had become Rebecca, and Li had become Benny, and Malachy hadn't changed his name but he'd certainly changed his style. And of course Regina herself had become Harry, Harmonica, adopting and reinventing her street gang alter-ego. But Viger was Viger, still Viger. If a true appreciation of the qverse was achieved through transformation then Viger had missed the point altogether. The matriarch was a static entity: not only old-school but also, pitiably, old-world.

'Singer thinks she knows the game,' Gig went on; 'she thinks she owns the game. She thinks she knows us, too— the way we work. The way you work. We're loners, sir. We do our business as far away from other people as we possibly can. So what Singer won't expect is us banding together. In the bedroom, maybe, since neither of us have many scruples in that department…but not when it comes to *work*.'

'Did you just insult me?'

'If I insulted you, sir, then I insulted myself too. And exposed myself to shame and ridicule and complete humiliation. Um. If you're into that sort of thing.'

Harry laughed. 'No wonder people hate you.'

They'd fallen easily into conversation; too easily, really. As if they were old friends. As if what they'd shared in virtual reality had crossed over, completely, into the real world. And this *was* a qverse conversation: no preamble, just the facts. Straight up, straight down the line. Harry appreciated that. She also appreciated that he was quick and easy and didn't *bitch*, which was more than could be said for the duo she'd abandoned in the food court. Most of all she liked the fact he understood the simple requisite of revenge. To people like us, Harry thought, payback isn't a choice but an imperative. You don't have to question it or analyse it. Like throwing a punch, like beating an automaton—*it just happens.*

'I want to do this with you, sir,' said Gig.

I want to do this with you, sir—she liked the way he said it.

She said: 'Okay.'

* * * *

There was no plan. Just two people with a similar goal and similar hang-ups and an unspoken understanding. You'll achieve nothing by doing this, Carter, Harry thought. You'll shut her down, *maybe*, but in a few weeks—a few days with

Benny's help—INTROMET will be up and running again. Look at it rationally: in the end, there's no point. Except to appease your smarting pride. Except to add a dash of excitement to your corporate life. Because that's always been your problem: you get a kick out of picking fights with people bigger and stronger than you...

'Watch it,' she warned herself. 'You're channelling Benny.'

And saw a humourless irony in that, as she entered the qverse in Benny's skin.

Or rather, *under* Benny's skin: Lucas had installed his masking hardware in Harry's neurocap. Which was the clever part of the not-plan, inspired by Gig's hack MO. (Isn't it obvious how he did it? Joaquin had said. He had someone on the inside...) Briefly Harry felt something not-solid pass over her face, tangible as a sheath of spiderwebs, blotting out and blinding. For a second there she was immersed in him, her ex- husband's virtual phantasm—(her speech unit clicked over, tuning itself to his voice; her scalp itched as her neurocap reorganised its wiring; and in the whirring dark of Benny Soo's internal mechanics Harry found she could almost *smell* him, that bitter starch-and-coffee scent that followed him everywhere)—but then the moment passed and the sensation of the mask with it.

When Harry opened her eyes she was standing in a private entrance portal: a small pastel-hued room identifiable as INTROMET territory only by the tiny company logo embossed in the lower right corner of each wall. It was completely empty and completely silent. There were no visible exits. Could this be a puzzle of some kind, she wondered, a Benny Soo trick to weed out unworthy trespassers? How do you escape a room with four walls and no door?

Riddle-savvy Harry looked up. A mirrored ceiling reflected her blank Benny-gaze.

No ready exit there. Harry pursed her lips. Can't go over it. Can't go under it. Which meant... She laid a hand against the wall. The code budded pinkly at her touch then burst outward in fine, fair petals that curled slightly at the edges like thin slices of ham. Each lip exposed was edged in wet gloss, some actually dripping with glutinous, earthy oil. It was a visceral thing, this opening, feminine in a gross, primordial way. Harry guessed Benny had designed it shortly after the divorce: the images were choked-up with obsession and hatred.

Digging in her fingers, she unpicked his code like you'd pick at a scar or a loose thread. It wasn't a difficult shell to crack—but then, cracking it clearly wasn't meant to be the hard part. Once destabilised, the walls came away in chunks, fleshily, grotesquely, some pieces as large as a human head. It occurred to Harry (as she waded through the shit, this gelatinous pink goo that slopped lasciviously against her thighs with a noise like punched meat) that every time Benny entered the qverse he had to first pull apart this room of saturated *femaleness*.

A deconstruction of his desire.

She guessed it was a form of therapy recommended by one of his high-priced psychoanalysts—or maybe cold-hearted Malachy Memphis was behind it.

(Li, man, to get her out of your system, you've got to *rip* her out of your world...)

Then the room dissolved and she was out. Out *where*? Harry wasn't entirely sure, but anything was better than wallowing about in her ex-husband's self-pity. Wiping clumps of pink from her hands, she caught a glimpse of a strange bell-shaped room, branded as INTROMET property, its ceiling grooved with cables like the ribcage of a whale... before she was swarmed by security programs. Her external visuals blanked out automatically and a series of bright lights fizzed on her control screen. Clearance codes checked, traces confirmed, passwords authorised, messages of authentication sent and received. INTROMET was processing her.

Harry waited. She trusted Lucas. She trusted his hardware and she trusted his plaincode and she trusted his clever masking idea and it looked now as if she'd entrusted him with her life, too. Which (in retrospect) might not have been a smart move, given that the kid was a compulsive liar. But she trusted in Benny, also: she trusted that Benny would never make a program that didn't work. (Even if, in innocence, he had constructed it for an entirely different purpose.) While the INTROMET security programs wormed their way over the complexities of the Benny-mask, Harry played it cool.

The security programs had just begun to disperse when Harry saw Viger Singer entering the qverse, a faint white bleep on her control screen, attracted like a moth to Benny's peculiar trace-signature. God, not *her*, Harry thought. Not her and not *yet*—I haven't had enough sleep to bluff my way out of a one-on-one with her... But the matriarch moved away almost as soon as she had appeared. Luck or design? Harry wondered.

She got her answer a minute or two later when she registered Gig's presence smoking up the Badlands, a pretty spot of pink flickering amongst flailing tendrils of codeshell black. Yellow half-moon ripples—signifying the emission of powerful laser flares—bounced away from his pink spot every four seconds. Looked like Gig was kicking up a fuss in the middle of Viger's stomping ground. From what Harry could tell he'd already demolished three of Viger's lesser defences. And had triggered every alarm on the way— alarms which were probably deafening Viger with their siren-screams.

Nicely done, McGuiggen.

The security programs were gone now. Harry stood in a whale's belly filled with switchboards and monitors. Aside from the bizarrely bloated arch of its ceiling, the room was simple and uncluttered. Like everything else in the qverse it had been designed this shape for a reason: it was a functional symbol. Harry thought: Jonah. Who was thrown overboard for being bad luck and was saved by God's grace—that was the story, wasn't it? Jonah, whose biblical tribulations mirrored the hardluck story of every Eurotrash migrant who'd washed up on SouthAsia's shores with a dream of corporate prosperity.

So this was Viger's secret place, Viger's INTROMET heart. It was evocative and pathetic. It stunk of insecurity and self-absorption. It was embarrassing to be there. What was it about the qverse that made people so *open*? That made people so willing to wear their neurosis on their sleeves? It made Harry feel sick. She hated Viger all the more intensely for being *human* under that scalpel-cut façade. Also, she hated Benny for being exploited (again).

And she hated Eleanor for her audacity, and Joaquin for his arrogance, and hated the qverse itself for encouraging the lot of them—but that was beside the point...

So.

Carter.

What was the point?

What was the question?

More importantly: *Why* was the question and *why* did it seem so obvious, now, that there were holes in the plot? That things had unravelled too far, beyond the rind, beyond the pith? Because if this brain-hacking scheme was reliant on *character*, then wasn't Viger's character—so prominently, so proudly presented in every element of her works—just another part of the puzzle, and not its root? Say there are layers to this mystery, Carter, (as there are layers to plaincode) and in stripping them you reveal a different secret each time. So *Viger Singer* may be the answer to layer three, but not necessarily layer four (or five!). And perhaps,

Carter, if you dig a little deeper with your long black fingers, you might find another culprit altogether…

In INTROMET's heart, in Viger Singer's fantasy, in Benny Soo's skin, Harry sat down.

And thought about this at length.

And presently came to the conclusion that she did not care. You could spend your whole life looking at plaincode and never understand it. You could spend years on a riddle and never solve it. You could spend a week on some crass matriarch whodunit and by the end the details of the answer didn't matter, so long as you *had* an answer.

She ran a hand over the INTROMET switchboard. The contract Benny, Rebecca and Viger had signed made the rules perfectly clear. To destroy one matriarch you'd need to convince the other two to set aside their differences for long enough to pull the plug. Or you could beg the matriarch's world-weary sidekick to cut the power from their generators, creating a territory blackout.

Or you could steal his identity and his insta-access and do it your own damn self.

It was easy. All the right answers were supposed to be.

Harry started turning Viger Singer off.

* * * *

16

gig

Gig's mission was a Petegin prototype—Seek and Annoy.

He plummeted into INTROMET like a stone, sending up a white cone of grainy pixel-dust when he hit the ground. When the dust cleared he saw he had landed on a pale, sun-bleached plain overlooking INTROMET's headquarters, a view half-shadowed by a reaching dark. Outside in the real world it was not yet noon, but it was coming on dusk in the Badlands, a dreary grey dusk without moon or stars. Time in INTROMET ran to a European schedule. Overhead the clouds thinned and ribboned across a horizon visibly contoured like the inside of a basin. Distantly something shrieked, a sound simultaneously prehistoric and manufactured.

Although his neurocap dimmed or drowned out most of his real-world sensations, Gig was still aware of a prickling of sweat at the base of his spine. It was the size of the territory spread before him that unnerved him, not the creature's scream. This is *all Singer*, he realised. From here to the end of the world, this is Singer. She is in every blade of grass, in every leaf on every tree; her presence is written ineradicably into the plaincode of every Badlands monster. I am standing in the palm of her hand. To someone like Singer I must seem as tiny and insignificant as an ant.

And this is the woman Harmonica thinks we can hack!

Harmonica and Gig against the odds and the gods, he thought, wrinkling his nose at the childish cadence of the phrase. Christ, I've become so bloody *heroic*.

His SWIFTWATER control screen revealed he was equipped with a state-of-the-art laser—a whole arsenal of them, in fact. He chose one arbitrarily and closed the control screen. The weight of the laser did not feel comfortable in his hand but it sure felt better than holding nothing at all. Tentatively he danced its silver flare across the earth. At a mere touch the sands crisped and melted into translucent ripples like bacon fat, then turned a glassy opaque. Threads of evaporating code spooled into the air like cigarette smoke.

To get Singer's attention (and hold it) he would have to break something, and break it loudly. Shredding large sections of Badlands territory with a ridiculously overpowered laser would, Gig felt, probably do the trick. He was in the process of recharging his laser for the main event when something landed on his shoulder.

He slid his gaze sideways. Sitting on his shoulder was a tiny silver harlequin, no bigger than his index finger, similar to the china-doll miniatures Sandra McGuiggen kept on the lounge-room mantelpiece—saving in one important regard:

the harlequin's facial features were Asiatic, not Anglo. Its costume was exquisitely detailed, each patch fringed in elegant cross-stitch. A black scarf covered its eyes. If there was a specific symbolic connection, Gig couldn't pick it, but he understood the gist. Phoun Swiftwater had come to him as a blind fool.

'Hi funny boy! Quick-quick, tell me truth. What you think?'

The harlequin struck a pose and Gig grimaced. 'Cute skin?'

'Skin? Silly boy. Not a skin but an *enabler.* A switch. A wire. I am the current and you are the plug. No. Better: I am the gateway of my own self. You like that? It some profound poetry shit I read in magazine. Or maybe I pick it up from Descartes—that dumb Anglo talk crazy circles, make your head ache to listen. How is my funny Gig boy this morning? Look to me like you is all geared up for a hack. A super big hack. Hey, you finding my cap okey? Calibration working smoothly? That no factory model you wearing. I make that whole cap by hand. All modifications, all extras. Because you a very special hack.'

'And I guess those 'very special' modifications you gave me included a spook module or two,' Gig said bitterly. 'Not to mention a handful of trace-location programs that let you find me wherever I'm hiding.'

'No,' said Phoun, giggling. '*That* shit come standard.'

'Jesus Christ. You're sick, Hayashi, you know that? You're like one of those sadists who hang around funerals. You get high seeing others fall. Hell, I don't even know who you're rooting for: us or Singer. Honestly, I'd rather not know.'

'You pretty full of yourself if you think you come this far without my help. Don't you know I always there behind the scenes? I am magician behind the curtain. I show you the right way!'

'That's what worries me. You haven't exactly been an unbiased resource.'

'You not exactly unbiased yourself.'

Gig switched off the laser and let it swing loose and limp from his fingertips like a pendulum, patiently clocking virtual time. The silver harlequin struck a defensive, square-shouldered pose. 'Oh you think you only one who suffers!' it squeaked. 'So you not super popular in qverse world right now! So couple of hacks try beat you up. Well big deal, as you SouthAsians say. What about me? What about poor Princess Phoun? I close all of SWIFTWATER just to clear my name! Every minute pass I losing money! Who fault that? I tell you: all fault of INTROMET and stinky Viger Singer. That who you should be mad at, not me.'

'Oh yeah?'

'What in your head now?' Phoun whined. 'Funny boy having second thoughts? Funny boy putting two and two together and making sixteen? Hey, hey. Maybe you on Viger's side now. Maybe you thinking me and Benny Soo are working together. That way work too, you know—fit evidence perfect! Me and Benny Soo, we set Viger up. We plan it out perfect. We use clever psychology. He infiltrate INTROMET. I infiltrate your head. We want to get rid of

Singer but keep our hands clean, so we invent a special program, bribe some goons, kill a qverse low-life and trick Viger into investigating—'

'You wouldn't have done it like that,' said Gig. 'Too many variables and uncertainties. That isn't your style.'

'Maybe Benny not involved then. Maybe you thinking it the matriarchs playing God, using you as pawns. I see it, obvious. Like in so many Western fairy-tales, when big chief-king chooses a champion to fight in his stead. We all want the qverse so we each select a hack. Viger pick Ray-gee-neh: she the loudest and bestest hack of all time! Rebecca want Talobos: a steady, smart hack, quick as weasel, crafty as fox. And I choose you. Gig. Not because you are particularly talented but because I know Ray-gee-neh's weakness is sassy NorthAsian boys and because the best way to unhinge an insecure egotist like Talobos is to pit him against a plainly unworthy opponent. And I can count on my little friend Lucas, too, to turn the screws on Ray-gee-neh. (Unlike Viger and Rebecca, my main weapon is psychology!) We matriarchs decide on our champions and send them into battle. But nothing happens—you too self-absorbed! You fight your own fights, not ours! So Viger gets idea: we make up bogus mystery, you three investigate, first one right wins! All get invited to participate in top secret mission—'

'I notice that you're always the villain,' said Gig. 'No matter which story you tell.'

Phoun snorted. 'Okey then Mister Smarty-pants. Say there is no criminal. Or say we are all criminals, equally bad.

What you do then? Play favourites? Take potluck? Or do what Ray-gee-neh tells you? Hey, funny boy, you finally lure sexy American into your home! Fry Singer, maybe you get laid!'

'I'm not like that. I'm not that kind of person.'

'Wake up to the world, McGuiggen. You never know the real truth about anything. You never see the whole, only the parts. So in the end everyone is 'that kind' of person. All make decisions based on limited information. Decisions and judgements. Some of them more right than others. Look at yourself, funny boy. You are arguing all solemn and righteous with a fully charged laser in your hand, while your leggy American co-conspirator is poised to flick switches in the heart of INTROMET. You tell me straight-face you are not making judgement just by being here.'

'I could walk away.'

'No,' said Phoun. 'No, you couldn't. Ha ha. Okey I tell a lie. You can take off your cap. You can go back to the real world. But not much different will happen. Wheels already in super-fast motion!'

'And you win whatever happens, right?'

The harlequin raised its tiny shoulders in a disarming shrug. 'Look on bright side. At least I like you. When you get right down to it, we both on same side.'

Gig swallowed and looked away. Below him the towers of INTROMET glinted like pyres in the fading sunlight. Am I on your side? he wondered. Is this what it was all leading to? A choice between matriarchs—*my* choice between matriarchs. If you can call *this* a choice: like everything else in the qverse, Singer and Swiftwater are near-copies of each other. Two crazy women pumped up on power. Even their goons are alike: Singer's Dee and Dum are scalpel-cut clones of Swiftwater's well-dressed blonds. It's like that old American saying: Same shit, different bucket.

'You're telling me nothing matters,' he said.

The harlequin grasped the loose fabric at its thighs and dropped in a pigeon-toed curtsey. Then, without pausing to straighten, it bounced off his shoulder and slid down his upper arm, easily navigating the sharp curve of his elbow. From there it skipped six brisk steps to his wrist and pirouetted, one leg extended, like a music-box ballerina. Faintly he heard chimes, played in a rising scale, and on the highest note—a note on the very fringe of hearing—the harlequin spread its gloved fingers beneath its chin, puckered its silver lips, and blew Gig a kiss, which gained form and flopped into the air like an ungainly butterfly to settle on his head.

Gig stared. The harlequin pointed a toe and vaulted into the air with Olympic precision, somersaulted once, and dove headfirst into Gig's laser, vanishing completely into the matte-black handle. Raw electricity fizzed in the harlequin's wake—*silver* electricity. Cautiously Gig tapped the laser against his thigh. Phoun's voice echoed up to him from inside, 'Ha ha funny boy,' each syllable reverberating as if she were speaking through a metal tube.

Then the laser turned itself on.

Gig turned it off on impulse. The laser turned on again. Gig turned it off and held down the switch; the laser turned on to spite him and its own motorised coding and cut a bright gash through the ground at his feet. Immediately the earth peeled back and the air became effervescent with escaping bubbles of plaincode. Gig shrieked; the laser bucked; Gig cursed it; the laser sliced a second hole through the ground; Gig cursed Phoun; the laser made another hole, which was followed by another; and another; and another; and as the laser slashed its merry way across the Badlands Gig was tugged along with it, like a master attempting to rein in an enormous and exceptionally capricious dog.

Someone said: 'Do you have a licence for that thing?'

Abruptly the laser stopped slashing and hummed malevolently in Gig's palm.

'V-Viger? I mean, Ms Singer?'

'Pardon me for interrupting your little game, McGuiggen,' said the matriarch thinly—standing cool and sexy in her own skin, on her own turf. 'But I couldn't help but notice you're destroying large sections of my territory. Of course I wouldn't find that so offensive if you weren't—' She paused for dramatic (comic?) effect. '—using SWIFTWATER hardware.'

Gig said, weakly, 'I'm here about the case.'

'Oh, *everyone* is here about the case. That's the only reason anyone wants to talk to me these days. They want to tell me about Arnold Lee. That's what you want to say, isn't it? You want to tell me how to kill a man in virtual reality. So please, Felix, tell me. Is it through a special program or is it done by hypnosis? Is there a problem with hardware, or has the hardware been switched? Is it a genuine answer or is it an answer contrived to win you one million dollars? I'm dying to know. Everyone is dying to know.'

Her skin wore a little black dress. She spread a slim white hand over her chest, beneath the shoestring straps, and hugged her shoulder.

Gig said, 'This has gone too far.'

'Sweetheart, I always go too far. I always let things get out of hand. I always get the wrong idea. I always make the wrong impression. I always trust the wrong bloody people. It's a bad habit. Habits, plural. Why are you carrying a SWIFTWATER laser, McGuiggen?'

She was so cool. She was so huge. She made him feel smaller than the smallest thing.

'You killed people!' he blurted. 'You killed Arnold Lee and Nelly Georges. You killed Eric and Bradley and you killed Zhadesh, you killed my cousin's *boyfriend*—'

Viger laughed and the sun flickered. Gig caught it out of the corner of his eye, like the pre-emptive blink of a dying bulb. On. Off. On. Off. Somewhere out there Harmonica was chewing up code, realigning generators—and Viger must have realised, too, because her laughter stopped abruptly. 'I killed people?' she murmured. 'I'm not going to dignify that. Tell me why you're carrying a SWIFTWATER laser.'

'You should be locked up. You're an insane megalomaniac. Do you think I'm stupid? That we're all stupid? Did you really think you were going to get away with it? Jane Cragg told me what you asked her to do. Remember the WAB? Remember that? You wanted to see how far you could go before people noticed something was astray. Well guess what, Viger Singer!' Wildly he stabbed a finger in the air—anything to pull her attention back to him. 'We *noticed*! We noticed *everything*.'

'Good grief. Are you on drugs?'

He calmed down, took deep breaths. 'It's AR in VR,' he persisted. 'Numbness. Hallucinations. Parkinson's. That's how you did it. With your fancy bloody Biocheck watches!'

'And where did you get your information from?'

'DI Karlsen! Jane Cragg! Tara Lee! Phoun! Even Malachy Memphis—' He realised, too late, the trap he'd fallen into.

'Second-hand information? Oh, you must be joking. You're telling me that you actually *listened* to these people? My *enemies*?' Her tone was lazily amused. 'Do you know how much they hate me? How much they'd like to see me fall? Why, I expect all the information you discovered just fell right into your lap, didn't it? Hints and clues. I am disappointed in you, McGuiggen—I thought you were a clever, resourceful young man, not the gullible type. Didn't you ever wonder if you'd been set up?'

'All the damn time.'

The matriarch sniffed regally. 'If there was another soul around listening to your babble, I'd be well within my rights to sue you for slander,' she said. 'And I'd take you for every penny you owned, rich boy—you mark my words. So I suggest unplug your neurocap and try to sleep off whatever illicit substance you're currently under the influence of. Come back when you're in possession of your senses. Frankly, I don't have time for this kind of disturbance.'

'Why are you denying it? I *know* it's the truth!'

'Do you?'

He hesitated. Only for a second, but she noticed and laughed.

'You're pathetic,' she said. 'I should never have chosen you.'

'This isn't over, Singer—'

'Oh, darling, I rather think it is.' Smirking, Viger flipped him the ultimate insult: a pre-recorded auto-eject message. 'Felix McGuiggen of SouthAsia, if you do not vacate INTROMET property within the next thirty seconds, you will be forcibly ejected by a team of trained INTROMET secops; all materials left on INTROMET property by you will be forfeit to INTROMET INC.; your behaviour will incur a three week ban from all INTROMET properties which will commence from this day, June 4th, 2062, onward—'

He fried her.

* * * *

Later Harmonica would explain it to him—the practicable *mechanics* of Viger Singer's demise. She would say: 'Phoun closed down all SWIFTWATER territories and rerouted their power into a single channel (a specially programmed portable skin) which she then plugged into the containment-zone of your neurocap's laser (designed by SWIFTWATER for this ulterior purpose), charging it to react at the exact moment that Viger Singer ejected you from

INTROMET territories and inadvertently exposed herself through the opening of a new exit (designed for the purpose of removing unwanted quantities, such exits are always created codeshell-less); Phoun blasted a hole through the ejection program and, by default, a hole through Viger Singer; and having destroyed the majority of Viger's defensive codeshells (codeshells already weakened significantly by my efforts in the control room), Phoun trained her artillery on Viger herself, on Viger's own neurocap, and (in simple, layman's terms) shot the *entire digitalised construct of* SWIFTWATER *through Viger Singer's head...*'

* * * *

But it went through *his* head first.

Brilliant, this Brutus-blade of SWIFTWATER. It did not hurt him, but it *hollowed* him. He felt power, but it happened in the third person. He was detached from it. It ran through the inside of him. He *experienced* power as a purr of light and static, a rush of colour, a prolonged and perverse synthasia. Fireworks sparked down his spine and crackled in his joints. Colours shot threads of rainbow through his head. Beams burst from his nose and ears and navel. He was a creator and a destroyer. He was a body, electric.

Images flashed before his eyes, the lingering ghosts of unmade SWIFTWATER creations: a flailing intestine of q-

Topian walkway, a storm-sky shot with religious propaganda, a street of orange houses and the white crest of a ski-slope. Also faces, an assembly of typically SWIFTWATER skins: bug-eyed anime dolls and over-pumped hunks with unreal hairstyles. But more intensely Gig saw Phoun, who was at that moment *all things*, an eternal ethereal banshee-howl of energy that beat an angry pulse through his body like the dissonant rev of a shuttle engine.

He thought: Maybe there's another story. Maybe Phoun did it. All by herself.

Then he thought: Maybe *I* did it. To myself.

Then he thought: Who cares who did it? I can't even remember what they *did* in the first place.

He recognised then that he had been standing all this time on the fringe of something he would never understand. It was a picture too big for him to conceive of. He lost hope and, as consequence, lost interest.

To hell with you women. To hell with you all.

Gig had no trouble getting out. He left his neurocap switched on and simply pulled it off his head.

* * * *

Harmonica wasn't in the basement when Gig came out. Ruth Nameri was. Sitting still and straight-backed on an overstuffed beanbag, his cousin was fiddling restlessly with a crumpled FOR Q newsletter. The headline: PROUD WARRIORS OF THE QVERSE: DEATHS IN VIRTUAL REALITY—the usual Memphis tripe jumbled up with the truth. The cheap typesetting ink had blackened Ruth's fingers and cheeks. Loosed from its usual sloppy ponytail, her dark hair shadowed her face.

(I am the current and you are the plug.)

Gig left the SWIFTWATER neurocap on a computer chassis, its spindles spitting static shards into the place where his head had once been. Silently he watched Ruth: she looked as small as he felt. He laughed. The sound came out tinny and fake. A wave of nausea overcame him—he dashed into the makeshift basement bathroom and vomited convulsively, hanging heavily from the towel-rail. He returned to Ruth, wiping the bitter taste from his mouth with the edge of a ragged sleeve. She had not moved. Her mouth was a straight but somehow uneven line.

'Well,' he said loudly, suddenly, 'I'm glad *that's* over!'

And he went upstairs, to find the mother of all hacks raiding his cupboard.

It was noon now (how long had he been in there?) and the venetian blinds streaked sunlight through the kitchen. The radio sang country and western with an outback twang. Fuffy the cat licked his paws on the counter-top, his tail curled in a listlessly unanswerable question mark. Three open jam-jars (marmalade, strawberry, raspberry) sat in a row on the table beside the toast rack. Placed in the centre of this domestic idyll, the black witch of q appeared strangely innocuous, almost maternal. An unlit cigarette flipped forward and backward through the fingers of her right hand; she was absently flicking at a lighter with her left.

If in the qverse, he would have first asked permission to join her, an ingrained courtesy all mid-level hacks afforded their superiors. But this was his house—his *mothers'* house. He pulled out the chair opposite her with shaky hands and sprawled on it. Briefly Harmonica's gaze settled on him, then passed on to the window and the neatly trimmed grass beyond. It felt a little like a dismissal. Troubled, Gig touched his ankle to hers under the table and was reassured when she did not pull it away.

'I unplugged ages ago,' she said presently. 'Cut Singer down to ten-percent power and jammed a few of her key systems. Then spotted Misoka lurking around the Badlands like a bad Japanese smell and figured it was time to port out. When the matriarchs get mad it's never pretty. You weren't around in forty-eight—Misoka wiped out three quarters of TEEK because Benny wouldn't let her go to a school disco. Anyway I came up here and made toast. One of your mothers—the slightly mad Scottish one—showed me where everything was.'

'I don't get it,' said Gig.

'My ex-husband called five minutes ago, wanting to know if I had anything to do with the blow-outs throughout the qverse. I filled the sink with water and dropped in my phone. Let him shout at me through the water.' She shrugged, sighed. 'Don't look so damnably glum, kid. We succeeded. Or at least we survived, which is a success of a sort. And the experience was entertaining, at least. I've never seen a proper matriarch fight since Rebecca and Viger went head-to-head a decade ago. Over planned sex-rooms. Bloody company politics—'

'Phoun is currently in the qverse injecting high-voltage electricity into Singer's *brain*. That isn't exactly business as usual in the office, sir.'

This time she had caught the tremor in his voice—that surfacing hysteria—and turned fully to face him. 'Gig,' she said.

'Harmonica, sir?'

'I want to explain something to y—'

'I think Phoun is killing Singer, sir. I think I helped.'

Saying it out loud made his belly ache: the words were heavy with gravity. (Phoun killed Singer. I killed her, too.) He endured a sick, plummeting sensation like the descent of a too-fast elevator and nearly vomited again. He made a bad assassin: he didn't have the stomach for it. As he fought back another rush of nausea a vision of Singer came to him: the black-haired beauty twitching spastically on the barren Badlands earth, her long body enveloped by electric flame. At each spasm she flashed a skeletal x-ray through her skin.

It was a cartoon set-up, funny and horrible, but he found he could neither laugh nor cry. It occurred to him he might be in shock or suffering some other variety of post-Phoun trauma.

'Hey, kid. Cool it. You won't get anywhere in this world if you puke every time you fry someone. If Singer's dead, she's dead—and she had it coming. If not, I guess you'll get to fight her again someday. Probably sooner than later.'

Harmonica covered his hands with hers, sandwiched them tight, something soft prevailing in the sharp lines of her face. 'The reason I survive everything,' she said slowly, 'is because I walk away and I don't look back.'

'But it was my fault, sir. Phoun might have been in my laser, but I was the one who actually *shot* Singer. I pulled the trigger. They could put me in jail if she dies. People can die from being fried. Or they get brain damage. Ruth showed me articles on it. God, this isn't company politics! It's warfare. It's murder. It's a *massacre*.'

'I survive because I don't think about stuff like that. I don't want to know about it. No matter what happens, I just keep on walking. I'm a hard bitch but I'm alive. That's the important thing.'

He sobbed, 'Stop talking that way!'

'I like you,' said Harmonica. 'But this could break you.'

She withdrew her hands, lit her cigarette and stared again out the window. Smoke ribboned from her nostrils and dissipated in the sunlight. A shuttle passed overhead and the radio hiccuped on a high note. When she next spoke she was Harmonica again—big business, corporate mogul, hard-as-nails, heart-like-a-swinging-brick Harmonica. A woman who never held hands, who never consoled her adversaries, and who would probably never love a limp-wristed emotional wreck like Felix 'Gig' McGuiggen. Briskly she said, 'This has been nice, kid, but I've got to get back to Sydney. My boy is there and I don't trust Joaquin's babysitting skills for a minute. Like as not he's got Lucas pottering around a strip-club by now.'

'I still owe you twenty dollars, sir.'

'I'll bill you.'

'But I—'

'I'll bill you, Gig.'

'Please don't go,' he said. 'Please stay. I'm sorry I'm like this. I'm sorry I'm not like you.'

'Why should I stay?'

He had many answers but knew intuitively the one she wanted to hear. He pulled it together, played it up, played it cool. 'Because if you don't, Carter,' he replied, affecting a swaggering, pulp-Western bravado, a cowboy's laconic drawl, 'I'll fry every one of your companies. Starting with the WAB. This virtual town ain't big enough of the both of us. Don't make the mistake of underestimating me, sir. In the course of the Lee investigation I acquired a state-of-the-art custom-made SWIFTWATER cap with better lasers than even Benny Soo could dream up. Not to mention a backstage room-pass from your pal Misoka and a fair understanding of plaincode. Reckon I put the fear-of-Gig into the qverse locals, too. And made some contacts even an old hack like you would be jealous of. Give me a week, sir, and I'll be able to code rings around you.'

'You like me that much, huh.'

'No shame in that.'

'No shame at all.' She dug out a card from her purse (REGINA CARTER, QVERSE CONSULTANT, CENTRAL SYDNEY) and slid it across the table to him. 'That's my name and my number. Give me a call if you're in my neck of the woods.

Can't promise to be sober but I can promise to be hospitable. Which is more than I promise most.'

'Thank you.'

'Be seeing you, Gig.'

* * * *

At the front door she made to wave and he grabbed her wrist and kissed her. Not a needy kiss but a kiss that *needed* to be kissed. A kiss somehow imbued with the day's current of confusion, as sudden and brilliant as an afterthought. Clumsy, also. They pushed and pulled on the porch, evenly matched in height and weight (although she wore heels). Tongues struggling for supremacy. Twice he actually stumbled, stepping on his own frayed laces. Her nails (manicured, red) snarled in the thin cotton of his t-shirt. She tasted like marmalade and toast.

When they pulled apart he found he couldn't even pretend to be apologetic. It was just something he had had to do.

* * * *

It was the reflections that got to you, he decided later. The qverse tricked you into thinking it operated under the same law as the real world. But virtual reality had no moral high ground. Ethics were a matter of personal taste. In their ineffable female wisdom the matriarchs had determined the meaning of right and wrong, and had managed to fuck that up just as royally as they'd fucked up their lives. If you could steal, cheat and con in the qverse without legal repercussion, it followed (in qverse logic) that murder was not a crime but a sound business move. As they said—as *everyone* said—it was all a matter of perspective.

Gig found these thoughts strangely consoling, but not as consoling as the rest of Honoria's Asahi beers. It struck him that drinking in the afternoon was a very macho thing to do and this made the experience all the more enjoyable.

He became popular around one o'clock. First to phone was Phoun, who out-waited the busy-tone twice before giving up. The recorded message she left on the lounge room wallscreen was cute and flirty and promised him super-big dollars if he chose to join Team SWIFTWATER. Next was Lucas Carter-Soo. The kid had begun to plead for the hack low-down ('Jo says that INTROMET and SWIFTWATER are dead and that the detonation has *your* trace all over it.') when he was distracted by the arrival of some Chinese take-out. Like mother, like son. Gig killed the connection while Lucas bartered cheekily with the delivery boy.

Tara Lee called but the line was bad, and static drowned out what might have been a thank-you. A self-conscious DI Karlsen buzzed him a text-only message: DID I MAKE A FOOL OF MYSELF? -MINNA. Oddly he also received two text-only messages from an INTROMET address. Which meant that either Singer was alive and well or that her identical minions were understandably pissed off by her demise and of a mind to dispense a little retribution. Gig deleted both messages without reading them. The not-knowing bothered him but he knew now that ignorance was a fair measure of security.

Quietly he reflected that he had not really found any answers. He did not know who Rebecca Descartes was or how the qverse had begun. He did not really understand how AR in VR worked. He knew next to nothing about the killer program Lucas had mentioned and he was still lousy with women, that kiss with Harmonica notwithstanding. He said aloud, 'I'm a hard bastard, but I'm alive. That's the important thing,' and was disappointed by the childish pitch of his voice.

Something crashed in the basement.

Gig took his beer and Sandra's nine-iron golf club and investigated, fearing the worst. But it was only Ruth. She was surrounded by scrunched paper rags and shards of Gig's SWIFTWATER neurocap. The cap's translucent shell had shattered into curved, triangular pieces like a broken Easter egg. It clicked in an instant: the magazine, the cap, Malachy Memphis. Zhadesh, Zhadesh.

His cousin wept.

Gig went to her, saying in a new voice, 'It's okay. It's going to be okay.'

* * * *